DATE DUE

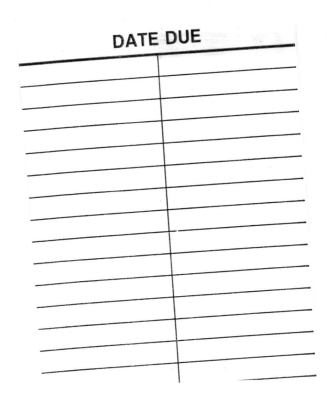

MOSSFLOWER

When the clever and greedy wildcat Tsarmina becomes Queen of a Thousand Eyes and ruler of all Mossflower Woods, she is determined to govern the peaceful woodlanders with an iron paw, bringing every otter and hedgehog, every mouse and squirrel whimpering to his knees.

But the brave mouse Martin and quick-talking mousethief Gonff meet in the depths of Kotir Castle's dungeon. With the aid of all the woodlanders, the two escape and resolve to end Tsarmina's tyrannical rule. Joined by Kinny the mole, Martin and Gonff set off on a dangerous quest for Salamandastron, mountain of dragons, where they are convinced that their only hope, Boar the Fighter, still lives . . .

READ ALL OF THE BESTSELLING NOVELS OF REDWALL . . .

Redwall
The book that inspired a legend—the first novel in the bestselling saga of Redwall! The epic story of a bumbling young mouse who rises up, fights back . . . and becomes a legend himself . . .

Mossflower
Brave mouse Martin and quick-talking mousethief Gonff unite to end the tyrannical reign of Tsarmina—who has set out to rule all of Mossflower Woods with an iron paw . . .

Mattimeo
Slagar the fox embarks on a terrible quest for vengeance against the fearless mouse warrior Matthias, cunningly stealing away what he most cherishes: his headstrong son, Mattimeo . . .

Mariel of Redwall
After she and her father are tossed overboard by pirates, the mousemaid Mariel seeks revenge against searat Gabool the Wild . . .

Salamandastron

When the mountain stronghold of Salamandastron comes unde
attack, only the bold badger Lord Urthstripe stands able to pro
tect the creatures of Redwall . . .

Martin the Warrior

The triumphant saga of a young mouse destined to beco
Redwall's most glorious hero . . .

The Bellmaker

The epic quest of Joseph the Bellmaker to join his daughter,
Mariel the Warriormouse, in a heroic battle against a vicious
Foxwolf . . .

Outcast of Redwall

The abandoned son of a ferret warlord must choose his destiny
beyond the walls of Redwall Abbey . . .

Pearls of Lutra

A young hedgehog maid sets out to solve the riddle of the missing pearls of legend—and faces an evil emperor and his reptilian
warriors . . .

The Long Patrol

The Long Patrol unit of perilous hares is called out to draw off
the murderous Rapscallion army—in one of the most ferocious
battles Redwall has ever faced . . .

Marlfox

Two brave children of warrior squirrels embark upon a quest to
recover Redwall's most priceless treasure from the villainous
Marlfoxes . . .

The Legend of Luke

Martin the Warrior sets out on a journey to trace his heroic
legacy: the legendary exploits of his father, Luke . . .

Lord Brocktree

The mighty badger warrior Lord Brocktree must reclaim the mountain land of Salamandastron from the army of a villainous wildcat . . .

Taggerung

The otter Taggerung, realizing he's not cut from the same cloth as the vermin clan who raised him, embarks on a journey to find his true home and family . . .

Triss

The brave squirrelmaid Triss plans a daring escape from the enslavement of the evil ferret King Agarnu and his daughter Princess Kurda . . .

Loamhedge

Young haremaid Martha Braebuck, wheelchair-bound since infancy, embarks on a quest to the mysterious abbey of Loamhedge to find a cure for her condition . . .

Rakkety Tam

Mercenary warrior squirrel Rakkety Tam MacBurl quests to rescue kidnapped Redwall maidens and thwart the plans of the murderous wolverine known as Gulo the Savage . . .

High Rhulain

Young ottermaid Tiria Wildlough travels to the mysterious Green Isle and joins a band of outlaw otters to help rid the land of the villainous wildcat chieftain Riggu Felis . . .

Eulalia!

A young haremaid embarks on a quest to find Gorath—the heir to the lordship of Salamandastron—held captive by the Sea Raider Vizka Longtooth . . .

Doomwyte

The young mouse Bisky leads his friends on a quest for the jeweled eyes of the Great Doomwyte Idol—into the realm of the fearsome Korvus Skurr, the black-feathered raven . . .

MOSSFLOWER

Brian Jacques

ACE BOOKS, NEW YORK

THE BERKLEY PUBLISHING GROUP
Published by the Penguin Group
Penguin Group (USA) Inc.
375 Hudson Street, New York, New York 10014, USA
Penguin Group (Canada), 90 Eglinton Avenue East, Suite 700, Toronto, Ontario M4P 2Y3, Canada
(a division of Pearson Penguin Canada Inc.)
Penguin Books Ltd., 80 Strand, London WC2R 0RL, England
Penguin Group Ireland, 25 St. Stephen's Green, Dublin 2, Ireland (a division of Penguin Books Ltd.)
Penguin Group (Australia), 250 Camberwell Road, Camberwell, Victoria 3124, Australia
(a division of Pearson Australia Group Pty. Ltd.)
Penguin Books India Pvt. Ltd., 11 Community Centre, Panchsheel Park, New Delhi—110 017, India
Penguin Group (NZ), 67 Apollo Drive, Rosedale, North Shore 0632, New Zealand
(a division of Pearson New Zealand Ltd.)
Penguin Books (South Africa) (Pty.) Ltd., 24 Sturdee Avenue, Rosebank, Johannesburg 2196,
South Africa

Penguin Books Ltd., Registered Offices: 80 Strand, London WC2R 0RL, England

This is a work of fiction. Names, characters, places, and incidents either are the product of the author's imagination or are used fictitiously, and any resemblance to actual persons, living or dead, business establishments, events, or locales is entirely coincidental. The publisher does not have any control over and does not assume any responsibility for author or third-party websites or their content.

MOSSFLOWER

An Ace Book / published by arrangement with Hutchinson Children's Books, Ltd.

PRINTING HISTORY
Philomel Books hardcover edition / 1988
Ace mass-market edition / November 1998

ISBN: 978-0-441-00576-5

ACE
Ace Books are published by The Berkley Publishing Group,
a division of Penguin Group (USA) Inc.,
375 Hudson Street, New York, New York 10014.
ACE and the "A" design are trademarks of Penguin Group (USA) Inc.

PRINTED IN THE UNITED STATES OF AMERICA

33 32 31 30 29 28 27

Late autumn winds sighed fitfully around the open gatehouse door, rustling brown-gold leaves in the fading afternoon.

Bella of Brockhall snuggled deeper into her old armchair by the fire. Through half-closed eyes she watched the small mouse peering around the doorway at her.

"Come in, little one, and close the door."

The small mouse did as he was bidden. Encouraged by the badger's friendly smile, he clambered up onto the arm of the chair and settled himself against a cushion.

"You said that you would tell me a story, Miz Bella."

The badger nodded slowly.

"Everything you see about you, the harvest that has been gathered, from the russet apples to the golden honey, is yours to enjoy in freedom. Listen now, as the breeze sweeps the last autumn leaves off into the world of winter. I will tell you of the time long ago before Redwall Abbey was built in Mossflower. In those days there was no freedom for woodlanders; we were oppressed cruelly under the harsh rule of Verdauga Greeneyes and his daughter Tsarmina. It was a mouse like yourself who saved Mossflower. His name is known to all: Martin the Warrior.

"Ah, my little friend, I am grown old. So are my comrades; their sons and daughters are fathers and mothers now. But that is life. The seasons still look new to young eyes, the food tastes fresher in the mouths of the young ones than it does in my own. As I sit here in the warmth and peace it all lives again in my memory, a strange tale of love and war, friend and foe, great happenings and mighty deeds.

"Gaze into the fire, young one. Listen to me and I will tell you the story."

BOOK ONE

Kotir

1

Mossflower lay deep in the grip of midwinter beneath a sky of leaden gray that showed tinges of scarlet and orange on the horizon. A cold mantle of snow draped the landscape, covering the flatlands to the west. Snow was everywhere, filling ditches, drifting high against hedgerows, making paths invisible, smoothing the contours of earth in its white embrace. The gaunt, leafless ceiling of Mossflower Wood was penetrated by constant snowfall, which carpeted the sprawling woodland floor, building canopies on evergreen shrubs and bushes. Winter had muted the earth; the muffled stillness was broken only by a traveler's paws.

A sturdily built young mouse with quick dark eyes was moving confidently across the snowbound country. Looking back, he could see his tracks disappearing northward into the distance. Farther south the flatlands rolled off endlessly, flanked to the west by the faint shape of distant hills, while to the east stood the long ragged fringe marking the marches of Mossflower. His nose twitched at the elusive smell of burning wood and turf from some hearthfire. Cold wind soughed from the treetops, causing whorls of snow to dance in icy spirals. The traveler gathered his ragged cloak tighter, adjusted an old rust-

ing sword that was slung across his back, and trudged steadily
forward, away from the wilderness, to where other creatures
lived.

It was a forbidding place made mean by poverty. Here and
there he saw signs of habitation. The dwellings, ravaged and
demolished, made pitiful shapes under snowdrifts. Rearing high
against the forest, a curious building dominated the ruined settlement. A fortress, crumbling, dark and brooding, it was a
symbol of fear to the woodland creatures of Mossflower.

This was how Martin the Warrior first came to Kotir, place
of the wildcats.

In a mean hovel on the south side of Kotir, the Stickle family
crouched around a low turf fire. It gusted fitfully as the night
winds pierced the slatted timbers where mud chinking had not
been replaced. A timid scratch at the door caused them to jump
nervously. Ben Stickle picked up a billet of firewood, motion-
ing his wife Goody to keep their four little ones well back in
the shadows.

As the Goodwife Stickle covered her brood with coarse bur-
lap blankets, Ben took a firmer grip on the wood and called
out harshly in his gruffest voice, "Be off with you and leave
us alone. There's not enough food in here to go around a decent
hedgehog family. You've already taken half of all we have to
swell the larders in Kotir."

"Ben, Ben, 'tis oi, Urthclaw! Open up, burr. 'Tis freezen
out yurr."

As Ben Stickle opened the door, a homely-faced mole trundled by him and hurried across to the fire, where he stood
rubbing his digging claws together in front of the flames.

The little ones peeped out from the blankets. Ben and Goody
turned anxious faces toward their visitor.

Urthclaw rubbed warmth into his cold nose as he talked in
the curious rustic molespeech.

"Vurmin patrols be out, burr, weasels 'n' stoats an' the loik.
They'm a lukken fer more vittles."

Goody shook her head as she wiped a little one's snout on
her apron. "I knew it! We should have run off and left this
place, like the others. Where in the name of spikes'll we find
food to pay their tolls?"

Ben Stickle threw down the piece of firewood despairingly.

"Where can we run in midwinter with four little 'uns? They'd perish long afore spring."

Urthclaw produced a narrow strip of silver birch bark and held a paw to his mouth, indicating silence. Scratched on the bark in charcoal was a single word: *Corim*. Beneath it was a simple picture map showing a route into Mossflower Woods, far from Kotir.

Ben studied the map, torn between the chance of escape and his family's predicament. The frustration was clear on his face.

Bang! Bang!

"Open up in there! Come on, get this door open. This is an official Kotir patrol."

Soldiers!

Ben took one last hasty glance at the strip of bark and threw it on the fire. As Goody lifted the latch the door was thrust forcefully inward. She was swept to one side as the soldiers packed into the room, out of the winter night chill. They pushed and shoved at each other roughly. A ferret named Blacktooth and a stoat called Splitnose seemed to be in charge of the patrol. Ben Stickle sighed with relief as they turned away from the burning strip of bark and stood with their backs to the fire.

"Well now, dozyspikes, where are you hiding all the bread and cheese and October ale?"

Ben could scarce keep the hatred from his voice as he answered the sneering Blacktooth. "It's many a long season since I tasted cheese or October ale. There's bread on the shelf, but only enough for my family."

Splitnose spat into the fire and reached for the bread. Ben Stickle was blocked from stopping the stoat by a barrier of spear hafts as he tried to push forward.

Goody placed a restraining paw on her husband's spikes. "Please, Ben, don't fight 'em, the great bullies."

Urthclaw chimed in, "Yurr, baint much 'ee c'n do agin spears, Ben."

Blacktooth turned to the mole as if seeing him for the first time. "Huh, what're you doing here, blinkeye?"

One of the little hedgehogs threw the sacking aside and faced the stoat boldly. "He came in for a warm by our fire. You leave him alone!" Splitnose burst out laughing, spraying crumbs from the bread he was eating. "Look out, Blackie. There's more of 'em under that blanket. I'd watch 'em, if I were you."

A nearby weasel threw back the covering, exposing the other three young ones.

Blacktooth sized them up. "Hmm, they look big enough to do a day's work."

Goodwife Stickle sprang fiercely in front of them. "You let my liddle ones be. They ain't harmed nobody."

Blacktooth seemed to ignore her. He knocked the loaves from Splitnose's paws, then turning to a weasel he issued orders. "Pick that bread up, and no sly munching. Deliver it to the stores when we get back to the garrison."

Waving his spear he signaled the patrol out of the hut. As Blacktooth left he called back to Ben and Goody, "I want to see those four hogs out in the fields tomorrow. Either that, or you can all spend the rest of the winter safe and warm in Kotir dungeons."

Urthclaw kept an eye to a crack in the door, watching the patrol make its way toward Kotir. Ben wasted no time; he began wrapping the young ones in all the blankets they possessed. "Right, that's it! Enough is enough. We go tonight. You're right, old girl, we should have left to live in the woods with the rest long ago. What d'you say, Urthclaw?"

The mole stood with his eye pressed against the crack in the door. "Yurr, cumm 'ere, lookit thiz!"

While Ben shared the crack with his friend, Goody continued swathing her young ones with blankets. "What is it, Ben? They're not comin' back, are they?"

"No, wife. Hohoho, lookit that, by hokey! See the punch he landed on that weasel's nose? Go on, give it to 'em, laddo!"

Ferdy, the little one who had spoken up, scuttled over and tugged at Ben's paw. "Punch? Who punched a weasel? What's happening?"

Ben described the scene as he watched it. "It's a mouse—big strong feller too, he is. They're tryin' to capture him ... That's it! Now kick him again, mouse. Go on! Hahaha, you'd think a full patrol of soldiers could handle a mouse, but not this one. He must be a real trained warrior. Phew! Lookit that, he's knocked Blacktooth flat on his back. Pity they're hangin' on to his sword like that. By the spikes, he'd cause some damage if he had that blade between his paws, rusty as it is."

Ferdy jumped up and down. "Let me see, I want a look!"

Urthclaw turned slowly away from the door. "Baint much

use, liddle 'edgepig. They'm gorrim down now, aye, an' roped up too. Hurr, worra pity, they be too many fer 'im to foight, ee'm a gurt brave wurrier tho.''

Ben was momentarily crestfallen, then he clapped his paws together. ''Now is the time, while the patrol's busy with the fighter. They've got a job on their paws, draggin' him back to the cats' castle. Come on, let's get a-goin' while the goin's good.''

A short while later, the fire was burning to embers in an empty hut as the little band trudged into the vast woodland sprawl of Mossflower, blinking water from their eyes as they kept their heads down against the keen wind. Urthclaw followed up the rear, obliterating the pawtracks from the snowy ground.

2

Gonff the mousethief padded silently along the passage from the larder and storeroom of Kotir. He was a plump little creature, clad in a green jerkin with a broad buckled belt. He was a ducker and a weaver of life, a marvelous mimic, ballad writer, singer, and lockpick, and very jovial with it all. The woodlanders were immensely fond of the little thief. Gonff shrugged it all off, calling every creature his matey in imitation of the otters, whom he greatly admired. Chuckling quietly to himself, he drew the small dagger from his belt and cut off a wedge from the cheese he was carrying. Slung around his shoulder was a large flask of elderberry wine which he had also stolen from the larder. Gonff ate and drank, singing quietly to himself in a deep bass voice between mouthfuls of cheese and wine.

> The Prince of Mousethieves honors you,
> To visit here this day.
> So keep your larder door shut tight,
> Lock all your food away.
> O foolish ones, go check your store
> Of food so rich and fine.
> Be sure that I'll be back for more,
> Especially this wine.

At the sound of heavy paws Gonff fell silent. Melting back into the shadows, he huddled down and held his breath. Two weasels dressed in armor and carrying spears trudged past. They were arguing heatedly.

"Listen, I'm not taking the blame for your stealing from the larder."

"Who, me? Be careful what you say, mate. I'm no thief."

"Well, you're looking very fat lately, that's all I say."

"Huh, not half as podgy as you, lard barrel."

"Lard barrel yourself. You'll be accusing me next."

"Ha, you're in charge of the key, so who else could it be?"

"It could be you. You're always down there when I am."

"I only go to keep an eye on you, mate."

"And I only go to keep an eye on you, so there."

"Right, we'll keep an eye on each other, then."

Gonff stuffed a paw in his mouth to stifle a giggle. The weasels stopped and looked at each other.

"What was that?"

"Oho, I know what it was—you're laughing at me."

"Arr, don't talk stupid."

"Talking stupid, am I?" Indignantly, the weasel turned away from his companion.

Gonff quickly called out in a passable weasel-voice imitation, "Big fat robber!"

The two weasels turned furiously upon each other.

"Big fat robber, eh. Take that!"

"Ouch! You sneaky toad, you take this!"

The weasels thwacked away madly at each other with their spearhandles.

Gonff sneaked out of hiding and crept off in the opposite direction, leaving the two guards rolling upon the passage floor, their spears forgotten as they bit and scratched at each other.

"Owow, leggo. Grr, take that!"

"I'll give you robber! Have some of this. Ooh, you bit my ear!"

Sheathing his dagger and shaking with mirth, Gonff unlatched a window shutter, and slipped away through the snow toward the woodlands.

Oh fight, lads, fight,
Scratch, lads, bite,
Gonff will dine on cheese and wine,
When he gets home tonight.

Martin dug his heels into the snow, skidding as he was
dragged bodily through the outer wallgates of the forbidding
heap he had sighted earlier that day. Armored soldiers clanked
and clattered together as they were dragged inward by the ropes
that restrained the prisoner, none of them wanting to get too
close to the fighting mouse.

Blacktooth and Splitnose closed the main gates with much
bad-tempered slamming. Powdery snow blew down on them
from the top of the perimeter walls. The parade ground snow
was hammered flat and slippery by soldiers dashing hither and
thither, some carrying lighted torches—ferrets, weasels and
stoats. One of them called out to Splitnose, "Hoi, Splittie, any
sign of the fox out there?"

The stoat shook his head. "What, you mean the healer? No,
not a whisker. We caught a mouse, though. Look at this thing
he was carrying."

Splitnose waved Martin's rusted sword aloft. Blacktooth
ducked. "Stop playing with that thing, you'll slash somebody
twirling it around like that. So, they're waiting on the fox again,
eh. Old Greeneyes doesn't seem to be getting any better lately.
Hey, you there, keep those ropes tight! Hold him still, you
blockheads."

The entrance hall door proved doubly difficult as the warrior
mouse managed to cling to one of the timber doorposts. The
soldiers had practically to pry him loose with their spears. The
weasel who had been given charge of the bread kept well out
of it, heading directly for the storeroom and larder. As he
passed through the entrance hall, he was challenged by others
who cast covetous eyes upon the brown home-baked loaves. It
had been a hard winter, since many creatures had deserted the
settlement around Kotir after the early autumn harvest, taking
with them as much produce as they could carry to the woodlands. There was not a great deal of toll or levy coming in. The
weasel clutched the bread close as he padded along.

The hall was hostile and damp, with wooden shutters across
the low windows. The floor was made from a dark granite-like
rock, very cold to the paws. Here and there the nighttime guards

had lit small fires in corners, which stained the walls black with smoke and ashes. Only captains were allowed to wear long cloaks as a mark of rank, but several soldiers had draped themselves in old sacks and blankets purloined from the settlement. The stairs down to the lower levels were a jumble of worn spirals and flights of straight stone steps in no particular sequence. Half the wall torches had burned away and not been replaced, leaving large areas of stairs dark and dangerous. Moss and fungus grew on most of the lower-level walls and stairs.

Hurrying along a narrow passage, the weasel banged on the storeroom door. A key turned in the lock.

"What've you got there? Loaves, eh. Bring 'em in."

The two guards who had been fighting were sitting on flour sacks. One of them eyed the bread hungrily. "Huh, is that all you got tonight? I tell you, mate, things are getting from bad to worse around here. Who sent you down with them?"

"Blacktooth."

"Oh, him. Did he count them?"

"Er, no, I don't think so."

"Good. There's five loaves. We'll have half a loaf each—that'll leave three and a half. Nobody'll notice the difference."

They tore hungrily at Goody Stickle's brown oven loaves.

Upstairs, Martin had managed to wrap one of the ropes around a stone column. Soldiers were jeering at the efforts of the patrol to get him away and up the stairs. "Yah, what's the matter, lads, are you scared of him?"

Blacktooth turned on the mocking group. "Any of you lot fancy having a go at him? No, I thought not."

The door opened behind them, and snow blew in with a cold, draughty gust. A fox wearing a ragged cloak trotted past them and up the broad flat stairs to their first floor. The soldiers found a new target for their remarks.

"Hoho, just you wait, fox. You're late."

"Aye, old Greeneyes doesn't like to be kept waiting."

"I'd keep out of Lady Tsarmina's way, if I were you."

Ignoring them, the fox swept quickly up the stairs.

Martin tried to make a dash for the half-open door to the parade ground but he was carried to the floor by weight of numbers. Still he fought gamely on.

The jeering soldiers started shouting and calling humorous advice again. Blacktooth tried freezing them into silence with a stern glance, but they took no notice of him this time.

Splitnose sniffed in disgust. "Discipline has gone to the wall since Lord Verdauga's been sick."

Fortunata the vixen waited nervously in the draughty antehall of Kotir. A low fire cast its guttering light around the damp sandstone walls. Slimy green algae and fungus grew between sodden banners as they slowly disintegrated into threadbare tatters suspended from rusty iron holders. The vixen could not suppress a shudder. Presently she was joined by two ferrets dressed in cumbersome chain mail. Both bore shields emblazoned with the device of their masters, a myriad of evil green eyes watching in all directions. The guards pointed with their spears, indicating that the fox should follow them, and Fortunata fell in step, marching off down the long dank hall. They halted in front of two huge oaken doors, which swung open as the ferrets banged their spearbutts against the floor. The vixen was confronted by a scene of ruined grandeur.

Candles and torches scarcely illuminated the room; the crossbeams above were practically lost in darkness. At one end there were three ornate chairs occupied by two wildcats and a pine marten. Behind these stood a four-poster bed, complete with tight-drawn curtains of musty green velvet, its footboard carved with the same device as the shields of the guards.

The marten hobbled across and searched the satchel Fortunata carried. The vixen shrank from contact with the badly disfigured creature. Ashleg the marten had a wooden leg and his entire body was twisted on one side as if it had been badly maimed. To disguise this, he wore an overlong red cloak trimmed with woodpigeon feathers. With an expert flick, he turned the contents of the satchel out on to the floor. It was the usual jumble of herbs, roots, leaves and mosses carried by a healer fox.

Approaching the bed, Ashleg called out in an eerie singsong dirge, "O mighty Verdauga, Lord of Mossflower, Master of the Thousand Eyes, Slayer of Enemies, Ruler of Kotir—"

"Ah, give your whining tongue a rest, Ashleg. Is the fox here? Get these suffocating curtains out of my way." The imperious voice from behind the curtains sounded hoarse but full of snarling menace.

Tsarmina, the larger of the two seated wildcats, sprang forward, sweeping back the dusty bedcurtains in a single move. "Fortunata's here. Don't exert yourself, father."

The vixen slid to the bedside with practiced ease and examined her savage patient. Verdauga of the Thousand Eyes had once been the mightiest warlord in all the land . . . once. Now his muscle and sinew lay wasted under the tawny fur that covered his big, tired body. The face was that of a wildcat who had survived many battles: the pointed ears stood above a tracery of old scars that ran from crown to whiskers. Fortunata looked at the fearsome yellowed teeth, and the green barbarian eyes still alight with strange fires.

"My Lord looks better today, yes?"

"None the better for your worthless mumbo jumbo, fox."

The smaller of the two seated wildcats rose from his chair with an expression of concern upon his gentle face. "Father, stay calm. Fortunata is trying hard to get you well again."

Tsarmina pushed him aside scornfully. "Oh, shut up, Gingivere, you mealy-mouthed—"

"Tsarmina!" Verdauga pulled himself into a sitting position and pointed a claw at his headstrong daughter. "Don't talk to your brother in that way, do you hear me?"

The Lord of a Thousand Eyes turned wearily to his only son. "Gingivere, don't let her bully you. Stand up to her, son."

Gingivere shrugged and stood by silently as Fortunata ground herbs with a pestle, mixing them with dark liquid in a horn beaker.

Verdauga eyed the vixen suspiciously. "No more leeches, fox. I won't have those filthy slugs sucking my blood. I'd sooner have an enemy's sword cut me than those·foul things. What's that rubbish you're concocting?"

Fortunata smiled winningly. "Sire, this is a harmless potion made from the herb motherwort. It will help you to sleep. Squire Gingivere, would you give this to your father, please?"

As Gingivere administered the medicine to Verdauga, neither of them noticed the look of slyness or the wink that passed between Fortunata and Tsarmina.

Verdauga settled back in bed and waited for the draught to take effect. Suddenly the peace was broken by a loud commotion from outside. The double doors burst open wide.

3

Ben Stickle nearly jumped out of his spikes as Gonff bounded out from behind a snow-laden bush in the nighttime forest.

"Boo! Guess who? Hahaha, Ben, me old matey, you should have seen your face just then. What are you doing trekking round here in the snow?"

Ben recovered himself quickly. "Gonff, I might have known! Listen, young feller me mouse, I haven't got time to stop and gossip with you. We've left the settlement at last and I'm lookin' for the little hut that the Corim keep for the likes of us."

The mousethief winked at Urthclaw and kissed Goody cheekily. "Ha, that place, follow me, matey. I'll have you there in two shakes of a cat's whisker."

Goody shuddered. "I wish you wouldn't say things like that, you little rogue."

But Gonff was not listening, he was skipping ahead with the little ones, who thought it was all a huge adventure.

"Is it a nice place, Mr. Gonff?"

"Oh, passable. Better than the last place you were in."

"What's that under your jerkin, Mr. Gonff?"

"Never you mind now, young Spike. It's a secret."

"Is it very far, Mr. Gonff? I'm tired."

"Not far now, Posy me little dear. I'd carry you if it weren't for your spikes."

Goody Stickle shook her head and smiled. She had always had a special soft spot for Gonff.

The Corim hut was well hidden, deep enough into the forest to avoid immediate discovery. Urthclaw said his goodbyes and trundled off to find his own kind. Ben watched him go as Gonff lit the fire. He nodded fondly. "Good old Urthclaw, he only stayed at the settlement because of us, I'm sure of it."

When the fire was burning red, Goody sat around it with Gonff and Ben. The four baby hedgehogs poked their snouts from under the blankets to one side of the hearth.

"Have you been stealing from Kotir again, Gonff? What did you pinch this time?"

The mousethief laughed at Goody's shocked expression. He threw a wedge of cheese over to the little ones. "It's not pinching or stealing if it comes out of Kotir, mateys. It's called liberating. Here, get your whiskers around that lot and get some sleep, the four of you."

Ben Stickle sucked on an empty pipe and stirred the burning logs with a branch. "Gonff, I do wish you'd be careful. We can live on what we have until spring arrives. Goody and I would never forgive ourselves if you got caught taking cheese and wine inside that cat's castle."

Goodwife Stickle wiped her eyes on her flowery pinafore. "No more we wouldn't, you young scallawag. Oh my spikes, I dread to think what'd 'appen if those varmin catchered you, Gonff."

Gonff patted her very carefully. "There, there, Goody. What's a bite of food and a warm drink between mateys? The young uns need their nourishment. Besides, how could I ever forget the way that you and Ben brought me up and cared for me when I was only a little woodland orphan?"

Ben took a sip of the wine and shook his head. "You be careful, all the same, and remember what the Corim rule is; bide your time and don't let 'em catch you. One day we'll win old Mossflower back."

Goody sighed as she went about making porridge for the next morning's breakfast. "Fine words, but we're peaceable creatures. How we're ever goin' to win our land back against all those trained soldiers is beyond me."

Gonff topped up Ben Stickle's beaker with elderberry wine and gazed into the flickering flames, his normally cheerful face grim. "I'll tell you this, mateys: the day will come when something will happen to change all this, you wait and see. Some creature who isn't afraid of anything will arrive in Mossflower, and when that day arrives we'll be ready. We'll pay that filthy gang of vermin and their wildcat masters back so hard that they'll think the sky has fallen on them."

Ben rubbed his eyes tiredly. "A hero, eh. Funny you should say that. I thought I saw just such a one earlier tonight. Ah, but he's probably dead or in the dungeons by now. Let's get some sleep. I'm bone weary."

The little hut was an island of warmth and safety in the night, as the howling north wind drove snowflakes before it, whining and keening around the gaunt trees of winter-stricken Mossflower.

4

Struggling wildly between two stoats, the captive mouse was dragged into the bedchamber. He was secured by a long rope, which the guards tried to keep taut as he dodged and jumped, scratched and bit, first letting the rope go slack, then dashing forward so the two guards were pulled together; as they collided he leaped upon them, biting and kicking despite the rope that pinned his paws to his sides. A ferret guard from the door came running in to help. Between the three of them they managed to pin the warlike mouse upon the floor. They lay on top of him, trying to avoid the butting head and nipping teeth. The mouse was breathing heavily, his eyes flashing reckless defiance at his captors.

Verdauga sat up straight, sleep forgotten as he questioned the two stoats. "Make your report. What have we got here?"

One of the stoats freed his paw and threw a quick salute. "Lord, this one was caught within the bounds of your lands. He is a stranger, and goes armed."

A weasel marched in and placed the traveler's ancient rusty sword at the foot of the bed.

Verdauga looked from under hooded lids at the sword and the sturdy young mouse upon the floor. "It is against my law to carry arms or to trespass upon my domain.''

The mouse struggled against his captors, shouting out in a loud, angry voice, ''I didn't know it was your land, cat. Tell your guards to take their claws off and release me. You have no right to imprison a freeborn creature.''

Verdauga could not help but admire the obvious courage of the prisoner. He was about to speak, when Tsarmina grasped the battered sword and stood over the captive with the point at his throat. ''You insolent scum! Quick now, what is your name? Where did you steal this rusty relic?''

As the guards pinned the struggling mouse down, his voice shook with fury. ''My name is Martin the Warrior. That sword was once my father's, now it is mine. I come and go as I please, cat. Is this the welcome you show travelers?''

Tsarmina forced Martin's head back with the swordpoint. ''For a mouse, you have far too much to say to your betters,'' she said contemptuously. ''You are in Mossflower country now; all the land you can see on a clear day's march belongs to us by right of conquest. My father's law says that none are allowed to go armed save his soldiers. The penalty for those who break the law is death.''

She beckoned the guards with a sleek catlike movement. ''Take him away and execute him.''

Lord Greeneyes' voice halted the guards as he turned to his son. ''Gingivere, have you nothing to say? What shall we do with this mouse?''

''Some say that ignorance of the law is no excuse,'' Gingivere answered without raising his voice. ''Even so, it would be unjust to punish Martin; he is a stranger and could not be expected to know of us or our laws. Also, it would be too easy for us to slay him. He seems an honest creature to me. If it were my decision I would have him escorted from our territory, then given his weapon. He would know better than to come back again.''

Verdauga looked from son to daughter. ''Now I will give you my decision. There are enough cowards in the world without killing a brave creature for so little reason. This Martin is a true warrior. On the other side of the scales, if we were to allow him to roam free as the wind on our land, this might be read as a sign of our weakness. It is my judgment that he be put in the cells to cool his paws awhile. After a time he can be set free, provided he is never again so rash as to trespass in my domain.''

Snap!

Everyone present heard the sharp report. Furious at being overruled, Tsarmina had set the sword between the jamb of the door and the stone doorway. With a huge burst of energy she threw her weight against the venerable weapon. Suddenly it broke; the old blade rang upon the floor, leaving her holding the shorn-off handle, which she tossed to a guard.

''Here, throw him in the cells with this tied around his neck. If ever we do release him, then others will see him and realize how merciful we can be. Take the wretch away—the sight of him offends my eyes.''

As the guards tugged on the rope, Martin stood firm resisting them. For a moment his eyes met those of Tsarmina's. His voice was clear and unafraid. ''Your father made a just decision, but yours was the right one. You should have killed me when you had the chance, because I vow that I will slay you one day.''

The spell was broken. The guards hauled on the ropes, dragging Martin off to the cells. In the silence that followed, Tsarmina slumped in her chair and sniggered. ''A mouse kill me, indeed! He's not even worth worrying about.''

Verdauga coughed painfully. He lay back on the pillows. ''If you think that, daughter, then you have made a grave mistake. I have seen courage before; it comes in all shapes and sizes. Just because he is a mouse does not make him less of a warrior than me. He has a fighter's heart—I saw it in his eyes.''

Tsarmina ignored her father and called to Fortunata. ''Vixen, mix Lord Greeneyes a stronger potion. He needs sleep after all the excitement. Gingivere, give father his medicine. You are the only one he will take it from.''

Fortunata gave Gingivere the beaker containing the prepared draught. Tsarmina nodded to her, and they left the room together. Outside in the corridor the wildcat gripped the fox's paw in her powerful claws. ''Well, did you fix the medicine?''

Fortunata winced in pain as the claws sank in. ''Twice. Once before the mouse came in, and just now before we left. He's taken enough poison to lay half the garrison low.''

Tsarmina pulled the vixen close, her cruel eyes burning. ''Good, but if he's still alive in the morning you had better prepare some for yourself. It would be a lot easier than facing me if you fail.''

The cells were deep beneath Kotir. They were ancient, smelly, dark, and dank. Martin the Warrior was hurled into his prison by the two guards who had dragged him down passage and stairway. He had fought every inch of the way and they were glad to be rid of him. Martin lay with his cheek resting on the cold stone floor where he had been flung. As the door clanged shut behind him, one of the stoats peered through the door grating, turning the key in the lock. ''Thank your lucky stars, mouse. If Lady Tsarmina had had her way, you'd be in the darkest wettest cells farther down the passage. It was Lord Greeneyes' wish that you should be put in a good cell, aye, and given bread and water to eat and some dry straw to lie on. Huh, he must have taken a shine to you. He's a strange one, old Verdauga is.''

Martin lay still, listening until the sounds of the guards' heavy paws receded and he was alone. Standing up, he took stock of his new surroundings. At least there was light coming in from a torch that burned on the far corridor wall. Feeling a slight draught, he looked up. There was a high narrow grille slitted into the wall near the ceiling. Martin changed position, still looking upward, until he could see a star shining outside in the night sky. It was his only link with freedom and the outside world. He sat, resting his back against the wall, huddling down in his ragged cloak to gain a little warmth. The rest of his cell was just the same as any prison: four bare walls and precious little else, no comfort or cheer to be gained from anything here. He was a prisoner, alone in a strange place.

The warrior mouse slept, overcome by weariness. Sometime before dawn he was wakened by paws thrusting something over his head and around his neck. Still half-asleep, Martin tried to grab hold of his assailants. He was roughly kicked to one side, then the door clanged shut as the key turned in the lock again. Leaping up, Martin ran to the door. The stoat guard peered through the grating, chuckling and wagging a paw at him. ''You nearly had me that time, mouse.''

The warrior mouse gave an angry snarl and leapt at the grating, but the stoat backed off, grinning at his futile attempt. ''Listen, mouse, if I were you I'd keep pretty quiet down here, otherwise you might attract Lady Tsarmina's attention—and I don't think you'd like that. You just sit tight and behave yourself, then maybe in time somebody like Gingivere will remember you're here and have you released.''

As the guards trooped off, Martin saw they had left a load of clean straw in one corner, also some bread and water. Instinctively he moved towards it, and felt something clunk against his chest. It was the sword handle dangling from a piece of rope around his neck. Martin held it in front of his eyes, staring at it hard and long. He would wear it, not because he had been sentenced to as a mark of shame, but to remind himself that one day he would slay the evil cat who had broken his father's blade.

Settling down in the dry straw, he drank water and gnawed upon the stale bread hungrily. He was about to fall asleep again when shouts and commotion broke out upstairs. Pulling himself level with the door grille, Martin listened to the sounds that echoed in the silence of the cells.

''My Lord Greeneyes is dead!''

''Lady Tsarmina, come quick, it's your father.''

There were loud stamping of spearbutts and the sounds of mailed paws dashing hither and thither, coupled with the slamming of doors.

Tsarmina's voice could be heard in an anguished wail. ''Murder, murder. My father is slain!''

Ashleg and Fortunata took up the cry. ''Murder, Gingivere has poisoned Verdauga!''

A tremendous hubbub had broken out. Martin could not hear clearly what was going on. A moment later there was a sound of heavy pawsteps on the stairs; it sounded like a great number of creatures. Martin pulled to one side of the grille and saw it all. Led by Tsarmina, a mob of soldiers carrying torches marched down the corridor, Ashleg and Fortunata visible among them. As they passed the cell door, Martin glimpsed the stunned face of the gentle wildcat Gingivere. He was bound in chains. Blood trickled from a wound on his head. Their eyes met for a second, then he was swept by in the surge of angry soldiers, their faces distorted by the flickering torchlight as they chanted, ''Murderer, murderer! Kill the murderer!''

Martin could no longer see them, owing to the limited range of his vision through the grille, but he could still hear all that went on. Some distance down the corridor a cell door slammed and a key turned. Tsarmina's voice rose above the noise. "Silence! I will say what is to be done here. Even though my brother is a murderer, I cannot harm him. He will stay locked up here until he lives out his days. He is now dead to me; I never want to hear his name spoken again within the walls of Kotir."

Martin heard Gingivere's voice trying to say something, but it was immediately drowned out by Ashleg and Fortunata starting a chant that the soldiers took up at full pitch. "Long live Queen Tsarmina. Long live Queen Tsarmina!"

As the mob passed by Martin's cell again, he drew back. Above the roars he heard Tsarmina, close by the door, speaking to Ashleg. "Bring October ale and elderberry wine from the storerooms. See that there is plenty for everyone."

Shutting his ears against the sounds of the revelers, Martin lay upon the straw with the sword handle pressing against his chest. Now that his last hopes were gone, it looked like being a long hard winter.

5

Across the lea, beneath the leaves,
When countrylands wake up to spring,
Hurrah here comes the Prince of Thieves,
Hear every small bird sing.
So daring and so handsome too,
He makes a wondrous sight,
But if he comes to visit you,
Lock up your treasures tight.

Sunlight sparkled on the chuckling stream that had lain iced
over and silent all winter. Snowdrops nodded agreeably to cro-
cus on the warm southerly breeze. Spring was everywhere.
Golden daffodils and their paler narcissus relatives stood guard
between the budding trees of Mossflower Woods; evergreens
that had endured the dark winter took on a new fresh life.

Gonff was returning from another successful visit to Kotir.
The wine flasks bumped and banged against his broad belt as
he skipped nimbly through the flowering woodlands, singing
aloud with the heady intoxication of springtime.

Cuckoo, cuckoo, good day, my friend, to you.
O sly one you know best.
To lay in others' nest,
Is a trick you often do.
But I am smarter, sir, than you,
Cuckoo, my friend cuckoo.

The blood coursed madly through Gonff's young veins like
the waters of a brook, gurgling happily and generally making
him so light-headed that he turned somersaults. Every so often
he would pull a reed flute from his tunic and twiddle away with
the sheer joy of being alive on such a morning as this. With a
great whoop Gonff threw himself into a thick tussock of grass
and lay with the perspiration rising from him in a small column
of steam. Overhead the sky was a delicate blue with small white
clouds scudding on the breeze. Gonff imagined what it would
be like to lie upon a small fluffy white cloud and allow himself
to be buffeted about in the sunny sky.

"Whooooaaa, look out, zoom, bump, whoof! Out of the way
you big clouds." The little mousethief held tight to the grass,
swaying from side to side as he played out his game of make-
believe.

He did not notice the two weasels dressed in Kotir armor
until too late. They stood over him looking grim and officious.

Gonff smiled impudently, aware of his clunking wine flasks.
"Er, aha ha. Hello, mateys, I was flying my cloud, you see . . ."

The larger of the two prodded him with a spearbutt. "Come
on you, on your paws. You're wanted at Kotir."

Gonff winked at him cheerily. "Kotir? You don't say! Well,
how nice! Listen, you two good chaps, nip along and tell them
I'm busy today but I'll pop in early tomorrow."

The spearpoint at Gonff's throat discouraged further light
banter. The smaller of the two weasels kicked Gonff. "Up you
come, thief. Now we know where the best cheeses and elderberry wine have been going all winter. You'll pay for stealing
from Kotir."

Gonff stood slowly. Placing a paw on his plump little stomach he looked from one guard to the other with an air of in-
nocence. "Me, steal? I beg your pardon, sirs, did you know
the head cook has given me permission to borrow what I please
from his larder? Actually, I was going to return the favor by

sending him some good recipes. I understand his cooking leaves something to be desired.''

The large weasel laughed mirthlessly. ''Shall I tell you something, thief? The head cook has personally vowed to skin you with a rusty knife and roast what's left of you for supper.''

Gonff nodded appreciatively. ''Oh good, I do hope he saves some for me . . . ouch!''

Prodded between two spears, he marched off with the guards in the direction of Kotir.

A pale shaft of sunlight penetrated between the iron bars of the high window slit. The walls of the cell dripped moisture, and sometimes the faint trill of a skylark on the flatlands reached the prisoner. Martin knew that this was the onset of full, burgeoning springtime. His face was haggard, his body much thinner, but his eyes still shone with the warrior's angry brightness.

Martin rose and paced the cell with the sword handle about his neck; it seemed to grow heavier with time. Fifteen paces, whichever way he went—from door to wall or from wall to wall, it was always fifteen paces. He had paced it many times as the days and weeks grew into months. Gingivere was too far away to converse with, besides, it only made the guards angry. They stopped his bread and water for attempting to speak to the one whose name it was forbidden to mention. Now Martin believed that he really had been forgotten and left here to die under the new regime of Tsarmina. He stood in the shaft of weak sunlight, trying not to think of the world of blue skies and flowers outside.

''Get the little devil in there quick. It'll be less trouble to feed two at once. Ouch, my shin!''

Lost in thought, Martin had failed to hear the approach of guards bringing a prisoner to his cell door.

''Aargh, leggo my ear, you fiend. Hurry up with that door before he bites my lug clean off.''

''Ouch. Ow. He nipped me! Keep him still while I find my key.''

There was more shouting and scuffling as the key turned in the lock. Martin ran to the door but was immediately bowled over by another figure, which shot through the doorway straight in on top of him. Together they fell over backward, as the cell door slammed shut again. The two prisoners lay still until the pawsteps of the guards retreated down the corridor.

Martin moved gingerly, easing aside the body that had fallen
on top of him. It giggled. He pulled his cellmate into the shaft
of sunlight where he could view him more clearly.

Gonff winked broadly at him, played a short jig on his reed
flute, then began singing,

I knew a mouse in prison here,
More than a hundred years.
His whiskers grew along the ground,
And right back to his ears.
His eyes grew dim, his teeth fell out,
His fur went silver-gray.
"If my grandad were here," he said,
"I wonder what he'd say?"

Martin leaned against the wall. He could not help smiling at
his odd little cellmate.

"Silly, how could the grandfather of a hundred-year-old
mouse say anything? Sorry, my name's Martin the Warrior.
What's yours?"

Gonff extended a paw. "Martin the Warrior, eh. By gum,
Martin, you're a fine, strong-looking fellow, even though you
could do with a bit of fattening up. My name's Gonff the Thief,
or Prince of Mousethieves to you, matey."

Martin shook Gonff warmly by the paw. "Prince of Mousethieves, by the fur. You could be the King of the Sky, as long
as I've got a cellmate to speak to. What did they throw you in
here for?"

Gonff winced. "Stop squeezing my paw to bits and I'll tell
you."

They sat down on the straw together, Gonff massaging his
paw. "They caught me running down the larder stocks of wine
and cheese, you see. But don't you worry, matey, I can open
any lock in Kotir. We won't be here for too long, you'll see.
Leave it to Gonff."

"You mean you can—we can—escape from here? How,
when, where to?" Martin's voice tumbled out, shaky with excitement.

Gonff fell back against the wall, laughing. "Whoa, matey,
not so fast! Don't worry, as soon as I get things organized we'll
say byebye to this dump. But first, let's get you fed. They

should be ashamed of themselves, keeping a great lump like you on bread and water.''

Martin shrugged and rubbed his hollow stomach. ''Huh, what else is there? I was lucky to get bread and water sometimes. What do you suggest, fresh milk and oatcakes?''

''Sorry, matey. I haven't got milk or oatcakes. Would cheese and elderberry wine do you?'' he asked seriously.

Martin was lost for words as Gonff opened his tunic and spilled out a wedge of cheese and a flat canteen of wine.

''Always keep this for emergencies or trading. Here, you may as well have it. I've had enough of cheese and wine for a bit.''

Martin needed no second bidding. He wolfed away at the cheese, slopping wine as he gulped it into a full mouth. Gonff shook his head in wonder as the wine and cheese vanished rapidly. ''Go easy, matey. You'll make yourself ill. Take your time.''

Martin tried hard to take the good advice, but it was difficult after so long on starvation rations. As he ate he questioned Gonff. ''Tell me, what have I walked into around here, Gonff? I'm only a lone warrior passing through; I know nothing of Mossflower and wildcats.''

The mousethief scratched his whiskers reflectively. ''Now, let me see, where to begin. Since long before I was born the old tyrant Verdauga Greeneyes, Lord of the Thousand thingummies and so on, has ruled over Mossflower. One day long ago, he swept in here at the head of his army. They came down from the north, of course. The fortress must have been what attracted him. To woodlanders it was nothing but an old ruin that had always been there; Verdauga saw it differently, though. This was a place of plenty where he could settle, so he moved straight in, repaired it as best as he could, called the place Kotir and set himself up as a tyrant. There were none to oppose him; the woodlanders are peaceable creatures—they had never seen a full army of trained soldiers, nor wildcats. Verdauga could do just as he pleased, but he was clever: he allowed our creatures to live within his shadow and farm the land. Half of everything they produced was taken as a tax to feed him and his vermin.''

''Didn't anyone fight back?'' Martin interrupted.

Gonff nodded sadly. ''Oh yes, even now there are old ones who are still too frightened to tell of how Verdauga and his cruel daughter put down the poorly organized rebellion. Those who were not massacred were thrown into this very prison and left to rot. I'm told my own parents were among them, but I don't know the truth of it. When the rebellion was broken, Verdauga proved what a clever general he was. He actually made a kind of peace with the woodlanders. They were allowed to live within Kotir's shadow and farm the land. He said he would protect us from further attacks by bands wandering down from the north. We were partly enslaved then and very much disorganized. Not having any proper fighting strength and with all the rebellious fighters out of the way, most creatures seemed just to accept their lot. Then last summer Verdauga became ill. Since he has been sick, he has left the running of the settlement to his daughter, Tsarmina. Unlike her father, she is cruel and evil. Woodlanders have been driven too hard out on the fields and not allowed enough to live on. Hedgehogs like Ben Stickle and his family dare not run away; where could they go, with young ones to care for? However, things became so bad that a lot of them took the chance and escaped from the settlement. As the numbers grew less, Tsarmina demanded more and more from the few. I tell you, matey, it's a sad tale.''

They sat side by side, watching the shaft of sunlight striking the cell floor. Martin passed the wine to Gonff. "What do you know about the wildcat called Gingivere?"

Gonff took a sip of the wine and passed it back. "I know he never took part in any killing. Woodlanders always hoped that Verdauga would pass the reins to him. He's supposed to be a good sort, for a wildcat, that is. Now you take the sister, Tsarmina. She is pure evil—they say that she is far more savage than Verdauga. I've heard the gossip around Kotir when I've been visiting here, matey—do you know, they say old Green-eyes is dead and his son in prison here, so that means Tsarmina must be the new ruler now."

Martin nodded. "It's true. I saw and heard it myself. Gingivere is in a cell far down the corridor. I tried to speak to him but it's too far away." The warrior mouse banged his paw against the wall in frustration. "Why doesn't somebody do something, Gonff?"

The mousethief tapped the side of his nose and lowered his voice. "Sit still and listen, matey. Now the last families have left the settlement, we're making plans. All the scattered families and woodlanders have banded together out there in Mossflower Woods. They're learning to become strong once more, and the old spirit of defeat is gone now. We have real fighters training, otters and squirrels, besides hedgehogs and moles and the likes of me. We've even got a badger, Bella of Brockhall; her family used to rule Mossflower in the good old days. You'll like her. Together we form the Council of Resistance in Mossflower—Corim, see, take the first letter of each word. Ha, we're getting stronger every day."

Martin felt the excitement rising within him again. "Do you think that the Corim know we're locked up here. Will they help us to escape?"

Gonff winked broadly, a sly grin on his face. "Sssshhhhh, not so loud, matey. Wait and see."

He passed the wine flask across to Martin. "Tell me something, matey. Why do they call you warrior? Where are you from? Did you live in a place like Mossflower? Was it nice?"

Martin put the wine to one side and lay back, staring at the ceiling. "Where I come from, Gonff, there are no forests, only rocks, grass, and hills. Aye, that's the northland. I never knew a mother. I was brought up by my father, Luke the Warrior— my family have always been warriors. We lived in caves, constantly under attack by roaming bands of sea rats who came inland. You were forced to defend your cave, your piece of land, or be overrun. There were other families like us. I had lots of friends—there was Thrugg the Strong, Arrowtail, Felldoh the Wrestler, Timballisto."

Martin smiled at the memory of his companions. "Ah, it wasn't so bad, I suppose. All we seemed to do was eat, sleep and fight in those days. As soon as I was tall enough I learned to lift my father's sword and practice with it."

He touched the broken weapon strung about his neck. "Many's the enemy learned his lesson at the point of this sword—sea rats, mercenary foxes too. One time my father was wounded and had to stay in our cave. Ha, I remember all that summer, fighting off foes while he lay at the cave entrance preparing our food and calling advice to me. Then one day he took off with a band of older warriors to meet the sea rats on the shores of the waters far away. They were supposed to make an end to all invading rats forever. It was a brave idea. Before he went he gave me his trusty old sword, then he left carrying spear and shield. My father said that I should stay behind and defend our cave and land, but if he did not return by late autumn then I was to do as I felt fit.''

Gonff nodded. ''And he never returned?''

Martin closed his eyes. ''No, he never came back. I defended our land alone, against all comers. That was when they started calling me Martin the Warrior instead of Son of Luke the Warrior. I left it as late as I could that autumn; then there seemed no point in defending a cave and land just for myself. I started to march south alone. Who knows how far I would have got if I hadn't been stopped at Kotir.''

Gonff stood up and stretched. ''I'm glad you did stop here, matey. I'd hate to be sitting in this cell talking to myself. I'd sooner talk to a warrior like you.''

Martin passed the wine back. ''Aye, and I'd sooner be locked up with a thief like yourself than wandering about alone, matey.''

6

It was strange that at the very moment Gonff and Martin were discussing Corim, the council of that name was talking of them. Ben Stickle's humble home was crammed with woodland creatures, the largest of whom was a badger, Bella of Brockhall. She presided over the meeting. Also present were the Skipper of otters, Lady Amber the squirrel Chief, Ben Stickle and Billum, a dependable mole who was deputizing for his leader. Seated by the fire, Beech the squirrel answered council questions.

"Where did you see Gonff captured?"

"Westerly, over near the fringe by Kotir."

"Whatever was Gonff doing to let himself get captured?"

"Oh the usual, skylarkin' and foolin' about."

"You say it was two of Verdauga's soldiers."

"Aye, no doubt o' that. In uniform and carryin' spears."

"Where were you when all this took place, Beech?"

"Sittin' up an old oak not far off."

"Did you hear what they said?"

"Heard 'em say they was takin' him off to Kotir. Of course, you know Gonff. Treated it like a big joke, he did. No doubt they'll have wiped the silly grin off his whiskers by now down in old Greeneyes' cells.''

Lady Amber nodded at Beech. "Well done. Anything else to report?''

"No, marm. I followed them as far as I could, then I spotted Argulor perched in a spruce. Couldn't say if he was awake, so I decided to come back here, knowin' there was a gatherin' of Corim.''

Ben Stickle winked at Beech. "Aye, it's late noon, too. There's a pot of spring vegetable soup, cheese, and nutbread. D'you think you could manage some, Beech?''

The squirrel winked back at Ben, bobbed his head respectfully to the Corim leaders and was gone before further questions could be thought up.

Bella rubbed huge paws across her eyes and sat back with a grunt of despair. "Well, here's another pretty pickle our mousethief has got himself into. Any suggestions?''

Amber clucked disapprovingly. "If I had my way, I'd leave the silly creature to stew his paws in Kotir awhile. That'd teach him a lesson.''

There were murmurs of agreement.

The Skipper of otters whacked his rudderlike tail against the hearth. "Belay that kind o' talk, mates. You all know that the little uns would have gone hungry many a time, 'cept for the thief.'' Skipper gave a good-natured chuckle. "That Gonff is my kind of mouse, a true messmate. A bit light of paw, but good-hearted and an able-bodied shanty singer.''

Ben Stickle raised a paw. "I vote we rescue Gonff. We'd be ashamed to call ourselves true woodlanders, leaving one of our own in Kotir prison.''

Billum lifted a velvety paw. "Hurr, do moi vote count whoil gaffer Foremole's not yurr?''

Bella thought for a moment while they all digested the meaning of the rustic molespeech. "Of course, Billum. After all, you are Foremole's deputy and the Corim respect your judgment as a sensible mole.''

Billum squinted his round eyes with pleasure at the compliment.

By a show of paws the vote to rescue Gonff was unanimous. Then there was a temporary respite for refreshment, while the assembly helped themselves to bowls of Goodwife Stickle's famed spring vegetable soup, farls of warm nutbread and ripe yellow cheese.

Lady Amber smiled fondly at two little hedgehogs who were trying to look very fierce and brave, knowing that she was always ready to recruit warriors into her band. She dealt with them as if they were two bold squirrels.

"Show me your paws. Hmm, you'd probably make good climbers after some training. You certainly look tough enough. Goody, are these two young villains very strong?"

Goodwife put down her ladle and wiped her paws on her apron. "Ho my, yes. Ferdy and Coggs are two of the strongest. Why, you wouldn't believe your eyes if you saw these two a-gatherin' up all those great heavy dishes and washin' pots. There's no two hogs more powerful."

Much smiling and winking was in evidence as Ferdy and Coggs gathered bowls, grunting with exertion as they proved their strength by scouring a large cauldron between them.

Buckling down to the business of Gonff, the Corim set about planning his escape.

Argulor had returned to Mossflower. No creature could say why he had deserted his mountain stronghold in the far West; maybe it was that he enjoyed the comfort of woodlands where prey was far more plentiful. Argulor was a golden eagle of great age. He had grown too slow and short-sighted to pursue small creatures, so staying within handy range of Kotir and Verdauga's troops suited him. But the frightening strength and savagery of an eagle had not deserted Argulor, and if the chance of a larger animal came his way he took it, with curving talons and fierce hooked beak. Ferrets, rats, weasels and stoats made good eating, and besides, there was a pine marten living in Kotir. Admittedly it was a bit battered and bent, but Argulor had never tasted pine marten before and was determined that one day he would do so. The eagle and the wildcats had crossed trails many times over the years. Each had a healthy respect for the other. With the exception of Tsarmina. Whenever Argulor was sighted circling the sky over Kotir, Verdauga's daughter incited the soldiers to fire arrows and throw stones at the great bird, offering rewards to the creature that could bring him down. Argulor was not unduly worried by a mob of vermin loosing missiles at him, as he could outdistance anything they chose to throw. Sometimes he would hover on a thermal, slightly out of range, trying with his failing eyesight to catch a glimpse of the desired marten, or Tsarmina, whom he hated. Bright spring sunlight warmed his wings as he wheeled above the fortress.

Ashleg cringed behind his wildcat mistress as she stood glaring upward at the soaring eagle. "Shoot, you fools! Not over there, idiots! There, see, right above your thick heads."

The soldiers continued firing without success. Tsarmina grabbed a particularly slow ferret and cuffed him soundly about the head. Hurling the smarting creature to one side, she picked up his bow and notched an arrow to the string. Taking careful aim, she paused a moment as the eagle swooped lower. Swiftly she loosed the barbed shaft with a powerful hiss of flighted feathers. To the surprise of the watchers, Argulor wheeled to one side then shot upward in pursuit of the arrow. Up he went until the shaft had reached its peak of flight, then wheeling quickly inward the eagle caught the arrow in his talon and contemptuously snapped it. Zooming downward, he flew low enough to stare for a second at Tsarmina, then he beat the air with massive wingstrokes, flying away into the blue yonder.

Tsarmina would have vented her rage upon Ashleg, but he had vanished inside when he saw the eagle diving.

"Get out of my sight, you useless lot of buffoons!"

The soldiers followed Ashleg with all speed, each trying not to be last as Tsarmina was in the mood for making examples.

The wildcat stood alone pondering a question: where had she seen that same look of vengeance and fearlessness before? The mouse, that was it! She could not even recall his name; anyhow, he probably hadn't lasted the winter down in the cells.

Tsarmina watched a furtive figure coming across the parade ground, ducking and weaving, flattening itself in the shadows. She snorted scornfully; it was only Fortunata. "Frightened of a blind old eagle, vixen?"

"Milady, I was ducking the arrows and stones of your soldiers as they came down, but that was a good shot of yours," Fortunata said in a fawning voice. "A pity that the eagle caught it in midair."

The vixen jumped sharply to one side as Tsarmina fired an arrow from the ferret's bow. It landed where her paw had been a moment before.

Tsarmina notched another arrow, her eyes glinting cruelly. "Right, let's see what you're best at, fox—catching arrows or getting inside with a civil tongue in your head.''

She bent the bow back and giggled wickedly at the sight of Fortunata beating a hopskip retreat.

Sooner or later the Queen of the Thousand Eyes had the final say in all things.

Something rattled through the slit window above Martin and Gonff. In the semigloom they groped about in the straw until Gonff found the object.

Martin could not conceal his disappointment. ''Goodness me, a stick. How helpful. We could take this place single-pawed with a stick. What a useful thing to send us.''

It was not a stick. Gonff ignored his cellmate and set about undoing the thin wire that bound the bark parchment to the slim blade. He unfolded the parchment and moved into the light, where he read aloud the message it contained.

> Gonff.
>   Here are your tools. Leave by the woodland side of Kotir at the first light of dawn. We will be waiting to cover for you.
>
>   Corim.

Gonff laughed quietly as he destroyed the message. ''This is what we've been waiting for, matey. Of course they don't know about you. The plan is only supposed to cover my escape, but don't worry, we'll sort it out. The council will be glad to have a real trained warrior on their side. Now, d'you see this silly old bit of wire and this little knifeblade? Well, they're going to get us out of here, matey. These are the tools of an honorable thief.''

Martin clasped Gonff's paw warmly. ''I'm sorry, Gonff. All I did was stand here making stupid remarks. You are the expert. From now on you have an assistant who is willing to learn from your experience. In fact, you've got a real mate, matey.''

Gonff laughed and winced at the same time. ''Righto, matey, the first lesson is not to break the expert's paw by crushing it 'cos you don't know your own strength. Let's settle down now. When is the next guard patrol due?''

''In about an hour's time, regular as clockwork since I've been here. After that, there'll be nobody by until two hours after dawn when they bring the bread and water.''

"Good, that gives us time for a little rest," Gonff said, stretching out comfortably on the straw.

Martin lay down, willing himself to relax against the flood-tide of excitement building inside him. Gonff played on his flute awhile, then he began singing softly.

> Pickalock pickalock, you'll regret the day,
> When you took a mousethief and locked him away.
> Sillycat, look at that, it's two for one,
> The thief and the warrior
> By dawn will be gone.

Martin lay with his eyes closed, listening. "Who taught you that song?"

Gonff shrugged as he packed his flute away. "Nobody. Songs just spring into my head. Silly, isn't it. Sometimes old Goody Stickle says that it's Mossflower singing through me. Now and then she'll say it's a sight of seasons the sun hasn't yet shone upon."

Martin savored the phrase as they lay in the straw. "A sight of seasons the sun hasn't yet shone upon, eh. I like that, matey, your friends sound like nice creatures."

Gonff chewed on a straw. "You'll like Goody Stickle. If I did have a mother one time, then she couldn't be any nicer than Goody. Wait till you taste her spring vegetable soup, or her oat and honey scones, piping hot and oozing butter, or her apple and blackberry pudding with spices and fresh cream, or just her new yellow cheese with hot oven bread and a stick of fresh celery, aye, and a bowl of milk with nutmeg grated on top of it . . ."

The straw slipped from Gonff's lips. Martin was glad that he had dozed off. All that delicious mention of food had set his mouth watering like a stream. He was positive that he would like Goody Stickle. In fact, she would never be short of a constant admirer if her cooking was half as good as Gonff described it.

7

It was still three hours to dawn as the rescue party headed by Amber and Skipper left the Stickle dwelling. Goody pressed parcels of food upon them, clucking worriedly. "Now I don't want to hear of anyone a-gettin' theirselves catchered by those madcats. They'll eat you for sure."

Amber the squirrel Chief smiled as she hefted a pack of food. "Don't fret your spines, Goody. We're more likely to be laid low by the amount of rations you're making us take than by an enemy."

Skipper peeked inside his pack. "Marm, my old stummick'd sink in a stream if I ate half o' this. I'd be down at the bows for a week."

The small band of tough, capable woodlanders were paw-picked from Amber's squirrel archers and Skipper's otter crew. They stood about checking weapons. The otters twirled slings and selected stones, some of them balancing light throwing javelins. The squirrels waxed bowstrings and belted on full quivers.

Ben Stickle remarked to his wife, "As fine a body o' wood-landers as I've seen. Let's hope they can be of help to our little Gonff."

Ferdy and Coggs strolled out to join the band. The two small hedgehogs wore cooking pot helmets and blanket cloaks, each carried a piece of firewood, and they scowled in a warlike manner as they stood among the squirrels and otters.

The Skipper of otters clapped a paw to his brow and staggered about in mock fright. "Strike me colors, if it ain't two bloodthirsty savages. One glance at these two'd put a wildcat off his skilly an' duff for life!"

Ferdy and Coggs strutted about, tripping on their blankets but still managing to maintain fierce grimaces. Concealing a smile, Lady Amber took the two would-be warriors by their paws and positioned them outside the Stickle house. She placed one on either side of the doorway, where they stood scowling and stabbing the air with their firewood weapons. The otter and squirrel band dutifully scowled back in recognition of two fellow fighters.

Skipper gave them a broad wink and waved his muscular tail for silence. "Belay the gab and listen to me now. These here rough-lookin' coves has offered to spill some blood 'n' guts over at Kotir, but what I say is, leave the easy work to us, we'll manage that. What we need is two ruffians who'll stop at nothin' to patrol round this cottage and guard it while we're gone. I'll tell you otters 'n' squirrels, 'tis hard and dangerous work, so I'll leave my packet of tuck to keep you two villains alive while you're on watch here. That's if you think you can manage the job."

Ferdy and Coggs stood to attention, spikes bristling, cheeks puffed out with authority, practically bursting with enthusiasm. They saluted officiously as the rescue party moved off in the direction of Kotir.

Amber sniffed the light breeze. "Not more than two hours to daybreak now."

Skipper wound a slingshot about his paw. "Aye, marm. That'll give us enough time if we move along handy."

On the fringe of Mossflower, Kotir stood dark and forbidding, the very embodiment of evil and tyranny, awaiting the dawn.

Martin sat bolt upright at the sound of a bird on the outside. He shook Gonff soundly. "Wake up, sleepyhead. It'll be dawn in less than an hour."

The mousethief sat up. Rubbing his paws into half-opened

eyes, he looked upward to the narrow strip of sky through the barred window slit. "Time to go, matey."

Gonff took out his slim knifeblade. Sliding it into the keyhole of the cell door, he twitched it back and forth. "Oh good, an easy one."

With both eyes closed and a smile of pleasure on his chubby face, he jiggled the blade until there was a metallic click. "That's it, matey. Give it a shove."

Martin pushed the door, but it refused to open. "It's still shut. What's gone wrong?"

Gonff tested it carefully, pushing until he heard a slight rattle. "Bolts. I'll need a boost—can you hold me up, matey?"

Martin braced his back against the door, cupped his paws and squared his shoulders. "Try me."

The mousethief climbed up and balanced on his friend's shoulders.

Martin bore his weight patiently, hoping that Gonff's talents would do the trick. "How does it look up there?" he asked anxiously.

Gonff's voice came back punctuated by odd grunts of concentration. "No real problems, matey. Leastways, nothing that a Prince of thieves can't handle. Ha, rusty old bolts, shove a bit of greasy cheese on 'em with my knifeblade, loop the wire round the bolt handle, then it's just a matter of wiggle and jiggle and tug until it comes loose, like this one. Ha, got it!"

Martin squared his shoulders once more as Gonff sought a new position. "Now for the other lock. Hee-hee, this beats scrabbling and climbing up doors, a good strong matey to stand on. Martin, you're as solid as a rock."

"Maybe," Martin grunted. "But I'm not as thick as one, so stop prancing about on the back of my neck like that. I've been standing here for ages."

Gonff was never short of an answer. "Ages, huh? You've not been there ten seconds, and the job's near done. I've known clumsy thieves and burglars who'd keep you there until you grew gray whiskers. Just thank your lucky stars you've got an honest thief like me to look after you, matey. Look out, here it goes!"

Suddenly the door swung open, and they both tumbled in a heap out into the passage. Gonff was laughing uproariously. Martin clapped a paw across his noisy friend's mouth.

"Sssshhh! You'll have the guards coming down to check on the din."

Martin closed the door carefully and rebolted it.

Gonff was halfway along the passage when he noticed Martin was not with him. Glancing back, he saw his friend standing by a cell far down the corridor. It was Gingivere's cell, and Martin was speaking to the wildcat.

"Gingivere, do you remember me? I'm Martin the Warrior. When I was taken prisoner you were the only one who tried to help me. I've not forgotten that, even though we're on opposite sides. I've got to go now, but if there's a way that I can help you when I'm free, then I will."

Gingivere's voice reached Martin. He sounded weak and despairing. "Save yourself, Martin. Get far away from this place and my sister."

Gonff pulled Martin away, calling as he went, "I'm Gonff, the Prince of Mousethieves. We've got to go now, but if you've helped my friend then I'll try and help you someday."

As they hurried along the corridor, Gingivere's voice echoed behind. "Thank you. Good fortune go with both of you friends."

They reached the end of the passage and mounted the stairs. Gonff was panting slightly, so Martin waited while he regained his breath. The stairs were built in a spiral. At the top was a wooden door. Gonff held up a paw for silence as he eased it open. It was all clear. They stepped out into a broad hallway which stretched away to the left and right of them.

Martin scratched his head. "Which way? Left or right?"

Gonff placed his slim blade on the floor and spun it. They stood watching until it stopped. "Left. Come on, matey."

Continuing down the hallway, they saw a high window with the morning sunlight streaming through onto the top of a flat wide stairway. Gonff groaned. "Oh no, we're late. We've mistimed it because of that dark cell. Ah well, if we hurry they may still be waiting outside for us. Which way now?"

As the steps took a turn they were in a smaller hall with a door at either end. The sound of Tsarmina's voice could be heard. They froze. "If one word of this ever gets out, just one, you vixen and you Ashleg, I'll see you both hanged in chains over a roasting pit. The army will only follow the rightful leader, and now that my brother is in the cells, that's me. I am Queen of the Thousand Eyes. I rule Kotir and Mossflower."

The escapers backed down onto the stairway they had just ascended, the echoes of Tsarmina's voice all around them as they ran round the turn of the steps.

Martin and Gonff crashed straight into Tsarmina, Ashleg and Fortunata, who had unknowingly been walking up the stairs behind them!

In the shrubs and small trees that bordered the woodland edge of Kotir the otters and squirrels lay low. It was full bright morning, long past the dawn. Birds were singing. The sun beamed over bright greenery dotted with daphne, spurge laurel and late winter jasmine.

Oblivious to the beauty around him, Skipper lay whispering to Amber. "We can't hang the anchor round here much longer, marm."

Amber stared at Kotir's gloomy walls. "You're right, Skip. We could be spotted in broad daylight from those walls quite easily. Where in the name of the fur has that little thief got to?"

"We can only give him a little longer." Skipper shrugged resignedly. "Then we'll have to push off and try another day."

A young dark-colored otter came wriggling through the grass on his stomach and saluted them. "Huh, you're never goin' to believe this, Skip, but there's a whole fleet of mice dressed in funny-lookin' robes comin' this way through the woods. Never seen ought like it in all me born days."

Skipper and Amber looked quizzically at the scout. "Where?"

"Sort of circling from the south. Look, there!"

Sure enough, he had spoken truly. Through the trees a band of mice were marching, all dressed in green-brown robes, complete with cowls and rope ties about the middle.

Amber shook her head in amazement. She signaled a squirrel in a nearby tree. "Quickly, take this otter with you. Get over and tell that bunch of ninnies to get down flat. Don't they know where they are?"

Before the pair dashed off, Skipper spoke. "Stay with 'em. Soon as it's safe, take 'em in tow. Go to Brockhall—that should be large enough. Get in touch with Bella, and tell her about them. Say that me and Lady Amber will be in touch afore nightfall. Off y'go."

Amber watched them bound away, ducking and weaving.

Besides the army of Kotir, there was always Argulor to watch out for. She turned to Skipper. "What a prize bunch of boobies! Imagine parading around Kotir in broad daylight. Where d'you suppose they've come from?"

The otter snorted. "Search me. Bella will probably know as she's done a fair bit of roaming in her time. Huh, talkin' of time, I think it's nearly run out for young Gonff if he doesn't show himself soon."

Even at this early morning hour the warmth from the sun had lulled old Argulor into a drowsy sleep. The eagle perched high in a spruce, partially leaning against the trunk. In his sleep he groaned pleasurably, ruffling his plumage slightly to let the glorious warmth seep through to his ancient flesh and cold bones. If only there was a place that had no cold winter or damp windy autumn, just eternal spring followed by summer.

Life passed Argulor by as he slept the day through on his perch. It passed by more importantly in the forms of an otter and a squirrel leading a band of robed mice directly beneath the very tree where he slumbered.

It would have been hard to tell who was more surprised, the escaping prisoners or the wildcat and her minions.

Immediately they collided, Tsarmina gave a yowl of rage and more by luck than judgment seized Gonff's leg. This was followed by a more anguished yowl as Martin whipped the blade from Gonff's belt and stabbed Tsarmina sharply in the paw, forcing her to release his friend.

"Follow me!" Martin grabbed Gonff and ran back up the stairs, giving Fortunata a good slash across the rump with the blade as he went. The vixen collided with Ashleg, and they fell in a jumble. Tsarmina tripped over them. She struggled to extricate herself, screaming curses and raking the unlucky pair with her claws.

"Blockheads, idiots, out of my way."

Martin and Gonff dashed headlong down the hall. Taking the door to the right, they dived inside, slamming it shut behind them.

It was the late Lord Greeneyes' bedchamber. With the shouts of their pursuers ringing closer the escapers scuttled for cover beneath the large canopied bed.

"We can't stay here long!" Martin panted as he felt about in the darkness and found Gonff's paw.

"Don't worry, matey. Get ready to make a bolt when I shout."

There was no further opportunity for conversation, as the door banged open. Tsarmina pushed her creatures before her and closed the door. She was licking her wounded paw. Fortunata, who had suffered a loss of dignity, tried not to rub at her wounded rump. Ashleg stumped about, trying to sound helpful.

"At least we know we've got them cornered in here somewhere."

"Somewhere," echoed Fortunata. "But where?"

Tsarmina lowered her voice as she called the other two close. "We don't know how much those mice overheard. They must not leave this room alive. Let us search every corner thoroughly."

Stretched out flat beneath the bed, Martin could see the paws of their pursuers. He watched as they dispersed in separate directions, then turned toward Gonff.

In the name of mice! That little thief was the absolute limit. Gonff had actually closed his eyes and appeared to be napping. Martin prodded him urgently. The three hunters were getting closer to the bed as other hiding places were discounted.

"Ashleg, have you checked those wall hangings properly?"

"Yes, Milady. Maybe they're up on top of the bed canopy."

The pine marten was actually leaning against the side of the bed now. Gonff patted Martin reassuringly as he wriggled silently past him. The warrior mouse could only watch in dumb suspense as his daring little friend went to work.

Gonff carefully pulled the end of Ashleg's long cloak beneath the bed, slitted it expertly with his blade and crawled a short way toward the bedhead, where a tall, heavy folding screen stood to one side. Working quickly, he tied the slit ends of the unsuspecting marten's cloak around one leg of the screen.

Gonff did three things almost in one movement. He pricked Ashleg's good paw viciously with his blade, grabbed Martin and shot from beneath the bed, roaring as they went.

"There they go! Stop 'em!"

Pandemonium ensued. Ashleg screamed and lurched forward. The heavy screen went with him; it tottered and fell.

Tsarmina managed to leap out of the way, but the vixen was
not so lucky, she was struck by the screen. Half-stunned, she
pushed it away. The cumbersome screen toppled sideways into
the fireplace, falling directly into the grate, which held the embers of a previous night's fire. In a trice the room was a thick
choking mess of ashes, cinders, dust and smoldering embers.

Martin and Gonff pushed the door open. Two weasel guards
who had heard the noise in passing came thundering into the
room as Martin and Gonff hurried past them out into the hall.
Behind them the shouts reached a crescendo as unprotected
paws came in contact with a floor strewn with red-hot embers.

This time Martin took the lead as they went straight down
the hall and through the door at the opposite end.

They found themselves in an upper messroom full of soldiers, stoats, ferrets and weasels, all eating breakfast at a long
trestle table with a window at one end. Taken completely by
surprise, the soldiers sat gaping at the two fugitives.

"Stop those mice! Kill them!" Tsarmina's enraged shouts
reached them as she ran toward the mess.

Gonff sized up the situation at a glance: the unexpected was
called for. Without a second thought he pulled Martin with him.
They ran across the room, bounded from a vacant seat up onto
the tabletop and dashed madly along it, scattering food, drink
and vessels everywhere as they went. Together the thief and
the warrior leaped through the open window into empty space
with a loud defiant shout.

"Yaaaaaaaahhhhhhh!"

Skipper and Amber both heard the cry.

So did Argulor.

It came from the north side of Kotir, not far from where the
woodlander squirrel scout stood perched in a tree. He bounded
down and made his report to Amber. "It's Gonff, but there's
another mouse with him. They jumped from the upper barracks
window."

"We'd better get round there. Are they hurt?"

"No, but talk about lucky, they landed right in the foliage
of a big old yew growing on that side."

Amber leaped up. "Get Beech and the others. We'll have to
get them out of there double quick. Skipper, you bring the crew
and give us cover."

Argulor launched himself from his spruce, flapping ponderously. Once he was airborne his natural grace and ability took over. Circling to gain height, he squinted over to where the sounds had come from. The yew's upper foliage was shaking. The eagle soared downward to see if it was anything edible.

Inside the messroom, Tsarmina laid about herself with a sturdy wooden ladle. "Don't stand gawping, you dimwitted toads! Someone get out there and capture them!"

There was an immediate stampede to grab weapons and buckle armor on. Nobody seemed disposed to leap out of the window, though they all tried to look as if they were helping in some way.

Tsarmina flailed the ladle about in a fury. Suddenly a bright young stoat, more reckless than his comrades, saw a chance to distinguish himself in the eyes of his mistress. He bounded up onto the table.

"Leave it to me, Milady. I'll stop them." Striking a gallant pose, the stoat ran to the window ledge and stood nerving himself for the leap.

Argulor soared low, close to the yew. His rheumy eyes could not distinguish much between the crisscross branches. He was about to abandon hope of a quick meal and turn away on his huge wing span, when suddenly a fat juicy stoat with an expression of heroic duty upon its face jumped out into midair, straight into the talons of the wheeling eagle.

Argulor gave a screech of delight, which contrasted jarringly with the stoat's ragged squeal of dismay. The old eagle flapped joyfully off to his spruce branch with the tasty burden.

Gonff wiped perspiration from his whiskers. "In the name of mice and crab apples, that big feller nearly had us there, matey!"

Martin pointed to the open window. "It's not over yet. Look!"

Tsarmina stood glaring at them. The mess was crowded with frightened creatures, none of whom would venture near the window.

Ashleg shuddered and clutched at his clammy fur. "Did you see those claws, ugh, the size of its beak!"

Tsarmina swung him round by his cloak. "Shut your blathering face and get me my bow and arrows. Just look at that for a prize piece of impudence."

Gonff was pulling faces at the wildcat Queen. He blew out

his cheeks, stuck a paw to his nose and rolled his eyes in the most ridiculous manner.

Tsarmina snatched up a spear and flung it, but the weapon was deflected by the close-knit yew branches. A well-aimed arrow would do the trick, she thought. "Where's that dithering woodenleg with my bow and arrows?"

Eight sturdy red squirrels came bounding through the yew branches as easily as walking a paved path. They split into two groups of four, each taking charge of the two escapers.

Lady Amber came swinging in. She spoke sternly to Gonff. "Now none of your shenanigans, young thief. You, whoever you are, just relax and leave the rest to us. You're in safe paws."

Before he could say a word, Martin was seized by paws and tail. He felt himself tossed about like a shuttlecock. Never in his life had he descended from a height so swiftly, or with such ease; it was like being a flower petal on a gentle breeze. In a trice he and Gonff were on firm ground.

A horde of armed soldiers poured out of Kotir. Martin sought about for a weapon, anything to defend himself with. There was a whirring sound, and the first four soldiers running forward seemed to relax, lying down upon the grass as if they were taking a nap. Two more went down. Martin saw a line of otters swinging slings; they were hurling large river pebbles with deadly accuracy.

A big burly otter came running to them. Gonff clasped his strong tattooed paws. "Skipper, I knew me old messmate wouldn't leave his favorite thief in the lurch. Oh, by the way, this is Martin the Warrior. He's my friend, y'know."

Skipper signaled his crew to retreat, waving to Lady Amber as he fitted another stone to his slingshot. "Ha, welcome aboard, Martin. Though how an honest fellow like you came to be mixed up with this little buccaneer, I don't know."

Skipper introduced Martin to Lady Amber, who said rapidly, glancing anxiously about her, "Pleased to meet you, I'm sure, Martin. Skipper, I don't like this, they're planning something . . ."

As Amber spoke, a horde of soldiers bearing Thousand Eye shields came streaming out of the main door with Tsarmina leading them. There were far too many to contend with.

Amber muttered to Skipper, "Take Martin and Gonff. Break and run for it. We'll cover you."

Tsarmina was furious. She guessed what was happening: the squirrels were taking a stand while the otters slipped off into Mossflower with the fugitives. She issued orders to a ferret Captain named Raker. "Stop here with a platoon and face the squirrels. I'll take the rest and circle around them, and we'll cut them off. They won't realize I'm following, so they'll slow down a bit when they think they're in the clear."

Raker saluted. "As you say, Milady. Here you, Scratch, and you, Thicktail, take your squads and follow the Queen."

The two weasel Captains saluted with their spears, then detailed their creatures to follow Tsarmina. The wildcat had bounded off alone, taking a wide loop south and back east.

Nothing aggravated Raker more than squirrel resistance fighters; they were like smoke in a breeze, here and gone. He took aim and heaved his spear at their leader, but it was a complete waste of time. Amber stood back drily, twirling her sling, and ducking as she let the spear graze harmlessly past. Directing her troops back across the open ground, she loosed a heavy pebble at tremendous speed. Raker threw his shield up in the nick of time, staggering backward as the stone struck his shield and bounced off. When the ferret lowered his shield it was as if there had never been a squirrel inside Kotir's grounds.

They were gone into Mossflower.

High in the branches of the trees that fringed the woodland, squirrels shook with silent laughter at the dumbfounded expression on Raker's face. He shook a mailed paw at the trees. "Come out and fight, you cowards!"

One last thunderous hail of stones, arrows and javelins sent the Kotir soldiery scurrying for cover.

The treetops rustled and swayed. Distant laughter told the enemy that the squirrels were swinging away through the sunlit upper terraces of leafy Mossflower.

8

Bella of Brockhall's huge striped face lit up with pleasure. "Well, this is a rare and unexpected pleasure, Abbess Germaine. Come in, all of you, welcome to Brockhall."

Abbess Germaine led the Brothers and Sisters of Loamhedge into Bella's ancestral home, down the long twisting passage into the massive cavelike main hall, whose ceiling was the arched roots of the great oak above Brockhall. They made themselves at home around the wide hearth, whilst Bula the otter and Pear the squirrel, who had acted as their guides, explained to Bella what had taken place.

The badger listened carefully, settling back in her old armchair. "I had an idea something like this would happen. That's why I left Goody Stickle's and came home here. Nothing ever goes as planned with Gonff. Still, not to worry, that young rip will be as right as rain, you'll see. First things first. Let's get you all fed. You must be famished. I was baking a batch of chestnut bread. It'll be ready soon. I'll make some celery and fennel stew with hazelnut dumplings and get a cheese up from the storeroom. Now stop looking noble, the pair of you. I know what growing otters and squirrels are like. You can wait here after you've eaten until the rest get back. Fetch bowls from the shelf for our guests. That's it, make yourselves useful."

Eagerly the woodlanders did as they were bid, then they sat with the Loamhedge Brothers and Sisters.

Bella rose and embraced Abbess Germaine. "My old friend, we were many summers younger when last we ate together."

The Abbess placed a thin, worn paw over Bella's hoary pad. "Yes, the seasons are born anew, but alas we grow older, my friend."

"But not you, Germaine," Bella chuckled. "You look as young as ever. What news of Loamhedge?"

The Abbess could not prevent a tear trickling onto her gray whiskers. "Loamhedge, what magic in that name. But the happy times there are gone like leaves down a stream. You heard of the great sickness?"

Bella nodded. "I had heard something from travelers, but I thought it was far south. I did not think it had found its way to your home."

Germaine shook and closed her eyes as if trying to ward off the memory. "Only those you see here escaped. It was horrible. Everything it touched withered and died, I could not . . ."

Bella patted the old mouse gently. "There, there, no need to say more. Try to forget it. You can call my home your own, for you and your mice, as long as you like, and please don't thank me—you'd do exactly the same if I needed shelter. In fact you did, many years ago, when I was young and liked to travel."

The two old friends went to the kitchen and began preparing the meal. Bella told Germaine of all that had taken place in Mossflower. "This is a sad and oppressed place you have come to, though once it was happy under the rule of my father, Boar the Fighter. I was still young then. I returned from my wanderings with Barkstripe—he was my mate; we met far to the southeast and returned to stay with my father at Brockhall. I think that father was waiting for this to happen. My mother was long ago gone to the gates of Dark Forest; she died when I was a cub. Boar the Fighter was a good father, but a restless spirit. He had tired of ruling Mossflower and wanted to go questing, just as his father, Old Lord Brocktree, did before him. One day he left here and Barkstripe ruled in his stead. Those were good seasons. We had a cub, a little male called Sunflash because of his forestripe, which had an odd golden tinge. He was a sturdy little fellow.

"In the autumn of that year the wildcats arrived. Verdauga and his brood took over that old ruin of a fortress. There was no one to oppose him, and he brought with him a vast horde of wicked vermin. At first we tried to fight back, but they were so cruel and merciless that they completely crushed us. Barkstripe led a great attack upon Kotir, but he was slain, along with many others. Those who did not escape into Mossflower were caught and left to rot in Verdauga's prisons. Alas, that was all long ago. We have learned to keep ourselves safe here in the thick woodlands now."

Germaine drew loaves from the oven on a long paddle. "Where is your son, Sunflash? He must be quite big now."

Bella paused as she laid the bread to cool. "While I was ill and grieving for Barkstripe, our son stole out of here one night. They say he went to Kotir to avenge his father's death, but he was far too young. Sunflash has never been seen or heard of since. Many, many seasons have gone by since then, so I think that one way or another my son ended up at the gates of Dark Forest with his father."

Outside in Mossflower the afternoon shadows began to lengthen over the trees that were budding and leafing, promising a thick emerald foliage for the summer. In another part of Mossflower not far from Kotir, a mailed tunic and tabard bearing the Thousand Eye device slipped carelessly from a high spruce branch and landed in a crumpled heap on the forest floor. Argulor shifted from claw to claw as he preened his pinions, carefully arranging his long wing feathers. A good fat stoat would be extremely welcome, but pine marten . . . ah, that was a delight he had yet to savor. Argulor would wait. His time would come; a marten with a wooden leg could only run so fast in any direction. The eagle snuggled down into his plumage, glad that the spring nights were kind to young and old alike. It was good to visit old hunting grounds again.

9

The evening chorus of birdsong fell sweetly upon Martin's ears as he strolled along through the woodlands with Skipper and Gonff, reveling in his new-found freedom after the long winter in Kotir prison. The otters were never still; they were playful as puppies, bounding and cavorting through the trees and bushes. Skipper was instructing Martin in the art of the sling-shot. He was delighted to have such a keen pupil and took every opportunity of amazing the warrior mouse with his expertise. Casting a pebble high into the air, Skipper reslung a second pebble and shot it, hitting the first one before it had time to fall to earth. The otter shrugged modestly. "It's only tricks, me hearty. I can teach you them anytime. Ha, I'll bet afore the summer's through you'll be able to sling a pebble across any villain's bows."

Gonff was great friends with the otters. He wholeheartedly shared their recklessness and sense of madcap fun. The little thief imitated their nautical mode of speech perfectly, telling Martin that he was, "As likely a cove as ever pirated vittles from Kotir's galley."

Martin enjoyed himself. Having been a solitary warrior for so long, he found it a pleasant change to be in the company of

such gregarious friends. Skipper presented him with his own
personal sling and pouch of throwing pebbles. He accepted the
gift gratefully. The otters were naturally curious about the broken sword hilt Martin kept strung about his neck, so he told
them the story, and was taken aback by their hatred of Tsarmina. Though, as Skipper remarked, "Wildcats never bothered
us. Once our crew is together, there ain't nothin' on land or
afloat that'll trouble otterfolk."

Looking about, Martin could quite believe it. Gonff danced
on ahead with two otters who did a hornpipe as he sang.

I'm a mouse with a very long tail,
With a heart and voice to match.
I've escaped from the pussycats' gaol.
They'll find me hard to catch.
So, away, through the grass, the flow'rs and leaves,
Like smoke on the breeze, the Prince of Thieves.
Let's cheer for the day when we will see
The Mossflower country safe and free.

Martin was tapping the happy tune from paw to paw when
he saw that Skipper had dropped back a few paces. The otter
was standing with an air of intense concentration, swaying from
side to side, sniffing the breeze. At a sign from him, Gonff
stopped singing and the entire crew grew silent.

Skipper said in a gruff whisper, "Some beast's a-comin,
mates. Not from astern, mind. Over yonder there. Birds stopped
singin' over that way first. Ha, I'll wager it's the cat." Skipper
pointed. They could soon make out shapes moving from tree
to tree. As the intruders drew nearer, it was plain to see they
were Kotir soldiers in full armor, led by Tsarmina, a barbaric
figure wearing a splendid cloak and a helmet that covered her
head completely except for slitted eye, ear and mouth apertures.

At Skipper's growl of command, the otter crew spread themselves out in fighting formation, faces grim, weapons at the
ready. Skipper stood fearlessly out in the open where Tsarmina
could see him, paws folded across his chest, a sling hanging
from the right one, loaded and ready. Tsarmina halted a short
distance away. She stretched out a paw, letting a wickedly
sharp claw spring dramatically forth to point at Martin and
Gonff.

"The mice are mine, otter. I will take them from you."

Skipper's voice was hard as flint. "Back off, cat. You're on my quarterdeck now. This is Mossflower, not Kotir."

"All the land belongs to me," Tsarmina said imperiously. "I am Tsarmina, Queen of Kotir and Mossflower. These mice are escaped prisoners. Give them to me now, and I will not punish you. Your creatures will be allowed to go unharmed."

A thin smile played about Skipper's mouth. "Go and chase your mangy tail, pussycat!"

The breath hissed from between Tsarmina's teeth at the otter's fearless impudence. She raised a paw to her soldiers, who began fitting arrows to bowstrings. As they did, some sixth sense tingled through the wildcat and she looked up. Lady Amber stood in a tall elm, in her paw a light javelin poised for throwing. Reacting instinctively, Tsarmina grabbed the nearest soldier to her—a ferret.

There was a swish and a thud. She felt the impact as the luckless soldier took the javelin that was intended for her.

The squirrel Queen concealed her disappointment at the lost opportunity by aiming another javelin and calling out, "Unstring those bows quick, all of you. She can't hold him in front of her for long, and this next one will get her between the eyes if you don't obey me right now!"

Tsarmina, still holding the ferret with the spear protruding from his lifeless form, said urgently out of the side of her mouth, "Do as the squirrel says."

They obeyed instantly.

Tsarmina let the ferret fall, twisting the body as she let go of it. Skipper was backing off into the bushes with his crew. He waved up to Amber. "Thankee kindly, marm. D'you mind keepin' a weather eye clapped on 'em while we push off?"

Suddenly the wildcat plucked the javelin from the fallen soldier and flung it up at Lady Amber.

"Cut and run crew!" Skipper shouted as he bolted off with the rest. Amber had momentarily relaxed the javelin in her paw; she ducked in the nick of time as her weapon came hurtling back at her. Tsarmina did not wait to see if she had scored a hit but took off after Skipper and the crew, yelling, "This way! Cut them off through the bushes!"

Martin and Gonff ran with the otters, Skipper urging them on as they pounded through the undergrowth. "Hurry now, crew. Amber can't hold 'em off forever—there's too many of 'em. Hark, they're back on to us."

Tsarmina was no fool; she had sensed the direction they would take. Accordingly, she retreated then came back at a tangent to cut down the distance on an angle. Suddenly Martin and Gonff found themselves on the banks of a broad fast-flowing river with steep grassy sides. Skipper stamped his paws and sighed. "Belay, we nearly made it. Too late, here they come!"

Tsarmina and her troops broke through the trees and came hurrying along the bank toward them.

Martin could see there would be no talking this time. He drew his sling, as did the otters around him. They let fly the first volley before their foes had time to notch arrows or raise spears. The hail of stone caught the enemy head-on. Rock clattered on armor as Tsarmina threw herself flat yelling at her soldiers, "Down, get down and return fire!"

Martin saw two otters felled by heavy spears. Now Skipper's crew was trapped between the open stretch of bank and the river. The otter crew rattled off another salvo of rocks.

This time Tsarmina had anticipated it; she had the front rank take the stones on their shields, while another rank behind hurled their spears over the tops of the shield-bearers. Some of the spears went too far, but one found its mark: an otter standing up with a whirling sling dropped back, killed by a well-aimed throw.

Reinforcements arrived, with Lady Amber bringing squirrel archers through the trees to fire at the Kotir troops from behind.

Skipper saw Tsarmina's forces turn to face the new foe. He seized his chance. Martin found himself grabbed by the otter leader, while Gonff was clasped by a big otter named Root. "Take a good breath, messmate. We're goin' for a swim!"

The entire otter crew took a short bounding run and dived into the river with a loud splash.

Tsarmina was facing the squirrels with an arrow notched to a bow. She spun round and loosed the shaft, catching the last otter in the back before it hit the water. Despite this, the otter still managed to submerge and get away.

Lady Amber found that she was losing troops. She decided on a quick withdrawal now that the otters had escaped. Ducking the arrows and spears, the squirrels took off through the trees.

Tsarmina howled her victory to the sky. Running to the water's edge, she called a halt to those soldiers who were aiming weapons into the river. "Enough! Cease fire! They're gone. Stand still, everyone."

The troops stood fast as the wildcat peered into the depths. They watched Tsarmina draw back from the river's edge. She was scratching at her fur as if trying to dry herself, shuddering as she muttered, "Urgh! Dark, damp, wet—water everywhere, swirling, swirling. Ugh!" When she was away from the water, Tsarmina recovered her composure. Throwing off her helmet and cloak, she slumped moodily at the foot of a beech tree. Night had crept up unawares. The soldiers stood watching, puzzled at their Queen's strange behavior. Tsarmina stared back. "Well, what are you all gawping at? Brogg, Scratt, listen carefully. I want you to go back to Kotir, see Fortunata, and tell her to bring the Gloomer to me. I want you back before dawn. Get going, the pair of you!"

Brogg and Scratt stood rooted; terror loosened their tongues. "The Gloomer, Milady? Surely you don't mean . . ."

"Lady, he's completely mad!"

Tsarmina rolled herself in her cloak and settled down beneath the tree. "I know he is, idiots. But I'll get a sight madder if you don't move yourselves. Now be off! Guards, set up a sentry on river watch. If anything happens, let me know straightaway. Otherwise I'm not to be disturbed until Fortunata arrives with the Gloomer. If Brogg and Scratt are still here, give them a good whipping with bowstrings for idling." Tsarmina settled down to sleep, lulled by the sounds of the two ferrets crashing and blundering off through the undergrowth.

Nothing could escape the Gloomer in the water. The wildcat Queen had tasted victory that day. She was not about to let it all slip away because of incompetent soldiers. The Gloomer must be brought here quickly to consolidate her triumph.

10

The whole world was black, icy cold, airless, and wet.

Martin concentrated on holding his breath. When he ventured to open his eyes, it became a murky dark gray, but he could sometimes make out shapes moving around him. He began to wish he were anywhere but beneath a river—even back in his cell at Kotir. At least there had been air to breathe there.

Skipper's strong paws gripped him relentlessly by the scruff of his neck. Water rushed by them, roaring in his ears as the powerful swimming otter dragged him along.

Fresh air, just one breath, he wished, one lungful of good clean air.

Skipper held Martin tighter as he began to wriggle in panic. Bubbles of air were escaping from his mouth, an iron band was crushing his skull. Why was Skipper drowning him?

Martin opened his mouth to shout, but the water came pouring in. With a huge rush accompanied by much barking and shouting, the otters broke the surface, shaking their coats.

Skipper hefted Martin's body and tossed him out upon the bank. The warrior mouse lay coughing and gasping, gulping in vast quantities of clean fresh air. Never again would he take such a wondrous gift for granted.

All around him otters were whooshing playfully in and out of the water, ducking one another and generally behaving as if the whole thing were a great lark. Martin looked about until he sighted Gonff. Immediately he dashed across to his friend. Gonff had not fared as well as he on the underwater journey; the little thief lay face down on the bank, his body looked forbiddingly limp and still. Root, the big otter who had borne Gonff underwater, began pushing and pumping at Gonff's inert form with his strong forepaws.

Martin felt a surge of panic. "Is he all right? He's not drowned? He'll live, won't he?"

Root laughed and gave Martin a huge wink. "Bless yer life, matey, he's fine. Little thief, stealin' our river-water like that. Here, he's comin' around now."

A moment later Gonff was spluttering and shaking indignantly. "Root, you great clodhopping water monster, I'm sure you took the long way around to get here. Have I coughed all that water back? Yuk! Bet I lowered the river level by a foot or two, matey. Oh, hello Martin. Well, how d'you like Camp Willow?"

Martin had not looked at his surroundings. Now that the danger was past, he took stock of where they had beached. It was a large, sandy, shelflike area, the roof of which was a mass of gnarled willow roots. Phosphorescence from the swift-flowing water palely illuminated the cave system of the underground bank. A canal ran through the middle of Camp Willow, emanating out of the gloomy darkness of hidden caves and bolt holes in the rear.

Skipper watched proudly as Martin gazed about. "You won't find no better 'ccommodation for an otter anywhere, Martin. Camp Willow was built by otter paws."

Martin nodded shrewdly. "A right fine job they did of it, too, Skipper."

The Skipper of otters swelled out his barrel-like chest. "'Andsome of you to say so, mate, but belay awhile and I'll call muster."

It soon became apparent that three of the crew were dead, possibly four; nobody could account for the fact that a young female called Spring was missing. Skipper's face was grim as he called two young males, Duckweed and Streamer, to search the river for the missing one. With barely a ripple, the two plunged back into the water and were gone.

Martin and Gonff were given rough barkcloths to dry themselves. They sat upon the bank with the otters around a bright
fire, eating thick wedges of carrot and parsley bread, which they
dunked in a steaming bowl of river shrimp and bulrush soup,
seasoned with fiery ditchnettle pepper. It was delicious, but
extremely hot.

The otters munched away happily, laughing at the two mice
and calling out old river proverbs.

"Haha, don't taste no 'otter to an otter, matey."

"The more 'otter it is, the more 'otter otters likes it."

Martin and Gonff swigged cold water and laughed along
with the crew.

Not long before they settled down to sleep, Duckweed and
Streamer returned. They emerged, dripping, into Camp Willow.
Between them they were supporting young Spring. Streamer
had removed the arrow from Spring's back. Fortunately, she
was not badly hurt.

Skipper was delighted to see her, and he dressed the wound
carefully. "Ho, 'tis me, little matey Spring. Never you fear,
young un. If they gave you an arrow, we'll pay 'em back with
a shower of javelins. You get some vittles and a good rest.
You'll be right as a river rock tomorrow."

Spring told them what had happened.

"When I got hit I didn't swim away for fear of leavin' a
blood trail in the water, so I swam a little ways then laid under
a bush hangin' over the bank. I slapped a good pawful o' mud
on my wound to stop the bleedin' and lay waiting. I knew Skip
wouldn't leave me long afore he sent help. I was that close to
some of those vermin sittin' on the bank that I could have
reached out and laid a flipper on 'em. They were all talkin'
about somethin' called a Gloomer—said that the cat had sent
messengers to Kotir to fetch this Gloomer thing."

Skipper patted Spring. "Well done, matey. You get some
sleep now, and don't fret your 'ead about nothin'. Old Skip'll
take care of it."

Root struck his thigh with a heavy paw. "Ha! The
Gloomer—I might've knowed it, Skip. What'll we do now?"

The fire burned low in the Stickle dwelling as Goody tidied
around before going to join Ben outside. It was a peaceful
spring night. Ben knocked his pipe out on the gatepost.
"Should be a fair day on the morrow, old girl."

They both stood nodding. Suddenly Goody threw up her paws. "Well, in the name of Stickles, will you just look at those two liddle 'ogs a layin' there."

Ferdy and Coggs had really taken their sentry duty to heart. They had rigged up a tent from a blanket and branches. Nearby lay a jug of strawberry cordial and a half-finished apple pie which they had requisitioned from Goody's cupboard. The two little hedgehogs lay with their arms about each other, snoring uproariously, cooking pot helmets askew, mouths wide open.

Ben chuckled fondly. "I do believe we'll sleep sounder in our beds, Goody, knowin' we've got these two terrors to guard us through the night."

As Goody folded the blanket away, Ben carried Ferdy and Coggs inside.

Still asleep, Ferdy waved his stick. "Who goes there? I'll fight the six of you!"

11

At Kotir, Fortunata was also sleeping peacefully, until the banging of spearbutts against her chamber door brought her yawning and shuffling from her bed.

"Who's there? Go away and see Ashleg about it, whatever it is."

Brogg and Scratt stood aside as Cludd, the weasel Captain of the guard, kicked the door open. "Come on, fox. You're wanted by Queen Tsarmina. She's camped by the River Moss."

Fortunata rubbed her injured rump. "Couldn't Ashleg go? I'm injured."

Cludd's stolid face was expressionless. "No, the Queen wants you there by dawn. You're to bring the Gloomer with you. Brogg and Scratt'll lend a paw."

Fortunata recoiled with fright and distaste. "The Gloomer! I thought that horror had died years ago or gone away." Cludd pointed his spear at the vixen. "Come on now, no nonsense. You know what Milady's like if you disobey her orders. We'll make sure Gloomer's well secured."

Fortunata had no choice. In a foul temper, she followed the three soldiers down corridors and flights of stairs to the very bowels of the fortress.

Far beneath the cells there was an underground cavern and a great lake. The only one who ever went down to the lake was the guard who was detailed to feed the Gloomer. Once a week he would take down the refuse from the barracks, leaving it a respectable distance from the post to which Gloomer's long chain was attached at the lake's edge.

Verdauga had captured Gloomer and brought him to Kotir long ago. The monster water rat was robbed of normal sight after years of swimming in the dark murky waters of the lake. It had little hearing and no speech at all. None of this mattered while it still possessed the instincts of touch and smell; the Gloomer was a killer, savage and mindless, particularly when there was fresh meat to be had.

Fortunata was frightened; this was no place to be in the night hours. Gingerly she picked up the chain. The rattling iron links echoed eerily around the cold musty cavern, and what little courage the fox had failed her. She dropped the chain, looking imploringly toward Cludd. "I'm only a vixen. This will take a creature strong and brave as a Captain of the Guard."

The obvious slyness of the remark did not escape Cludd, yet he swelled slightly at the flattery. Taking the chain firmly, he nodded at the others. "Right. Stay out of the way and leave this to me. I know how to deal with Gloomer."

Tugging hard on the rusty chain, Cludd splashed it up and down in the water as he pulled. The underground lake rippled, and there was an audible gasp of shock from the three onlookers as the Gloomer's monstrous head appeared from the depths like the worst kind of vision from a bad dream. The eyes were staring, sightless white marbles veined with blood-red streaks, the snout ribbed and scarred like a wet black patch of leather. What little fur there was on the head was plastered flat. Water ran off it as the mouth opened wide.

Even Cludd felt his paws shaking as the Gloomer swam toward land. The sightless eyes were fixed upon the weasel Captain as if they could actually see him. The mouth worked hungrily open and shut, purple blubbery lips drawn back to reveal curving greeny-yellow fangs spread this way and that, the very oddness of them adding to their revolting appearance.

Cludd dropped the chain and picked up his spear, his voice shaking noticeably. "Here, Brogg, Scratt, grab your spears and do as I do. Keep driving that thing in a circle around the post."

Gloomer paused for a moment in the shallows, water dripping from its ugly bulk, the hideous head moving to and fro as it scented the soldiers and pinpointed them by their sound and movement. Then in a sudden rush Gloomer charged with an awesome turn of speed.

The trio were highly nervous but ready. Dodging and prodding Gloomer with spearpoints, they kept the monster pursuing them clockwise around the post, Cludd bawling instructions as he ran.

"Don't stop, whatever you do. Keep it moving!"

Fortunata was impressed; the plan was simple but effective.

The trio skipped, jumped and ran as Gloomer pursued them mindlessly. It was not until the entire chain had been wound around the post that Gloomer was forced to stop. The post shook with the beast's maddened efforts to push forward. Brogg and Scratt kept their spearpoints at its back, so it could not unwind the chain by going in the reverse direction. Cludd leaned his weight against the chain to keep it tight, and called to Fortunata, "Get the leads attached to the collar, quickly!"

With icy fear coursing through her veins and an expression of extreme distaste on her face, Fortunata obeyed. Cludd strained at the chain, watching Fortunata impatiently. "Stop dabbing and primping, fox. Get those leads fastened, or I'll loosen this chain."

Fortunata secured the last of the three heavy greased leather halters around the short, powerful neck, which already bore a studded iron collar. Detaching the chain, she jumped backward and made for the stairs. "There. It's done! I know which way to go. You three get hold of the leads and follow me."

Cludd called out sternly, "Get back here, lily liver, I'm not going anywhere. Captain of the Guard's my job. If the Queen had wanted me, she would have said. Come on, take one of these leads."

Immediately Fortunata picked up the lead; Gloomer moved toward her. She hurried swiftly ahead to keep Gloomer from her. Brogg and Scratt stood on either side and slightly back, pulling their leads tight, straining to control Gloomer. Cludd watched them go, glad he had completed his distasteful task.

Fortunata led the way. Having lived in Mossflower all her life, she was familiar with the area. She increased her pace to keep the maximum distance between herself and the huge gray and black beast. Gloomer snuffled and tugged, this way and that; Brogg and Scratt strained on the leads to keep it going the right way. The moon over the woodlands shone through the trees on the reluctant trio and their monstrous charge as they blundered and crashed through Mossflower, disturbing the peaceful night, tainting it with evil.

12

Martin was awake before dawn. He fed the fire and sat by it.
Skipper came and sat with him. "Now then, messmate. You've
got a face on you like a wet waterbeetle's grandad. Why so
worried?"

Martin smiled half-heartedly. "Oh, it's listening to those sto-
ries that the crew were telling about the Gloomer, I suppose.
It's all my fault for coming here and causing trouble for you,
Skipper."

The big otter gave Martin a hearty clap on the back that
nearly sent him head over tail. "Ha harr. Bless your little 'eart,
me old warrior. You don't want to listen to that scuttlebutt.
Was that all you was afeared of? You come with me and I'll
introduce you to our Stormfin."

"Stormfin?"

"Aye, Stormfin, matey. Come 'ere to the back of the cave."

In the darkness of the cavern recess, Skipper showed Martin
a sluicegate that blocked the canal across its middle. There were
narrow spaces in the gate, allowing the water to flow through.
At one side was a hollow log.

Skipper picked up a cudgel and passed it to Martin. "Listen,
mate, that big pussycat may 'ave a Gloomer, but us otters got

a Stormfin. You start thumpin' that there log and I'll raise the sluicegate. Stay clear of the water's edge, though."

Mystified, Martin began banging the log. The eerie sounds bounced off the cavern walls as Skipper raised the gate clear of the water.

The otter nodded sagely. "That'll warn anyone who's in the water to get out, Stormfin's comin'. Watch the canal, now, and don't forget to stay clear."

Far back in the darkness something was beginning to come forward. A smooth wave rose; it slopped over the sides as the water was pushed along by some tremendous force. Martin was about to question Skipper when the otter lowered the gate slightly, and the water began roiling and bubbling. A long shape, like a section of tree trunk, smooth, with a many-spiked dorsal fin emerged.

Martin gasped and jumped back. "That's Stormfin?"

"Aye, this is Stormfin, matey. Me and my brother trapped him long ago." Skipper leaned forward and patted the giant pike's fin, causing it to lash its tail. The water boiled into a white foam as the otter leaped back laughing.

"Hohoho! Take a look, Martin. You wouldn't like to cross that cove's path if you was out a swimmin', now would you?"

Martin leaned forward. He saw the powerful bony head with its muddy eyes and long hooking underjaw. The mouth opened slightly. He had never seen so many teeth in one mouth; there were row upon row of jagged backward curving rippers, needle-sharp and milky white. Stormfin seemed to be smiling in anticipation. With a flick of his mighty silver-and-black-banded bulk he butted his head against the lowered sluicegate, anxious to be freed into open water.

Skipper stood with both paws on the gate lever. "Right then, you old buccaneer. Don't eat him too quick, now; you'll make yourself sick."

Martin helped Skipper to weigh down upon the lever. The sluicegate lifted. Stormfin rushed through, creating a miniature tidal wave as he traveled. Skipper left the gate open.

"He'll be back in a few days. We coax him in with tidbits. Pity there ain't more'n one Gloomer. That pike has a terrible appetite."

Panting and rasping, the Gloomer dragged on the leads. The trio looked toward Tsarmina as they dug their paws into the turf and were dragged helplessly toward the River Moss.

Fortunata began to panic. "Milady, quick, give the word, or it will have us in the water!"

Tsarmina extended her paws and raised them as if starting a race. "Right, you three, when I let my paws drop the—"

Too late. Gloomer snapped the lead Fortunata was holding and the two guards were pulled over on their faces. Immediately they let their leads go; Gloomer splashed noisily into the water.

The monster water rat swam about in slow circles, scenting and feeling vibrations in the river current. Without warning it dived, heading in the direction of Camp Willow.

The soldiers of Kotir ran alongside the bank, following Gloomer's progress and shouting excitedly.

"Look, he's after something. Hey, Gloomer, eat an otter for me!"

"Don't eat 'em, kill 'em all, Gloomer! Rip them to bits!"

A ferret who had run ahead of the rest called back to his comrades, "Something's coming! I think it's the otters. No, wait, it's a big fish of some sort."

Swift chevrons of water rippled out to both sides of the bank as Stormfin sped downstream like a great arrow.

Gloomer thrashed the water as he swam upstream, feeling his prey getting near.

Closer and closer the leviathans came toward each other. Gloomer lifted his snout clear of the water, sucking in a huge gasp of air. He submerged again and waited, facing the oncoming foe, mouth slightly agape, claws at the ready.

Stormfin looked as if he was smiling. The underslung jaw clamped shut, pointing at his adversary like a battering ram, he piled on extra speed, drew his fins in tight and came at Gloomer like an arrow from a bow. The onlookers on the bank saw a spout of water shoot high like a geyser as the combatants crashed together.

Gloomer had the breath driven from him as Stormfin struck his ribs. Disregarding the pain, the rat sought the pike with his teeth, feeling his heavy claws rake searingly through its scales.

With the madness of battle upon him, Stormfin rose clear of the river, swishing his tail in a mighty leap; then twisting in midair, he launched himself back into the water like a downward torpedo with gaping teeth. Gloomer was waiting. He pushed his head clear of the river, sucked in a quick breath and locked jaws with the descending pike. The surface boiled in a welter of cascading water, shimmering scales and ragged fur, the whole scene streaked with blood.

They snapped and bit at each other, locking jaws, rolling over and over, now letting go, now seeking another hold, contorting madly. Gloomer had the pike by the tail. He chewed voraciously. Pain seared through the big fish, but Stormfin had his enemy by the stomach, and ripped viciously.

Tsarmina dashed up and down the bank with a spear at the ready. She could not throw it for fear of hitting her destroyer. Mud boiled up from the bottom to mix with the flotsam of combat. Silver scales and gray black fur became indistinguishable in the melee.

Now Gloomer had latched his claws into Stormfin's side and bitten deep into the pike's dorsal fin. Stormfin thwacked away at Gloomer's injured side with his heavy tail like a stout paddle. He had severed Gloomer's tail and was tearing ferociously at the rat's hindquarters.

The need for breath forced Gloomer to relinquish his hold momentarily, and Stormfin slid off like a wraith, following the current. Gloomer surfaced and gulped in several grateful breaths.

Dementedly Tsarmina shouted from the bank, "Gloomer's won! Where's the pike? Is it dead?"

Fortunata was caught up in the excitement. "It must be, Milady. Nothing could stand against the Gloomer for long."

The soldiers raised a ragged cheer. It was immediately stifled as Stormfin came back to the attack!

Driving low, hard and fast, the big pike crashed into Gloomer with staggering force, catching him unawares. The huge rat had the breath smashed from his lungs as he was battered swiftly up against the far bank. Falling back into the water, he swallowed liquid instead of air. Still lashing out with tooth and claw, Gloomer was unconsciously inflicting injuries on the pike, but the damage was done.

Stormfin knew every inch of his river. He slid into a deep pit beneath the bank and attacked the rat's soft underbelly with the mad power of one who feels victory in sight. Gloomer scratched blindly at the rock either side of the underwater hole, missing his adversary's head completely. Baffled, he tried to turn away.

Stormfin's jaws clamped tight on Gloomer's back legs. The

monster pike backed water as he dragged the rat backward down the pit with him. The watchers on the bank saw Gloomer's front claws emerge wildly from the water, grasping at thin air before they vanished beneath the surface.

The destroyer from Kotir was beaten. Stormfin had finally won!

Tsarmina shot several arrows into the area where the pike had pulled her rat down. The soldiers stood about on the bank, shuffling awkwardly and fidgeting. A sense of foreboding hung over them after the defeat of Gloomer. Fortunata tried to stroll casually out of sight, knowing the wildcat Queen would be looking for a scapegoat to vent her wrath upon.

"Get back here, fox. Don't try to slink away." Holding out her paw, the wildcat Queen snapped at a stoat close by, "Give me your spear."

Keeping her eyes fixed on the quaking vixen, Tsarmina accepted the spear. She swung it around until the point was at Fortunata's throat. "So, nothing could stand against the Gloomer, eh, fox?"

The terrified fox could think of nothing to say. She merely gulped.

Tsarmina swung the spear away and dipped it into the river. She fished about for a moment then whipped the point out of the water. Looped over the spearpoint was the collar once worn by the Gloomer. Tsarmina hurled the weapon. It whizzed past Fortunata and buried itself in an ash trunk, quivering with bright droplets of water shaking from it.

From somewhere along the river came the deep, barking laugh of an otter.

The wildcat's cloak swirled about her as she tore the spear from the tree and ran to the water's edge brandishing it.

"Laugh, yes laugh all you like, but stay hidden while you value your miserable lives. I am Tsarmina, Queen of the Thousand Eyes. Before I am finished with Mossflower, every creature who defies me will wish that its mother had never given birth to it. The crying and the dying will be loud and long. Now let me hear you laugh at that!"

As Tsarmina finished her speech, Fortunata leaped forward. The vixen was thinking of ingratiating herself with her Queen by adding a few words to the speech.

"Thus speaks the mighty Tsarmina, ruler of all Mossfl—"

As Brogg turned from the river's edge he collided with the

leaping fox. Their heads clashed painfully. The weasel staggered back a step and trod on the hem of the vixen's cloak. They tripped, landing ungraciously in the mud of the shallows.

The otters' laughter was mingled with the chuckling of squirrels.

13

The sun was at its zenith in the woodlands. Young bees droned fuzzily around the flowers in anticipation of their first summer. A venerable oak of massive girth and height towered above the surrounding trees. Beneath its spring foliage of small green leaves and below its aged trunk was Brockhall, the ancestral home of badgers. The solid, intricate root structure of the oak provided ceiling beams, wall columns, shelves and in some places flooring for the beautiful old dwelling. A door was set between the fork of two roots at ground level. From there a long passage ran downward with rooms leading off it—Bella's private study, small sitting rooms, a nursery and small infirmary. At the other end the passage opened out into the main hall. This was large and well-appointed, with a hearth, fireplace, full dining board and small seated alcoves around its walls. Several doors led off the main hall; to the left was the master bedroom and dormitories, while off to the right was the larder, kitchens and storerooms, behind which lay the bolt hole or escape door, constructed with typical woodland common sense.

Brockhall had been built by badgers in the dim past, and they had taken great pains that everything should be just the way woodland badgers like it to be. Great care and the skill of many craftbeasts had provided every conceivable comfort in the underground mansion; there were elaborate wall torches and beautifully carved furniture (again, much of this cut into the living root to blend with the surroundings). The walls were lined with fawn-and pink-colored clay, baked to give it a fine rustic atmosphere. Here and there throughout the chambers were large overstuffed armchairs of the type badgers prefer, each with a fuzzy old velveteen pawstool, often used by young ones in preference to the small polished maple chairs made specially for them. Overall it was an admirable country seat which could easily accommodate the entire Corim membership.

All the woodlanders were gathered to meet the mice who had journeyed from Loamhedge; it was an occasion for feasting. The Council of Resistance in Mossflower leaders sat in the main hall, infants were taken to the nursery, and friends went to help with the cooking and preparation of food in Bella's much admired kitchen. Though the badger was not short of provisions, she always welcomed the addition of otter, squirrel and mole food. All had arrived well burdened. Bella liked tasting other dishes, after cooking for herself all the time.

Gonff introduced her to Martin. She greeted him warmly.

"Martin, welcome, friend. We have heard of you already from Ben Stickle. I believe you gave a Kotir patrol a taste of your warrior skills single-pawed, before they managed to capture you. We shall be grateful if you would share your talents with us in the times that lie ahead. Tell me, did you come from the northlands?"

Martin nodded as he shook Bella's big paw. The badger smiled knowingly. "Ah, I thought so. You probably cut your eyeteeth on rats and foxes. I've heard all about the warrior mice from up north. Come and meet some friends of mine from the south."

Bella took them to the kitchen, where they were introduced to Abbess Germaine, who was presiding over the preparations. From there Gonff took Martin to be introduced to Ben and Goody Stickle.

The two hedgehogs were overjoyed to see Gonff back safe. They patted him furiously on the head, as their spines prevented them hugging anyone other than fellow hedgehogs.

Goody patted and scolded Gonff at the same time. "Oh, my goodness, thank mice you're back, you liddle rip. Don't go ever gettin' yourself locked up like that again. Me 'n' Ben was plain worried for you, Gonff.''

Ben was patting Martin's head enthusiastically. ''Heed what Goody tells you, Gonff. 'Tis for your own good. Be more like young Martin here—only get yourself caught when there's nought else for it.''

Goody nodded in agreement, trying to look severe, but Gonff caught her by the paws and danced her about.

You've been more than a mum to me,
And you brought me up very well
I'm a little mousehog to thee.
My Goody, no words can tell,
When I see your old prickle face—

''Get on with you, you thievin' liddle fibber!'' Goody shooed Gonff off, wiping her eyes on her old flowery apron.

Gonff flung a paw across Martin's shoulder. As they strolled away smiling, Ben sniffed loudly. ''Can't fail to like that little rogue, some'ow.''

''Silence, woodlanders, please.'' Bella called out, ''Could you all find a seat? The food will be served after the talking has been done.''

The hall was full, creatures occupying seats, shelves, hearth and floor. Skipper banged his tail. The hubbub subsided, and he nodded for Bella to continue.

''Thank you. Welcome, one and all. As you can see, there are many new friends in our midst, not the least of whom is Martin the Warrior. He and Gonff recently escaped from Kotir prison in a very brave and daring manner.''

Heads turned to look at Martin. There were winks, nods and pawshakes.

''Also I have great pleasure in introducing some mice that you may not know of yet,'' Bella continued, ''Abbess Germaine with her Brothers and Sisters of Loamhedge. I am sure the Abbess would like to say a word.''

There was general applause as the old mouse stood up.

''My mice and I wish to thank you from the bottom of our hearts for allowing us to settle in your beautiful Mossflower country. We are a peaceful order of builders and healers; in our own tradition we are wise in the ways of mother nature. Please feel free to come to us with your families, the sick, injured, or just fretful little ones. We will do all we can to help. The only price we ask is the gift of your friendship. Perhaps one day when this land is free of the tyranny which shadows it, we can work together to raise a mighty building, giving settlement and security to all who wish to dwell peacefully within its walls.''

The Abbess sat down amid loud cheering and many offers of help from decent, hardworking family creatures. Order was nearly restored when a young squirrel voice piped up, ''Caw, is that roast chestnut with cream and honey I can smell?''

''Indeed it is, made to an old Loamhedge recipe, too.'' Abbess Germaine called back, ''Is the talking finished, Bella?''

''It certainly is, Abbess. I haven't had Loamhedge roasted chestnuts in many a season. Stay where you are, everyone. The food is ready.''

Suddenly a fat dormouse leaped up with a squeak of fright. ''Ooh, the floor's moving!''

''Don't be afeared, matey.'' Skipper laughed. ''That'll be Foremole arrivin'. He's smelled the vittles, too.''

Willing paws united to lift a floorstone. There was a moment's silence, the earth trembled slightly, then a huge pair of paws with powerful digging claws broke through. Seconds later they were followed by a dark velvety head with tiny bright black eyes, a moist snout, and a gruff whiskery mouth.

''Boy urr, a mornin' to 'ee, do be sorry bouten tunnel. Cooken smells roight noice.'' Foremole popped out like a black furry cannonball, followed by a score and a half of grinning moles. Like their leader they all spoke in heavy rural molespeech.

''Ho urr, 'lo Bella stroip'ead.''

''Yurr, be that chesknutters oi smell?''

''Hoo arr, oi gets powerful 'ungered a-tunellen.''

''Harr, morrow to 'ee, Skip. 'Ow do 'ee do.''

The industrious moles were loved by all the woodlanders. Infants shrieked with laughter at their quaint speech, and the moles would smile, speaking more broadly, if that were possible.

Exclamations of admiration and delight greeted the food as it was served. After all, who could resist roast chestnuts served in cream and honey, or clover oatcakes dipped in hot redcurrant sauce, celery and herb cheese on acorn bread with chopped radishes, or a huge home-baked seed and sweet barley cake with mint icing, all washed down with either October ale, pear cordial, strawberry juice or good fresh milk.

Martin muttered through a mouthful of cake and milk, "In the name of mice, I'd have been a cook and not a warrior if I knew food could taste this good."

Gonff grinned, trying to answer through a face crammed with chestnut, honey and strawberry juice. "Mmmfff, shoulden talk wiff y'mouff full."

Bella sat with the Corim leaders. As they ate they talked. "I think for the future we should all live together here in Brockhall—at least all those that can't climb trees and swim rivers. They'd be caught by Tsarmina and her army sooner or later."

"Aye, marm, good idea," Skipper agreed. "They can't be found out here; the cat knows nothing of Brockhall. But that doesn't mean my crew and Lady Amber's band. We don't strike our colors and run at the first sign of trouble."

"Nobody doubts your courage, Skipper," Abbess Germaine interrupted. "But maybe we're jumping ahead a bit. With all the woodlanders hiding out here, the cat will have little to do except sit on her tail. Why not form a good spy network and see what she is up to? Maybe then we can form a plan of action. What do you think, Martin? You're a seasoned warrior?"

Martin had been listening. He cleared his mouth. "I think all your ideas are good and sensible. Let's try them. But peace is not found like a pawful of nuts or an apple. The wildcat is here, and Kotir won't go away if we close our eyes. Sooner or later we will have to fight to rid the land of them. Only then can we talk of building and peace."

Skipper and Amber both clapped him on the back.

"Let us attend to one thing at a time," Bella advised. "First, we need a good spy to keep us informed. If we know our enemies, we will know their weaknesses."

Ferdy and Coggs marched up, trying to look warlike yet secretive at the same time. "We've heard you're looking for two good spies, Miss Bella."

Before any laughter could start, Skipper was up and marching around inspecting them. They stood stiffly to attention, knowing a good officer when they saw one. Skipper eyed them up and down.

"Ho yes, I remember you coves—two of the fiercest fellers as ever stood guard at the Stickle place. I heard weasels and ferrets was a-shakin' in their skins at the thought you might attack Kotir. Shall we let 'em be spies, Lady Amber?''

The squirrel looked serious, shaking her head. ''Spying is too tame for these old wardogs. I think that with the good job they did at Stickle's we should promote them to Captains of the Home Guard at Brockhall.''

The two little hedgehogs nearly burst with pride. They set off to make themselves badges of office.

Gonff threw in a suggestion. ''The best spy I know is Chibb.''

Objections flooded in.

''Chibb's not one of us.''

''He's a bird.''

''He'll want payment.''

''I wouldn't trust a robin.''

''Why not one of our own?''

Bella pounded her chair until a heavy dust cloud arose and silence was restored.

''Gonff is right. No one could get closer to Kotir than Chibb. If he wants payment, then so be it, we'll pay him. I think it's a good idea.''

''Hurr, a burd 'tis, we'ns say let Chebb be a spoiy. Save us'ns doin' the job. Asoides, we doant'ave wingers to floiy wi'.''

The Foremole's logic was irrefutable. Unanimous agreement was given by a show of paws.

Chibb it was to be.

Ben Stickle had the final word. Being one of the last to leave the shadow of Kotir, he received a sympathetic hearing.

''I don't know much about fightin' and spyin' but I still think it's a good idea. One thing I do know, me an my missus an our liddle family won't be goin' back to slave for no cat and her soldiers. We'd be as well off dead as havin' to do that again. But we'd all best listen to the good Abbess here. Let's not jump too hasty; war means creatures gettin' theyselves killed. If it must come to that, then so be it, but meanwhiles let's keep level heads about us, concentrate on safety for now. Aye, that an keepin' ourselves an' our families safe. I want to see my little ones grow to farm their own food and not have soldiers comin' around to tell us that our land is theirs an' takin' toll and tax of over half the vittles we have. That ain't fair nor right. Mind, though, we've got time on our side. I know that

Kotir larders must be run down considerable since we all left. Huh, the cat and her soldiers can march about all season, but there's no one left to order about and they ain't no farmers, that's sure. They'll starve without others to do their labor.''

14

The sun beat down on the soldiers of Kotir as they stood in serried ranks upon the parade ground. Each creature stood stiff as a ramrod, and all wore every available piece of equipment, including heavy spears, shields and full packs stuffed with rocks strapped to their backs.

Blacktooth licked a drop of sweat that rolled past his lip. He muttered to Splitnose, "Huh, what's all this about? It was the Gloomer lost the battle, not us. As far as I can see, we didn't do too badly against those river wallopers and tree jumpers."

Splitnose twitched his eyelid against an inquisitive fly. "You're right there, Blackie. Sometimes I think I'd like to pack in all this soldierin' lark at Kotir."

Behind them in the next rank, Brogg could not resist a titter. "Heehee, just you try it, stoat. Where would you go on your own, eh? Nah, she'd have you dragged back and made an example of."

Scratt in the rank behind Brogg agreed. "Aye, you're right there, Brogg, but there's not many would pass up a chance of sliding off from here and starting up somewhere else. Perhaps we might form a little group sometime and try it."

Blacktooth was skeptical. "Oh yes? Let me tell you something, Scratt. That'd be worse than going off on your own, it'd be mutiny or mass desertion—and you know how Tsarmina'd punish that little lot.''

Scratt knew only too well. ''Death!''

Blacktooth chuckled humorlessly. ''Right. Deader than a fallen log. Huh, you'd be glad to be so when she finished with you, bucko.''

Cludd's heavy voice bellowed out across the parade ground, ''Silence in the ranks! No talking back there!''

Scratt muttered under his breath, ''Oh dry up, slobber-chops. You weren't even out in the forest when we had to fight.''

''No, he was back here with his nightie on, snoring like a dead dog,'' Splitnose sniggered.

''I won't tell you again. I said, silence in the ranks!''

From the rear of the army a complaining voice called out, ''I reckon we've been stood here nearly two hours now. What for?''

Other voices began complaining before Cludd could silence them.

''Aye and why the full uniform and rock packs? Are we supposed to roast alive?''

''Pretty daft, if you ask me. I'm only a storeroom guard.''

Tsarmina prowled silently out of the main door onto the sun-lit parade ground. An immediate deafening silence fell over all.

She signaled to Cludd.

The Captain of the Guard bellowed to the sweating troops, ''Tribute to the Queen followed by twelve circuits of the square at the double. Begin!''

With a loud shout, ferrets, stoats and weasels roared in unison.

''Tsarmina, Queen of Mossflower!''

''Slayer of enemies!''

''Lady of the Thousand Eyes!''

''Conqueror of all creatures!''

''Ruler of Kotir!''

''Daughter of Lord Greeneyes!''

Breaking off, they commenced running in a swift trot around the parade ground, paws punished by the harsh gravel, muscles aching with the strain of the heavy packs and cumbersome weapons.

Tsarmina watched impassively, remarking to Ashleg,

"Daughter of Lord Greeneyes. Who said that was to be kept among my list of titles?"

Behind her back, Ashleg looked at Fortunata and shrugged.

The wildcat Queen stared fixedly ahead as her troops lumbered by on their second circuit. "Well, I'm still waiting for an answer. Who said that my troops should be shouting about my dead father instead of me? Am I not capable of ruling Kotir alone?"

Fortunata got in ahead of Ashleg. "There has never been a more capable ruler than you, Milady. On my oath as a healer, it was not I who arranged your title list."

Tsarmina rubbed her injured paw thoughtfully. Behind her, Ashleg's wooden limb made nervous little shifting noises.

"What have you got to say for yourself, marten?"

"Your Majesty, I thought that—"

Tsarmina's snarl overrode Ashleg's nervous muttering. "Thought? Who gave you permission to think? Get out on that parade ground this instant!"

The unhappy Ashleg stumped out, knowing it was useless to plead or argue.

Tsarmina halted the march on its next circuit. They ground to a halt in front of the marten. She called out to Cludd, "Keep Ashleg in front of the army. First rank, point your spears at that marten. All of you, remember this: I am no longer called Daughter of Lord Greeneyes. That title is dead. It will be replaced by the name Tsarmina the Magnificent."

At a wave of Cludd's spear the army chanted aloud, "Tsarmina the Magnificent!"

Ashleg looked around nervously. He was standing out in front of a rank of gleaming spearpoints, all pointed at his body. The marten gathered his cloak up, knowing the cruel command that was imminent. Tsarmina's snarl cut across his thoughts. "At the double. Carry on!"

Fortunata stood to one side, knowing that a careless word could have placed her alongside the hapless marten.

Ashleg tried not to think. Desperately he dragged himself along in a frantic hop cum hobble, in front of the lethal spears. Madly he tried to gain a little ground, only to realize that he was hard put to keep what lead he had from the relentlessly double-marching soldiers.

Tsarmina laughed mockingly and she dug Fortunata in the

ribs. "Ha, thumpitty clump, eh, fox. How long d'you reckon he'll last?"

"Not long at that rate, Milady. Look at him trying to keep ahead of those spears. Ashleg mightn't be too bright, but at least he's obedient and loyal."

Tsarmina sighed moodily; her fun had been spoiled. "Hmm, you're right, I suppose. Tell Cludd to call a halt."

Fortunata waved a signal to the stolid weasel Captain. Cludd halted the troops at the very moment Ashleg fell face forward on the gravel, his tortured body unable to travel another pace. He was sobbing pitifully for breath.

Tsarmina prowled purposefully out in front of the ranks, ignoring Ashleg, who was dragging himself painfully toward the indoor coolness of the entrance hall. The wildcat Queen faced her command as they stood in the gravel dust with heaving chests.

"Look at you. See how you have grown fat and lazy, slugs, worms! As from today, all of this will change. Believe me, or die. Mice, two silly little mice, have escaped my prison. Together with a rabble of woodlanders, they have made fools of you all."

Nervous paws crunched the gravel as Tsarmina's fury and scorn lashed them.

"I'll take revenge for the insult to my majesty. Mossflower will be drenched in the blood of any creature who will not obey me, whether it be a woodlander or a soldier of Kotir!"

Fortunata shuddered inwardly at the mad light that shone in Tsarmina's eyes as her voice rose in the sunlit stillness.

"Cludd, Ashleg, Fortunata, you will split the army four ways. Take a group each. I will stay here to guard Kotir with the remainder. You will go into the forest and hunt out every last woodlander. Take them prisoners. Any that resist, kill. Kotir will grow strong again with prisoners to serve it. We will enslave them. The flatlands to the west will be cultivated and farmed. My father was too soft with those creatures. They took advantage of his good nature in letting them live outside the walls in a settlement. That's what encouraged them to desert: too much freedom. Well, I'll tell you all right now, no more settlements. It'll be the cells for them this time; separate cells, punishment, that's what they'll be here for. We will hold their young as hostages. To stop any uprising, they will toil from dawn to dusk—or their families will starve. Go now, and remember, this time there will be no failure.''

There was a hurried clanking and stamping from the already armored and kitted troops. Orders were called amid wheeling and marching. In a short time Tsarmina stood alone on the empty parade ground, staring at a single fallen spear.

Whoever had dropped it would be far too scared to come back and retrieve it. She stooped and picked up the weapon as something whooshed by close overhead.

Argulor!

As big and powerful as she was, Tsarmina did not wait around to challenge the eagle. Taking a swift run, she vaulted through a ground-floor window, using the spear shaft as a pole. Peering out, she saw Argulor circle away to his perch, well out of arrow range.

The wildcat Queen was glad that no one had witnessed her retreat.

15

Chibb the robin watched the little procession of woodlanders marching southward. He had no doubt that they were coming to visit him. They were carrying food. If they were not coming to see him, then what right did they have wandering about Mossflower carrying bags of candied chestnuts?

He was different from other birds. For the sake of his little fat stomach, Chibb had overcome all barriers. Greed was the one motive that drove him to sell his spying skills to others—greed, tempered with wisdom. Chibb would never sell his services to Kotir, as he had narrowly escaped being eaten by weasels and such on more than one occasion.

The woodlanders used Chibb whenever they had cause to, sometimes to locate a missing young one, more often than not to find out what was going on in other parts of the forest. Chibb did not come cheaply, however. The fat robin had a fondness amounting to a passion for candied chestnuts.

He watched the party below him: Martin, Lady Amber and a young Loamhedge mouse called Columbine were in the lead; Gonff and Billum the mole trailed behind, both carrying small barkcloth bags of candied chestnuts. Chibb could not take his bright eyes off the bag that Gonff was bouncing playfully in his paws.

"Ha, candied chestnuts, eh, Billum. What's the good of giving these to old Chibb, just for a skinny bit of spyin'? I'll bet me and you could scoff these between us and get their spyin' done for 'em easy enough."

The trusty mole caught the bag in midair as Gonff tossed it. He crinkled his velvet face in a deep chuckle.

"Ho hurr hurr! Liddle wunner they send oi t'keep watch on 'ee, you'm a villyen, Maister Gonff. Keepen 'ee paws outten 'ee chesknutters, or oi tells Miz Bell offen 'ee."

Gonff threw up his paws in mock horror and ran to catch up with Martin, complaining aloud. "The nerve of Billum! Fancy not trusting honest old Gonff—me, that was sent on this mission specially to keep an eye out for greedy moles. I'll bet I end up getting scragged by you lot, trying to keep those chestnuts safe. There's no room for an honest thief these days."

Martin chuckled as he watched Columbine from the corner of his eye. The pretty young fieldmouse was laughing merrily, obviously taken by Gonff's roguish charm. Martin encouraged her by putting in the odd word or two on his friend's behalf.

"Be careful of that fellow, Columbine. He's not one of your Loamhedge order. If you don't watch Gonff, he'll steal the whiskers from under your nose."

Columbine's eyes went wide with amazement. "Would he really?"

Gonff winked at Martin. Cartwheeling suddenly, he shot across Columbine's path so close that he brushed by her face. With a squeak of shock she put up her paws. Martin shook his head seriously.

"You see, they don't call Gonff the Prince of Mousethieves for nothing. Have you counted your whiskers?"

Columbine put her paws up then dropped them smiling. "Oh really, you two!"

Gonff bowed and produced two thin strands. "What do you think these are, O wise beauty?"

Columbine's mouth fell open. "But, I didn't feel a thing."

Billum had caught up. He chuckled and scratched his snout. "Nor oi wagers you didden, missie. They whiskers is offen Gonff. Tha's 'ow you'm never feeled owt."

Lady Amber pointed at a long-dead elm covered in ivy. She held up her paw for silence. "Hush now. This is Chibb's home.

We don't want to frighten him off. Gonff, you do the talking.''

Gonff rapped upon the trunk of the elm and shouted up toward a hole left by a broken branch, "Hey, Chibb! Come out, you old redbreast. It's me, Gonff."

There was no response. Gonff tried again. "Come on, matey. We know you're in there. What's up? Don't you want to earn some candied chestnuts?"

Billum opened one of the bags and selected a large nut. "Harr, may'aps you'm roight, Gonffen. Us'ns could ate chesknutters an' do 'ee job ourselfs."

The mole popped the dark sugar-glazed nut into his mouth, licked the sweetness from his digging claws and chomped away with an expression of rapture on his homely face. "Umff, gurr, oo arr, mmmmm!"

Much to Columbine's amusement, Gonff did likewise, imitating perfectly the mole speech and gesture.

"Hurr, oo arr, Billum, these yurr be furst-clarss chesknutters. Hoo arr, that they be."

They had eaten a nut apiece when a bout of nervous coughing erupted from the branches of a nearby rowan. "Err, harrumph, ahem hem!"

Chibb puffed out his chest importantly, ruffling his feathers to increase his stature. He paced a branch with wings folded behind him in a businesslike attitude. Politely he cleared his throat once more before speaking.

"Harrumph, ahem, 'scuse me. Let me warn you before we proceed any further, if anyone eats another nut I will judge it an insult, then of course you will have to take your business elsewhere, ahem."

"Please consider what I say before answering." Martin responded in an equally formal tone. "I have been authorized to make you an offer. Here are our terms: you, Chibb, will spy on Kotir and find out what plans are being made by Tsarmina against the woodlanders of Mossflower. The Corim wish to know all details of any reprisals or attacks directed at our creatures. For this you will be paid two bags of candied chestnuts now and a further two bags upon bringing back your information. Is that agreed?"

Chibb cocked his head on one side. His bright eye watched Gonff as he picked crumbs of chestnut from his whiskers with his tongue. The robin coughed nervously.

Columbine had assessed the situation correctly. She interrupted in a more friendly tone. "Of course the nuts will be carefully counted, Mr. Chibb. The bags will be completely filled. I will see that four more nuts be added as an interest for the two that have just been eaten, and another four added as evidence of our good faith in your well-known skills."

Chibb shifted his claws and fixed Columbine with a quizzical stare. "Ahem, hem, you are the one from Loamhedge they call Columbine. I shall do business with you, harrumph, 'scuse me. These others are not required for our dealings."

Lady Amber breathed a sigh of relief. Chibb could be incredibly pompous and stubborn; thank the fur for the good sense and initiative shown by Columbine.

The robin flew down and bowed courteously to the Loamhedge mouse. "Aherrahem! There is, however, one small matter that may cost an extra nut or two . . ."

Billum nudged Gonff. "Oi 'spected thurr moight be, hurr hurr."

Chibb ignored the mole. "Harrumph, yes, there's the question of the eagle, Argulor. Ahem, as you know, he is back in the area of Kotir. This puts an, ahem, element of risk upon my espionage activities."

Columbine nodded in agreement. "Indeed it does, Mr. Chibb. I appreciate this. Should you be attacked or injured in any way by large birds, we propose in doubling your fee. Do we have a bargain, sir?"

Chibb was almost dumbfounded by this generous offer. He held out a claw to Columbine. "Er ahem, a bargain, Miss Columbine. A bargain indeed!"

Paw shook claw. Lady Amber interrupted to give details of the spying mission to the robin, Gonff tossed the two bags expertly up into Chibb's home in the elm, and goodbyes were made all around as the friends departed. A few paces into the undergrowth Lady Amber held up a paw.

"Hush! Listen!"

Silently they tried to stifle their laughter as the sounds of Chibb reached them. The robin was stuffing himself with his fee, coughing with excitement as he crammed candied chestnuts into an already overflowing beak.

"Ahemcawscrunffmmmharrumphcrunch!"

Martin held his sides as tears from stifled laughter ran down his cheeks. "Hahaha, oh dear, listen to that. Oh, the little glutton! Columbine, whatever possessed you to offer him a double fee like that?''

Columbine leaned up against a tree, helpless with mirth. ''Well I, oh, heeheehee, I could have offered him ten times the fee, if I'd thought, ohahaha. Imagine a robin coming back to claim a fee after being attacked by a golden eagle, haha-heeheee. There wouldn't be enough of him left to make a smear on Argulor's beak. That eagle could scoff Chibb in a half-mouthful, haha-haha!''

Tsarmina stood at a barred window in full view of Argulor's perch.

''I'm here, you great feathered blindworm,'' she called.

Argulor took the bait; the fierce instinct of his ancestors would not allow him to do otherwise. The eagle launched from his perch with a blood-chilling screech, diving like a great winged missile at his insolent tormentor.

Tsarmina danced triumphantly and laughed aloud at the sight of the half-blind eagle smashing against the barred window. ''Haha, you blundering old feather mattress. Dozy farmyard fowl.''

Argulor struggled awkwardly on the narrow window ledge, trying to marshal his wings into a proper flying position to regain what was left of his dignity. The great eagle slipped from the sill, landing on the ground. He had to resort to an ungainly lopsided shuffling run to attain flight.

Tsarmina purred aloud and dug her claws into a rug, opening and closing them, reveling in the pretense of pinioning helpless woodlanders in her needlelike grip, puncturing imaginary hides. Suddenly she whirled over, tossing the rug high in the air. Leaping upon it, she rent it fiercely with her savage strength. Fragments of the flayed rug flew about the room as she ripped and slashed. Hairs and fibers floated in the sunlit shafts from the bars, dancing with golden dust motes on their way to the floor.

Filled with exuberance, the big cat paced restlessly. Soon a bunch of woodlanders would be marched in, sniveling and bound, to await her pleasure.

And what pleasure! Some she would deal with personally; otters, yes, she would take them down to the Gloomer's lake and see how well they would swim bound up and weighted with stones—that would teach them manners. There were one or two squirrels that could do with jumping lessons from the battlemented roof of Kotir. As for the rest, well, there were always plenty of good hard work and the cells.

Tsarmina sprang down the stairways and the dripping passages of her fortress, heading for the cells, where sunlight seldom penetrated. Two stoat guards tried hastily to come to attention as their Queen hurtled past, but they were knocked spinning sideways.

Picking himself up from a pool of slimy water, one of the stoats rubbed his head where it had banged against the wall.

"By the fang! What d'you suppose is wrong with her, this time?"

His companion felt gingerly at the sore beginnings of a lump on his snout. "Huh, your guess is as good as mine. One thing I do know, she's not down here for the good of our health. We'd better get straightened up before she comes back this way."

Tsarmina ran from cell to cell, peering through the bars at the hostile interiors as she muttered aloud, "Yes, good, this is ideal. They'll soon learn obedience down here. Males in one cell, females in another and young ones in a special prison all of their own, where they can be heard but not seen by their parents. Haha, I must remember that: heard but not seen. Well, what have we here, all alone in the darkness?"

Gingivere was fading into a gaunt skeleton. The once glossy coat was ragged and graying, his whole body had an air of neglect and decay about it, except the eyes. They fixed Tsarmina with such a burning intensity that she was forced to look away.

"Well, well, my one-time brother, I thought perhaps that you had perished by now in this unhealthy atmosphere, dark, cold, damp, with little to eat. But cheer up, I'll find you an even darker and deeper prison when you move out to make room for the new lodgers I'm planning. How would that suit you?"

Gingivere stood clasping the cell bars. He stared at his sister.

Tsarmina shifted nervously. Her previous mood of euphoria rapidly disintegrating, she became irritable.

"Never fear, my silent, staring brother. I can soon fix up other arrangements for you. A sword, perhaps. Or a spear during the night to deepen your sleep."

Gingivere's eyes burned into Tsarmina, and his voice was like a knell. ''Murderer!''

Tsarmina broke and ran, pursued by the voice of her brother like a spear at her back.

''Murderer! You killed our father! Murderer! Murderer!''

When the sounds of Tsarmina's flight had died away, Gingivere let go of the bars and slumped to the floor, hot tears pouring from his fevered eyes.

After their trek through Mossflower to find Chibb, the little party was ready for food. Now that all the woodlanders were billeted at Brockhall, mealtimes were like a constant feast, so many different dishes were contributed. A pretty posy lay in the middle of the festive board symbolizing the coming together in springtime to oppose the reign of Kotir.

Gonff was conscious of Columbine watching him. Bella had given the little mousethief permission to sing grace, and he stood up boldly and sang aloud,

> Squirrels, otters, hedgehogs, mice,
> Moles with fur like sable,
> Gathered in good spirits all,
> Round this festive table.
> Sit we down to eat and drink.
> Friends, before we do, let's think.
> Fruit of forest, field and banks,
> To the springtime we give thanks.

The woodlanders began passing food. As Gonff sat down, he winked at Columbine, showing no sign of modesty.

''Good, eh? That's an ancient chant that has been sung through the ages. I composed it a moment ago for today.''

Gonff was so pleased with himself that Columbine could not help laughing with him at his outrageous statement.

Martin had sat at many tables—farm tables, inn tables, and, more often than not, any handy flat piece of rock where he could lay his food. Now he sat back and surveyed the board before him with wonder. Bulrush and water-shrimp soup provided by the otters; a large flagon of Skipper's famous hot root punch; hazelnut truffle; blackberry apple crumble; baked sweet chestnuts; honeyed toffee pears; and maple tree cordial, a joint effort by hedgehogs and squirrels. The Loamhedge and Mossflower mice had combined to provide a number of currant and berry pies, seedcake and potato scones, and a cask of October ale. By far the biggest single offering was a colossal turnip 'n' tater 'n' beetroot 'n' bean deeper 'n' ever pie with tomato chutney baked by the Foremole and his team.

Normally a solid trenchermouse, Martin would have stuck to deeper 'n' ever pie, but Gonff encouraged him and Columbine to sample some of everything.

"Here, matey, how's that for October ale? Columbine, try some of this hot root punch. How d'you like seedcake? Try some of this, both of you. Come on, have a wedge.

"Hey, Martin, d'you reckon you'd get the better of one of these toffee pears? Come on, get stuck in, stuck in, hahaha.

"Put that hot root punch down, Columbine. You look as if your face is on fire. Try some of the maple tree cordial."

Ferdy and Coggs sat nearby, hero-worshipping Martin and Gonff.

"Tell you what, Coggs. If ever I come across a broken sword I'm going to hang it round my neck, just like Martin the Warrior."

"Huh, fancy trying to keep old Gonff locked up in Kotir! I'll bet he could come and go with both paws tied. You know, I think I look a bit like Gonff."

"Of course you do. I look like Martin—pretty quiet and very brave—or I will be when I'm older. Just wait and see."

"Come on, matey. We've eaten enough. Let's go off together and invade Kotir before we get sent to bed. We can slip away quietlike."

In the hubbub and confusion of the feast, nobody noticed the two baby hedgehogs take their leave.

16

A crescent moon hung over the warm spring night, casting its cloak over the light early foliage of Mossflower Woods. Indifferent to the woodland floor carpeted with dark green grass, dotted with bluebell and narcissus, Fortunata stopped in her tracks and held up a paw for silence. Immediately she was bumped by Brogg and Scratt, two weasels who did not stop fast enough. Ferrets and weasels in their turn blundered sleepily into each other.

Fortunata bared her teeth impatiently. "Stand still, can't you. I think I hear something."

The patrol held its collective breath and listened intently. Scratt dropped his shield with a clang. They all jumped with fright. Fortunata cursed at the hapless weasel, but he was tired and weary of listening to pointless orders.

"Ahh, what's the difference, fox? We're on a right fool's errand in this jungle, I can tell you. Huh, tramping about all day in full kit and armor, without anything to eat, and not a sight or sound of a living thing, except the sign of our own pawtracks that we keep coming across. What are we supposed to be doing out here, anyhow? That's what I'd like to know."

There were murmurs of agreement. Fortunata cut in quickly

to stem any ideas of mutiny. "All of you, get the soil out of your ears and listen to me. Can you imagine what will happen if we march back to Kotir empty-pawed? Well, can you? By the claw, it doesn't bear thinking about. Imagine the Queen—d'you think she'll say: 'Oh, you poor creatures. Didn't you find any of those naughty woodlanders? Well, never mind, come in and take off your armor, sit by the fire and have a bite to eat.'"

One particularly stupid ferret grinned hopefully. "Oh, that would be nice."

Fortunata was about to give him something painful to think about when she heard the noise once more.

"Ssshhh! There it is again, coming right toward us. Right, this is your chance to carry out the mission properly. I want you all out of sight. You lot, get behind those trees. You others, hide in the bushes. When I give the signal, come out whacking. Use your spear handles, shields, branches—anything. I want them taken alive. Here they come! Hide quickly."

As the soldiers dropped out of sight, a cloud obscured the moonlight. At that moment a band of dark shapes came into view.

The vixen ran out shouting, "Now, up and at 'em, troops!"

Spurred on by Fortunata, the soldiers dashed from hiding. They charged with a roar into the midst of the intruders, dealing out heavy blows, kicking, biting, scratching and pounding away at the enemy. The air was rent with blows, screams, thuds and yells of pain.

Exulting in the chaos of the ambush, Fortunata seized the nearest figure and thrashed it unmercifully with her staff.

Thwack, bang, crack!

"Yeeow, aargh, oo mercy, help!"

It was only when she kicked out savagely and splintered the wooden leg that the vixen realized she was close to slaying Ashleg.

"Stoppit! Halt! Pack it in, you fools. We're fighting our own!" Fortunata yelled at the top of her lungs.

When the clouds moved, moonlight illuminated a sorry scene. The soldiers of Kotir sat about on the grass, moaning pitifully. Broken and fractured limbs, collective bumps, bruises, sprains, missing teeth, blackened eyes, contusions and some very nasty scratches were much in evidence.

Ashleg sat on the ground, nursing his wrecked wooden leg.

"You booby, you knothead, you nincompoop of a fox, you, you . . . !"

"Er, sorry, Ashleg. But how were we to know? Why didn't you signal that you were coming?"

"Signal, you brush-tailed blockhead! I'll give you a signal!" The marten flung his broken wooden leg, catching Fortunata square on the tip of her nose.

"Yowch! You twisted little monster, there was no call for that. We thought you were woodlanders; it was a genuine mistake."

Ashleg rubbed a swollen ear. "Woodlanders! Don't talk to me about that lot! We've patrolled this forest until our paws are sore. Not a solitary mouse, not so much as the hair off a squirrel's tail or the damp from an otter's back."

The vixen slumped down glumly beside him. "Same here. Where d'you suppose they've vanished to?"

"Huh, search me. Tsarmina will skin us alive when we get back."

Scratt threw down his spear and sat with them. "Aye, you're right there. Ah well, maybe we'll have more luck when it gets light. We may as well camp here. At least we can search around for roots and berries."

Fortunata and Ashleg looked at each other.

"Roots and berries . . . Yuk!"

Chibb the robin circled the crenellations of Kotir in the dawn light. There was not a lot to interest the little spy; the garrison was still asleep. He noted each window and what was inside: snoring ferrets, slumbering weasels, dozy stoats, even Tsarmina in her upper chamber, stretched out in splendor upon a heap of furs. The wildcat Queen was dreaming troubled dreams of water, muttering to herself, pushing the air as if it were water enveloping her. Chibb flew down and lighted on the parade ground near the wall. Keeping a watch for the eagle, he set about breakfast. From a small bag slung about his neck he selected a candied chestnut; not one of the big smooth ones, but a small wrinkled nut that had lots of sugar in the cracks. Chibb liked them better that way.

Chibb noted that he was near something which looked like a drain outlet, a hole cut into the wall at floor level. He hopped inside, peering about curiously. It went slanting downward as far as he could see. Nibbling the nut daintily, the fat robin explored the tunnel. It was quite dry underclaw.

Chibb cocked his head to one side, listening to the sounds of ragged breathing from further down the tunnel. "Ahem, hem, must be somebody still asleep."

Working his way farther down, he found his progress arrested by three vertical iron bars set into the tunnel. This was no drain; it was the upper window of a cell. Chibb edged up to the bars and peeped down. He was looking into the burning eyes of an emaciated wildcat seated below upon the damp stones.

"Humph, harrumph, hem, 'scuse me."

Gingivere shaded his eyes, staring upward at his strange visitor. "Please don't fly away. I won't harm you. My name is Gingivere."

The robin cocked his head airily on one side. "Ahem, humph. You'll excuse my saying so, but you don't appear to be in any position to harm me. Er, ahem, must go now. I'll drop by and see you another time."

Chibb beat a hasty retreat back up the tunnel. The wildcat with the staring eyes had quite unsettled him. At the edge of the tunnel the robin ate the last of his nut, then flew off back to Brockhall to report his findings.

The day promised to be fine and sunny. Chibb flew high, knowing that the sun in the east would shine in the eyes of predators looking west. He took not the slightest interest in the woodland floor far below. Had he flown lower, he would have noticed Ferdy and Coggs lying in a patch of open sward, fast asleep, their paws about each other, blissfully unaware that a short distance away Cludd was making an early start at the head of his patrol.

Bella was up and about early that morning, being a light sleeper. She received Chibb's information about Gingivere being imprisoned. This was already known to the Corim through Martin and Gonff, yet it gave Bella pause for thought; Kotir was now definitely ruled totally by the cruel Tsarmina.

Martin joined her for an early morning stroll in the woodland before breakfast. The badger had matters to discuss with the warrior mouse.

"War is coming to Mossflower, Martin. I can feel it. Now that we are all at Brockhall, the defenseless ones are safer, but I listen to the voices at Corim meetings. The squirrels and otters are not satisfied with merely resisting Kotir's rule—they want to challenge it.''

Martin felt the broken sword hanging about his neck. ''Maybe that is no bad thing, Bella. Mossflower rightfully belongs to the woodlanders. I will do all I can to help my friends live without fear.''

''I know you will, little warrior, but we are not strong enough. We have few who are trained in the art of war. If Boar the Fighter, my father, were still ruling here, there would be no question he would fight and lead us to certain victory.''

Martin noted the sad, faraway look in the badger's eyes. ''He must have been a mighty warrior. Does he still live?''

Bella shrugged. ''Who knows? He followed his father, old Lord Brocktree, to go off questing. This was before Verdauga and his army arrived in Mossflower. My mate Barkstripe was slain in the first battle against Kotir and my son Sunflash lost to me forever. Barkstripe was more farmer than warrior. Had it been Boar the Fighter that faced Kotir, we would have won, I am certain of it.''

Martin turned his steps back to Brockhall.

Goody Stickle was standing in the doorway, rubbing her paws together anxiously. As they approached, Bella spoke to Martin in a whisper. ''Tell nobody of our conversation. I must talk to you further about certain important matters, maybe later.''

Martin nodded. ''I will look forward to it, Bella. You have aroused my curiosity. Hey, Goody, why are you looking so worried?''

Goody fussed with her apron. ''Mornin' Miz Bella. Mornin', Martin. 'Ave you seen ought of those two liddle 'ogs of mine in the woods?''

''Ferdy and Coggs?'' Bella shook her head. ''No, Goody, I'm afraid we haven't. Is anything wrong?''

The hedgehog gnawed her lip. ''Well, they ain't slept in their beds last night. Asides that, there's two oatfarls, a good wedge o' cheese and some of my best blackcurrant cordial missin' from the larder.''

Martin could not help smiling at the thought of the two little would-be warriors. ''All that for breakfast! They'll go bang one of these days. I wouldn't worry too much, Mrs. Stickle. Knowing those two rascals, they'll be back by lunchtime for more food.''

Ben Stickle emerged into the sunlight. "Aye, Martin's right, m'dear. Don't you go a-botherin' your old 'ead. Ferdy and Coggs is like new button mushrooms—they always turn up at a good meal."

Ben sat against a tree, chuckling as he filled his pipe.

Gonff and Columbine came out to join them, the mousethief patting his stomach.

"Better hurry up, mateys. There'll be no breakfast left soon. Hey, Goody, I hear that Ferdy and Coggs are missing. We'll help you to look for them. Don't worry, they're probably somewhere nearby playing soldiers."

Goody knotted her apron strings anxiously. "Thank you, Gonff. Oh, I do 'ope they've come to no 'arm, Ben. Get up now and 'elp Gonff 'n' Columbine. I won't be 'appy until I see their mucky liddle snouts agin."

Ben stood up and stretched. "So be it, Goody. Come on, you two."

Bella reassured her. "Now don't start getting upset, Goody. I'll send all the woodlanders out looking. They'll find them. Martin and I will stop here at Brockhall in case they come back while everyone's out searching."

Goody smiled gratefully, although she was close to tears. "Thank you kindly, Miz Bella. I'll go and start cookin' the lunch."

Shortly thereafter, Bella addressed a large party of willing helpers.

"Listen now, friends. Ferdy and Coggs must be found before nightfall. Split up into small groups, search everywhere, and pay particular attention to small dens and possible hiding places—they may be lying asleep somewhere. Above all, be careful. There may be Kotir vermin abroad in Mossflower. Don't shout out too loud or make unnecessary noise. Report back to me or to Martin. Off you go now, and good luck."

The woodlanders dispersed, eager to begin. Each creature searched in the best way it knew; squirrels swung off into treetops where they could scan the ground below, otters made their way to the water to scour the banks and creeks, mice and hedgehogs ploughed into the undergrowth. Moles trundled through last autumn's deep loam. The search was on.

•   •   •

A blackbird in a sycamore raised its amber beak in a hymn of joy to the sun. Ashleg blundered into wakefulness. Shivering from the damp, he hopped into the sunlight and leaned against a tree. Scratt joined him, but not before he had aimed a sly kick at the sleeping Fortunata.

"Oi! Are you going to lie there all day, lazybones?"

The weasel drew his paw swiftly back from the vixen's snapping jaws. Far more used to sleeping in the open than the Kotir soldiers, she had dug herself into the soft loam of the forest floor.

"Mind who you call lazybones, fathead. I've been lying awake here for the past two hours listening to you snore like an ailing toad."

Ashleg closed his eyes, letting the warmth of the sun seep through his damp cloak. With a sigh of resignation he remembered the quandary they faced.

"Can't you two stop squabbling long enough to give a thought to the mess we're in? We've beaten each other up, slept through the whole night without posting a single sentry, and now we've got to go back to face Tsarmina sometime today. Look, if we must argue, at least let's argue about something useful. What's to be done about this whole fiasco?"

Fortunata shook loose loam from her cloak, showering them. "Well, there were three patrols sent out to search this forest. Where have Cludd and his lot got to?"

As if in answer to the vixen's question, Cludd came marching through the undergrowth at the head of his column. Scratt was the first to notice him.

"Oi, Cludd, over here. Where in hell's teeth did you get to? We haven't seen you since we left the fortress."

The weasel Captain stuck a paw in his belt and leaned upon his spear, smirking knowingly.

"Oh, we've been doing our job, don't you worry, Scratt. Huh, what happened to you lot? Did a pile of trees fall down on you?"

"It was nothing, really—a little mistake, could have happened to anybeast." Ashleg tried to sound casual. "Let me tell you, though, we haven't seen hide nor hair of a living creature in this rotten maze of trees. We're rightly in for it when the Queen sees us."

Cludd smiled confidently. "Speak for yourself, Ashleg. We won't be returning empty-pawed. Oh no, not us."

"Why, what d'you mean?" Fortunata interrupted eagerly. "Who have you captured? Where?"

Cludd sneered at the fox. "Oh hello, vixen. You look as if you've been enjoying yourself. By the way, what happened to the old wooden leg, Ashy?"

The marten was using a forked branch as a crutch, and he stamped it down bad-temperedly.

"Listen, weasel, will you stop waffling around and tell us what you've got, instead of standing there looking pleased with yourself?"

Cludd beckoned with his spear. "Right. Show 'em lads."

The ranks of the patrol parted, revealing two small hedgehogs. They were gagged and trussed upside down, slung upon poles carried by four soldiers.

Ferdy and Coggs were well and truly captured!

17

Bella paused, gazing at the run of the grain on the tabletop. She was remembering times long gone.

"Where did old Lord Brocktree and Boar the Fighter go questing?" Martin asked softly. The badger gave her answer in a single word: "Salamandastron."

"Salamandastron?" Martin repeated the strange-sounding word.

Bella nodded slowly. "Aye, the fire mountain, secret place of the dragons."

Martin's eyes went wide with wonderment. "Bella, don't stop now. Carry on, please."

The badger smiled wistfully. "Ah, little Martin the Warrior, I see that same strange fire kindled in your eyes, just as it was with my father and his father before him. Why must Salamandastron always weave its spell upon the brave? I can see your desire to travel there; that is as I wanted it to be."

Martin furrowed his brows. "You want me to travel to Salamandastron? But why?"

Bella leaned close, emphasizing each word with a tap of her paw on the table. "Since Boar left Mossflower, we have lived under virtual siege. First there was the rebellion, when many brave woodlanders lost their lives; then there was the settlement with its slummy hovels and tolls, and soldiers harassing the creatures that had to endure living there. I know it seems fairly safe out here in Brockhall, but will it always be so? Now that Tsarmina rules Kotir, we can never be sure what she will do next. Ben Stickle hit the nail on the head when he said Kotir could not last without creatures to supply it with rations. Will the cat start to search Mossflower for us? She will have to do something before next winter; she has a full army to feed. Martin, I feel that we are living on a knife's edge here. Ben Stickle wants peace, Skipper wants war, the Abbess wants peace, Lady Amber wants war. Boar the Fighter is the rightful ruler of Mossflower. I cannot leave here; I have responsibilities to our friends the woodlanders and the Corim. Who could I send? Martin, there is only you. You have traveled, you are an experienced warrior, you are the one I will stake my trust on. Don't rush to give me your answer now. I want you to think about it. This is a very dangerous mission, and I will understand if you wish to stay here. My home is your home!

"I believe that my father still lives. You must bring him back to Mossflower to break Tsarmina's regime. Together under the leadership of Boar the Fighter we will defeat Tsarmina."

The spell was broken by Lady Amber, who came striding in with a face that was so grim it heralded bad news.

"Ferdy and Coggs are lost for sure. We've scoured high and low, all of us. It's as if the forest has swallowed them up."

Bella scratched her stripes reflectively. "Have you seen Chibb?"

"Yes. He's been around Kotir. Nothing to report, really. I sent him on a wide patrol of the woods. Maybe he'll bring news before nightfall."

The searchers returned at noon. Goody had busied herself setting out a salad luncheon on the sward outside Brockhall. Woodlanders ate in silence, avoiding any mention of the lost young ones while Goody was about. Shortly they set off again to resume searching. It was not a happy day in Mossflower. Martin was torn with a desire to help the searchers and curious to find out more about the mysterious place called Salamandastron. The former won; by early noon he was out searching with the others, knowing that Bella would tell him more that night.

• • •

Tsarmina stood at her high chamber window, watching the perimeter of the woodland where the trees thinned out into shrubs and bushes. There they were, at last!

The ragged columns tramped out of the woodlands with Cludd bawling orders at them.

"Come on, you sloppy mob, smarten yourselves up into proper ranks. Right markers, lead off. Tidy that pace up there. I'll not have you lolloping into the garrison like a load of hedgehogs on daisychain day. You there! Yes, you! Liven your ideas up, me laddo, or I'll liven them up for you with my spear."

The Captain's voice drifted up to Tsarmina. She could see plainly that there had been no losses among her troops. Neither had there been any mass of captives taken. In a sudden outburst of vicious temper, she slashed a wall curtain from top to bottom with her wicked claws, before storming out down the stairs to the parade ground.

The three platoons staggered to an untidy halt in the courtyard. Wearily they bumbled their way into formation, shouldering weapons and showing Thousand Eye shields front and center. Tsarmina checked her rush in the doorway and strode gracefully out with sinuously waving tail and baleful eye. A tremor rippled the ranks as they stood stiffly to attention, all eyes front. They saluted jointly.

"Hail, Tsarmina, Wildcat Queen of the Thousand Eyes, Ruler of all Mossfl—"

"Save your breath, fools. You'll get your chance to speak when I say and not before." Tsarmina prowled between the ranks, missing nothing, not even the two pitiful forms that lay bound on the gravel.

Fortunata stood rooted to the spot, feeling the Queen's feral breath raising the hairs on the nape of her neck.

"Well, fox, it seems that you all had a cheery spring outing in the woods. I notice that half the patrols are injured in one way or another. Tell me, did those two small woodlanders put up such a ferocious battle?"

Tsarmina continued circling Fortunata, her voice at a level of dangerous calm. "No need to worry now, eh, fox? We've caught their two champion warriors this time. What, if I may ask, was your heroic part in all this?"

Fortunata's limbs trembled with the effort of standing motionless. "It was Cludd who caught them, Milady. He found them asleep in a tent made from a blanket. Ashleg and I helped to bring them in."

Tsarmina repeated the phrase slowly. "You helped to bring them in. I see. Good work!"

The pine marten was next to receive Tsarmina's attention.

"Ah, my fearless friend Ashleg, you must be in great pain. Did one of those two bold rogues nibble through your wooden leg?"

"No, Majesty. That happened when my patrol was attacked by Fortunata's command in the night," Ashleg blurted out, surprised at the shrillness of his own voice.

Tsarmina widened her eyes in mock horror. "How awful! We attacked ourselves in the dark. No doubt it was all a little mistake."

"That's right, Milady, just a bit of a mistake, it could have happened to anyone, really." Fortunata's protest sounded hollow.

The wildcat turned her back on the whole scene. Paws akimbo, she stood staring out toward Mossflower. When she eventually spoke her tones dripped sarcasm and controlled rage.

"Get out of my sight, all of you idiotic scum. Down on your bellies and crawl back into the barracks like the worms you are. That way I won't have to look at your thick gormless faces slobbering excuses at me. Go on, clear off, the lot of you! Fortunata, Ashleg, Cludd—bring the prisoners up to my chamber."

Less than a minute later, Argulor stirred on his spruce branch and blinked owlishly, unaware that he had missed the chance of snatching a quick meal from the parade ground. He dozed off again in the hot afternoon sun as Chibb shot across the front of him, bound for Brockhall and safety. The tiny redbreasted spy had not missed a single word or movement of what took place on the parade ground.

A group of sad-faced creatures sat in the main hall of Bella's home.

Gonff tossed the blanket and empty cordial jar on the table in front of the Corim leaders. "Found 'em over to the west, about halfway between here and Kotir. The place stank of weasel and ferret. Lots of tracks—a big party, I'd say. Anyone go more news?''

Bella looked around the searchers who had returned, check ing that the Stickles were not present. She kept her voice low ''Chibb saw them trussed up on the parade ground at Koti earlier today. There's no doubt about it: Ferdy and Coggs hav been taken prisoner. They were carried off to the wildcat' chamber for probable questioning.''

Skipper slammed a paw against the hearth. ''Mates, doesn't bear thinkin' about, those two pore little fellers in th vermins' brig.''

Columbine's voice had a sob in it. ''What'll we tell Ben an Goody, poor creatures.''

Gonff was in no doubt at all. ''Tell 'em we'll rescue littl Ferdy and Coggs back straightaway. That's what we'll do, ma teys!''

There was a roar of approval.

Bella called for silence. ''Please, Gonff, be sensible. I'm cer tain that the Corim will agree to mount a rescue operation a soon as possible. But let us not run off or do anything reckles in the meanwhile. It would only end up in more prisoners bein taken, or lives being lost.''

''Bella is right,'' Abbess Germaine put in. ''I suggest tha you let me preside over the rescue operation. We can use al of you, especially Chibb; he will be of more value to us nov than ever before. Meanwhile, let us keep our hopes high an tempers in check. Bella is very busy working on somethin else for our benefit with Martin, and they must be exclude from the rescue attempt.''

Bella was astonished. She looked blankly at Germaine.

The old Abbess smiled back at her. ''I too was out takin the air in the woods early this morning.''

Bella bowed to the Abbess. ''Thank you for offering you help, old friend.''

Bella and Martin retired to the study. Immediately Bell closed the door, Martin turned to her.

''Bella, I have decided. I will find Boar the Fighter—I wil undertake the journey to Salamandastron.''

Bella took hold of the warrior's paws. ''Are you sure yo want to do this thing, Martin?''

Martin nodded firmly. ''For you and all my friends in Moss flower, I will find this strange place, even if it is at the world' end. And I will bring back your father Boar the Fighter.''

The door swung open. Gonff entered, rubbing a paw to his ear.

''Funny things, doors. Sometimes it's as if they're not there, and you can hear everything. By the way, Miss Bella, I'm surprised at you. Fancy sending my matey off on a quest without an able-bodied assistant.''

Martin hesitated. He looked to Bella. ''I'd feel a lot safer with a good thief along.''

The kindly badger smiled. ''Of course. Careless of me. Welcome, Gonff. We may need a brain as sharp as yours.''

They sat on the edge of a scroll-littered desk, while Bella settled comfortably into a dusty old armchair. She sighed and looked from one to the other.

''Well, I wish I knew where to begin. Fighting badgers have been going off questing for Salamandastron as far back as memory goes. My grandfather, old Lord Brocktree, went off when I was very small, then later he was followed by my father, Boar the Fighter.''

''Is there any record of whether they ever found it, or are there any maps of the way to Salamandastron?'' Martin interrupted.

Bella stroked her stripes thoughtfully. ''There must be a map somewhere. Both Lord Brocktree and Boar seemed to know where they were going. One thing I do know, it would be far too difficult to find the place of dragons without some form of key or map. You would need directions.''

Gonff smiled disarmingly. He picked up a bundle of scrolls from the desktop.

''Well, mateys, the solution is simple. Let's find the map!''

It had been a confused and frightening day for the two little hedgehogs. Since they had been taken by Cludd's patrol, not a word had passed between them. Both lay on the floor of Tsarmina's room, trying to forget the pains that shot through their bound-up paws and the filthy-tasting gags tied roughly across their mouths. Ferdy snuffled through his nostrils for breath and exchanged glances with Coggs.

What must Goody and Ben be doing?

Would the Corim leaders organize a search and a rescue?

What lay ahead they could only guess, but it wasn't going to be very pleasant.

Tsarmina sat watching impassively as Ashleg cut the captives' bonds and relieved them of their gags. Ferdy and Coggs lay quite still, fighting back tears as the circulation was painfully restored to their swollen limbs.

Cludd stirred the inert forms with his spearpoint. "Huh, they're fit enough, Milady. Wait'll their tongues loosen up, and we'll see what they've got to say for themselves."

Coggs rolled closer to Ferdy. "Don't tell the villains a thing, matey. Let's be like Martin and Gonff: brave and silent." His voice was barely above a whisper.

Fortunata kicked out cruelly at Coggs. She regretted it immediately as her paw came into contact with his sharp little spines.

"Silence, prisoner. Don't you know you're in the presence of Her Majesty Queen Tsarmina?"

Ferdy curled his lip rebelliously at the vixen. "She's not our Majesty—we're woodlanders."

Tsarmina leaned forward to the two little creatures lying at the foot of her chair. Bringing her face near them she slitted her eyes venomously. Baring her great yellowed fangs and extending her fearsome claws, she gave vent to a sudden wild growl.

"Yeeeggaarroooorrr!"

Ferdy and Coggs clutched at each other, their eyes wide with terror.

Tsarmina laughed and leaned back in her chair. "Now, my two tiny woodland heroes, let's begin, shall we?"

The wildcat's expression became almost benevolent as she took a tray of food from a table and sat with it in her lap.

"You, Ferdy—or is it Coggs? Wouldn't you like some milk and biscuits? A rosy autumn apple, perhaps? Or maybe you prefer dried fruit and nuts? Look, they won't hurt you."

Tsarmina bit into an apple, washing it down with a draught of milk.

The two small hedgehogs gazed longingly as she ate. They had not tasted food since dawn that morning.

Tsarmina selected a biscuit. Tossing the apple aside, she nibbled daintily, flicking crumbs from her whiskers.

Ferdy licked his lips. Coggs nudged him warningly. "It's probably all poisoned. Don't touch it."

Tsarmina placed the platter on the floor close to them. "Silly, if it were poison I'd be ill by now. Try it yourself, it's all from my special store. All I want is that you tell me about your woodland friends."

Coggs yawned and muttered wearily, "Don't tell her anything, matey. Not a word."

Ferdy yawned.

Tsarmina sat watching the two young captives. Their eyelids were beginning to droop, so she decided to try another angle. Stretching luxuriously, she yawned and snuggled deep in the big cushioned chair.

"I'll bet you two are tired. Mmmm, wouldn't it be nice to lie down on a bed of clean fresh straw and sleep for as long as you please? You can, too. It's quite simple, really. Just tell me about your friends—who they are, where they live, and so on. I won't harm them, you have my word. They'll thank you for it later when they are truly free. What do you say?"

Ferdy blinked hard, fighting back sleep. "Our friends are already free from you."

Tsarmina controlled her mounting temper by burying her claws in a russet apple. "That's as may be. But consider your own position. You two aren't free, and you're not likely to be, until you get some sense into your heads and answer my questions. D'you hear me?"

The wildcat's threats fell upon deaf ears. Ferdy and Coggs lay with their heads resting against each other, nodding slightly as they snored. They were both fast asleep.

Cludd touched them gently with his spearbutt. "Huh, it beats me why you don't string 'em both up and give 'em a taste of your claws, Milady. That'd soon make them talk."

Tsarmina's voice was tinged with heavy sarcasm. "You would think that, thickhead. How long d'you suppose they'd last with that treatment? These two are valuable hostages. Carry them down to the cells and lock them up for the night. We'll see if they are hungry enough to talk business tomorrow."

Gingivere heard the sound of an upstairs door opening. Someone was coming.

It was Cludd, accompanied by Ashleg and Fortunata. A key turned in the lock of the cell to the wildcat's immediate left. He heard Cludd's voice giving orders.

"Right. One in here, and one in the cell on the other side of the prisoner whose name must not be mentioned by Milady's order. They must be kept apart.''

When the trio had departed, Gingivere reflected upon this new development. Whoever the prisoners were, he knew that Chibb the robin would be interested next time he visited Kotir.

18

Young Dinny the mole knocked upon Bella's study door with his heavy digging claw.

"Hello, who is it?" Gonff's voice rang out from within.

"Hurr, it be Young Din. Miz Goody sent oi with these yurr viddles furr 'ee."

Martin opened the door and admitted the mole balancing a tray of food. Young Dinny blinked. The inside of the study was a mass of dust, scrolls, open drawers and general confusion. As Bella took the tray from the mole, Gonff leaped upon him from the desktop. They rolled about together on the floor, wrestling and hugging each other at the same time. Gonff laughed joyfully.

"Young Din, where've you been keeping yourself, me old diggin' mate?"

Dinny gained the upper paw and sat on Gonff. "Wurr you'm been, zurr Gonffen? You'm a-getten' fatter, hurr."

Gonff introduced his mole friend to Martin while struggling to heave Dinny off. "Matey, this is Young Dinny, the strongest mole in Mossflower."

The young mole allowed Gonff to get up. He smiled modestly as he shook paws with Martin.

"Naw, oi baint the strongest. Moi owd granfer Dinny, 'ee be the moightiest mole in these yurr parts, even tho' 'ee seen many summers. Oi be 'onored to meet 'ee, Marthen."

Martin took an instant liking to the friendly mole. They sat and shared the food while Bella explained the nature of the search.

Dinny gazed around at the masses of dusty scrolls littering the room. "Oi'd best lend a paw or winter'll be upon uz afore 'ee foinds owt."

The search was proving long and fruitless. Cupboards were turned out, the desk was emptied, shelves were scoured without success. The bulk of the scrolls were mainly old Brockhall records. Some were Bella's recipes, others dealt with woodland lore—none of them filed in any system. Bella brushed dust from her coat and sighed.

"I'm afraid it's all a bit higgledy-piggledy. I've been meaning to put them in order for some seasons now, but I never had time to get around to it."

Martin banged his paw on the desktop in frustration. "If only we knew ex . . . oof!"

A secret drawer shot out from the desk, catching the warrior mouse heavily in his stomach. He sat down, surprised and winded.

Bella took the single yellowed parchment from the drawer and read its contents aloud.

To the mountain of fire where badgers go,
The path is fraught with danger.
The way is long and hard and slow,
Through foe and hostile stranger.
The warrior's heart must never fail,
Or falter on his quest.
Those who live to tell the tale,
First must turn the crest.

Gonff looked bemused. "Is that all?"

Martin took the parchment and scanned it carefully on both sides. "Yes, that seems to be it."

Bella sat in her chair with an air of resignation. "Well, there doesn't appear to be much to go on."

Dinny tapped the parchment with his digging claws. "Hurr,

it be a start, tho'. This yurr's a clue may'aps.''

Martin brightened up, "Of course, it tells us how to start. Look: 'Those who live to tell the tale, first must turn the crest.' Bella, you would know, what does it mean by, 'turn the crest'?''

The badger pondered awhile. "I think it refers to the Brockhall shield—that's the badger family crest. It takes the form of a shield with the great oak of Brockhall on one half and the stripes of a badger on the other. Beneath it is a scroll bearing our family motto: To serve at home or afar.''

"But where is this crest and how do we turn it?" Gonff asked, scratching his whiskers.

Bella stood up. "I know of at least two places where it may be seen. The first is on the door knocker of Brockhall, and the second over the hearth in the main hall. Come on, let's try them both.''

The four friends trooped out to the front door, where Bella seized the rusty iron door knocker and twisted it sharply. The old metal snapped under the considerable strength of the badger, who stood holding it in her paw with a slightly guilty expression.

"Oops! I think I've broken it.''

Young Dinny shrugged. "Never moind, Miz Bell, moi granfer'll fix it for 'ee. Whurr's t'other un?''

The crest over the hearth was carved into the top lintel of the wide fireplace. Martin turned to Bella.

"I think I'd better try this one. My paws aren't as heavy as yours. Could you lift me up there, please?''

Bella obliged by picking the warrior mouse up as if he was a feather and placing him on the broad lintel.

Martin leaned over, gripping the protruding crest that had been carved on the fire-blackened oak-root beam. He tried turning it without success. Gonff climbed nimbly up beside him.

"Here, matey, let me try. Maybe you haven't got the magic touch." From his pouch the mousethief drew a piece of cheese and rubbed it around the edges of the crest.

"Give it a moment for the grease to work its way into the cracks. It shouldn't take long—this mantel's quite warm from the fire.''

Gonff's talents had not been wasted. After a short interval

he wiped his paws upon his jerkin and gave the crest a skillful twist. It moved!

"Here, matey, lend a paw. Jiggle it from side to side with me, like this. Pull outward as you do."

Martin assisted Gonff. The entire crest started to move outward. Bella stood ready to catch the hollow wooden cylinder—it dropped into her waiting paws.

Martin and Gonff eagerly clambered down from the lintel.

Dinny danced about excitedly. "Gurr, do 'urry, Miz Bell. Is it the map of Sammerlandersturm?"

The badger looked gravely at the young mole. "Haste will only put us on the wrong track, Dinny. Let us take each step carefully."

Bella upended the cylinder and peered into its open end. "Here, Gonff, there's a scroll inside. Your paws are a lot more nimble than mine—see if you can get it out without damaging it."

The clever mousethief had the parchment out and opened in a twinkling. They studied the writing; it was a bold and heavy old-fashioned style. Bella smiled.

"The paw of my grandsire old Lord Brocktree did this. You must understand that only male badgers went to Salamandastron. Each one left clues for his son to follow. This was written for my father Boar to solve. Unfortunately, Boar had no son to leave a map for, so after he had solved Lord Brocktree's riddles he carefully replaced everything in the hope that one day another young son of our house would find them."

Bella sniffed and looked away. "Alas, maybe my little one Sunflash might have followed these clues, had he been here today."

Young Dinny rubbed the back of his velvety paw against Bella's coat. "Hurr, doant fret 'eeself Miz Bell, us'ns foind it furr 'ee."

Martin had been toying with the wooden cylinder. He shook it and tapped the sides. Some leaves fell out.

"Look, Bella. What do you suppose this means?"

The badger shrugged. "They're just old leaves. Let's see what the parchment says."

Boar is badger, named after wood,
Not after forest but trees.
Where did you play on a rainy day?

Where did I eat bread and cheese?
Search inside, stay indoors,
Look up and find the secret is yours.
Your castle your fort,
Or so you thought.
The way is in four trees.
The way is in Boar in Brockhall
Under ale, under bread, under cheese.

Martin leaned back against the fireplace. "Phew! That's a right old riddle and no mistake."

Back in Bella's study, they sat pondering the evidence. A long time passed and still they could not even begin to unravel the complicated thread of the poem. Gonff was becoming disgruntled. He lay on the floor, drumming his paws against the armchair.

"Huh, woods and trees and bread and cheese, rainy days and castles and forts. What a load of old twaddle!"

Dinny had commandeered the armchair again. He sat back with eyes closed lightly as if taking a nap.

"Keep 'ee paws still, Gonffen, oi be a-thinken."

Bella pursed her lips and crinkled her brow. " 'Boar is badger named after wood.' I never knew my father was named after a wood."

Gonff rolled over onto his back. "If he was named after the wood, he'd be called Mossboar or Boarflower or Mossboarflower . . ."

Martin silenced the mousethief with a stern look. "Please, Gonff, we're supposed to be solving the riddle, not fooling about. The second line tells you that Boar is not named after the forest, but after the trees."

"Oi baint never 'eard of no Boartrees, nor oi 'spect 'as moi granfer," Dinny chuckled.

Bella agreed. "Neither have I, there's elm and birch and sycamore and all kinds of trees, but no Boartree. I wonder if that's an old nickname for some type of tree?"

Gonff sat up. "Say that again, Bella."

The badger looked at him, puzzled. "What, you mean about Boar being a nickname for some kind of tree?"

"No, I think I see what Gonff means," Martin interrupted. "You said there were all kinds of trees, like elm, birch, sycamore, and so on. Dinny, where d'you think you're off to? I thought you were helping us to solve this riddle.''

The young mole trundled out of the study, calling over his shoulder. ''Burr, that be 'zackly wot oi'm a-doen, goen t'get they owd leafs wot you'm founden afor.''

''Of course! The leaves!'' Gonff leapfrogged over Dinny's back before he was out of the door. Dashing back into the main hall, he scrabbled about collecting the leaves while Dinny followed up, berating him.

''Yurr, that be moi idea, zurr Gonffen, 'ee gurt mousebag.''

They brought the leaves back to the study between them. All four looked at the dried, withered specimens despondently.

''They're only dead leaves, many seasons old, but what are they supposed to mean?''

Bella touched them lightly with her paw. ''Well, let's see. There's four leaves here—an ash, an oak, a rowan, and a beech. There's nothing written or sketched on them. What do you make of it, Martin?''

The warrior mouse inspected the leaves. He arranged them in patterns, turned them over and rearranged them, shaking his head.

''I don't know. Ash, beech, rowan, oak; rowan, oak, beech, ash. Search me.''

Gonff smiled in a highly superior way. ''Listen, matey, it's a good job I'm a Prince of leaf-puzzle solvers. Try this: beech, oak, ash, rowan!''

''Is this another one of your jokes, Gonff?'' Bella asked, eyeing him sternly.

Gonff placed the leaves in order, still smiling. ''If it is a joke, then it's a very clever one, you'll admit. Beech, oak, ash and rowan in that order, can't you see, it's the first letter of each one. B then o then a then r, spells Boar.''

Bella shook his paw warmly. ''You're right. Boar is badger, named after wood. And look at this line lower down: 'The way is in four trees.' ''

Dinny clapped his paws together with excitement. ''O joy, now we'm agetten sumwheres. Roight, thinken carps on.''

''Yes. Look at this line: 'Search inside, stay indoors.' At least we know the map is somewhere in Brockhall; we don't have to go out scouring the woods.''

''But where indoors?''

''Where Boar played on rainy days.''

"Boar the Fighter, playing?"

"Ho aye, 'ee must've played when he'm a liddle un."

"Good thinking, Din!"

"Now, 'where did I eat bread and cheese?' D'you think that'd be Boar having his lunch?"

"Nay, that'd be thy granfer, Miz Bell."

"Of course. Boar was very close to old Lord Brocktree. It's quite probable he'd be playing around near him while Brocktree was eating."

"Aye, but there's the difficult bit: 'Your castle your fort'. Where's there a castle or a fort inside Brockhall?"

"No no, look at the next line; 'Or so you thought.' Didn't you ever play make-believe with something when you were little?"

"Haha, I still do, matey."

"Hurr, we'm know that, zurr. Coom on, Miz Bell. Show us'ns whurr Bowar did play when 'ee wurr a liddle un."

They wandered haphazardly from room to room. Every so often Bella would stop, look about and shake her head, muttering, "I'm not too sure, my father never talked too much about playing when he was little. Besides, I wasn't even born then."

Martin paused between the passage and the main hall. "Then think for a minute. Did your father ever say where Lord Brocktree went to eat his bread and cheese?"

"Hmm, not really. I expect he ate it at the table like any civilized creature would do indoors."

"The table!"

They hurried into the main hall to where the huge dining table stood.

Gonff rapped it with his claws. "Well, a good stout table, looks like it's made from elmwood. What do we do now?"

Bella had a faraway look in her eyes. "Wait, I remember now. Lord Brocktree was a crusty old soul. I recall my father telling me that he refused to eat at this big table, said he needed a spear to reach for things from the other end. So one day he made a table of his own, just big enough for him to sit at and handy, so that his bread and cheese and ale were all close to paw. It's out in the kitchen. Grandfather loved the heat from the oven. Besides, he used to dip his bread into any pans of sauce that were cooking. He liked it out there."

Standing in the kitchen was the very table Bella had told

them about. Gonff climbed on top of it and stood looking upward.

"Doesn't make sense, matey. All I can see is the ceiling. The riddle says: 'Look up and find the secret is yours.' "

Bella sat in the chair, spreading her paws across the table. "This is it. The answer is in this table somewhere. Look, my grandfather made it from beech, oak, ash and trimmed it with rowan wood. Do you know, I can picture my father sitting at this table just as his father did before him, eating bread and cheese and drinking October ale."

Martin had not spoken. He was staring at Bella as she sat at the table. It came to him like a flash.

"While you played underneath it. It probably had a table cloth on it then."

Bella smiled at fond memories. "Yes, a big white one. I would pretend it was my tent."

The warrior mouse scrambled underneath the table.

"Not Boar the Fighter, though. He'd probably pretend it was a fort or a castle. Ha, here's an odd thing. Underneath here is covered with a few pieces of chestnut bark. Pass me your knife, Gonff."

Martin worked away underneath the table, cutting the chestnut bark and tossing it out. The other three inspected each piece of bark for clues without success. Dinny sniffed it and raked it with his claws.

"O foozlum! Thurr baint nuthen yurr."

"There's something here though. It's the map!" Martin's voice could not conceal his delight. He came tumbling out with a pale bark scroll in his paws. "It was laid between the bark and the table. Look, it's covered with strange writing."

Bella took the scroll. "Haha, this is ancient badger script. Right, back to my study. I'll have to translate it. Thank you, my friends. This is the route to Salamandastron. Once we've solved it, you are on your way!"

19

Gingivere hacked away at the cell wall. As soon as the guards
had gone, he set about trying to communicate with the prisoners
on either side of him. From the damp mortar between the stones
of his cell he had prised loose a spike that had a ring attached
to it for securing unruly prisoners. Armed with the spike, the
wildcat selected a damp patch on one adjoining cell wall, and
worked furiously at the mortar around a stone which was not
quite so big as the others forming the barrier. Soon he had it
loose. Digging and jiggling, he pulled and pushed alternately
until the rock slid out, aided by a shove from the prisoner on
the other side. A small wet snout poked through.

"Hello, Ferdy. It's me, Coggs."

Gingivere smiled, glad to hear the sound of a friendly voice.
He patted the snout encouragingly.

"Sorry, old fellow, it's not Coggs. I'm Gingivere—a friend.
Coggs is in the cell on the other side of me. You stay quiet
and I'll see if I can get through to him."

"Thank you, Mr. Gingivere. Are you a wildcat?"

"Yes I am, but no need to worry. I won't harm you. Hush
now, little one, let me get on with my work."

Ferdy stayed silent, peering through the hole at Gingivere,

who was hacking stolidly at the opposite wall. It took a long time. Gingivere's paws were sore from grappling with the stone, chipping the mortar, and pulling this way and that until the rock finally gave and shifted. With Gingivere pulling from one side and Coggs pushing from the other, the wallstone plopped out onto the floor.

"Hello, Mr. Gingivere. I'm Coggs. Is Ferdy there?"

The wildcat shook the paw which protruded from the hole. "Yes, Coggs. If you look you'll see him through the hole from his cell."

The two little hedgehogs looked through at each other.

"Hi, Coggs."

"Hi, Ferdy."

"The guards will be coming shortly with bread and water for me," Gingivere interrupted. "I'll share it with you. Go back into your cells now and stay quiet. When Chibb arrives tomorrow I'll let him know you two are here."

Gingivere replaced the stones without much difficulty. He sat awaiting the guards with his daily ration of bread and water, realizing for the first time in a long and unhappy period that he was able to smile again.

A questing-o the friends did go,
Companions brave and bold,
O'er forest, field and flowing stream,
Cross mountains high and old.
These brave young creatures journeying
Along the road together,
While birds did sing throughout the spring,
Into the summer weather.

"Gonff, will you stop prancing about and caterwauling while we're trying to solve this chart? Dinny, chuck something at that fat little nuisance, will you, please?"

Martin scratched his head as he and Bella turned back to the scroll. Young Dinny obliged by hurling an armchair cushion that knocked the mousethief flat upon his bottom.

"Thurr, thad'll keep 'ee soilent apiece, zurr Gonffen. You'm a roight liddle noisebag, stan' on moi tunnel, you'm arr."

Gonff lay on the floor, resting his head upon the cushion; he hummed snatches of further new verses he was planning. Martin and Bella pored over the writing on the scroll, gleaning the information and writing it upon a chart with a quill pen. The wording was in ancient badger script that only Bella could translate.

Young Dinny called out from Bella's armchair, where he was ensconced, ''Wot we gotten so furr, Marthen?''

Martin read aloud:

Given to Lady Sable Brock by Olav Skyfurrow the wild-goose, after she found him injured in Mossflower and tended his hurts. The beacon that my skein find its way to the sea by is called the strange mountain of fire lizard.

Here Martin had marked a star with the word thus: *Sala-mandastron.

We of the free sky do wing our way there. But if you be an earth walker, it will be a long hard journey. Here is the way I will tell you to go. I begin as I fly over Brockhall:

Twixt earth and sky where birds can fly,
I look below to see
A place of wood with plumage green
That breezes move like sea.
Behind me as the dawn breaks clear,
Woodpigeons come awake,
See brown dust roll, twixt green and gold,
Unwinding like a snake.
So fly and sing, the wildgoose is King.
O'er golden acres far below,
Our wings beat strong and true,
Where deep and wet, see flowing yet,
Another snake of blue.
Across the earth is changing shape,
With form and color deep,
Afar the teeth of land rise up,
To bite the wool of sheep.
So fly and sing, the wildgoose is King.
Beyond this, much is lost in mist,
But here and there I see
The treachery of muddy gray,
'Tis no place for the free.
O feathered brethren of the air,
Fly straight and do not fall,

Onward cross the wet gold flat,
Where seabirds wheel and call.
So fly and sing, the wildgoose is King.
The skies are growing darker, see
Our beacon shining bright.
Go high across the single fang
That burns into the night.
We leave you now as we wing on,
Our journey then must be
Where sky and water meet in line,
And suns drown in the sea.
So fly and sing, the wildgoose is King.

Gonff came across and stared at the scroll. "Well, old wot-sisname Skyfurrow was nearly as good a bard as me. Bet he wasn't half as clever a thief, though, matey."

Martin shook his head. "It's certainly a strange route to follow, given in goose song, written in ancient badger, and translated into common woodland. Do you think we've missed anything, Bella?"

The badger looked indignant. "Certainly not. It's all there, word for word. I'll have you know that female badgers are great scholars, though I must say it all looks very cryptic to me."

Young Dinny clambered out of the armchair and squinted at Martin's neat writing.

"Urr, triptick, wot be that? Stan' on moi tunnel, it be wurse'n maken 'oles in watter, ho urr."

Gonff stifled a giggle. "You certainly have a way with words, Din. Ah well, let's get our thinking caps on and imagine we're all Skyfurrows."

Martin clicked his paws together. "Right! That's exactly what we have to do. Imagine the ground from up above as if we were birds."

Tsarmina stood watching the dawn break over Mossflower from her chamber window. Mist rose in wisps from the treetops as the sun climbed higher in a pale blue cloudless sky. The wildcat Queen was highly pleased with her latest plan; the woodlanders must have realized the two baby hedgehogs were missing, and they would send out search parties. Tsarmina detailed Cludd and another weasel named Scratch, acting as his deputy, to patrol the woods, along with a picked group of twenty or so.

They would travel light, unhampered by the usual Kotir armor. They could act as a guerilla force, lying in wait to capture any woodlanders they came across and sabotaging resistance wherever they encountered it.

She watched them slip out of the perimeter gate, armed with their own choice of weapons and equipped with rations. The wildcat Queen curled her lip in satisfaction. There was no need to try interrogating her two prisoners further at the moment; let them stay in their cells until they were starving. It was always easier to interview creatures who had not eaten for a few days. Two small hedgehogs trying to pit their wits against the Queen of the Thousand Eyes—what chance did they have?

Scratch was a fairly observant weasel. He jabbed skyward with his dagger.

"See that robin, Cludd?"

Cludd noted that Scratch had omitted to call him Captain. He looked up, but Chibb had flown from view.

"What robin? Where?"

Scratch sheathed his dagger. "You've missed him now. I could have sworn it was the same bird I've noticed hanging about outside the barracks a few times. Always ends up somewhere near the ground, hidden."

Cludd was reluctant to believe that Scratch was more alert than he.

"Hmm, it might be summat or nothing. Woodlanders don't usually have much to do with birds. Still, we'd best be on the safe side. Hoi, Thicktail, make your way back to Kotir and tell Milady about that robin. Don't breathe a word to anyone else, though. I don't want Ashleg or that fox stealing any of my credit."

Thicktail saluted, and jogged off in the direction of Kotir.

Scratch looked at the thickly wooded area they were in. "Perhaps we'd better lie low here awhile. That way we can have a rest while we keep our eyes and ears open, eh, Cludd?"

Cludd knew the idea was a sensible one, but Scratch was beginning to annoy him with his insubordinate manner.

"Aye, I was just thinking the same thing myself. Right, lads, pick good hiding places and keep your eyes and ears open. But just let me catch anyone snoozing and I'll have his tail for a bootlace. That goes double for you, Scratch."

As the special patrol dispersed among the trees, Scratch stuck out his tongue at Cludd's back, muttering beneath his breath, "Cludd the clod thick as mud."

Thicktail did not like being out in Mossflower alone, even in broad sunny daylight. The stoat scurried through the trees looking furtively from left to right; as he went he repeated Cludd's instructions aloud to himself, "Tell the Queen that there's been a robin redbreast hanging about Kotir grounds. It flies down low and vanishes near the floor. Cludd thinks that it might be something to do with those woodlanders. Now, I'm to say nothing to Fortunata or Ashleg. Huh, if they ask me I'll just tell them that I had to come back because I sprained my paw. I'd better practice limping on it just in case."

Argulor was making a wide sweep from Kotir over the forest; this way he could fool anyone at Kotir into thinking he had flown away. He was about to circle back when he heard the voice below him and saw a stoat limping about in the undergrowth.

"I must tell the Queen that a robin has seen Cludd hanging about. No, that's not right. I must tell the robin that Cludd has been hanging the Queen . . ."

Argulor did not require perfect sight to tell him where his next noisy meal was. He dropped like a stone to the forest below.

A stone with talons and a curving beak.

Bella's study was still awash in a litter of old documents. They slid from the desk, which still had its secret drawer hanging askew. Several food trays stood balanced here and there amid the dust. The scroll and four leaves that had led the friends to the route lay on the arm of the big armchair, where Dinny sat snuggled in its deep cushioned seat. Bella leaned against the desk. She did not mind the young mole borrowing her favourite chair, though he did seem to be growing rather fond of it. Martin paced up and down. At each turn he had to step over Gonff. The little mousethief lay stretched out on a worn carpet that covered the study floor. Martin was having trouble imagining himself as a bird. The mere mention of heights made the groundloving Young Dinny feel sick and dizzy. Gonff, however, was displaying a fine aptitude for a mousebird.

"Ha, 'I look below to see a place of wood with plumage green that breezes move like sea.' It's as plain as the whiskers on your face, mateys. He means good old Mossflower Woods, right where we are.''

Bella closed her eyes, picturing herself in flight. ''Hmm, I suppose that our woods would look like water moving in the wind from above. Carry on, Gonff. What's next?''

''Er, 'Behind me as the dawn breaks clear, woodpigeons come awake'.''

''Burr, doant you uns see, dawnbreak, sunroise. Gooseburd be a-tellen us'ns to traverse westerly,'' Young Dinny called out from the armchair.

Martin shook Dinny's paw. ''Good mole! Of course, if the sun rises in the east and dawnbreak is behind him, then he must be traveling due west. Well solved, Young Dinny.''

The mole gave a huge grin, settling deeper into the armchair. ''Ho urr, this yurr young mole ain't on'y a digger. Oi seed they woodenpidger waken at dawnen, gurr, turrible noisebags they be, all that cooen. Goo on, wot's next bit o' poartee?''

Gonff continued, ''The poetry says, 'See brown dust roll twixt green and gold, unwinding like a snake.' ''

Bella nodded knowingly. ''Aha, friend Olav gave me an easy one there. I know the very place. Between the woods and the flatlands south of Kotir, the road has a twist in it. I've walked down it many times and thought it was just like a snake trying to slough its skin.''

Gonff shuddered at the mention of snake. ''So, mateys, we walk through the woods, heading west, and cross the path below Kotir. Then there's only one way we can go. Straight out across the flatlands and the open plains, like the poem says, 'O'er the golden acres' to where the 'snake of blue' lies—brr, snakes.''

''That's no snake, Gonff,'' Martin interrupted. ''It's the same as Bella's winding road, but this one is blue—it's a river. What puzzles me is the teeth of land eating the wool of sheep line.''

Bella stretched and yawned. ''Whoo! I think we must be going stale sitting around this dusty old room. Sheep and land, wool and teeth . . . Ah well, maybe we can't see the wood for the trees, but whatever it is, you'll know it when you see it. What do you want to do? Sit here half a season solving riddles, or follow the clues you already have and work the rest out as you go along? The supplies are packed and ready, you have your weapons, wits and youth to help you along—what more do you want?''

Gonff supplied the answer. "A good matey to walk by your side through thick and thin."

"You'ns baint leaven this yurr mole behoind."

Martin and Gonff laughed heartily, Bella bowed apologetically to the mole.

"Forgive me, Dinny. I did not know you wished to go questing."

The young mole heaved himself up onto his hind paws. "Burr, you try 'n' stop oi, Miz Bell. Tho' oi do 'ate to take leave of yon armchurr."

20

The Corim plan was beautifully simple.

A party of woodlanders would set out with haversacks of provisions from a point near to Kotir, and Chibb was to be given the rations one sack at a time. That way he could make short journeys to the cell window, passing the food in to Gingivere. Abbess Germaine had reasoned it all out: the woodlanders were helping by carrying the food, Chibb would not be overtaxed by making many long flights and Gingivere would secretly share the rations with Ferdy and Coggs. Later, there would be time to mount a rescue operation, but it needed a great deal of careful planning between the Corim leaders.

In the hour before dawn the two parties sat eating an early breakfast provided by Ben and Goody Stickle: hot scones, fresh from the oven, with butter and damson preserve and mugs of cold creamy milk.

"Mmmff, lookit those otters and squirrels packin' it away. You'd think they was a-goin' away nigh on three seasons," Ben Stickle mumbled through a mouthful of hot scone.

Goody topped up his beaker with milk. "Listen to the leaf a-callin' the grass green. You're worse'n any of 'em, Ben

Stickle. Just you mind those two liddle 'ogs of mine don't go
'ungry. See they gets their rations.''

Skipper tucked a spare scone in his sling pouch. ''Don't fret
your head, marm. They'll both take on a cargo of vittles afore
evenin' bell.''

Lady Amber raised her tail and waved it. ''Righto. Form up,
woodlanders carrying provisions in the center, squirrels and
otters forming guard on flanks and scouting ahead. Martin, your
party can walk with us part of the way.''

The sun was not yet up as they left Brockhall through the
still slumbering forest. Both parties stole silently into the trees,
waving goodbye to Bella, Abbess Germaine and Goody Stickle
who stood on the sward outside Brockhall.

The old Abbess tucked her paws into the long sleeves of her
habit. ''Let us hope that both parties are successful.''

Goody Stickle blinked back a tear. ''Let's 'ope my Ferdy
and Coggs gets their proper nourishment.''

Bella watched the last of the party vanishing into the thick-
nesses of Mossflower.

''Aye, and let us hope that Martin can bring back my father
Boar the Fighter, to save us all and free us from the vermin of
Kotir.''

It was close to midday. Scratch and Cludd lay beneath an old
hornbeam. All around the troops lay hidden, most of them
sleeping soundly. Cludd had spotted one or two soldiers and
was about to recall them to duty with his spearbutt, when
Scratch suddenly put a claw to his lips for silence and pointed
to a break in the trees.

The woodlanders marched by the sleeping soldiers, unaware
that they were being watched. Skipper strode boldly in the lead,
twirling his sling. Some of the otters had relieved the carriers
of their loads. They strolled along, conversing with the Loamhedge mice. In the middle terraces of sycamore, plane and elm,
Lady Amber swung from bough to limb with her archers.

Scratch and Cludd watched the passage of the curious band
in silence. Cludd hoped that none of the soldiers would waken
noisily; he could practically taste reward and promotion. Rubbing his paws together in excitement, he nudged his companion.

''By the claw, that lot can only be headed to one place—
Kotir. Wait'll the Queen hears about this, eh, Scratch.''

As he rose, Scratch shoved him roughly back down. "Ssshh! Look over there."

Coming through the trees in a slightly different direction, Martin, Dinny and Gonff marched along a path that would take them due west, skirting Kotir on its south side. Columbine had walked with Gonff, but now their paths were to part and she hurried away to join the others. As Cludd watched he made a mental note to pay Scratch back for banging his nose down into the dirt. Unaware of his Captain's displeasure, Scratch listened to the strains of Gonff singing his farewell to Columbine as she waved to him with a kerchief.

> Goodbye, Columbine.
> Now your path and mine
> Must part in the woods of Mossflow'r.
> Keep a lookout each day,
> For I'll be back this way,
> In the noontide or cool evening hour.

Scratch cackled. Fluttering his eyelids, he picked a daisy and sniffed it gustily. "Aaahh, isn't that romantic, now? The young mouse singing farewell to his sweethear . . . ouch!"

Cludd rapped him smartly between the ears with the flat of his spearblade. "Shut your trap, nitwit. D'you want the whole forest to hear you? Those three aren't going to Kotir. Oh no, they're bound for somewhere else. Now listen, greasy ears, here's what I want you to do. Take two others and follow them. Don't let them out of your sight. Find out where they're going and why, then report back to me."

Scratch rubbed the top of his head indignantly. "Oh yes. Go off and follow those three. Who knows where they're going, or how long it'll take? Huh, you must think all the acorns have dropped off my tree, Cludd. I know where you'll be, mate—grabbing all the glory for yourself. 'Yes three, Milady, no Milady, three bags full Milady. I saw them first, Milady, so I've sent daft old Scratch off chasing the odd three.' Hoho, I'm on to your little game, weasel."

Cludd seized Scratch roughly by the ear and began twisting savagely. "So! Open rebellion, eh, Scratch. Now listen to me, you scruffy half-baked excuse for a soldier, if I have to report your disobedience to Her Majesty, she'll have you staked out on the parade ground for eagle meat, d'you hear me? Now get going, wormbrain. Here, you two, Blacktooth ferret and Split-nose stoat, grab weapons and supplies. Go with Scratch. Jump to it, that's a direct order from me.''

The sulky-looking trio skulked off, muttering.

"Old bossy boots Cludd, eh.''

"Huh, how he ever got to be Captain, I'll never know.''

"Take that spear away and he'd fall over flat on his nose.''

"Aye, Tsarmina's pet, the baby-hedgehog catcher.''

Cludd waited until they were gone, then shouldered his spear. "Right, me laddos. Up on your paws. We'll take the shortcut north back to the garrison, then Milady can arrange a warm welcome for her woodland visitors.''

Cludd put the remainder of his force into a swift jog trot. Soon the spot where the three paths had crossed was deserted as the last soldier vanished into the bright leafy shades of Moss-flower.

Toward evening, Tsarmina grew restless. She had the two pris-oners brought up from the cells. The wildcat Queen was reluc-tant to admit to herself that she could not get the better of two little hedgehogs. Hunger, she decided, was a great tongue-loosener.

Ferdy and Coggs stood before her, their eyes riveted to the big tray of crystallized fruit and nuts.

Tsarmina popped one neatly into her mouth, delicately lick-ing the sticky sugar coating from her claws one by one.

"Mmm, delicious! I'll wager that either one of you two young 'uns could eat this entire tray in one go. Come on, now. Don't be shy. First to talk a bit of sense gets them all.''

Coggs licked his lips. Ferdy grasped his paw and spoke out for them both.

"Huh, I'd swap all that lot for just one slice of our mum's apple pie.''

Tsarmina smiled winningly. "Of course you would. I sup-pose your mum makes the best apple pie in all Mossflower?''

Coggs wiped his damp whiskers with the back of a paw. "Oh, I'll say she does. Hot out of the oven, with fresh cream poured on until it floats.''

Tsarmina nodded agreeably. "Lovely. That's just the way I like it. By the way, what do they call your mother?''

Ferdy was caught completely off guard. "Goody.''

"Goody what?'' The wildcat Queen kept up a friendly purr.

Coggs kicked Ferdy and interrupted, "Goody, goody. We love our mum's apple pie, and that's all we've got to say!"

Tsarmina scowled irritably and pushed the tray of sweetmeats away. "Guards! Take these two little fools and lock them up again. They'll learn what hunger is a week from now."

As they were marched off, Coggs shouted bravely, "Aye, and you'll see how woodland warriors can still behave two weeks from now, cat."

Far below at the prison window bars, Chibb earnestly discussed the new plan with Gingivere.

Gonff was first to complain as evening fell over the woodlands. "Phew, it's a while since I trudged this far, mateys. What d'you say, this looks a likely place for the night, then we can get a fresh start in the morning?"

Young Dinny inspected the site. It was a dead chestnut stump, with a small hole between the two main roots.

"Hurr, oi knows this yurr gaff. Slep' yurr many a noight. 'Ee'll do."

Martin crouched as he made his way into the confined space. "Just about enough room for the three of us. We'd better call it a day. Break out some supper, Gonff."

While Gonff set the food out, Dinny scooped loam around the entrance, leaving a small space for observation. The mole had no sooner finished his task when he held up a paw.

"Usher now. Cum by 'ere an' lookit."

Silently they gathered round and watched as Scratch blundered noisily through the undergrowth, followed by Splitnose and Blacktooth.

"Haha, look out. The bogey Cludd's behind you."

"Fat chance! He'll probably be stuffing his face back at Kotir."

"Aye, and getting ready to sleep in a dry bed, too."

"No sign of the mice and the mole yet, Scratch?"

"It's getting so dark I can't see my own paws, let alone mice and a mole. Come on, let's get clear of this forest while we can. If we reach the road, there's a dry ditch where we can camp the night."

"Hey, Blacktooth, stop scoffing those rations. There'll be none left for us."

"Aah, there's plenty. Anyhow, I'm starving."

"You're starving! I haven't had a bite since breakfast myself. Here, give me that food."

"No, I won't. Leggo, you big grabber!"

"Here, I'll take charge of that, you two. Garr, you greedy nits, it's spilled all over the place now. You've dropped it."

"It wasn't me, it was him. He shoved me, clumsy paws."

"Clumsy paws yourself, greedy guts. Take that!"

"Owoo! I'll report you to Cludd when we get back."

"Oh, go and report your mother."

In the hole beneath the chestnut tree the three friends held their sides in silent mirth, tears running down their whiskers as they watched the antics of the searchers, who fumbled and bungled their way off into the darkness, still arguing and fighting.

"Gurr, moi goodness, us'ns been 'unted by those 'oller'eads. Burr, yon vermints cudden 'unt their way outer a shallow 'ole."

Gonff handed cheese to Martin. "No wonder. Did you hear who their boss is, matey? Old Cludd the clod. He couldn't order his own two ears to stand up straight."

Martin put his supper to one side. "Maybe not, but he was smart enough to spy on us without our knowing it. I think we should treat them as enemies. That way we won't be caught off guard. Anyhow, let's get some supper and sleep. We've got a long day ahead tomorrow."

From the window of her high chamber, Tsarmina's eyes pierced the night with the keenness of a predator. She saw Cludd and his special patrol hurrying to Kotir from the north fringes, then sweeping her gaze in an arc she noted a movement at the south edge of the forest.

Woodlanders!

Tsarmina rushed to the table and rang her little bell vigorously. A ferret named Raker came scurrying in.

"Quickly, alert the entire garrison. Have them form up inside the barracks awaiting my orders. Tell them to be silent. Send Cludd to me. He'll be arriving shortly."

Raker wondered how Tsarmina knew of Cludd's imminent arrival, but he did not dare ask her how. He held up his Thousand Eye shield in a smart salute.

"Right away, Milady."

Tsarmina peered intently at the band of otters, mice, and hedgehogs. She noted the ripple in the treetops—squirrels too. This time she had the element of surprise on her side. She did not intend wasting it. Now they would learn the meaning of the word fear.

Halfway down the stairs she bumped into Cludd, who was dashing up to her chamber to make his report.

"Milady, I have gathered some expert knowledge on the movements of the woodla—"

"Yes, I already know. Form your patrol up and get down to the main barracks quickly."

"But, Majesty, there was a robin flying through the woods and I told Thic—"

Tsarmina whirled upon the slow-witted weasel. "Robin? What rubbish are you spouting now? What d'you think I care about a robin? Get out of my sight, you useless lump."

Cludd stood, bewildered, on the stairway as she brushed past. There was no point in trying to talk to Tsarmina when she was in one of her moods.

The highest tree near the south side of Kotir was a stately elm. Chibb was perched in its branches when he sighted the wood-landers.

"Ahem, harrumph! Over here, please, and keep quiet. We don't want any eagles waking up."

Skipper threw a smart nautical salute with his tail. "Ahoy there, mate. Is everything shipshape?"

Chibb paced to and fro upon the branch. "Ahem, well I must say it appears to be, harrumph. Though I have my doubts."

Lady Amber dropped in beside him, and the nervous robin leaped with fright.

"Madam! Ahem, kindly have the goodness to announce your presence in a less startling manner."

Ben Stickle and the rest were unloading packs of rations at the foot of the elm. Columbine looked upward at the robin.

"D'you know, Ben, for some reason I feel as uneasy as Chibb."

Ben loaded the packs on the squirrels, who scampered up the trunk as if it were level ground.

"Aye, m'dear, I know 'xactly how you feel. I don't like this place one little bit meself."

As if to punctuate the hedgehog's remark, an arrow whistled out of the darkness to stand quivering in the elm bark.

"Ambush! Everyone take cover!" Lady Amber called aloud from her vantage point.

Immediately, the mice and hedgehogs were screened by a wall of otters. Skipper bounded to the fore, ducking a spear as he swung a sling loaded with several stones.

"Over yonder, crew. By those thickets. Give 'em a rattlin' good broadside, mates."

Ranks of brawny otters made the air rain heavy with hard river stones.

The dinting and thudding of rock upon armor and pelt was mingled with screams and cries from the ambushers.

When the fusillade slackened, Tsarmina sprang forward, urging her attackers onward. "Charge. Rush them now. Up. Charge!"

The soldiers pounded toward the woodlanders, yelling and shouting threats as they waved pikes, spears and javelins.

Lady Amber watched coolly. She notched an arrow to her bow-string as, all around her in the high branches, squirrels followed her example. She laid her tail flat along the bough of the elm.

"Steady in the trees there. Let them get well into the open, then watch for my signal."

Though one or two otters were down with spear wounds, Skipper had heard Amber and he backed up her strategy. "Otter crew load up. Don't sling until the arrows are loosed."

Now the Kotir army had covered over half the distance, Fortunata slacked off, dropping back with Ashleg and Cludd. Tsarmina alone led the field. Confident that the charge would carry the full distance, she turned to yell further encouraging words to her troops.

Lady Amber decided they had come far enough. Her tail stood up like a banner as she called, "Archers, fire!"

The waspish hiss of arrows halted the advance in its tracks, the back and middle ranks colliding with the fallen in front.

"Slings away hard, crew!" Skipper's wild call boomed out across the melee.

A second volley of stones flew thick and fast into the confused soldiers.

Now Tsarmina was forced back into her own ranks. Furiously she began snarling out orders.

"One rank crouching, one rank standing. Give me a wall of

shields to the front and carry on advancing. Poke spears out between the gaps in the shields. Quick, fools. Fortunata, group archers at the rear. Tell them to fire over our heads into the woodlanders. Hurry!''

Realization that they were in danger of being under serious attack galvanized the Kotir troops into action.

Ben Stickle and Columbine were crawling about, whispering to the noncombatants.

''Friends, help the wounded. Go with them quickly and quietly around the back of this tree. Foremole has arrived with help.''

They slid away, with Skipper's crew masking their retreat.

The soldiers were firing arrows now. They rattled off tree trunks and stuck into the earth, some finding their mark among the woodlanders. The shield-fronted advance moved slowly but steadily forward.

Skipper and Amber had coordinated their firepower. After the otters loosed stone and javelin, the squirrels shot their arrows, each giving the other a chance to reload, while keeping up continuous fire.

''Slings away!''

''Archers, fire!''

Brush and Birch were two big competent squirrels. Following Lady Amber's directions, they swung off toward Kotir's furthest side, carrying as many ration packs between them as possible. Chibb flew with them. All three were silent, and unseen by those in the fray below.

Cludd's bellow urged the soldiers forward. ''Come on, you lot. Stir your stumps, you laggards. Keep pushing on. We'll have 'em soon. You can have an otter apiece shortly.''

A stoat winced as a rock bounced off his spearshaft, sending shocks of pain through his claws. ''Huh, I'll have a mouse or a wounded hedgehog, mate. Let Cludd and the Queen tackle those big otters.''

His companion, a weasel, nodded agreement. ''Aye, let them have the glory. We'll be satisfied with the pickings.''

Seconds later he was silenced by an arrow.

Lady Amber was beginning to get worried. She called down to Skipper, ''We're almost out of arrows up here, Skip. There's too many of 'em. We can't stop their advance; it looks as if we've had it.''

Skipper's tongue was lolling as he tore off two large rocks from his sling.

''There's nothing for it, marm. We'll just have to see how many of 'em we can take with us.''

21

Early morning was enveloped in white mist. It clung to tree
and bush like a gossamer shawl, sparkling with dewdrops in
the promise of a hot sunny day ahead.

Eager to be on their way, the three friends broke fast as they
traveled. Martin unpacked scones for them, Gonff doled out a
russet apple apiece, and Dinny vanished into the mist, reap-
pearing with a canteen of fresh spring water.

Limbs loosened as the night stiffness receded. They stepped
out at a brisk pace to Gonff's latest marching chant.

> Sala-manda-stron, look out here we come,
> A thief, a warrior and a mole.
> Though the quest may take its toll,
> We'll march until we reach our goal,
> Sala-manda-stron.

The flood of morning sun penetrated the mists, melting them
into a yellow haze. Martin and Gonff struggled to keep
straight faces, listening to Dinny chanting the marching verse
in mole tongue.

"Salad-anna-sconn, lookit yurr'ee come."

Still in fine fettle, they reached the outskirts of Mossflower Woods. Pushing on through the fringes, they found themselves facing a brown dirt road, which curved and bent like a snake. Beyond it lay the far dim expanses of the flatlands shimmering in the heat. Between the path and the flatlands was a deep ditch, though because of the dry weather it contained only the merest trickle of water.

The companions kept silent, remembering that Scratch and his aides might well be somewhere nearby.

Gonff went back to the woods and returned with a long stout branch. Taking his knife, the mousethief trimmed off the twigs.

Martin watched with interest. "What are you up to, matey?" he asked, keeping his voice low.

Young Dinny knew. "Ee'm maken a powl t'jump ditcher. Squirrelbeast do et iffen they baint no tree to swing offen."

Martin took the pole and felt its balance. "Oh, I see. A vaulting pole. Good idea, Gonff."

Making sure his grip was firm on the pole near its top, Gonff leveled it in front of him.

"Me first, Dinny next, then you, matey. Watch me and see how it's done. I'm a prince of vaulters, y'know."

Gonff broke into a fast trot. With the pole held straight out, he sped across the road, then dipping the pole into the ditch he levered upward and out. Martin saw the pole bend, carrying Gonff high into the air. The momentum swung him easily across the ditch. He landed lightly on his paws and pushed the pole back to the mole.

Dinny held it gingerly, whispering to Martin, "Murrsey, oi 'ates a leaven owd earth, 'tis on'y burds be so fool'ardy. Arr well, yurr oi goo."

Dinny performed a waddling little shuffle, jabbed the pole into the ditch and rose slowly into the air. The impetus was not sufficient to carry him across; he wavered in the air and began dropping back. Martin made a mad dash. Catching the pole low down, he thrust against it and whipped back with all his force. Dinny was catapulted away from the pole across the ditch. He hit the far bank near the top and was grabbed by Gonff, who helped him to scrabble out. Dinny lay kissing the grass, thankful to be back on firm ground.

Martin's strength and fearlessness helped him to make the crossing with ease. He quite enjoyed the sensation of flying through the air. When Dinny was fully recovered, they commenced their journey into the flatlands.

They were not long gone when Blacktooth yawned and stretched himself in the ditch. The trackers had camped a short distance south of the vaulting area.

Splitnose rolled over in his sleep and slid from the narrow strip of dry bottom into the slimy shallow water.

"Yaaauugghhh! You lousy vermin! Who did that? Come on, own up!"

"Heeheehee! You did it yourself, puddenhead. It's a wonder you never carried on snoring."

"What, me, snoring? Have you ever heard yourself? Sounds like a goose gargling."

"Rubbish. I never slept a wink. Oh, I dropped off for a moment or two a while back. Funny, though. I dreamed I saw a mouse, just up that way apiece. Guess what? He flew across the ditch."

"Heeheehee oh ahaharr! He wasn't followed by Cludd pretending to be a swallow, was he?"

"Ha, you can laugh, fatty. But it was almost as if I was awake. The mouse flew, I tell you."

"Fatty yourself! That's what you get for hogging all those rations last night. It was a nightmare brought on by pure greed."

"It was not. It was more like a daymare brought on by the hunger. I'm starving."

Scratch ignored their arguing. Pulling himself from the ditch, he took a chunk of bread from his pack and began munching it.

Splitnose and Blacktooth stopped fighting to complain.

"Oi, that's not fair. You're supposed to be the leader. It's up to you to see we're properly fed."

"That's right. I've only got a stingy little bit of crust and it's sopping wet from that stinking ditch water."

Contemptuously Scratch threw a crust on the bank edge. "There you are. First out gets it."

The ferret and the stoat fought tooth and claw. They kicked each other down in an effort to be first out of the ditch. Blacktooth won. He grabbed the crust as Splitnose wailed piteously, "Give me some, Blackie. Go on. I'd give you half if I had bread."

"No you wouldn't, stoatface."

"Yes I would."

"Wouldn't."

"Would."

Blacktooth relented with bad grace. "Oh, here, scringetail. Don't pig it all down in one gobful."

"Aaahh, that's not fair. You've got the biggest half."

Scratch had wandered farther up the bank. He chewed on a young dandelion, pulled a face, spat it out and shouted, "Hoi, you two, stop bellyaching and look at this."

They ambled up, chewing the last of the crust. "What is it?"

Scratch shook his head in despair. "What do you think it is, loafbrains? Look, it's the track of those two mice and the mole. See, here and here, the pawprints are as clear as day. They're traveling west."

Splitnose found the pole and held it up triumphantly. "Aha, another clue. They must have used this to climb out of the ditch on."

"Oh chuck it away, bouldernose," Scratch sneered. "Huh, you'll be telling me next that they used it to fly through the air on. Come on, you two. At least we're on their trail."

From the topmost branches of a beech on the south side of Kotir, Chibb checked the straps on his pack before flying off to the cells. Brush and Birch watched him flying into the thin dawn light, then Brush readied the next pack.

"Shouldn't take too long, then we can nip back and see how the battle's going."

Birch looked to his quiver. "I'm nearly out of arrows. Bet the others are, too. Tell you what—you stay here and see to the robin while I swing back to base. I'll gather all the arrows I can lay my paws on from the stores and take them to our archers."

"Good idea. See you later, mate."

Around the back of the elm, it was only a short distance from the heavy loam of the woodlands. Foremole led the little party, Columbine and Ben bringing up the rear with Soilflyer, a champion young digging mole. "Hurr on'y a liddleways, now gaffers," he chuckled secretively. "'Uz diggers do 'ave a foin tunnel awaiten fer 'ee to excape thru."

Gratefully they were helped into the broad tunnel dug by the moles. As they progressed along it, Columbine could hear Soil-flyer filling in behind them. Up ahead, Foremole said comfortingly to some mice, ''Never 'ee fear, liddle guddbeasts. We'm a goen' to Moledeep. None may foind 'ee thurr.''

Tsarmina's determination was unabated. She pushed her forces ruthlessly forward.

''Come on. Can't you see they aren't sending over as many arrows or stones? Keep going. We've got them.''

Fortunata's ear throbbed unmercifully. The vixen was lucky that the arrow had not struck a bit lower, or it would have been her skull. Clamping a pawful of her own herbs to the wound, she looked up dismally as a large squirrel swung in laden with quivers of arrows. The fox dropped back a few paces, muttering beneath her breath, ''If you think you've got 'em, Milady, then go and get them yourself.''

Two of Skipper's crew were driving long sharp stakes into the ground at the base of the elm trunk. Earth had been piled around the stakes and leafy branches scattered on top. From a distance it looked for all the world like a crew of otters lying in wait, armed with spears.

The newly arrived arrows drove the Kotir soldiers back a short distance, despite Tsarmina's threats and blandishments. Lady Amber checked to see that the moles had got away with their charges.

''Is it ready, Skip?''

Skipper held up a paw. ''As ready as it'll ever be, marm.''

''Good. We'll fire a last couple of heavy salvos while you slip off with the crew. See you back at Brockhall.''

''Aye. Good huntin', marm. Come on, crew.''

Once again Amber's tail stood up straight. ''Archers, fire!''

Tsarmina and Cludd heard the command.

''Down flat, keep your heads down, shields up,'' Cludd bellowed to the soldiers.

When the invaders lifted their heads, the otters were gone. There followed an eerie silence, broken only by the rustle of the treetops. Tsarmina knew this was the squirrels retreating. She straightened up and ventured a pace forward. Cludd joined her.

''Ha, bunch of cowards, eh, Milady. Looks like they've run away.''

Tsarmina peered toward the mound at the base of the elm. "Maybe, maybe not. I think they might have set up some sort of trap, or is that a crew of otters armed with spears? Take ten soldiers and investigate it, Cludd. Go on, we're here to back you up."

Reluctantly Cludd selected ten creatures and set off gingerly for the enemy lines. He ducked once or twice when someone stepped on a twig. Finally he arrived at the mound. Knowing the danger had passed, Cludd kicked at a leafy bough, and prodded the mound with his spear.

"All clear, Milady. It was only a stupid trick to make us think they were still here."

"What about the squirrels, Cludd?" Fortunata sounded cautious.

The weasel Captain peered upward into the elm branches then hurled his spear straight up. Several soldiers dodged out of the way as it landed back, point up in the mound. A small amount of twigs and leaves fell with it.

"Not a hide nor hair of the lily-livered bunch!" Cludd puffed his chest out as he retrieved his spear.

Relieved and exultant, the soldiers of Kotir rose up, cheering and stamping about in a victory dance.

"We won, we won!"

"Won what?" Tsarmina's voice rose angrily above the celebration. "Fools, can't you see it's an empty triumph: no plunder, no slaves, no submission. They've vanished completely, and what have we gained? A few yards of woodland that belongs to me anyway."

The sudden volley of arrows slashed down, taking them unawares. Soldiers threw up shields, diving headlong for the undergrowth. Even the wildcat Queen had to beat an undignified retreat behind the elm tree she had conquered.

Once again the chattering derisory laughter of squirrels, as they swung off into the fastnesses of Mossflower, was all that remained of the woodlanders.

Gingivere had enlarged the two holes so that Ferdy and Coggs were able to squeeze through into his cell.

Gleefully they upturned the contents of the first pack.

"Good old mum's apple pie!"

"Ooh, elderberry cordial!"

"Look, cheese and hazelnuts!"

"Candied chestnuts, too. Hahaha, bet old Chibb didn't know about 'em."

"Come on, Mr. Gingivere. Here's some seedcake and milk. Let's have a secret supper together, then you can tell us the news from Chibb."

Amidst the laughter, Gingivere brushed away a tear from his eye. He was delighted with the company of his two little hedgehog friends, after the long lonely confinement following his father's death.

It was noontide when Martin and Dinny sat down to rest. Gonff stood surveying the vastness that surrounded them; undulating plain, flatland and moorland stretched away into the distance, the far horizon danced and shimmered in the unseasonal heat. Gonff thought he could detect a smudge on the horizon, but he could not be sure until they had traveled farther. The mouse-thief turned, looking back to where they had come from.

"Well, mateys, it's certainly a big wide world outside the woodlands and good old Mossflower. I can still glimpse it back there."

Dinny lay back chewing a blade of grass. "Hurr hurr, an' can 'ee still see yon liddle mousemaid a-waven to 'ee?"

Gonff shielded his eyes with his paw and played along. "Why yes, and there's someone else too. It looks like your grandad waving his stick. He wants that deeper 'n' ever pie that you stole from him."

"That wasn't Dinny," Martin yawned. "You probably stole it. See anything else?"

Gonff's whiskers twitched. "Aye, those three vermin that are tracking us. Looks like they've picked up our trail, matey."

Martin and Dinny leaped up, staring in the direction Gonff was pointing.

"There, see—a weasel, a ferret and a stoat. Now they've started to run. Why are they in a hurry all of a sudden?"

"Prob'ly cos they'm soighted us'ns, now we studd up," Dinny suggested.

"Aye, matey, you're right. Well, what do we do now, warrior? Stand and fight? You just say the word."

Martin gnawed his lip, stopping his paw from straying to the otter sling bound about his middle.

"No, that's not what we're questing for. We'd be losing

valuable time. It's our duty to find Salamandastron and Boar the Fighter, so that he can return with us to save Mossflower. The first thing a warrior must learn is orders and duty.''

Gonff strapped his pack back on. Dinny had not removed his. He was away and running, small velvety paws pounding the grassland.

"Coom on, 'ee two,'' he called. "Us'ns can lose they vurmin afore eventoid.''

The three friends ran in silence, measuring their stride and conserving energy. All that could be heard above the drumming of their paws was a descending lark and the chirrup of grass-hoppers in the dry grassland warmth. The high sun above watched the scene like a great golden eye. The hunted jogged steadily on, with the hunters rushing behind to close the gap.

There was no infirmary for the wounded at Kotir. Soldiers lay about in the barracks, licking their hurts and tending to them-selves as best as they could. Cludd was quite pleased with himself. They had driven off the woodlanders and the army had not retreated, so what was all the fuss about?

He put the question to Ashleg.

"Try telling her that, weasel. Here she comes.'' The pine marten's cloak swirled about as he pointed to the stairs.

Tsarmina bounded into the barracks, crooking a claw at them. "You two, up to my room. Right away!''

There was little to be gained by arguing, so with sinking hearts they trooped up the stairway.

Fortunata was already there, her ear painfully swollen from the arrow wound. Ashleg could not resist a sly snigger.

"Heehee, looks like you need a healer, fox.''

Tsarmina swept in, just in time to hear the jibe.

"One more remark like that, woodenpin, and you'll need a new head. Now, what happened to my ambush in the woods?'' They stood dumbly, waiting for the storm to break. It was not long in coming.

The wildcat Queen cleared the table in one reckless sweep. Bell, dishes, ornaments, linen and food crashed to the floor.

"Nothing! That's what we gained from it all.''

She raged around the chamber, kicking over furniture, tear-ing at wall hangings and bending fire irons out of shape as her voice rose to a maddened howl.

"I saw them. Me! I set up the ambush, warned you, marshaled the army, led the charge and thought that you buffoons had the brains and courage to assist me. What did I receive? Not one original idea or scrap of encouragement."

Her whole body quivered with dangerous temper, then suddenly she slumped into a chair as if temporarily exhausted by her outburst. The quaking trio stood staring at the floor for inspiration as she scowled at them.

"Aahh, what business is it of yours, anyway? You're not supposed to think, only to carry out orders. It's my job to do all the brain work around here. I suppose nothing will bother you three until the food supplies run out. Oh, they won't last forever, you know. I've seen for myself; the stores are getting lower, since we were unable to levy tribute from the few that lived around our walls. That's the trouble with being a conqueror and having an army to feed: soldiers are no good at providing anything unless they can snatch it away from the helpless." She stretched and kicked moodily at a fallen goblet. "Well, any ideas?"

"There's always the two prisoners I caught, Milady." Cludd sounded half-apologetic.

Tsarmina sat bolt upright. "Of course, well done, weasel. Maybe you aren't as stupid as I thought. Prisoners, hmmm, yes. What do you think the woodlanders would pay as ransom for those young hedgehogs?"

Fortunata narrowed her eyes calculatingly. "Well, I've had more dealings with woodlanders than most. They're a soft, sentimental lot when it comes to young ones. I think that they'd give quite a bit to get them back safe."

"Safe, that's the key," Tsarmina purred happily. "Imagine if the woodlanders saw their babies exposed to real suffering or danger—we could practically name our own terms."

The trio relaxed visibly, now that their Queen was in a saner mood.

There was one other listener to the conversation who had no cause to rejoice: Chibb the robin, perched on the outside window ledge.

Splitnose was the first to slacken pace. He gradually slowed to an easy lope. Blacktooth joined him, leaving Scratch to make the running. The weasel stopped and turned. He curled his lip in disgust at the pair, who were now sitting on the grass panting. Scratch ran back energetically, drawing his dagger.

"Get up, you idle worms. Come on. Up on your paws, both of you."

Splitnose teased a passing ant with his claws. "Ah what's the point? They're well away. We'll never catch 'em now."

Scratch kicked out at Blacktooth. "I suppose you think the same, lazybones."

Blacktooth kicked back insolently. "Oh, give it a rest. You can't make us run."

"Right, so it's mutiny, eh!" Scratch looked from one to the other disdainfully. "Then here's something for you two buckoes to think about. One, if you don't get running, I'll stab the pair of you. Two, unless you decide to run, I won't share my rations with you. And three, think about when I make my report. The Queen will be pleased to hear how you two lay down on the job."

Wordlessly they rose and started running again.

Gonff trotted alongside his friends, his quick eye noting the landscape.

"It gets a bit hilly further on, mateys. We could drop down and hide in a dozen places. What d'you say? Shall we give 'em the slip?"

Martin glanced backward. "I'd rather not risk it. They've got us in plain view. No, best keep on until evening, then we can pick a good hiding place when it's dark and camp there the night. Are you all right, Dinny?"

The mole wrinkled his snout. "Doant loik a-runnen. Lucky oi'm stronger'n most. You'm keep a-goen, Marthen. Doant wurry over oi."

The noon sun gained intensity. Birds soaring on the upper thermals passed over the six tiny figures below, hunters and hunted.

To spur themselves on, Splitnose and Blacktooth played a game, shouting out their favorite dishes to each other. Scratch ran a length behind them, keeping his dagger drawn as an insurance against further rebellion. Despite himself, the weasel had to keep licking his lips, not being able to shut his ears against the ferret and the stoat.

"Some of those candy chestnuts and a flagon of cold cider. Could you manage that, Blackie?"

"Oho, could I! How about a baby trout grilled in butter with some of that woodland October ale?"

"Very nice. But have you tried blackberry muffins soaked in warm honey with a few beakers of iced strawberry cordial to wash 'em down?"

"Gaw! Stoppit, Splittie. You're reminding me of that time when old Lord Greeneyes had a plunder feast at Kotir. Those were the days! I had iced strawberry cordial in a big drinking bowl, with mint leaves floating on it and crushed raspberries too. I remember I sucked it all through a cornstraw. Whew, I must have supped enough of it to have a good bath in."

"Yurghh!" Scratch called out in disgust. "I was enjoying that until I had a vision of you, all covered in mud and muck, sitting in a bath of iced strawberry cordial with two mint leaves stuck up your snout and a pile of crushed raspberries shoved into your ears. Doesn't bear thinking about. Anyhow, why don't you two shut your traps and keep your eyes on those three ahead?"

Dinny was first to gain the low hills. He ran up one side and rolled down the other. Martin and Gonff joined in until all three were dizzy. They ran onward as the shadows began to lengthen. Gonff gradually dropped back. He was breathing heavily. When they turned to look he waved his paws.

"Keep going, mateys. Phew, this is much harder work than thieving."

Without hurting Gonff's feelings, they slacked their pace to match his. Martin noticed that the blob on the horizon they had seen earlier that day was not merely a low cloud bank.

"Look, Gonff. It's a range of mountains. Big ones, too. What d'you think, Din?"

The young mole squinted hard to bring the view into perspective. "Ho boi urr, that they be. Oi reckons that be whurr the teeth o'land reaches up to ate woolen sheeps, wi' they gurt 'eads in clouds."

"Clever, Dinny mate." Gonff nodded admiringly. "Exactly as the poem says: 'Afar the teeth of land rise up to bite the wool of sheep.' They look quite close, but don't let that fool you. We've got a fair bit of traveling to do before we reach them."

Dinny risked a backward glance through a fold in the hills.

"Hurr, they vurminbags be none closer oither. 'Spect us'ns be moightier runners."

Scratch had taken the lead again. He knew the others were hungry and sure to follow. Trying to keep their quarry in sight was difficult, as they were often hidden by the hills. Descending the first low hill, he stopped to extract a burr from his pad. The other two ran slap bang into him from behind.

"Clodhoppers!" he shouted. "How is it that you have all this open country to run in, yet you both manage to crash into me? What d'you think this is, a game of leapfrog?"

More bickering and backbiting ensued. Scratch ended the dispute by banging their heads together. "Look, it's nearly dark now and I've gone and lost 'em, thanks to you two oafs!" He gritted his teeth in frustration.

Martin and Gonff prepared the evening meal while Dinny enlarged a small hole on the far side of the final hill. In a short while they were happily installed in a superb little cave. Dinny had even dug a ledge halfway round for them to rest on. The three friends lay on the ledge, eating their supper and watching the crimson underbellies of purple cloud rolls as night took over from the long, hot day.

Scratch and his minions sat out in the open on top of the highest hill, hoping that they might catch sight of the others at next daybreak.

Night on the open lands was both cold and windy.

Chibb paced the mantelpiece at Brockhall, relating all he had heard at Kotir.

The Corim were worried by this new threat to Ferdy and Coggs. "Hmm, this is an unwelcome development." Lady Amber waved her bushy tail anxiously.

The robin ruffled his crimson breast feathers importantly. "Ahem, harrumph. On the surface it would appear to be so. However, our wildcat ally in the prison said to tell you that he may be able to forestall Tsarmina's plans awhile."

Bella looked up to the mantelpiece. "How will he manage that, Chibb?"

The robin folded his wings behind as he explained. "Well, ahem, 'scuse me. Gingivere has taken a stone from the walls on each cell, as you know. He proposes to hide both Ferdy and Coggs in his own cell, after sealing the wallholes up. That way, if the enemy do not think of searching his cell too closely, they will naturally suppose that the two prisoners have escaped.''

There was wholesale approval for the clever plan.

Skipper had an additional idea. ''Hark, now. What if we was to pretend that Ferdy and Coggs were safe with us? That'd take suspicion off Gingivere.''

''How will we manage that, Skip?'' Bella was curious to know.

''Easy, marm. We'll find two other little hedgehogs and disguise 'em, then let 'em be seen by someone from Kotir.''

''Good thinking, Skipper,'' Bella said with approval. ''But now we'll really have to think of how we can rescue Ferdy and Coggs. Gingivere's plan is brave and daring; however, it puts all three at great risk.''

Lady Amber shook her head. ''Where do we get two little ones that look like Ferdy and Coggs?''

''You may lend my little Spike an' Posy,'' Goody said from the doorway. ''Long as they don't come to no 'arm. Though I must say, they don't look a smidgeon like my Ferdy an' Coggs. I can tell my liddle ones apart like apples from nuts.''

Abbess Germaine tapped a paw to her nose. ''Two blanket cloaks, two saucepan helmets, a piece of stick each, like the swords of make-believe warriors. I think that would fool anyone from a distance, Goody. But what about a rescue attempt? Have we any kind of firm plan?''

''You leave that to old Skip, marm.'' Skipper laughed drily. ''Bula, you take charge of the crew while I'm away. I think I'll pay the Mask a visit.''

''What's the Mask?'' Several woodlanders voiced the question.

''You'll soon see!'' Bula winked.

22

Consternation reigned at Kotir.

A luckless stoat had been "volunteered" from the cell guards by Fortunata and Cludd, and he was pushed unwillingly into Tsarmina's chamber.

"Er, your Maj of the green Queenest, er upper of all ruler and lower Moss. Er, er . . . The prisoners have gone!"

"Gone! What do you mean, gone?" The wildcat Queen left her seat in a single bound and picked the stoat up by his throat.

"Yuuurrkkgghhaaaarrr . . .'Scaped."

Tsarmina threw the gurgling heap to the floor. Her voice echoed in the stairway as she dashed down to the cells.

"Escaped? Impossible! Guards, get down to the cells quickly."

The cells were searched.

The corridors were scoured.

The outer walls were surrounded.

The parade ground was gone over inch by inch.

The barracks were turned inside out.

Not a room, passage, cupboard, chamber, kitchen, guardhouse, or scullery remained unprobed.

Gingivere, however, was officially nonexistent. His cell was not searched. Nobody thought of looking in a prison cell that was already bolted and barred.

Except maybe Tsarmina.

Columbine sat up, rubbing sleep from her eyes.

Was it night or day? she wondered. How long had she slept in this warm dry cavern? Everything seemed so quiet and peaceful after the noise and panic of the battle she had witnessed. There was an old patchwork quilt covering her. She pushed it to one side as a little molemaid entered.

"Mawnen to 'ee. Wellcum t'Moledeep. Brekkist be ready."

She followed the mole into a larger cave, where Ben Stickle and the woodlanders who had been injured sat with the Loamhedge mice and the mole community.

Foremole waved her to a place between himself and a grizzled old mole whose fur was completely gray.

"Set ee by yurr, maid. This be Owd Dinny, t'other young rip's granfer."

Old Dinny nodded and continued spooning honeyed oatmeal.

Obviously the moles liked a good solid start to the day. There was a variety of cooked roots and tubers, most of which Columbine had never seen before. All of them tasted delicious, whether salted, sugared or dipped in honey and milk. (Some of the moles did all four.) The bread was wafer thin and tasted of almonds; small cakes patterned with buttercups were served warm. There were fluffy napkins and bowls of steaming rosewater to cleanse sticky paws. As Columbine nibbled at a rye biscuit and sipped fragrant mint tea, she could not help asking Foremole where all the huge deeper 'n' ever pies and solid trencherfood the moles seemed to favor were.

Foremole chuckled. He gestured at the table with a massive digging claw. "Ho urr, Combuliney. This yurr be on'y a loight brekkist for 'ee an' yurr friends. We'm fancied it up a bit for 'ee. Moles be only eaten solid vittles at even toid when they's 'ungered greatly."

Columbine nodded and smiled politely, trying to hide her amazement. "Oh, I see, just a loight brekkist, er, light breakfast."

As Columbine ate, she remembered Gonff. If only he were here amid this friendly company with her! She mentally wagered with herself that he would know the name and taste of every dish (and probably be jokingly chided for having stolen

many of them in bygone days). She pictured her mousethief
jesting with everybody, imitating molespeech and singing ballads as he composed them.

The young mousemaid heaved a sigh into her mint tea. It
dissolved in a small cloud of fragrant steam. Where, oh where,
was Gonff on this beautiful morning?

It was nearly midmorning when the "light breakfast" reached
its conclusion. Then, guarded and guided by the mole community, Columbine and her friends made their way back to
Brockhall by a secret woodland route.

Martin, Gonff and Dinny were wide awake by daybreak. They
crouched in the small cave, eating breakfast as they watched a
gray drizzly dawn. Packing the food away, the travelers
stamped life back into their numbed paws. Surprisingly, Gonff
was first to step outside.

"Come on, mateys. It'll brighten up by mid-morning. You
wait and see—I'm a Prince of Predictors."

Striding out, they left the low hills behind, to face yet more
flatlands. Wakened grouse whirred into the damp morning air
at their approach.

Sala-manda-stron,
Look where we've come from,
Three of Mossflower's best,
Marching out upon our quest:
Sala-manda-stron.

Scratch sighted the three dim forms through the layers of
drizzling rain.

"There they go. Come on, you two. I've got a feeling that
today's the day we catch 'em. Come on, move yourselves. The
sooner it's done, the quicker we'll get back to Kotir. Aye, good
solid food again, a long rest, and maybe a bit of honor and
glory."

"Huh, I'm soaked right through!" Splitnose complained.

"Me too," grumbled Blacktooth. "I never slept a wink
again. Sitting out on top of a hill, miles from anywhere in the
pouring rain, stiff all over, cold, hungry, shiver—"

"Shuttup!" Scratch interrupted bitterly. "Put a button on
your driveling lip. Look at me, I'm weary, saturated and
starved, but do you hear me whimpering on about it all the

time? Up on your paws, and try to look like you're the Queen's soldiers from Kotir.''

They trekked westward, pursuing the travelers.

Splitnose was muttering as he kicked a pebble along in front of himself. "Honor and glory, huh. Cludd'll get all that, and he can keep it, too. Now if it was honor cake and a mug of hot glory, that'd be a different thing.''

"Honor cake and hot glory drink? Don't talk such rubbish, soggyhead,'' Blacktooth laughed.

"Soggyhead yourself, drippynose.''

"Crinkleclaws!''

"Greasyfur!''

"Beetlebottom!''

"Stow the gab and get marching, both of you!'' Scratch told them.

True to Gonff's prediction, the rain ceased. Above the plains the sun came out to watch fluffy clouds sailing about on the breeze across a lake of bright blue sky.

Dinny sniffed the air, wiggling his claws. "Buharr, they's watter nearby, likely a pond or tarn. May'ap us'll catcher a liddlefish. Be gudd eaten, hurr.''

Martin looked sideways at Gonff. "How does he know there's water near? I can't smell a thing.''

The mousethief shrugged. "Neither can he, matey. Moles probably feel it through the earth with their digging claws.''

Dinny nodded wisely. "O arr, us'ns do smell lots o' things wi' us claws.''

Gonff winked at the warrior mouse. "That's the nice thing about moles, they always have a sensible explanation which we can all understand.''

The three friends laughed aloud. Dinny proved as good at predicting as Gonff. Midday found the travelers at the edge of a large pond. Bulrushes and reeds surrounded the margin, small water lilies budded on the surface. The glint of silver scales beneath the water promised good fishing. At first Martin was loth to stop but, realizing the valuable addition a fish would make to their supplies, he called a halt. While his friends went about fishing, the warrior posted himself on guard to watch for their pursuers.

Dinny sat on the edge of the bank, immersing his paws in the shallows with exclamations of delight.

"Oo arr, oo bliss 'n' joys. Hurr, this be the loif, Gonffen!"

The mousethief had cast a line baited with a tiny red mud worm. In seconds it was snatched by a voracious stickleback. "Ha, look, matey," he called. "I've got a bite! Come to Gonff old greedyguts."

Martin crept up behind them. He placed a paw gently on each of his friends' shoulders as he whispered to them, "Ssshhh. Listen to me. We are in great danger. Don't make a sound, if you value our lives!"

23

Skipper sat inside the curve of a big hollow log. He faced a slim gray otter, trying hard not to look where the strange creature's tail had once been.

"So then, Mask, how are you keeping, my brother?" he asked.

The Mask nibbled at some otter delicacies that his brother had thoughtfully brought along.

"Oh, I get by, Skip. Sometimes I'm a squirrel, sometimes a fox. Ha, I was even a half-grown badger for a while."

Skipper shook his head in amazement, gazing around the hollow log where the master of disguises lived alone. Many curious objects were carefully stowed there: make-believe tails, false ears, a selection of various whiskers.

The Mask watched Skipper with his odd pale eyes. Seizing a few things, he turned his back and made some swift secret adjustments. When he turned around, Skipper's mouth fell open in disbelief.

"Look, Skip. I'm a squirrel again!"

The otter chieftain marveled; this creature in front of him was surely an aged squirrel—thin, graying—but undeniably a squirrel, from its bushy tail and erect ears, right to the two large front upper teeth.

"Strike me tops'ls, Mask. How d'you do it?"

"Oh, it's no great thing," the Mask chucked quietly. "Actually, I'd look more like a treeflyer if I took a little more time and care with this disguise. This is only a quick change to amuse you."

Skipper whacked his tail against the side of the log. "Well, you could fool me anytime, shipmate."

Mask tossed aside the false tail and ears. Spitting out the two false front teeth, he readjusted his body. He was an otter again.

"Maybe I fooled you, maybe I didn't. But you're not fooling me, Skipper of Camp Willow. What do you want me to do?"

Skipper sat back, folding his paws across his chest. "I have a proposition to make to you, brother Mask. Sit still and hear me out."

Tsarmina glared through the cell aperture at Gingivere. The imprisoned wildcat sat in the darkest part of the cell. His fur was tousled, damp from the walls dewed his paws, his head drooped despairingly. Now and then his eyes would flicker rapidly. The wildcat Queen brought her face close to the bars.

"If you know what's good for you, you'll tell me all about how those two hedgehogs made their escape. Speak up. You must have heard or seen something—they were in the cells either side of you."

Gingivere leaped up, his voice a cracked singsong shout. "Hahaha! You let them escape so you can have their bread and water. I knew you wouldn't give me any. You're keeping it all for yourself. Oh, I saw you, sneaking along the passage. You let them go so that you could have all that bread and water for yourself. Heeheehee."

Tsarmina turned to Cludd. "Listen to that. He's completely crazy."

She swept off down the passage. Cludd stayed a moment, looking through the bars. He had never seen a completely crazy wildcat before, although he had seen his mistress dangerously close to that condition once or twice.

"No bread, no water, she's keeping it for herself." Gingivere continued his insane lament.

Cludd banged the door with his spear. "Quiet in there!"

"Atishoo!"

The sneeze came as Cludd was turning away. He whirled back. "Who did that?"

Gingivere grabbed a pawful of straw and sneezed into it. "Atishoo, choo! Oh, I'm sick and dying, sir. The cold and damp down here. Please get me extra rations of bread and water or I'll die."

Cludd rapped the door with his spear again. "Enough of that! You get the rations Lady Tsarmina allows. So stop moaning, or I'll give you something to moan about."

As the weasel Captain lumbered off down the passage, another sneeze rang out.

"Atishoo!"

On the wall above the cell door, two food haversacks hung from a spike driven into the rock. Ferdy and Coggs sat, one in each sack, their heads poking out like two fledgling housemartins in their respective nests.

Coggs reached across, trying to stifle Ferdy's snout with his paw, but another sneeze rang out.

"Atishoo!"

Ferdy blinked and rubbed his snout. "Sorry, sir. This bag has flour in it from the scones, and it's tickling my sn . . . sn . . . Ashoo!"

Reaching up, Gingivere lifted his little cellmates down from their hiding place. While there were no guards about, they could play and exercise.

Chibb flew to the window, dropping the latest supplies in. He caught the empty sacks that Gingivere tossed up to him. In the shaft of light the wildcat was looking strangely sane and healthy.

"What news, Chibb?"

"Ahemhem. The Corim have decided that you must soon be rescued, all three of you. How they propose to do it, I don't know yet."

Gingivere nodded. "I hope they realize that the longer they wait, the more dangerous it becomes for Ferdy and Coggs."

Chibb slung the empty sacks around his neck. "Ahem, I'm sure they do. At present the message is, keep on the alert and keep up your courage. You are not forgotten."

Chibb flew off swiftly. Gaining the woodlands, he paused to perch on a spruce branch as he adjusted the bags about his neck for easier flight.

Argulor belched dozily and glanced at the robin perched beside him. Chibb gave a jump of surprise, but did not forget his manners.

"Ahem, beg pardon." The fat robin darted from the branch like a flame-tipped arrow.

Argulor shifted his claws. Wearily he dropped his eyelids back into the slumbering position.

Were the small birds getting faster, or was he getting slower? The eagle dismissed the problem, reasoning that there were still plenty of soldiers in Kotir who were a lot slower than a single robin redbreast.

A lot tastier, too.

Dinny and Gonff sat quite still at the edge of the pond as Martin whispered to them, "Now, very slowly, look to your left. Do you see the female swan over there? She's sitting on her nest with her back to us. Right. Don't look, just take my word for it, in the open water to the other side there's a big male swan— it's her mate. He's not seen us yet, but he's headed this way and bound to sight us if we stop here, so let's move away as silently as possible."

With great care Gonff let the fish slip back into the water. He cut his fishing line. The three friends moved speedily, ducking behind the rushes with not a second to spare.

The huge white swan glided by them serenely. He was like a ship in full sail, an awesome spectacle, the snowy white body and half-folded wings complementing perfectly the muscular serpentine neck column surmounted by a solid orange bill and fierce black eyes.

Martin shuddered. He thought of how close they had been to death. The male swan was warlike and fearless, absolute monarch of his pond. Any creature who dared trespass upon these waters while his mate sat upon the three new-hatched cygnets in their nest was fated never to see the sunset. The white colossus swept by, continuing his patrol of the pond.

When he was past, the three friends slipped away. Gonff whispered a silent goodbye to the silver fish in the shallows. "We were both lucky that time, matey. Swim free."

A respectable distance from the water, Dinny untangled a streamer of duckweed from his paw.

"Boi okey, this'n's owd granfer near losed a dear liddle mole back thurr. Oi never see'd a skwon afore, gurt feathery burdbag they be, stan' on moi tunnel.''

They lunched on apples and bread, supplemented with some cow parsley that Dinny had discovered.

Blacktooth and Splitnose sighted the pond. They had been running ahead of Scratch after a particularly nasty bout of name-calling. The stoat and ferret had called Scratch a frogwalloper; this seemed to touch some hidden nerve in the weasel, and he took strong objection to the insult. The pair ran off, cackling gleefully as the weasel threw pebbles and earth clods after them.

"Come back here and say that, you cowardly custards. I'll give you frogwallopers when I get you!"

Running wide, they approached the pond at a different angle from that of the travelers. Blacktooth and Splitnose whooped with delight.

"Look, a river, a river! Truce, Scratch!"

Scratch joined them, the quarrel temporarily forgotten at the sight of the watery expanse.

"That's not a river, it's a pond," he pointed out. "This is more like it, a good fresh drink, a nice bath for our paws. Look, a swan sitting on a nest. Swan eggs—what a tasty idea!"

Splitnose was not so sure. "Er, don't you think that bird looks a bit big, Scratch?"

"So what?" the weasel snorted. "There's three of us and we've got spears. I bet swan eggs are lovely."

"Have you ever eaten one?" Splitnose asked.

"No, I've never even seen one, but I bet they're very big and good to eat."

"Well, all right, we'll back you up. How do you get the eggs?"

"Easy, just stand in the shallows and chuck our spears at the swan until it's forced to fly away, then we rob the eggs."

Buoyed by Scratch's confidence, they waded into the shallows. The female swan watched them fearlessly. She issued a warning hiss.

The would-be plunderers were enjoying themselves immensely.

"Ooh aahh. Hey, Blackie, doesn't this mud feel great when you squelch it with your paws?" Splitnose called.

"Aye, 'specially after all that running, mate. Just watch

this.'' Blacktooth flung his spear. It fell far short of the target.

Splitnose laughed scornfully, then threw his. It went a little farther, but still far short of the swan.

Scratch sneered contemptuously at their efforts. ''Huh, you two couldn't throw a frozen worm and hit the earth. Go and get some stones to fling at her. I can probably wade out that far and stab the bird.''

The ferret and the stoat waded back to the bank, and ran off to search for missiles.

Scratch ventured recklessly on until the water was around his middle. There was a crackle of parting rushes behind him. Scratch turned in the water. The giant male swan blotted out everything in his vision; he did not even get a chance to cry out or lift his spear.

Scratch was dead before he knew it!

Splitnose and Blacktooth returned to the water's edge, their paws full of rocks and earth clods.

''How'll this little lot do, Scratch?''

''Scratch, where are you?''

''Scratchy-watchy, you old frogwalloper, come out. We know you're hiding, we can see the rushes moving.''

The male swan came thundering out of the rushes in half-flight, churning up a bow wave as it hissed like a nest of serpents.

''Yooooaaaagggggghhhh!''

Only the speed of raw terror and the fact that they were racing away from the pond and its nest saved the lives of the panic-stricken pair.

''Owoowoowoo helpelpelp!''

The male swan webbed its way up onto the bank, beating its wings wide to the blue sky, hissing out its victory cry—a savage challenge to the distant runners.

The female settled securely on her babes in the nest. She preened her neck feathers, smiling with just a touch of smugness. Swans never laugh aloud.

Though they were a fair distance from the pond, Martin and his friends heard the anguished shouts on the breeze.

''Sounds like our followers from Kotir have ruffled someone's feathers, eh, Din,'' Martin remarked.

The mole looked grave. ''Skwons etted 'em, oi uxpect.''

Gonff placed a paw on his heart and sang slowly,

A weasel, ferret and a stoat,
Found a pond but had no boat.
Now they can't see the waters from
The inside of a swan.

Tsarmina stood at her high window, watching the squirrels. They had descended from the trees at the woodland edge. With them were two small hedgehogs clad in cooking-pot helmets and blanket cloaks.

Fortunata rapped lightly at the chamber door and entered.

"Milady, oh, you've already seen them."

Tsarmina did not even turn to look at Fortunata. She continued peering intently at the two little figures in the middle of the squirrel group.

"Are they taunting us, do you think?" she asked.

Fortunata joined her at the window. "No, woodlanders don't go in for that sort of display, Milady."

To her surprise, Fortunata found Tsarmina patting her approvingly. "Good thinking, fox. Shall I send out a party to try and capture them?"

Fortunata shook her head. "I'd advise against it, Milady. They'd only sweep off into the trees, making our soldiers look foolish. Squirrels always do."

Tsarmina smiled. She sat up on the window ledge, winking at the vixen. "Clever, very clever, Fortunata. You aren't as dull or slow-witted as Cludd and Ashleg. Listen now, I have better eyesight than you or any creature in Mossflower. I've been watching those two little hedgehogs, and there's something not quite right about them."

"Not quite right, Milady?" Fortunata was baffled, but she tried her best to look intelligent.

Tsarmina tapped a paw to her nose. "Exactly. They're playing little games with me, those woodlanders. But I have a game or two of my own to play. Tell me, you know these woods and their creatures better than anyone in Kotir, don't you?"

Fortunata was pleased that Tsarmina was confiding in her, but she began to feel uneasy. There was often an unpleasant sting in the tail of her Queen's schemes.

"I was born and brought up in Mossflower country, Milady. What is it that you require from me?"

"Fortunata, we are surrounded by blunderers." Tsarmina's tone was that of an old and trusting friend. "You are the only one I can really rely on. I never forget those who serve me well. I haven't forgotten that you helped me to be Queen with your knowledge of herbs. This is a big area to rule, and it becomes lonely. I could do with someone as wise and clever as yourself to share that rule. But first I am going to ask you to do me a favor. Think carefully before you answer, because on that answer rests our friendship. Will you do me this favor?"

The greedy fox fell headlong into the trap. "I am yours to command, Queen Tsarmina."

The wildcat ruler smiled like a cat with a bird. "Well said, friend. Now, what I want you to do is this . . ."

24

The Corim were startled.

Skipper strolled into Brockhall followed by a ferret. Before Lady Amber could fit arrow to bow, or Bella pick up a poker to strike the foe, Skipper addressed them heartily.

"Mates, don't get your ropes in a tangle. This 'ere ferret is an otter. Meet my brother, the Mask."

The Mask bowed low. Stripping the bindings from his ears, he removed the bark slivers that sharpened his muzzle, pulled out the wicked eyeteeth and undid his imitation tail.

Bella pounded the sides of her chair with a heavy paw. "Wonderful, he is indeed an otter. Welcome to Brockhall, Mr. Mask."

Abbess Germaine seated the otter, placing food and drink before him. "So you are the Mask. I have lived long and seen strange things, but never one as strange as you, though I hope you will forgive me for saying so, sir."

Mask shook the Abbess warmly by the paw. "It is a strange world, marm, you will forgive me saying, but never have I seen such friendly and gentle mice as you and your oddly dressed followers."

Skipper patted Mask on the back. "Friends, you wouldn't

161

believe your eyes if you saw old Mask in some of the getups I've seen him in.''

''Oh, tell us, Skip.'' Columbine leaned forward eagerly.

Skipper took a draught of cider from Mask's cup. ''I couldn't begin to tell you all this one's disguises, but just as an instance, he gave me the slip coming through the forest. I looked high and low for him. Ha, there was the old deceiver stood right next to me, up against a tree, got up as a piece of bark, would you believe!''

Spike and Posy clung to Columbine's habit, staring wide-eyed at the strange otter.

''Did you really, Mr. Mask, sir?'' Spike asked.

Mask chuckled as he fed them a slice of apple each. ''Oh, aye. That's an easy one. All you need is an old piece of bark as big as yourself and the right tree. You just stand there and think the same thoughts as the tree, and presto!''

''What others can you do, sir?'' Posy wanted to know.

''Oh, a fox, a squirrel, a hedgehog like you, even—you name it. Haha, otters are pretty hard to do, though. Funny tails, you see.''

''Could you be a bird?'' Spike inquired.

''Well, er, let's say I'm practicing that one, shall we?''

''A stoat or a rat, then?'' Posy persisted.

''No trouble. They're the easiest to do. It's all a question of studying shape, really.''

Abbess Germaine was impressed. ''You say you could look like a stoat, weasel or even a fox?''

The Mask winked. ''Indeed I can, marm. That's why I'm here.''

Early evening shadows were beginning to lengthen across the plain. Dinny looked to the mountains on the horizon, and judged the distance shrewdly.

''We'm be vurry close to yon mountings on t'morren, Marthen.''

The warrior mouse glanced toward the massed rock. ''So we will, Din. As to how we'll cross them, I'm at a loss. Look at the size of them. They almost disappear into the sky.''

''Don't you worry, mateys,'' Gonff said confidently. ''We haven't come this far to be beaten by an old stone hill. Besides, we don't have to worry about those vermin following us. The swans probably dealt with them.''

Dinny's snout rose into the air. "Oi'm a-smellen' more watter thru 'ee paws agin."

"What, more water, Din?" Martin asked.

"Burr aye. Runnen watter thiz toim."

"Best keep our eyes skinned for swans, eh, mateys," Gonff warned.

"Hoo arr, doant wanna see skwons no more."

Gonff was first to find the broad stream. It was not quite wide enough to be classed as a river. The mouse thief strode down the bank and recited aloud to the flowing waters,

O'er golden acres far below,
Our wings beat strong and true,
Where deep and wet, see flowing yet,
Another snake of blue.

Martin looked to the opposite bank. "It seems peaceful enough, but it's far too wide to cross here. We'll camp here tonight and scout the bank for an easier crossing in the morning."

The mild spring evening was very pleasant by the water. Dinny scooped out a circle while Martin set flint to the steel of his broken sword and started a small fire. Gonff repaired his fishing line. Within a short time he landed a plump young bream.

The three travelers sat around the fire, watching the fish grilling in a cradle of green reeds over the flames. Firelight flickered and danced in Dinny's buttonlike eyes.

"Warmff, hurr hurr. Oi do likes warmff."

Gonff tested the fish with his knifepoint. "It'll be ready soon, mateys. A little loaf apiece toasted up, some cress from the water's edge, a beaker of fresh streamwater, and we're snug for the night."

The stream gurgled and eddied ceaselessly toward the distant mountains as they enjoyed a spell of rest on its soft mossy bank.

Splitnose and Blacktooth had wandered aimlessly. Without Scratch to direct them they were lost. Night found the pair out upon the open plain, hungry, tired and thirsty. Splitnose lay down, snuggling sleepily against the grass. Blacktooth was restless.

"Huh, I'm not sleeping out in the open again. There must be a hole or a cave hereabouts. Might be a bite of grub, too."

"Oh lie down and get some rest," Splitnose murmured sleepily. "You're as bad as Cludd or Scratch. Get some sleep, and we'll see what it's like around here in the morning. I'm not moving. Might even sleep late, too."

Blacktooth moved off. "Right. You stay here. I'll be back if I can't find something better. I could swear there's water running nearby. I'll go and take a look."

"Mind the swans don't eat you," Splitnose called out, his eyes already closed.

Blacktooth was back sooner than expected. He danced about, giggling quietly to himself.

"Splittie. Hey, come on, snoreface. Wake up! Heeheehee, guess what I've found?"

The stoat grumbled as his companion shook him awake. "Two frogs and a dandelion. Now beat it, will you? I need sleep."

The ferret could not contain his excitement. "I found a big stream, a camp, a fire and food—and those two mice and the mole!"

Splitnose came awake. "Where?"

"Not far. Over that way a bit. Listen, if we're quick and quiet we can take them prisoner."

The stoat leaped up. "Great. You say they've got food and a fire?"

"Yes, half a roast fish, packs too, full of goodies," Blacktooth told him. "You know those woodlanders—they love their rations."

"We could march 'em back to Kotir."

"Heehee. Aye, could you imagine old Cludd's face when we walk in with three prisoners? The Queen'd prob'ly make us Generals. Oho, I'd give that Cludd a few dirty jobs to do. I'd make him jump!"

"Right, Blackie mate, lead me to 'em."

They sneaked silently across to the river bank armed with their spears.

The three friends lay asleep around the fire, unaware of the eyes that watched them from the top of the bank.

•   •   •

Fortunata struck deeper into Mossflower, aware that Tsarmina was watching her from the high chamber window.

The vixen had cast off her borrowed finery from Kotir, reverting to the frayed old healer's cloak and bag of herbal remedies. She leaned heavily upon an ash staff. Fortunata was more suited to this type of work; she preferred subterfuge to warfare. Besides, the rewards promised were greater.

Tsarmina moved from the window to ring her table bell. Cludd entered, saluting with shield and spear.

"Yes, Your Majesty."

"Get somebody to clean this room up, it's filthy. Drill the troops and keep them on the alert. They're not here to eat me out of house and home. Oh, get a foraging party together. We must keep something in the larders if we want to outlast the woodlanders."

Cludd saluted again. "It shall be done, Milady."

The wildcat Queen settled back in her chair. Now was the time to play the waiting game.

Columbine lay behind a screen of bushes, nibbling a green hazelnut. The mousemaid often volunteered to go on watch outside Brockhall, imagining herself to be the first to sight the travelers' return. That Gonff! He would probably come back singing at the top of his voice,

> I'm back, Columbine.
> Yes, now is the hour
> My good friends and I
> Will be saving Mossflower,

or some such cheery air. Columbine lay watching sunmotes dancing through dappled patterns of green leaves, dreaming of her thief.

Then she sighted the fox.

It was a vixen, dressed like a journeying healer. The fox cast about, sniffing here, inspecting a scuffed leaf there, obviously searching for somebody or something.

Columbine slid silently away from her hiding place. Once she was out of the fox's vision she took to her paws, dashing headlong back to Brockhall.

Shooing some little ones inside, she shut the door and bolted it. It was lunchtime. Loamhedge mice were serving up hazelnut cloister pudding with willowherb sauce. Columbine made straight for Bella.

"Fox, fox, coming this way!" she panted.

Skipper put a restraining paw on her. "Whoa there. What fox coming from where?"

"Out in the woods, coming from the northwest, sniffing and probing. It's a vixen. She'll find her way here soon unless we stop her."

Lady Amber mopped up sauce with a crust. "A vixen eh, did you recognize her, Columbine?"

"Oh yes, it's the one they call Fortunata, though she's disguised herself up a bit. I recognized her at the ambush."

"An old raggedy cloak and hood," Bella interrupted, "together with a bag of herbs and a staff?"

Columbine nodded.

"The old pilgrim healer disguise. Wearing a bit thin, eh, Mask," the badger chuckled drily.

The otter looked up from his pudding. "What are you going to do about her?"

Lady Amber reached for her quiver. "A swift arrow in the right place should save any argument."

Skipper pawed his sling. "Either that or a sharp rock on her stem."

Mask stood up, patting a full stomach. "Miz badger, why don't you let me deal with this? It may help with our escape plans for the prisoners."

Bella pushed food toward Columbine. "Here, little one, have some lunch. Go on, Mask, tell us the plan."

The otter had his back to them, he was selecting disguises. "I say, let her come, see what she wants, but don't let her know who I am. Pretend that I'm a newcomer."

When he turned to face the Corim, Mask was indeed a newcomer. He was transformed into the most evil slim gray old fox they had ever seen.

The Mask slid into Bella's study to complete his disguise. "Find the right tail, rub a little brown dust into my coat and see to the finer bits. Ha, she won't be able to tell me from her own grandpa when I'm finished."

"Right. We've got you. Don't try anything funny or we'll skewer this mole!"

Martin opened his eyes. The ferret and the stoat were standing over Dinny, their spearpoints at his throat. The warrior mouse was about to jump instinctively for them, but Gonff discouraged him.

"Do as he says, matey. They've taken us by surprise."

All three lay quite still. Blacknose smirked with satisfaction.

"I'll keep the mole pinned down, Splittie. Look through that pack over there, and see if you can find some cord."

Splitnose scuttled off and rummaged in the pack.

"Even better, mate. Look, a rope," he called.

"Give it here and keep your spear on the mole, stick him if he moves. Blacktooth wound the rope round the travelers. Binding them together, he tugged the end to make sure it was tightly secured.

Picking up his spear, he strutted around them. "Ha, you're our prisoners now. You'll pay for breaking the laws of Kotir and leading us on a wild-goose chase. Be still!"

Splitnose was emptying the supply packs out. "Heehee. Look, apples, bread, cheese, mmfff. Pie!"

Blacktooth threw extra fuel on the fire and crammed food wolfishly into his mouth, while menacing them with his spear.

"Hey, this is more like it, Splittie," he enthused. "Come and get warm by the fire."

Gonff winked at Martin and whispered, "Leave it to me, matey. I'll settle these two idiots."

Blacktooth yanked sharply on the rope's end. "No talking there. One more peep out of you and you'll be sorry, d'you hear me?"

Gonff shrugged as best as he could. "Don't worry, Captain. You've got us, all right. But please don't eat all our supplies, we'll have nothing left to keep alive on."

Splitnose threw an apple core at Gonff and bit into a cheese. "Ah, stop moaning, mouse. Look at us, we've lived on one skinny crust and grass for the last few days. Mmmm, this is good cheese. Hey, a fruitcake! By the claw, that'll do for me."

"Come on greedyguts, half for me." Blacktooth prodded Splitnose with his spear.

"Get your own, fatbelly," Splitnose retorted.

"Why, you gluttonous worm!"

"Ouch! You keep that spearpoint away from me, rotten-gums."

"That's the stuff, matey," Gonff called out encouragingly. "You show him that stoats are the bosses."

Blacktooth was about to stab Gonff with his spear when Splitnose jabbed him in the bottom with his spearpoint.

Martin took Blacktooth's side. "Don't let him do that to you, ferret. Get him."

Dinny supported Splitnose. " 'Ee be nowt but a gurt bully. Jump on furret's tunnel, skoat."

Blacktooth cracked Splitnose across the head with his spear-shaft. Splitnose retaliated by stabbing Blacktooth in the paw.

The three friends egged them on with loud shouts.

"You've got him now. Stab!"

"That's it. Keep him pinned down!"

"Get his throat with your teeth!"

"Shove him in the fire, quick!"

Filled with blind rage, the stoat and ferret battled all over the camp site, rolling through the fire, splashing in the shallows, stumbling against the captives, oblivious of all except the desire to win.

"Grr, take that, stoatswine!"

"Aarghh, you won't push me around anymore, ferret-face. Get this!"

Blacktooth fell, pierced by his opponent's spear. Splitnose backed off, dropping his spear, and stumbling farther into the shallows. Blacktooth pulled himself upright and staggered toward his foe, spear held outright. Splitnose blundered into deeper water, unarmed, holding his paws out pleadingly.

"Blackie, no. I didn't mean it!"

The ferret tottered unsteadily into the water, lifted the spear to throw and fell dead into the shallows.

Splitnose kept backing off as if in a daze. "I didn't mean to, Blackie. Honest. You can have half the c—"

Suddenly he was gone! All that remained was Blacktooth the ferret, face down in the shallows of the swirling stream.

The three friends had fallen over. They lay, bound, gazing at the water where Splitnose had been a moment before.

"Pitholes, matey, full of bottom mud," Gonff explained. "We'll have to remember that when we cross."

Dinny wriggled. "Us'll 'ave to set about thinken 'ow to free usselfs."

Martin wrenched round to face Gonff. "Any ideas?"

The mousethief smiled in the darkness. "Stay still. I can

reach my dagger. Didn't I ever tell you, matey, I'm a prince of escapers.''

Martin felt the blade sawing at their bonds. ''Aye, I seem to remember you saying something of the sort in the cells at Kotir, matey.''

The ropes fell away under Gonff's keen blade. He stood upright.

''I was right that time too, if you remember,'' Gonff pointed out.

Dinny straightened up. ''Hurr, tho' you'm 'ate to boast about et.''

They took stock of the damage. Martin threw a trampled cheese to one side.

''Huh, they've ruined our supplies,'' he said with disgust. ''Most of the food rolled into the water with them. Look, even the fish fell in the fire.'' He held up a smoking relic.

Gonff pushed Blacktooth's carcass into the fast-flowing water. ''It could've been worse, matey. At least we're alive.''

Dinny blew on the embers, adding dry reeds and wood. ''Ho aye, Marthen. Us'll make out awright, 'ee'll see.''

25

Fortunata followed a trail that led to a dead end. Some creature had skillfully covered most traces, but the vixen knew that there had been woodlanders here. The camouflagers had not been entirely successful in covering everything; there was still scent and the odd broken twig. She scratched about in the undergrowth, trying to reveal further clues.

"Lost something?"

The vixen was startled by the voice. She whirled around, attempting to discover its owner. All she saw was the silent woodland. Quite suddenly there was another fox standing alongside her.

"I said, have you lost something?" he repeated.

Fortunata weighed up the newcomer carefully. He was an old fox, patched gray and dusty brown, slim built and slightly stooped. But it was the eyes that caused her to shudder—weird, flat, shifting eyes. This was the most evil-looking of her species that the vixen had ever encountered.

"No, it's not something I've lost," she said, trying to sound unconcerned. "Actually, I was merely passing through here."

"Aye, me too. Maybe we can help each other," the old fox suggested.

"Yes, maybe we can. My name is Besomtail, the wandering healer, what are you called?" Fortunata asked.

"I'm Patchcoat. I come from far away to the east," he replied.

Fortunata nodded. He certainly looked like a patched coat. "Well, I come from the . . . er, southwest. Maybe that's why we've never met. I'm really hungry, though, Patchcoat. I expect you've seen tracks around here. Maybe there's a camp of woodlanders nearby. They usually give me food in return for my healing skills."

Patchcoat rubbed his lean stomach. "Aye, I'm hungry too. There's not much future in eating grass and drinking dew. Listen, Besomtail, maybe I can travel along as your assistant. I passed a place earlier today that might be just what we're looking for."

Fortunata's ears stood up. "You did? Where?"

The strange fox waved a paw. "Oh, round and about, you know. I didn't stop because those woodlanders always drive me off, for some reason. Huh, you'd think I was out to steal their young. It looked like a well-stocked hideaway. I expect I could find it again."

"I can't blame them driving you off, friend Patchcoat," Fortunata sniggered. "You certainly don't look anything like a baby fieldmouse on posy day."

Patchcoat threw back his head and laughed wickedly. "Hahaha, look at yourself, you raggedy-bottomed tramp. Any honest woodlander would run a mile from you. Let's join forces. Come on, how about it? You won't find the place without me."

Fortunata rubbed her whiskers as if she was giving the matter some earnest thought. Finally she thrust out a paw. "All right, Patchcoat," she agreed. "We'd better stick together, I suppose. Shake paws, fox."

"Aye. Shake paws, fox."

Left paw met left paw as they intoned the ritual of villains,

Shake paws, count your claws.
You steal mine, I'll borrow yours.
Watch my whiskers, check both ears.
Robber foxes have no fears.

Ben Stickle was observing the scene from the cover of a humped loam bank. He scurried off to report to the Corim that the Mask, alias Patchcoat, had made contact with Fortunata, alias Besomtail.

The Mask would lead Fortunata a merry dance through Mossflower before evening fell over the woodlands.

It was mid-afternoon when Chibb left the cell window at Kotir. Gingivere sat in the straw with his two little friends, patiently explaining the message sent by the Corim.

"Now, if a ferret looks like a ferret, or a stoat like a stoat, or a weasel looks like a weasel, don't trust them. But if a fox that looks like a fox says that his name is Mask and he's been sent by the Corim, we must do exactly as he says, quickly and without question."

Ferdy scratched his spiky head. "Supposing it's a stoat that looks like a weasel with a ferret's nose and a fox's tail, Mr. Gingivere?"

Gingivere pushed him playfully backward into the straw. "Then don't trust him, even if it's a Ferdy that looks like a Coggs with a Gingivere's fur, you little rascal. Hush now, there's somebody coming. I'd better get you back into your bags."

Two weasel guards passed along the corridor, chatting animatedly.

"So what did the foraging party bring back?"

"Not a single acorn. The Queen's not too happy, either."

"Well, that's only to be expected."

"Aye, but it made things worse when Cludd reported that one of our soldiers had been taken by that big old eagle."

"Who was it?"

"A stoat, they say."

"Ah well, as long as it wasn't a weasel."

"Aye. Can't stand stoats myself. Nasty sly creatures."

"Right. Not like us, mate. Anyhow, I'll bet if the eagle attacked one of our lads he'd weasel his way out of it somehow."

"Hahaha. That's a good one. Weasel his way out of it!"

The waters of the fast-flowing stream glittered in the afternoon sun. All day the three travelers had wandered along the bank, looking for a shallow fording place. Martin gazed up at the mountains. They were much closer now. He could see the green of vegetation at the base changing to basalt and slate-colored rock which soared upward to snow-covered peaks that seemed to support the sky like mythical columns.

Gonff was singing as he trailed his fishing line along.

O the day is fair and blue,
The mountains lie ahead.
Companions good and true,
Our enemies are dead.
I'm longing for the day,
O for that happy time,
When I'll return to say,
Sweet Columbine, you're mine.

As they trekked, Young Dinny dug up edible plants and roots to add to their supplies.

Martin sighted a bend ahead with steep sloping banks. "Come on, mates. The stream looks narrower there. Perhaps there's a way to cross."

He was right; just around the bend was a sight that gladdened their hearts.

A rope stretched across the water, attached at either end by a deep stake driven into the earth. On the opposite bank a white willow trunk lay in the shallows. Gonff twanged the tautened fibers of the rope.

"It's a ferry, mateys," he told them. "See on the other bank? Pity it isn't on this side of the water. Never mind, even if it means getting wet we'll cross on this rope."

Two pairs of unwinking eyes watched them from behind the log on the opposite shore.

Martin waded into the river, holding the rope as a guideline. "Come on, it's not too bad," he called. "Stay on this side of the rope, then the current won't sweep you downstream."

Dinny and Gonff followed his example. The going was not too difficult. Paw by paw, they began pulling themselves through the stream. Halfway across, it deepened. They were floating now, but still going forward, aided by the rope.

A shout rang out from the far bank, "Stop right there, strangers!"

A snake and a lizard emerged from behind the willow trunk.

"Looks like trouble, eh, Din," Gonff whispered.

Martin ignored the warning, continuing to pull himself forward.

Dinny called out a friendly hail. "Goo' day to 'ee. Us'n's on'y a crossen, no need t'be afeared."

The snake reared up, flickering a slim tongue. "Hssss. Nobody crosses without paying us. I'm Deathcoil and this is Whipscale. We are the ford guardians. Pay us, or pay with your lives."

Gonff caught up with Martin. "I don't like the look of those two. Has that snake got adder markings?"

Martin's warrior nature rose. Tightening his grip on the rope with one paw, he unslung the broken sword from around his neck.

"Looks a bit skinny and undersized to be a true adder, Gonff," he reassured his friend. "I'm pretty certain that the other one is only some kind of newt. Leave it to me. We'll soon find out."

It was now apparent to the ford guardians that the travelers were coming across.

"What've you got for us?" the lizard asked, his voice harsh and aggressive. "Come on, move yourselves. Up on the bank here, and empty those packs out. Quick, now!"

Martin's face was grim. "Listen, you two. You don't frighten us. We're travelers and we aren't carrying anything of value, but we'll fight if we have to, so you'd better stand clear."

The snake lowered his head onto the rope, glaring wickedly at them. "Hsss, fools, one bite from my fangs means death. If you have no valuables, then go back and get something to pay our toll with."

Martin yanked down on the taut rope, letting it go with a twang. The line sprang upward, vibrating. The snake was hammered on the lower jaw several times before he was tossed flat on the bank. "How's that for starters, worm," Gonff laughed. "Stand up straight, and I'll give you a taste of my dagger when I get ashore. Come on, Din."

The mole waved a hefty digging paw. "Oi'll make knots in 'ee, then oi'll teach yon glizzard sum manners."

The three friends bounded up on the bank, dripping but determined. Martin advanced, wielding his broken sword; Gonff drew his dagger as he and Dinny spread in a pincer movement; the mole whirled a pack loaded with plants and roots.

As they closed for combat, the snake flicked his coils at Martin. "Hsss, you'll leave your bones on this bank, mouse!"

26

Fortunata was becoming irate with her traveling partner. "By the fang, Patchcoat, I'm certain we've passed this same yew thicket three times today. What are you playing at, in the name of foxes?"

Patchcoat whirled upon the vixen, pulling out a long rusty knife. "Are you calling me a liar, Besomtail? Think I don't know where I'm going?"

The vixen backed off, licking dry, nervous lips. "Of course not, friend. I'm sorry, this forest looks all the same to me. I'm a healer, not a pathfinder, you know."

Patchcoat grunted, as he sheathed his knife. "Huh, I'm no trailmaster myself. I'm a mercenary by trade. I'd swap a good barracks for this lot any day. Never mind, not far to go now."

Fortunata pushed aside an overhanging branch. "A mercenary, eh? Soldier for hire. Well, you do right by me and I might be able to find you a good barracks. I could have you made into a Captain."

"A Captain, you say. Where at?"

The vixen winked. "Tell you some other time. Are we nearly there?"

"See that big oak?" Patchcoat asked, pointing. "It's got a

hidden door between the main roots. Follow me.''

At the sound of knocking, Bella opened the door of Brock-hall the merest crack. Skipper and Amber craned their necks to see the visitors as the badger called out gruffly, ''Who are you? What do you want?''

Fortunata made a fawning bow. ''My name is Besomtail. This is my assistant, Patchcoat. Are there any among you who require the services of a healer?''

Lady Amber showed her teeth. ''We don't need your mumbo-jumbo, fox. Now clear off, quick!''

''Oh, please have pity on us,'' Mask whined pitifully. ''We've fallen upon hard times. Foxes are always driven off, even when they have traveled far, seeking honest work. We do not mean harm to any creature. We are starving.''

Skipper winked at the badger. ''Oh, let 'em in, Miz Bella. Surely we can manage a bite and a sup for these two cruising fleabags?''

Bella opened the door wide. ''Come in, foxes. But mind you behave, otherwise you may find yourselves hanging by the tails from a high branch.''

Once inside, Fortunata's eyes roved ceaselessly, noting every detail of her surroundings. Abbess Germaine entered the room, accompanied by two small hedgehogs dressed in blanket cloaks and cooking-pot helmets.

''Ferdy, Coggs, take these two travelers to the kitchen,'' she ordered them. ''Ask Goody to feed them, please.''

Goody Stickle fed the unsavory duo some leftover spring vegetable soup with bread and cheese. They ate ravenously.

''Dearie me, it looks like you two ain't eaten since last harvest,'' Goody remarked. ''I'll cut more bread 'n' cheese, then you can earn your keep by scouring some pots and pans before you eat us out of house and home altogether. That'll save my old paws a job.''

Reluctantly the foxes finished their meal. Afterwards they faced the formidable stack of dirty kitchenware heaped in bowls of water.

The vixen curled her lip in disgust. ''You wash and I'll wipe.''

Mask shook his head. ''Oh no. A healer needs clean paws. You wash, and I'll do the wiping.''

As they worked, Mask whispered to Fortunata, ''What d'you make of this place, Besomtail?''

"Well, they've certainly got a comfy den here," she replied. "Well-stocked, too. But hark, Patchcoat, they're soft and innocent as new bread. Look how easily we got in here."

Mask tapped his nose knowingly. "A right bunch of woodland bumpkins, eh? One good squad of soldiers could tie their whiskers in knots."

Fortunata passed a large pan to be wiped. "How would you like to be in charge of that squad, Patchcoat?"

"Would this have anything to do with that Captain's job you mentioned earlier?" Mask whispered out the side of his mouth.

Fortunata wiped her paws on a towel. "Aye, it would. I've been watching you, Patchcoat. You're a fox after my own heart. Now listen carefully and stick by me. We can both come out of this as two rich and powerful foxes if we play both ends against the middle."

A fraction before both sides joined in combat there was a deep gruff shout from the reeds. "Whoooaaahhh, gerroutofit!"

A small, ferocious shrew, armed with a heavy hornbeam club, hurled himself roaring onto Deathcoil and Whipscale. He belabored them mercilessly with swift hard blows.

"What've I told you two filthy reptiles?" he shouted. "Gerroff my bank. Here, take this with you, and this, and this too!"

The snake and the lizard were thrashed into the stream.

"Ouch, ow, no, please, owoo, ooff!" they cried.

The bad-tempered shrew slammed his club down hard on Whipscale's tail. It flew off into the air, and he batted it into midstream with an expert flick.

In the water, a pattern of dirt floated away from Deathcoil, showing that under the dark bruises he was only a common grass snake.

The shrew turned to Martin and his friends, gesturing toward the unlucky pair in the stream. "See, a grass snake and a newt. Pair of nuisances. I've warned 'em before about threatening honest travelers. Go on, clear off you snotty vermin. Just let me catch you around here again, and I'll make you eat each other's tails!"

The snake and the newt were carried off by the current, hissing dire threats now they were out of reach of the shrew and his club. "You wait, you'll pay for this, you haven't seen the last of us."

A well-aimed stone from Gonff's sling bounced off the

snake's head; another from Martin stung the newt's severed tail stump.

The shrew nodded approvingly. "Slingmice, eh? Good shots. This club's my weapon. They won't be back for another dose of this."

Martin smiled. He liked the shrew's truculent manner.

"Thank you, sir," he said warmly. "I am Martin the Warrior. This is Gonff the thief, and this Young Dinny, our mole friend. We are travelers, as you see, bound on a quest to Salamandastron."

The shrew shouldered his club. "Sala what? Oh, you mean that big place t'other side of the mountains. Well, I'm called Log-a-Log Big Club. I own the ferry round here. You should have given me a shout, like this."

Log-a-Log cupped his paws around his mouth, bellowing out in a deep voice which echoed off the mountains.

"Logalogalogalogalog!"

Gonff put his sling away. "We would have if we'd known, matey. Do you live around here?"

Log-a-Log parted the reeds, revealing a cave hewn into the bank. "Aye. I live alone. I expect you're hungry; travelers always are. Come inside. I'll tell you all about it."

Inside the cave was a nest of untidy odds and ends. Fishing nets draped the walls, a fire smoldered in one corner, many tools lay all about a large, skillfully made boat that dominated the living area. An old black water beetle sat by the fire.

The travelers found seats amid the jumble, and Log-a-Log served them steaming bowls of freshwater shrimp soup with arrowhead bread and spring radishes. He sat stroking the beetle's back.

"I call this fellow Grubwhacker. He lives nearby, comes in and out of here for his food, just like a pet. That there is my boat. It's about finished. I was going to try it soon in the stream."

Martin felt the sturdy polished hull. "It's beautifully crafted, Log-a-Log. You know about boats, then?"

The shrew picked up a spokeshave. He took a sliver off the stern. "Ships, friend, ships. Though I'm a ferry-puller, like all my family, we used to live with our tribe on the banks of the River Moss, far to the north of here. One day, several seasons ago, we were invaded by sea rats who sailed inland. They took many of us captive and put us to the oars of their galley. Some died there, but I escaped. One night I slipped my chains and went overboard, just south of Salamandastron. I swam ashore. Do you see those mountains? Well, I couldn't cross them, so I walked around them. Ha, that took a season or two, I can tell you. Eventually I found my way to this place—the Great South Stream, I call it. One day I'll go back to my village, where the shores and flatlands meet the woods on the River Moss. Until then, well, here I am.''

Martin put down his bowl. "Then you've seen Salamandastron?"

"Oh aye, passed it a few times when I was in the galleys," Log-a-Log agreed. "Big mountain, fiery at night. Sea rats don't like it, though."

Martin nodded. "Yes, I've heard about the sea rats. My father went off to fight them up north. He was never heard of again. Tell me, Log-a-Log, do you know the way to Salamandastron?"

The shrew pointed with a ladle. "Over those mountains and due west."

Dinny was stroking Grubwhacker. "Hurr, can 'ee go thurr by stream, Gloglog?"

The shrew paced the cave with his lips pursed. Silently they watched him. Finally he stopped alongside Dinny and the beetle. Taking a loaf and a piece of cooked fish, he placed them upon Grubwhacker's back, where they could be carried without falling off. Log-a-Log patted his pet affectionately.

"Go on Grubwhacker," he told him. "Back to your missus and the little uns."

The beetle trundled off obediently.

The shrew turned to Martin and his friends. "Right. Load the boat up with supplies. I'll get the mast and sail ready to rig up."

Gonff stood up. "Why, matey, what are we supposed to be doing?"

Log-a-Log grunted as he heaved a heavy mast timber from the back of the cave. "We're going to see if that old stream will take us under the mountain. That's the shortest route to Salamandastron. I wouldn't chance it on my own, but now that I've got a crew . . .''

BOOK TWO

Salamandastron

27

Skipper hobbled into the dining room at Brockhall. He sat down with a sigh of relief, rubbing his tail and paws.

Fortunata and Mask were clearing away the lunchtime dishes. The sly vixen nodded toward Skipper and winked at her companion. Mask looked slightly bemused, but Fortunata winked again as she sauntered over to the otter.

"What seems to be the trouble, sir?" she asked solicitously. "Is it an old injury?"

Skipper shook his head and continued rubbing. "No, it's these pains I get in me paws and tail. The minute I come out of the water, or even after a rainshower these days, it starts throbbing right into me old bones. Ooh, the pains, matey. It's agony!"

Fortunata crouched in front of Skipper. "Here, allow me to take a look, sir. I'm a healer of pains."

First she stroked the fur on Skipper's paws, then she probed and tested with her claws. The otter put on a fine display of anguish.

"Ow, ooch," he exclaimed. "That's it, right there. You touched the very spot."

The vixen stroked her whiskers, looking very professional.

"Hmm, yes, I think you've got a touch of the stiffeners," she told him.

Skipper expressed concern. "The stiffeners? Float me tail, is that bad?"

Fortunata shook her head gravely. "It will be, if you let it get any worse. I've seen otters bent double with the stiffeners. Very, very, painful indeed."

"Can you cure me, Besomtail?" he asked.

Fortunata leaned against the table. "Feverfew, wormwood, extract of nightshade leaf to stop the pain, that's what you need. Plus, of course, a few other items that I don't normally carry with me."

"But you can get them?" Skipper asked hopefully.

Fortunata smiled at Mask. "Well, I suppose so. Though I'll have to go out into the woods to gather them. What d'you say, Patchcoat?"

Mask had caught on to the scheme. "Right, Besomtail," he said. "We'd better go out into the woodlands and hunt for the stuff. After all they've done for us here, it'd be a shame to watch this poor otter suffer when we can help him."

Fortunata kept her voice light and casual. "Of course we'd need a couple of helpers, creatures that aren't needed for other duties. What about those two little hedgehogs? I'll bet they'd love a romp in the woods."

Spike and Posy (disguised as Ferdy and Coggs) were eager to help. Goody Stickle wiped their snouts with her apron corner.

"Now mind you, don't go a botherin' the healers," she warned them. "Behave yourselves like two liddle gentle'ogs."

Fortunata patted them gingerly on their heads. "Oh, they'll be just fine with old Patchcoat and me, marm."

The healer and her assistant strode off, in the wake of the two small hedgehogs who scampered playfully ahead. Mask hitched the medicine bag around his neck as he trudged along with the vixen.

"Here, Besomtail, what are you up to now?" he asked. "I thought we were supposed to escape back to Kotir and tell this Queen of yours where the woodlanders are hiding out."

Fortunata ducked an overhanging branch. "That's exactly what we're going to do, Patchcoat, but there's no harm in bringing back a couple of escaped prisoners while we're about it.

You wait and see. It'll be an extra feather in both our caps, though I'd hate to be one of those young hedgehogs when Tsarmina has them back under her claws.''

Mask felt a cold hatred for the cruel vixen, but long practice had taught him to keep a straight face.

Fortunata watched the two little ones tussling happily in the loam. ''We'll get the credit for them, eh, mate.''

''You'll get what's coming to you today.'' Mask's voice had sunk to a grim whisper.

Fortunata only half-heard her strange companion. ''Eh, what's that?''

Mask looked around him. ''I said, I'm not sure if this is the way.''

''Oh no, don't tell me we're lost,'' Fortunata groaned.

Mask pointed to a fork in the trail. ''No, wait a moment, it's one of these two paths. Listen, I'll take this path to the right and keep an eye on these hedgehogs. You take the one to the left. If it's the real trail, you'll come across a fallen beech. Give me a call. If I find the beech on my trail, I'll give you a yelp.''

Fortunata parted from them, calling out to the hedgehogs, ''Be good, little ones. Stay with Uncle Patchcoat. I'll see you later.''

When the vixen was gone, Mask sat on a chestnut stump. He gave Spike and Posy a sugared hazelnut each.

''You're not really our Uncle Patchcoat, are you?'' Posy giggled.

Mask patted her gently. ''No, I'm not. And Besomtail isn't your aunt. But I don't think we'll be seeing her again.''

Spike stared gravely at the otter. ''Can we call you Mr. Mask again?''

Mask gave them his canteen to drink from. He wiped nut fragments from their faces with his false tail.

''Not until we're safe back at Brockhall tonight,'' he said firmly. ''Pretend for now that I really am your Uncle Patchcoat.''

Posy hugged the false tail to her comfortingly. ''You're a nice old Uncle Patchcoat.''

Beneath his disguise Mask blushed with pleasure.

Fortunata spotted the fallen beech ahead. She leaned against it with a sigh of relief.

''Phew! Thank the fang this is the right trail,'' she said aloud.

"Soon as I get my breath back, I'll give Patchcoat a call."

"You've done all the calling you're going to do, traitor!"
Lady Amber and ten squirrels dropped from the trees and stood
blocking the vixen's path, each with an arrow notched on a
drawn bowstring.

Instinctively Fortunata knew her plans had gone badly astray.
She cowered down with drooping ears.

"It was Patchcoat," she whined. "I wasn't going to harm
the little ones. He forced me to go along with his wicked plans.
He said that—"

"Silence, fox!"

Lady Amber dropped her bushy tail flat along the ground.

Ten bowstrings strained tighter.

The squirrel leader pointed an accusing paw at the trapped
spy. "We knew who you were from the moment you entered
these woods," she rasped. "When you left Brockhall today I
was only a treetop away from you. I heard every word that
passed between you and Mask."

Fortunata crouched low, trying to offer as small a target as
possible.

"No, you've got it wrong, he's Patchcoat the mercenary,"
she argued. "I don't know any creature called Mask. Wait, yes
I do, there's another fox named Mask. He lives over by Kotir—
a real evil creature. He's the one you want. I'll take you to
him."

"Spare me your lies, fox." Amber's voice was flat and
harsh. "You have lived the life of a traitor and earned the
reward of treachery. Tell your deceitful tales to whoever meets
you at the gates of Dark Forest."

Amber's tail flicked upright like a banner.

Ten arrows flew straight and true!

O for the life of a sailormouse,
It's better than Kotir gaol,
A rest for the weary traveling paws,
With the wind to drive our sail.
There's a shrew for skipper
Two mice for mates,
And a mole for a cabin boy.
When we sight Salamandastron,
We'll shout out loud, Ahoy!

Midafternoon on the waters of the Great South Stream saw the friends learning to handle the boat that Log-a-Log had named *Waterwing*. Martin was taking a turn at the tiller under the shrew's guiding paw, while Gonff charged about playfully trying to air his new-found nautical knowledge.

"Keep her downwind, me lads. Steady at the tiller there. Watch your larboard side, Cap'n Log-a-Log. Bring the helm a point to starboard. Steady as she goes!"

Dinny was definitely not cut out for a sailor's life. The young mole lay amidships clutching his stomach.

"Burr oo, 'ush 'ee, Gonffen. This yurr pore mole be a-dyen. Yurr, c'n oi goo ashore an' walk apiece, 'twould stopp 'ee wurld goen round."

Log-a-Log produced some herbs for Dinny to chew upon. After a while he felt better, but he kept up a steady stream of comments.

"Oi'd as soon be a gurt burdbag flyen in 'ee sky than sailen on this yurr streamer."

Martin watched the stream carefully. The mountains towered right over them now, blocking out the sky ahead.

"Log-a-Log, have you noticed the current? It's very swift here and getting heavier. We're moving along a bit too fast for my liking."

"Aye, I've noticed the stream is starting to take a steep downward course, Martin." The shrew looked worried yet spoke calmly. "Here, Gonff. Let's see you take the sail in and drop the mast. Better lend a paw, Martin and Dinny. I'll take the tiller."

As they worked, the water began to get very choppy. Crested foamheads began appearing around rocks which stuck up like jagged teeth in the swirling flow. Log-a-Log was stretched to his limit holding the tiller and maneuvering *Waterwing*. The little craft began to buck and tilt; water was splashing in heavily over the forward end.

"Leave the mast." The shrew's voice boomed out above the roar of water. "As long as the sail's down, bale her out before we're swamped. Hurry!"

Waterwing leaped about like a frenzied salmon. The thunder of the stream rose, echoing from the mouth of a dark tunnel forming overhead. Hanging bushes and vegetation clawed at the small crew, while rocks pounded dangerously at the sides of the boat. Without warning, they were swept deep into the tunnel. The stream became a waterfall.

In a mad torrent of boiling white water they were hurled over the brink of the chasm. *Waterwing* hung for a second in space, then plunged into the abyss. The mast struck the mountainside. It snapped with a resounding crack and came crashing down onto them.

Tsarmina stood in her usual position at the high chamber window, Cludd waiting dutifully at one side.

"Spring vegetables aren't much use, Cludd. Find out what the birds like to eat, and scatter some of it about. Set some traps and get the archers out. Fat woodpigeons, a juicy thrush or two—that's the sort of thing we need."

"Yes, Milady, I'll see to it right away." The weasel Captain trudged off obediently.

Tsarmina leaned farther out the window, scanning the wood fringe. "No, wait!"

A strange-looking fox emerged from the undergrowth, tugging two little hedgehogs along on a rope. It was plain to see he was in a hurry. Behind the trio, a band of otters and squirrels came dashing in pursuit. Looking backward at his pursuers, the fox tripped over the rope. The woodlanders dashed forward and pounced upon him.

Tsarmina shoved Cludd to the door. "Quick, quick. Get down there and grab the nearest troops. Help the fox. Hurry!"

The wildcat Queen raced back to the window yelling aloud, "Hold on, fox. We're getting help out to you. Keep hold of those hedgehogs!"

The stranger put up what appeared to be a good fight. Unfortunately, he was outnumbered. One group of woodlanders kept him busy defending himself, while several squirrels slashed the rope from the captive hedgehogs, bearing them off into the trees, away into thick wooded Mossflower.

Late again! Tsarmina slammed her paw hard against the windowsill.

Down below, Cludd and a party of soldiers raced toward the melee. The woodlanders broke off the attack, vanishing like smoke into the undergrowth.

Tsarmina was standing in the entrance hall as Cludd escorted the newcomer in. She peered closely at the odd-looking stranger.

Mask panted heavily, slumping down on his haunches. "Whew, those squirrels and otters fight like madbeasts!"

Tsarmina circled him. "You didn't do too badly yourself." There was grudging admiration in her voice. "What's your name? How did you come here?"

Mask looked up at the wildcat. "I'm called Patchcoat. You must be Queen Tsarmina of the Thousand Eyes. Fortunata told me about you."

"So, you've met the vixen. Where is Fortunata now?"

Mask shrugged. "Probably lying in the woods, full of squirrel arrows. She was too slow to keep up. I could have beaten those woodlanders to here easily if it hadn't been for that great dozy lump."

Stupidly, Cludd stepped forward. He prodded the strange fox with his spear. "You still haven't told Milady why you're here, fox."

With a deft movement, Mask grabbed the spear, thudded the butt into Cludd's midriff, bowled him over, and was standing on his chest with his dagger pressed against the weasel's throat.

"Listen, fatguts," he growled dangerously. "I'll make you eat that spear if you ever poke it at me again. Remember that. My name's Patchcoat the mercenary, see. I sell my blade to the highest bidder."

Mask stood on Cludd's nose with one paw and executed a neat turn to teach the weasel a painful lesson. Without even looking to see the result he turned to Tsarmina.

"Ha, you could do with some proper fighters, Queen. Especially if that oaf and Fortunata are a specimen of what you keep around here."

Tsarmina showed her great fangs in an approving smile. "Well, at last a real warrior. Welcome to Kotir, Patchcoat. I'm sure you'll do well here. Cludd, get up off the floor and give this fox your Captain's cloak to wear. From now on you'll take orders from him."

Sullenly Cludd undid his cloak, flinging it to Mask.

Ashleg stumped in with a band of soldiers. He threw a healer's bag upon the floor.

"We tried tracking those woodlanders, Milady," he reported sadly. "But they're well away. I found Fortunata east of here, full of arrows. Her body is out on the parade ground."

"Dead?"

"As a doornail, Milady."

"Then what do I want with a slain fox?" Tsarmina asked impatiently. "Throw it out in the woods for the eagle."

Tsarmina started back up the staircase. "Patchcoat, I'll be up in my chamber. Come up later. I'm sure we have plenty to discuss together."

Mask fastened on the cloak of Captaincy. "Aye, later, Milady. First I want to inspect these cells Fortunata told me about. Maybe I can discover how two young hedgehogs escaped from them so easily."

Tsarmina climbed the stairs pensively. This strange fox was certainly a lucky find.

28

Time stood still. Martin imagined he was back under the river in Mossflower being towed along by an otter. Everything was pitch-black and ice-cold. A million thoughts rushed through his brain, bringing memories flooding back: his father leaving to fight the sea rats . . . Tsarmina snarling at him . . . the kind face of Bella at Brockhall . . . Dinny chuckling as he wrestled with Gonff . . . Everything whirled together into one great maelstrom of crashing water, then there was silence.

Martin felt mossy ground against his wet back.

"Not dead, bring medicine, medicine," a sibilant voice was saying somewhere close.

The warrior mouse felt some vile-tasting liquid being poured between his lips. He opened his eyes.

He was lying on a broad ledge, which was covered in velvety moss. Soft light cast flickering luminous water patterns around the rock face. A mouse was standing over him, another crouched nearby. Martin took a second look. Surely these creatures could not be mice? They had very little fur, black leathery skin and, oddest of all, wings!

The one nearest pushed the bowl toward Martin with a black claw.

Martin smelt the putrid medicine and pushed it away. "No more, thank you. I'm all right now. Where am I? Who are you?"

"Lie still, lie still. We are the tribe of Lord Cayvear who is ruler of Bat Mountpit. You will not be harmed, not be harmed," the creature assured him.

Martin sat up; he felt wet but unhurt. "My name is Martin the Warrior. There were three others with me—a shrew, a mouse and a mole. Where are they? Have they been rescued from the water?"

The other bat shuffled over. "I am Rockhanger. This is Wingfold. We have found the angry one and the strong tunneller, but no other creature, no other creature."

Martin stood and leaned against the rocks. His head was aching and he felt a large bump between his ears.

"The other mouse is called Gonff. You'll know him easily. He's a cheeky little thief who loves to sing. He's my friend, and we must find him," he said anxiously.

Rockhanger felt with the edge of his wing across Martin's face and body. Martin recoiled and then stood still. Rockhanger was blind.

The bat chuckled; it came out like a dry hiss.

"No creature is blind who sees by touch. If I tried hard enough I would see you with my eyes, but the tribe of Bat Mountpit gave up the use of eyesight long ago. We can feel in the dark, feel in the dark."

The bats led Martin away from the ledge with its constant sound of falling water. They made their way along a network of caves connected by a series of passages. In the first cave they entered Martin found Log-a-Log and Young Dinny.

"Yurr, Marthen. Woip wet off'n'ee." The mole tossed him a heap of soft dried moss.

The warrior mouse dried himself vigorously, bringing the warmth back to his body.

"Has there been any news of Gonff?" he asked his friends.

Log-a-Log squinted in the pale light that diffused throughout the regions of Bat Mountpit.

"None at all," he said sadly. "We've lost *Waterwing* too, after all the work I put in on that boat."

Dinny wrinkled his snout. "Ho urr, c'n allus make 'nother bowt, but thurr be on'y one Gonffen."

A bat came in carrying food for them. "I am Darkfur. Eat,

eat. Our tribe are searching for your friend, for your friend.''

The three companions took the edge off their hunger with the food of the bats. There was hot mushroom soup and a drink made from some salty-tasting waterweed. The rest was not easy to identify, though it was quite palatable.

Martin ate automatically. A great weight hung upon his spirit. He could not imagine life without his mouse-thief friend at his side.

After the meal they rested awhile to recover from their ordeal. When Martin awoke, Log-a-Log and Dinny were still sleeping. There was an enormous bat standing over them. The stranger touched him lightly with a wingclaw.

''You are Martin the Warrior. I am Lord Cayvear, High Chief of the dark places. Welcome, welcome.''

Martin stood up and bowed. ''Thank you for looking after our safety, Lord Cayvear. Is there any news of our friend Gonff?''

''Not yet, not yet, but sometimes no news is good news,'' Lord Cayvear said reassuringly. ''My scouts are searching, searching.''

Martin paced the cave anxiously. ''Lord Cayvear, I cannot stay here feeling helpless while my friend may be in great danger.''

The great bat folded his wings. ''I know, I know. You would not be a true friend if you did, Martin. Come with me. We will search together. Let these two sleep on; it will do them good, do them good.''

Mask strode down to the cells with a businesslike air, his Captain's cloak swirling splendidly.

''Hey, where d'you think you're off to?'' a weasel on sentry duty in the corridor challenged him insolently.

The disguised otter rounded on the unfortunate guard, stamping his paw down hard in fine military fashion.

''Stand to attention when you address a Captain, you scruffy idle mud-brained scum.''

The weasel gulped, coming swiftly to attention. ''Sorry, Captain. I didn't realize . . .''

Mask stood, paws akimbo, sneering contemptuously. ''Chin in, chest out, eyes front, spear straight, shield up. Up, I said. So, you didn't realize. It strikes me there's been quite a bit of 'not realizing' going on down here. You probably didn't realize it when the prisoners escaped. Well, let me tell you, my mangy-furred laddo, things are going to be different around here. You'll learn to jump when you hear the name of Captain Patch-coat in the future. Either that, or you and your cronies will find out what double duties in full pack on half-rations mean. Do I make myself clear?''

The weasel banged his spearbutt resoundingly against the floor. ''Very clear, sah!''

''Right. Lead me to the wildcat's cell, then get back about your duties,'' Mask ordered sternly.

''Follow me, sah!''

Gingivere heard the rapid paws marching down the passage. With practiced ease he slung Ferdy and Coggs up into their haversacks and sat on the floor, looking forlorn.

The wildcat gaped vacantly through the bars at the evil-looking fox on the other side of the door grille.

When the sentry departed, Mask held up a paw to forestall questions. ''I am the Mask. The Corim sent me to free you. Are the hedgehogs with you?''

''Yes.''

''Good. Then be ready tonight.''

''You mean we're getting out tonight?'' Gingivere asked incredulously.

''Aye, if I can swing it. Tell Chibb there must be a good force of woodlanders waiting in the thickets on the east side. I've got to go now. Be ready tonight.'' Mask strode off down the passage, every inch the Captain of Kotir.

Ferdy and Coggs made the haversacks dance and wriggle.

''Hooray, we're going home tonight!''

''Who was that, Mr. Gingivere? Was it a fox?''

''You tell me, little Coggs. How the Corim could employ any creature so evil-looking, is beyond me.''

''Look at me, Mr. Gingivere. Do I look evil?'' Ferdy called, sticking his snout out of the haversack. ''I can, you know. All I do is shut one eye and pull my snout to the left, like this.''

''By the fur, you're frightening the life out of me, Ferdy. Best leave your snout alone or it'll stick like that.''

''Can we come down to play, Mr. Gingivere, please,'' Coggs pleaded.

''Not right now. Try and get some sleep up there. I'll call you when Mr. Mask gets back tonight. We'll need to be bright and alert if we're to make it back to your friends and family in Mossflower.''

Martin was astonished by the size of Lord Cayvear's domain. Bat Mountpit was vast and impressive, with chasms, tunnels, streams, caves, waterfalls, and underground lakes. Lord Cayvear pointed out his tribe. Those not searching for Gonff were farming great areas of edible roots, mushrooms and subterranean plants, while others fished the lakes.

But there was still no trace of Gonff the mousethief. Having climbed upward in the search, they spanned the high cave galleries, leading off a central pathway that rose steeply. At the top Lord Cayvear stopped. He turned, barring the path with outstretched wings.

''We go no farther, no farther,'' he stated.

Martin pointed upward. ''But, Lord Cayvear, I'm certain I can see the glimmer of daylight up ahead.''

The great bat was unmoved. ''So you can, Martin. So you can. The outside world may be reached from up there, but none may venture farther. There is a large bird of prey roosting higher up, far bigger than any bat. It is a killer. Many of my bats who went up that way were never seen again, never seen again.''

Martin gave one last dejected look at the slim shaft of light and turned back.

The little bats were curious and delighted with Dinny. They were under the impression that the mole was a fat bat without wings. Dinny liked the idea.

''Ho urr, batmousen. Oi do fly under 'ee soil. That's as 'ow oi wore moi wings out wi' all that diggen.''

The little bats laughed. ''Mr. Dinny, you are funny, funny!''

Martin called Dinny and Log-a-Log together to discuss their position.

''As I see it, there's one way into Bat Mountpit, and that's the way we came in. As for the way out, it's a high passage with an opening, but it's barred by some large bird of prey. Even Lord Cayvear fears to go up there.''

''Burr, do 'ee say wot sort of burdbag it be?'' Dinny asked.

Martin shrugged. ''That I don't know, Din. I only hope poor Gonff wasn't taken by it. Listen, we must find a way past that bird to continue the quest. Gonff would have wished it.''

Log-a-Log was not optimistic. "If the big bird could kill Lord Cayvear, what chance would we have?"

Martin unwound his sling. "Still, we've got to give it a try."

"You'm caint do it wi' slings, Marthen. But if yon burdbag is 'igh up, then oi knows an ole mole trick to cave 'im out," Dinny promised.

Lord Cayvear materialized out of the gloom. "How would you do it? What is your plan, your plan?"

"Urr, oi get'n b'neath 'im an' dig away 'ee nest, then push so it fall out'ards down 'ee mounting," the mole explained.

Lord Cayvear flapped his wings and flew upward, hanging upside down by his claws.

"Can you do it, do it?" His voice was an excited hiss.

Martin patted Dinny on the back. "Lord Cayvear, if this mole says he can do it, then rest assured, he can. Come on, we can give him some assistance."

Darkness had scarcely fallen over the woodlands. Treetops were touched by the fires of the setting sun, and evening birdsong was thinning out to the last few warblers. The thickets at the east side of Kotir were packed with squirrels and otters, each one personally paw-picked by Skipper and Lady Amber. The two leaders listened to reports coming in.

"Squirrels ready, marm; archers in the low branches. Beech and Pear along with Barklad and Springpaw, waiting to whirl the young uns off through the treetops to Brockhall."

"Full crew standing by, Skip. Bula and Root to one side in case we need decoys. All otters fully loaded—slings and javelins. We'll give 'em plenty to think about if it comes to a fight."

They lay in wait, watching the night grow older.

Bella and the Stickles, plus the Loamhedge mice, had stayed behind at Brockhall, the Corim decision being that this was a mission for the swiftest and most warlike.

Inside Kotir, Mask made his way down to the cell areas. Inwardly, the otter shuddered after his interview with the wildcat Queen. Tsarmina's grisly plan for victory over the woodlanders did not bear thinking about: enslavement, death and imprisonment. Nor did the expression of fiendish delight upon her face every time she talked of separating woodland families, locking infants in cells as hostages, wreaking a murderous revenge on otters and squirrels, putting the old and infirm out to the fields as enforced labor.

Mask went about his perilous game with a new determination.

Torches glittered in the brackets on the walls of the dismal cell passages. The stoat on sentry duty had been warned of the bad-tempered Captain Patchcoat. He had prepared himself well, even sweeping his part of the passage with a broom.

At the sound of the Captain's approach, the stoat came smartly to attention, awaiting orders. Mask came briskly along the passage.

"Hmmm, that's a bit more like it. Straighten that spear up a touch," he said, inspecting the sentry. "Good, anything to report?"

"All in order, Cap'n."

"Right. Get your keys out. The Queen wants a word with the traitor Gingivere."

"But Cap'n," the sentry gulped nervously, "Her Majesty gave strict orders that he was never to be mentioned again, only fed and kept under lock and key. That's what she said."

"Well, she's the Queen, mate," Mask chuckled, patting the stoat's paw. "If she decides to change her mind, who are you and I to say different? We're only common soldiers. But I like your style; you've a lot more sense than the buffoon who was on duty here earlier. You take your orders from me, soldier, and I'll see to it that you wear a Captain's cloak before long. Tell you what: you give me the keys. That way I'll take all the responsibility. You go and get your supper and have a game of shove acorn with your mates."

The stoat surrendered the keys willingly to Mask. Who said this new Captain was a bad-tempered fox? He saluted smartly.

"Thanks, Cap'n. Give me a call if you need help."

Mask marched off down the passage, calling over his shoulder, "No need, mate. You carry on. I can take care of a crazy half-starved cat anytime, or my name ain't Patchcoat."

Gingivere was ready with Ferdy and Coggs as the key grated in the lock. The door swung open to reveal the strange fox with the evil countenance.

"Quickly, now," he whispered, holding a paw to his muzzle. "There's no time to lose. Gingivere, you walk in front of me, I'll have my dagger out as if I'm marching you up to the

Queen's chamber. Ferdy, Coggs, get behind me, under my cloak, and keep as close to me as possible. Don't make a sound; your lives depend upon it.''

To the casual observer, it looked as if there were only two creatures walking along the passage, Gingivere and Captain Patchcoat. Ferdy and Coggs were completely hidden beneath the long Captain's cloak. They negotiated the cell area successfully. Twice they passed guards who, knowing Captain Patchcoat's reputation, saluted smartly, keeping their eyes to the front. Mask nodded curtly to them. The escapers carried on up two flights of stairs and into the main entrance passage.

Cludd strode out of the mess hall with another weasel named Brogg just as Mask and Gingivere were passing. Cludd was still smarting from his demotion. ''Watch this, matey,'' he winked cunningly at Brogg. ''I'll make old cleverwhiskers jump through the roof. You'll see.''

Mask's bushy imitation tail protruded from the bottom of the cloak that had once been Cludd's pride and joy. Sneaking up behind Mask, Cludd stamped his paw down hard and heavy on the tail, expecting to see Mask leap in the air and roar with pain. Instead, Mask carried on walking. The tail had fallen off; it lay trapped under Cludd's paw. The weasel stared open-mouthed at the false tail, its end covered with pine resin and two cunning twine fasteners.

It took the slow-witted Cludd a moment to catch on.

''Hey, you, Patchcoat! Stop! Stop him. He's no fox!''

Cludd ran forward. Mask tore down a wall hanging, throwing it over the head of his charging enemy. Cludd fell, stumbling and wriggling to unhamper himself. Gingivere swept up the two small hedgehogs and dashed for the main door, with Mask close behind. Together they charged the main door, both creatures slamming their weight against it. The door flew open, bowling Ashleg over as he stumped in.

The fugitives sped across the parade ground as the hue and cry was raised behind them.

''Escape! Escape! Stop them quickly. Kill them if you have to!''

The upper galleries were crowded with the tribe of Lord Cayvear. Martin stood ready with a heap of rocks and his sling. Log-a-Log was beside him, his shrew dagger drawn.

It was a tense moment as Dinny went up silently, paw by paw, until he was directly under the crack of light.

"What is your friend doing now?" Lord Cayvear whispered to Martin. "There is soil and moss up there, but many rocks, many rocks."

Martin watched the soft earth and small rocks beginning to slide down the incline. "He's digging inward then downward. That way, whatever is above will collapse and hopefully fall outward."

More moss, rock and earth came down in a moving scree. Dinny came with it, sliding on his back and keeping an eye on the light shaft. The young mole dusted his coat off.

"Hurr, hurr, clever oi. Marthen, see if 'ee c'n get summat to lever your 'ole with."

Martin turned to Lord Cayvear. "Have you got a long stout timber we could use as a lever?"

The bat chieftain conversed quietly with a band of his followers. They saluted and winged off from the high galleries.

"Be lot quicker an more suproisful wi' a gurt lever," Dinny explained to Lord Cayvear.

There was not long to wait before the bats returned bearing a stout piece of wood.

Log-a-Log fondled it, with tears in his eyes. "It's the keel of *Waterwing*, my lovely boat!"

Sure enough, the stout curving timber was the original birch-wood keel of *Waterwing*; the bats had salvaged it from the falls.

On Dinny's instructions, it was borne upward by an army of bats. They waited until he had clambered up and positioned himself at the hole, then slowly they fed the strong timber in, under the mole's guidance. When the timber was fixed to Dinny's satisfaction, he wedged it on either side and underneath with three rocks. Then the mole slid back down to his friends. Martin looked up; what Dinny had accomplished was a deep hole beneath the light shaft, with the boat keel sticking out of the excavation at a slightly upward angle.

Log-a-Log scratched his chin. "What happens now, Dinny?"

"Hurr, now 'ee baths fly oop thurr soilent loik and perch on yon lever's end."

Lord Cayvear began signaling his legions. Two by two the bats flew silently as cloud shadows, then perched on the end of the lever.

When eight of them were perched securely, the keel grated, moving fractionally downward. They shifted and tightened clawholds.

Two more bats landed on the keel. It stayed still.

Yet another two landed. This time it moved visibly.

Dinny turned to the assembly. "Hoo arr, arf duzzen more'll do 'ee. Best coom out o' way whurr it be safer."

Another two bats had landed, then another two. There was more shale and rock sliding down as the final two bats landed on the end of the overcrowded keel, proving Dinny's calculation totally accurate.

Suddenly the hole gave way and collapsed, pushed outward by the keel bearing down. The entire rock face shifted under the leverage. Bats flew in all directions. Through the dust the small shaft of light widened into a hole as big as a fair-sized cave entrance.

There was a screeching and hooting, and through the debris Martin glimpsed a huge tawny owl winging its way west then south.

Amid the rubble of the landslide, the bats raised a sibilant cheer. Dinny was carried above them up the scree to the opening, Martin and Log-a-Log helping to bear their friend.

The three travelers were breathing deeply in the cool sweet evening air when Lord Cayvear flapped up gracefully. He bowed deeply.

"My thanks to you and your friends, Martin. Against the bigeyes we were totally helpless, totally helpless."

"I know, Lord Cayvear," Martin nodded understandingly. "Even we could not have fought off a tawny owl that size—he was a real monster. Well, thanks to our Dinny, we can continue the quest and your tribe can live in peace and safety."

Log-a-Log offered some good advice. "What you must do is to bar the entrance with wood and make a door. Leave some small holes in it, and station sentries night and day. Then if any large birds try to roost, you can push them off with spears and long poles. I will tell you how this door can be made."

For the first time Martin and Dinny looked over the edge to the outside world below. There was nothing to see except heavy gray evening mist in layers on the ground.

Martin stepped back from the edge. "We couldn't attempt to climb down there at night, Din. Let's stop here with our friends tonight and continue the quest tomorrow. Oh, Dinny, if only Gonff had been here to see this."

29

The escapers ran toward the outer gates in the perimeter walls, hotly pursued by Cludd, Ashleg and a band of soldiers.

Tsarmina, keeping her usual vigil at the upstairs window, had armed herself with bow and arrow in the hope that she might spot Argulor disposing of Fortunata's remains.

When the hubbub broke out down on the parade ground, without hesitation she fitted an arrow to her bow and took aim at Gingivere's back. Coggs slipped from Gingivere's pawhold. He rolled into a ball, hitting the parade ground harmlessly. Gingivere bent to pick him up, as Mask dashed up from behind to see if he could help.

The Queen of the Thousand Eyes had already loosed the deadly shaft. As Gingivere picked Coggs up, he heard Mask grunt behind him. Thinking the otter was urging him to hurry, the wildcat dashed for the gates with his precious burden. He knocked the bar aside and pushed one gate open.

The woodlanders flooded in. Ferdy and Coggs were passed from paw to paw until they were out of the danger zone. Freed of his burden, Gingivere turned to see his rescuer staggering slowly across the parade ground as the Kotir soldiers closed in on him. With a fearsome cry and a bound, Gingivere was at

Mask's side. Holding him up, he supported the injured creature through the gate, while the otters and squirrels stood fearlessly in line on the open parade ground, driving Cludd, Ashleg and the soldiers back to the barracks under a hail of arrows, javelins and rocks.

Tsarmina joined Cludd in the main hallway with a band of reinforcements at her back.

"Come on," she shouted furiously. "They're easily outnumbered. We're not going to retreat from our own parade ground. Get out there!"

Cludd was enraged at being taken by surprise on his own territory. With a bellow he dashed recklessly out into the open.

Encouraged by Queen and Captain, the forces of Kotir flooded out across the open ground. Madly Tsarmina raced ahead of them, spurred on by her own fury.

Skipper and Lady Amber decided it was time to make a tactical withdrawal. Their mission was accomplished as far as getting the escape party out of Kotir was concerned; besides, the woodland troops were far outnumbered by the hordes of Tsarmina's soldiery. The far side of the parade ground was black with soldiers who swarmed forward regardless of missiles. The woodlanders fired a parting volley then ducked out behind the doors.

"Lively now, mates," Skipper roared. "Follow Gingivere and Mask. Make sure they get home safe. Amber and me'll slow 'em up a bit here."

As the gates opened outward, it was but the work of a moment for the otter and the squirrel to place two sizeable wooden wedges beneath each gate and bang them home firmly with rocks.

Thinking ahead, Tsarmina guessed that the gates would have been barred to slow her progress. Standing on the backs of several soldiers, she sprang up, gained a clawhold on top of the gates and vaulted over with great agility. Tearing out the wedges with feverish energy, she pulled the doors open.

The woodlanders had had no time to cover their tracks, so it was plain to see which route they had taken. Tsarmina pointed east into Mossflower. "Follow me, stay together and obey my commands. We might not catch them, but there's an even chance these tracks may lead to their hideout!"

• • •

Deep in the woodland shade, Mask and Gingivere were traveling slowly. The otter was breathing laboriously, often halting to lean against trees, but he insisted on walking unaided.

Gingivere was puzzled and concerned for his rescuer. "Mask, what's the matter, friend? Are you hurt?"

The strange otter gave a wry grin and shook his head. "I'm all right. Listen, that must be Skipper and the crew coming this way."

The otters were boisterously recounting their victory over Kotir.

"Ha, soldiers! Vermin, more like."

"Aye, it took two score our number to make us back off, eh, Skip."

"I must have used two pouches of rocks on their thick skulls."

"Hoho, I could throw one of 'em farther than they could hurl their own spears."

"What a bunch of blunderers! Good job they've got the cat to lead 'em, or they'd be lost in their own headquarters."

"Hey, you two. What are you doing hanging about here?" Skipper bounded up, twirling his sling. "Mask, me old shipmate. You did us proud back there."

"I think he's been hurt," Gingivere whispered in Skipper's ear.

Mask straightened up and began walking doggedly forward. "Leave me alone, I'll be all right."

"Look, Skip, it's his back!" Bula pointed to the wet patch spreading across Mask's cloak.

Mask staggered a few paces, then fell heavily.

Skipper dashed across and knelt by Mask. Gently, he drew back the cloak to reveal the broken arrow shaft protruding from the otter's gray fur. Tsarmina's arrow had found its mark, not in Gingivere as she intended, but deep in the back of Mask.

Skipper supported the wounded otter's head as he said encouragingly, "Hold on, matey. We'll get you back home and patch you up in a brace of shakes. Strike me colors, one measly arrow isn't going to stop a freebooter like you."

Mask shook his head, a slow smile playing on his lips. "Someone at the gates of Dark Forest must have put my name on that arrow. At least I made it back into Mossflower."

Hot tears sprang into Skipper's brown eyes. "Don't say that, messmate. It wouldn't be the same without you.''

Mask leaned close to Skipper's ear. ''Do me one last favor, Skip.''

''Anything. You just name it.''

''Promise me that you won't tell little Spike and Posy about this. Say that Uncle Mask has gone to live far away.''

Skipper wiped Mask's brow gently with his paw. ''On my affidavit, brother.''

The gray otter nodded slowly. His curious eyes clouded over as he lay back peacefully and went limp.

Skipper stood up. He sniffed, grubbing grimy paws against his eyes. ''Listen, crew. We're taking him back to the River Moss. He liked it there. We'll stow him under a willow on the bank, and that way he'll always be near the sound of the water he loved. Tie some slings together and make a stretcher, mates.''

Gingivere stepped forward. He picked Mask up from the earth, holding him firmly in his strong paws.

''Please let me have the honor of carrying him. He rescued us from Kotir prison. Ferdy, Coggs and myself, we owe him our lives.''

Skipper turned away. ''So be it.''

Thus passed the Mask, the strange one who lived alone in Mossflower, the otter who was master of many disguises.

30

Dawn had scarcely broken when Log-a-Log put the finishing touches to the main frame of the gate. Martin peered down from the edge of the hole in the mountainside, holding tight to Dinny beside him.

"So, this is what the other side of the mountain looks like, eh, Din."

"Ho urr, baint much to be seen tho, Marthen."

The sloping side of the mountain was visible, but beyond that the bottomland was a bed of thick white mist, as far as the eye could see.

Lord Cayvear joined them.

"What lies below, I do not know," he told them. "Thank you, Log-a-Log. Thank you for your good work. Soon my tribe will be safe once more. We will be complete masters of all Bat Mountpit, Bat Mountpit."

Log-a-Log patted the heavy timber frame, made mainly from the wreckage of *Waterwing*.

"Aye, no sign of that owl now, though this gate should keep it away. That, and a few sharp prods in its feathery bottom. Don't like owls myself."

• • •

The sun was up and shining bright within an hour, but instead of clearing the mist it seemed to make it thicker. Martin and his friends were eager to continue the quest. Politely they refused entreaties from the bats to stay as long as they wished, though with a tinge of regret because of the kindness and hospitality shown them by the tribe of Bat Mountpit.

Lord Cayvear presented them with haversacks of fresh food and drink. The great bat stayed inside the darkness of the exit hole with his tribe, away from the glaring sunlight.

Martin shook him heartily by the paw. "Now, put that barrier up as soon as we leave. Better safe than sorry, my friend."

The little bats clung to Dinny. "Fly back through the earth and visit us one day, visit us one day," they begged.

The mole was visibly moved. "Doant 'ee fret, little bat uns. Thiz yurr mole'll see 'ee sumtime."

Log-a-Log gave final instructions as to the care and maintenance of the gate. All three then stood for a moment in the awkward silence that often marks the parting of friends. Martin was about to say that Gonff would have composed a ballad for the occasion, but he turned away with a sigh. Adjusting the sword hilt about his neck, he faced the outer world.

They began the sloping descent with Lord Cayvear's whispered farewell in their ears.

"Our spirit flies with you. May you find what you quest for, what you quest for."

The going proved not too difficult. They dug their paws into the loose scree and shale, half-walking, half-sliding.

"If only Gonff were here," Martin could not help remarking. "He'd remember the exact words of the Skyfurrow poem. Let me see, now. 'Land lost in mist and gray-brown treachery'— or something like that. I can't recall it properly."

Dinny braked himself against a boulder. "Nay, nor do oi. Proper owd pudden 'eads us be, hurr hurr."

Log-a-Log took a chunk of rock and tossed it outward. It fell down into the mist, vanishing completely.

"Usually some kind of swamp or marshland under mist like that. We'd best keep our wits about us down there," he warned.

It was midday when they finally reached the bottom-land. The mist was dense and high above their heads. It blocked out the sky, leaving the travelers in a world of swirling fog. Dark squelchy moss and slimy weeds carpeted the ground, dotted with wide areas of evil-smelling fungus. Here and there small rivulets ran, as if trying to find a way out of this oppressive region.

Dinny gazed into the mist. "Yurr, be that summat moven over yon?"

They stopped to peer. Log-a-Log rubbed his eyes. "It might be. Then again, it might be the mist playing tricks. If you let your imagination run away with you, all sorts of shapes start popping up."

The travelers leaned against a large humped rock to take their noon meal. Martin broke off some bread. "I've got the strangest feeling that we're being watched," he said, chewing as he spoke.

Dinny tapped the rock. "Diggen claw be a-tellen oi that too, Marthen."

Suddenly, behind them, six huge toads bearing the ends of a twisted reed net leaped from the top of the rock. Passing right over the travelers' heads, they landed square on the ground, neatly trapping the three friends tightly underneath the net.

One toad poked a trident at them.

"Krryoik glogflugg glumbatt. Catchincaught threehere!"

Tsarmina pushed her party hard into the fastnesses of Mossflower. She halted frequently to sniff the earth or trace the pawprints in soft ground.

"No mistake, this is them, all right. Look here: my traitor brother, carrying something heavy, by these deep prints. Keep going. Dawn can't be too far off; we'll give those woodlanders a breakfast they won't forget."

High in a tree above Tsarmina's force, Barklad the squirrel sat muttering to himself, "Too many heads to count. Looks like most of Kotir has been mobilized to track us down."

He vaulted off across the high green terraces to make his report.

Cludd pointed with his spear. "Blood spots, Milady."

The wildcat Queen inspected sticky dark red flecks brushed off on the leaves of a lilac bush.

"Otter. That must be the one who tricked us into thinking he was a fox—Patchcoat. He took the arrow that was meant for Gingivere."

Cludd ground his teeth. "Patchcoat, eh? I want that one myself, wounded or not. He's wearing my Captain's cloak."

Tsarmina pushed onward. "Take who you please, but Gingivere's mine. Leave him to me," she ordered.

The soldiers marched forward confidently, made brave by sheer weight of numbers.

Not far from Camp Willow, the ancient gnarled tree that was its namesake bent lithe boughs over the clear flowing river. Beneath its branches the dawn light filtered through onto the party who had gathered round the last resting place of the Mask. Smooth river boulders in a cairn marked the spot; flowers and decorated otter slings were laid on the grave in tribute to a fallen comrade.

Skipper sighed heavily, turning away to join Lady Amber, who was listening to Barklad's report. Cold fury had overtaken the otter leader's grief; at his insistence there would be none but otters to face the oncoming hordes of Kotir. Lady Amber wisely acceded to her friend's wishes, but not before she had outlined a few plans of her own.

"Do what you have to, Skipper, and good luck to you. The whole of Kotir is abroad in Mossflower, so be careful. However, this is an opportunity we must not miss. I have sent messengers to Brockhall. No doubt the Foremole and his crew would welcome a chance to inspect Kotir while the cat's away. I will take my force to make sure they get there and back in safety. Agreed?"

Skipper greased his sling with slippery bark and checked the rows of dangerous-looking otter javelins sticking point down into the bank.

"Agreed!"

Ashleg was first to sight the river, heavily swathed in morning mist from bank to bank.

"We've been here before, Milady," he reminded her. "This is where we lost Gloomer. Surely this isn't where they have their headquarters?"

The Queen of the Thousand Eyes peered into the mists ahead. "No matter. This is where the trail leads; here is where they'll be. What's that?"

Cludd stood forward brandishing his spear. "It's that otter,

Milady. Look, the insolent hound is still wearing my cloak. Let me at him!"

Tsarmina nodded toward the spectral figure that stood wreathed in the mists.

"Get to it, Cludd," she commanded. "Obviously they know we've been following. I'll check around for surprises. We won't be fooled a second time. Oh and Cludd—"

"Yes, Milady?"

"See you finish the job properly, if you want to wear that cloak as a Captain again."

Hefting his spear Cludd advanced on the cloaked figure. "You just leave it to me, Majesty. Right, Patchcoat, let's settle this once and for all," he challenged.

Skipper stepped out of the tendrils of mist, shedding the cloak. "I'm ready for you, weasel. The one you called Patchcoat was my brother. You're not fit to lick his paws. I will give you your cloak back to take with you to the gates of Dark Forest; they have a special place for cowards there."

Stung by the insult, Cludd bellowed with rage as he charged.

Skipper allowed himself a grim smile of satisfaction. Flexing his powerful limbs, he hurled himself like an uncoiling spring at the oncoming weasel. Disregarding weapons, the two creatures locked together on the ground, snarling and tearing at each other like savage beasts.

Martin, Dinny and Log-a-Log struggled helplessly, floundering about in the net like fish out of water. The more they moved, the tighter they were entwined. Martin realized this, and lay still.

"I am Martin the Warrior," he called out. "These are my friends Dinny and Log-a-Log. Why have you done this to us? We mean you no harm. We are only travelers passing through. Turn us loose, please."

The toads turned to each other. They made unintelligible clicking and golloping noises, seeming to find the whole business highly amusing. Their leader jabbed warningly at the captives. "Krrrglug, yukyuk! Quiet-now, furmouse. Dampwatch-say comenow."

The prisoners were dragged unceremoniously along the muddy ground. Other toads came out of the mist to join the procession. When they finally reached their destination, the captives were surrounded by a veritable army of the creatures.

The leader threw the net ends over a stake driven into the ground. He spread his webbed claw membranes. "Krrplok! Seehere, onemole twomouse, Marshgreen saywhat?"

Seated on a huge fungus carved into the likeness of a high throne was a toad bigger than the rest. Far more repulsive, too. It had no warts and was a slimy wet green color. Its great translucent eyes filmed over as it blinked at the captives. Fireflies danced in opaque plant-holders, and four more toads stood guard around the throne with tridents. The big toad gave an ungainly hop down to the ground and stood in front of the trio, blinking ceaselessly, its great wobbly throat pulsating.

"Krrklok! Goodfind, Dampwatch. Furmouse make-happy Marshgreen."

Martin decided that politeness was at an end. They were being treated like trophies. The warrior mouse's voice was loud and angry. "See here Marshgreen, or whatever they call you. You've no right to treat us like this. Now set us free, this instant!" he demanded.

The assembly of toads gave a bubbly cry of shock at the blatant disrespect to their ruler.

Marshgreen inflated his throat until it swelled like a balloon. His eyes bulged like button mushrooms.

"Splakkafrott! Mouthshut mousefur. Cheekybeast. Takethree, throwin Screamhole."

The company of toads waddled and hopped excitedly, brandishing their tridents. "Krrrplakoggle! Screamhole, throwin Screamhole!"

"Look over there," Log-a-Log whispered to Martin. "I might have known it wouldn't be spring without those two weeds sprouting again."

It was the newt and the grass snake, Whipscale and Deathcoil. The unsavory pair saw they were noticed and grinned wickedly.

"D'you fancy standing on my tail again, shrew?"

"Oho, you three are in for it now."

Dinny shook the net. "Goo boil yurr'eads, sloibeasts."

Deathcoil stood almost on the tip of his tail. "Not until we've seen you thrown into the Screamhole with the Snakefish."

Before they had a chance to find out what Deathcoil was talking about, the trio were dragged along in the net once more. The journey was not so long this time; it was far speedier because the net was hauled by many more toads.

• • •

They halted at what appeared to be an overgrown well. Its large circular bore disappeared deep into the earth. Thick ferns drooped about the edges, growing down into the pit.

Marshgreen came waddling up with the snake and the newt. They were flanked by toads carrying firefly lanterns on their trident forks.

"Krrpook! Snakefish feedwell, Marshgreen bringyou furmouse," the toad ruler called down the dark wellhole.

A toad presented Marshgreen with an elaborately carved trident. He jabbed it ceremoniously at the captives in the net, then jabbed it three times toward the well. The assembled toads flattened themselves against the ground, chanting, "Snakefish mightyone, stayin Screamhole, eatup furmouse, leavealone Dampwatch!"

Martin and his friends lay apprehensively listening as the chant grew louder. Suddenly it stopped. The toads holding the net spilled it open, tugging it backward vigorously.

Martin, Dinny and Log-a-Log were shot forward through the tracery of overhanging ferns. Deep into the Screamhole.

Tsarmina had detailed her archers to scatter volleys into the trees and brush in case of concealed woodlanders. They fired off a desultory salvo, then all else was forgotten as they broke off to watch the battle between Skipper and Cludd at the water's edge.

Jaws locked, the combatants rolled over and over. Loam and sand flew in all directions as they bit, grappled and kicked, raking each other with heavy claws. The very ground shook at their wildness. Fur hung on the dawn air. Blood spattered into the river.

It was not too long before Cludd realized he was outmatched by the power and fury of Skipper; now he was fighting for his life. The weasel tried to pull free from the maddened otter, but to no avail. His breath sobbed raggedly in his throat as he strained to reach the spear he had dropped in the first charge. Skipper, aware of what Cludd was up to, squirmed over, rolling him in the opposite direction to the weapon. Suddenly Cludd grabbed a pawful of sand and ground it into his opponent's eyes. Temporarily blinded, Skipper furiously tried to clear his vision, unwittingly freeing Cludd. Seizing his chance,

Cludd bounded up and snatched the spear. With a savage scream he charged at his floored adversary, leveling the point at Skipper's unprotected neck.

Through a sandy haze, Skipper saw the weasel coming. He rolled to one side. As he did, his paw came in contact with the Captain's cloak he had shed upon the bank. Sweeping it up and over in one continuous movement, the otter netted Cludd, head and haunches. Falling over backward, Skipper felt the breeze of the spearpoint pass his ear.

He thrust upward mightily. All four paws connected squarely with Cludd's body. The weasel shot high in the air, enveloped by the cloak, landing with a cry of shock. His fall had been broken upon the otter javelins that stood fixed in the ground.

Otter javelins are pointed at both ends!

Chaos broke loose. Tsarmina hurled her troops forward at Skipper. A band of otters broke cover, stopping them with javelins and slingstones. Skipper bounded gracefully tail over ears into the river, followed by his crew, who took the liberty of rattling a last furious salvo at the soldiers of Kotir. Pushed on by those behind, several of the front ranks spilled into the water.

Tsarmina was among the first to go headlong into the river. Panic overtook the wildcat as she floundered in the water. "Out, get me out," she screamed. "Quick, before they loose the pike!"

Hurriedly she was dragged up onto the bank.

Farther upstream, there was a barking laugh of victory as Skipper's head broke the surface. "The weasel got his cloak back, cat. It's pinned to him."

The river closed with a swirl on the last of the otters. Tsarmina raced up and down the bank, snatching spears from her soldiers, hurling them vindictively at the water.

"Come out, woodlanders, stand and fight!" she challenged.

Brogg, the weasel companion of Cludd, had taken the opportunity of extracting the cloak from the javelins and his friend's body. He squatted at the river's edge, washing it through.

Few rips, bit of blood; still, it should clean up nicely, he thought.

Suddenly the cloak was being pulled into the water, dragging Brogg along with it. Ashleg kicked him soundly on the bottom.

"Leggo, fool. They've got the pike out."

Brogg had never let anything go so quickly.

Bella appeared on the opposite bank. "Stay out of our woods, cat," she said, pointing a blunt claw at Tsarmina. "Take your vermin away from Mossflower and leave us alone, or you will be defeated someday."

Tsarmina ran to the water's edge, but halted at the sight of a dorsal fin patrolling the river. Her voice was a hoarse scream.

"I am the Queen of the Thousand Eyes. I rule all Mossflower. One time I might have shown you mercy, but not now. This is war to the death—your death, badger! Archers!"

Before an arrow could be strung, Bella had gone.

31

The Screamhole was dark and slimy. Martin, Dinny and Log-a-Log landed with a splash in muddy water. The mole slipped upon a smooth bulky object.

"Yurr, wot be that?" he wondered aloud, as he spat out fetid water.

"Don't hang about down there, matey. Here, reach up and I'll give you a lift."

The voice belonged to Gonff!

Martin and his friends looked up. They could not see daylight or hear the toads. Above them was a hole in the pit wall; Gonff stood at its entrance, holding a firefly lantern in his paw. The little mousethief looked dirty and wet, but as cheerful as ever.

Martin was overjoyed. "Gonff, you old thief, is that really you?"

Their long-lost companion shook with silent mirth as he held up a cautionary paw. "Shush, matey. Not so loud. You'll wake up the big feller. Here, grab this vine and I'll pull you up."

Gonff hauled Martin up; together they pulled Log-a-Log and Dinny to safety. All three shook water from their coats and warmly hugged the little mousethief.

"Bring any rations with you, matey?" Gonff was hungry.

"Nay, 'ee toaden took'm all."

Gonff looked disgusted. "Oh, that warty lot. I might've known."

Log-a-Log sat in the dryest spot he could find.

"But how did you come to get down here?" he asked curiously. "We thought you were dead for sure when we lost you at the waterfall."

Gonff puffed his chest out indignantly. "Me, dead! Not likely. When I went over the falls I must have been washed right underneath the mountain by the currents. Next thing I knew, I woke up with the snake and the lizard standing over me. Foul reptiles, they'd bound me tail and paw. I was taken up in front of old Greenfrog, or whatever they call him. Huh, the filthy old swamphopper, he'd been listening to the snake and the lizard, and wanted to know where I'd hidden you three. Of course I told him to go and roast his fat green behind. That was when he lost his temper and had me chucked in here with old Snakefish."

"What's this Snakefish thing supposed to be?" Martin interrupted.

"Be? He's not supposed to be anything, matey. Snakefish is a giant eel. Big, you never saw the like. He's like a wriggling tree trunk. Here, watch this."

Gonff prised a rock loose from the clay. Leaning out, he hurled it at what looked like a smooth boulder sticking out of the water. In the dim light, the brown muddy mess churned, boiling, as thick coils looped and weaved, thrashing about with untold might.

Gonff shuddered. "That rascal nearly had me. I was saved by the vine hanging from this cave. Good job I'm a prince of climbers. I still keep checking the tip of my tail to make sure it's there—that's how close it was. Still, he's not a bad old sort, providing he keeps his distance. Oh yes, we've even had a conversation, Snakefish and me. He was the champion toad-scoffer in this part of the country, until they laid a trap for him and he fell in here. Poor old Snakefish can't get out now. Still, they keep him happy enough by slinging the odd enemy in here—the occasional fish, maybe a dead bird, passing travelers too, of course. Old Snakefish wallops the lot down, doesn't bother him."

Gonff leaned out, calling to the eel, "I said, it doesn't bother you, does it, big matey?"

The surface of the dim water parted with a whooshing up-heaval and the head of Snakefish appeared. It was something out of a nightmare: thick, wide, silver-black, and the color of yellow ivory beneath. A massive slablike head hissed and swayed, revealing countless teeth, pure white and needlelike. Two savage jet eyes watched them with unblinking intensity. Coils of flexible steely muscle rippled and undulated with a life of their own.

Snakefish spoke.

"One day I will find my way out of here, then I will taste the toadflesh again."

Dinny saluted with his digging claw. "Let's 'ope 'ee do, zurr. You'm scoff a few for uz. 'Spect you'm passen fond of 'ee toaden."

Snakefish clouded his eyes dreamily. "Aaaaahhhh meeeee. There's nothing so tasty as a brace of plump toads. Unless it's two brace."

Log-a-Log shifted his paws nervously. "Er, right first time, sir. Look at us, all string and fur. Ugh! Why don't you slip out for a toad supper?"

Snakefish reared up, pushing his coils against the smooth walls of Screamhole. There was no purchase for the great eel. He slid back into the water.

"See, I have given up trying," he said sadly. "Each attempt only makes these walls more smooth and slippery. Strength alone is useless down here."

Martin had the glimmer of an idea forming in his mind. He decided to risk broaching the matter.

"Listen, Snakefish, I have a proposition to put to you. Supposing we helped you out of here, would you leave us to go our way in peace without harming us?"

The great head submerged momentarily, emerging again beneath the hole. Martin felt that if Snakefish really tried he could reach them. The eel slid back a little to reassure them.

"If you could free me, I would leave you to go at liberty where you will," the eel promised. "I would rather eat toad than mouse. Besides, I need to take my revenge on the tribe of Marshgreen. But you had better decide quickly; before the passing of another day I will need to eat. Do you understand me?"

The warrior mouse replied for them all.

"We understand perfectly, Snakefish. Now, will you leave

us alone while we formulate a plan. I'll give you a call the moment we are ready.''

The sinister giant slid noiselessly back into the murky waters.

Gonff giggled nervously. ''Right, mateys. Thinking caps on, or it's mouse, shrew and mole pie for dinner tomorrow.''

Kotir was deserted. The entire garrison had been mobilized to pursue the woodlanders.

Abbess Germaine and Foremole stood at the window of Tsarmina's high chamber, looking out over the forest.

They had discovered little. Kotir was as grim and mean as any self-respecting woodlander could imagine it—damp and oppressive, riddled with dank crumbling rooms and passages where feeble torches guttered fitfully against fungus and moss-clad masonry. As to supplies, it was useful to know that they were at a low ebb in the fortress.

Foremole tugged his snout reflectively. ''Hurr, marm. Baint even wurth a-carryen off they mangeful vittles.''

Moles and mice had searched the stronghold thoroughly; it was an empty carrion nest.

Columbine wandered through the deserted armory with Old Dinny. All the weapons had been taken off by the soldiers of Tsarmina.

The Loamhedge mouse curled her lip in disgust. ''Oh, what's the point of wandering around a filthy evil jumble like this?''

The venerable grandsire of Young Dinny was too busy carrying out his own research to answer. He sniffed the floor between paving cracks, tapped upon walls, dug his claws into rotten beams, all the while muttering to himself, ''Burr, oi'm getten a feelen in moi diggen claws 'bout this yurr fort'ication. Oi'm bound to 'ave a sniff round yon cells.''

Columbine went up to join the Abbess in Tsarmina's apartments. She could not help noticing the vast difference between the luxurious trappings of the Queen's quarters in contrast to the squalor of the barracks.

''Abbess, I think I'd sooner live wild in the woods than endure this dreadful place. Have you seen the way she treats her soldiers?''

The Abbess ran a thin paw over the tawdry hangings and stained rugs, which Tsarmina had spoiled in her rages. ''Yes, child. Now you know the difference between the way these animals live in comparison to honest woodlanders.''

Foremole had only one word to express his disgust: ''Durt-bags!''

The Abbess looked pensive; an idea was forming in her mind.

''Columbine, this place is deserted. Why couldn't we take it?''

''Goodness, is this our peaceful Abbess speaking?'' the young Loamhedge mouse replied, with a twinkle in her eye. ''Actually, I was thinking the same thing myself earlier. The answer is that we are not warriors, and our forces are split; the otters and squirrels are out in the woodlands. Besides, we would find ourselves in the position of being unarmed and without food supplies. How long could a little party like ours last out?''

The old mouse shook her head wonderingly. ''Goodness, is this our little Columbine speaking? Strategies, supplies, lack of weapons, divided forces . . . Maybe you missed your true vocation, young maid. Perhaps you would have fared better as an army commander. I bow to your superior military knowledge, General Columbine.''

The young mouse laughed heartily and curtsied.

Old Dinny came shuffling in. The Abbess noticed he was looking highly pleased about something.

''Hullo, Old Din. My, my, you've got a light in your eye.''

Columbine clapped her paws. ''Oh, you've found something. Do tell us, please!''

The old mole tapped a paw to his snout, winking broadly.

''Do you'ns foller oi now. Oi'll show 'ee a gurt new way outten thiz stink.''

Mystified, they followed him. As they walked, they talked, and Old Dinny imparted a plan to Columbine and the Abbess.

Lady Amber stood in the thickets with Barklad. Together they watched the east gate.

Amber tapped the ground impatiently. ''Where in the name of acorns have they got to?''

''Shall I take a party in and bring 'em out, marm?'' Barklad asked, noting her anxiety.

Amber looked up to the high chamber window. ''No, give it a little while yet. But I tell you, Bark, I don't like hanging about this place. Look, they've not even posted sentries or lookouts at the window. How are we supposed to let them know if the cat and her troops are on their way back? Oh, where have they got to?''

"Roight yurr be'ind 'ee, marm!''

Startled, the squirrel swung round. There was Foremole, the Abbess too, and Columbine—everyone that had gone into Kotir, down to the last mole and mouse.

"By the fur, where did you lot spring from?''

Columbine stroked her friend's gray head. "It was Old Dinny—he found a secret way out. We went beneath the cells. It's a sort of cavern with a lake in it. We, or should I say Grandpa Dinny, found a moving slab, and underneath it was a tunnel that traveled along for a while then went up. We followed it and came up into a hollow oak stump—that one right behind you.''

Lady Amber curled her tail in amazement. "Well, I'll be treebound!''

The Abbess gave a wry chuckle. "If we put your discovery together with Old Dinny's plan, we may have a final solution to the problem of Kotir.''

Columbine could not help interrupting. "I'll bet Gonff, Young Dinny and Martin will have the solution too when they return from their quest with Boar the Fighter.''

"No doubt they will, child,'' the Abbess nodded. "But they have been long gone. Who knows when they will return. Bella has said that it is a long journey fraught with danger. Besides, how do we know that Boar the Fighter still lives? I do not wish to alarm you by saying this, but, all things being equal, we must have plans of our own. Merely sitting waiting on Boar's return will not help Mossflower; we must all act to the best of our abilities. Wherever your Gonff is at this moment with Martin and the young mole, you can wager that they will be giving of their utmost. Let us hope that they will be both safe and successful in their quest.''

They made their way back to Brockhall that fine spring noon, unaware that they were passing on a parallel course to Tsarmina and her returning army.

The wildcat Queen was in a foul temper. "I wouldn't give a pawful of mouldy bread for the lot of you, standing gawping while your Captain gets slain by an otter.''

From somewhere in the jumbled ranks a voice murmured

impudently, "Huh, I noticed you didn't leap forward to help Cludd."

Tsarmina whirled on the troops in a fury. "Just let me catch the one who said that! You bunch of buffoons couldn't even get a single arrow off at that badger. Oh no, you stood there like a load of frogs catching flies."

As she turned to press on, the voice continued muttering, "Well, you've got the biggest bow. Why didn't you use it?"

Tsarmina grabbed her unstrung bow from the pine marten and flailed indiscriminately about her.

"Ashleg, I want that cheeky beggar found," she shrieked. "I'm the Queen, d'you hear? I'll make an example of whoever it is."

The pine marten dropped back. Marching at the rear, he bobbed up and down to see if he could catch the cheeky one unawares.

When the army straggled wearily back into Kotir at midday, Tsarmina's temper had not improved.

"Ashleg," she commanded. "Dismiss this load of nincompoops. Send them to their barracks. I'll be up in my chambers."

Ashleg was stumping his way round to the front when the voice was heard again.

"Oh, that's nice, lads. Wish I had comfy chambers instead of a damp barracks."

Tsarmina turned to confront the sea of blank faces, but she stifled her reply and contented herself by elbowing her way savagely through the ranks to the main door.

"Dinny, I was thinking—could you burrow upward through the side of this cave?"

The mole tested the walls with his digging claws.

"Loik as not, Marthen. But 'ee'd need diggen claws loik oi to foller upp'ard if we'n all t'get outten 'ere."

Martin patted his friend's velvety back. "Good mole, Din. We only need you to reach the surface, then you can lower something down so we can all climb out."

Dinny wiped his paws. "Stan' outten this yurr mole's way. Yurr go oi!"

With a mole's undoubted digging skills, Dinny was soon burrowing inward and upward.

Martin reported the plan to Snakefish as Log-a-Log and

Gonff backpawed the freshly dug earth out of the way into the pit below.

Night and day were of little consequence in the misty world of the marshes. The toads had lingered awhile on the edge of Screamhole, but there was little to see, and their enjoyment was marred by the fact that no screams issued from the well. One by one they drifted off, back to the Court of Marshgreen. Deathcoil and Whipscale stayed, however. They sat by the Screamhole, waiting to hear the cries of their foes as Snakefish did his grisly work.

The newt felt the stump of his new growing tail.

"What's happening down there? Has the Snakefish gone to sleep?" he snarled.

Deathcoil stretched leisurely on the ground. "Patience! Have you ever known any creature to escape what happens in the Screamhole? Snakefish is probably feeling sluggish from lying in that muddy water for so long. He'll liven up when the hunger drives him. You'll see. Sit down here and wait a bit."

The unsavory pair stretched out side by side.

They had been dozing for some considerable time when the earth beneath them began trembling.

Deathcoil pulled to one side, rearing up. "Did you feel that? The ground's shaking."

The newt scampered out of the trembling area. "Quick, let's get out of here."

His companion slithered behind. "No, wait, it's only in that one spot," he called out. "The ground is quite still over here. Let's get behind that rock and see what happens."

In a short while, two digging claws and a moist snout broke through the ground surface. Young Dinny emerged from the earth, shaking soil from his coat. Going to the edge of the Screamhole well, he called down, "Doant wurry, soon 'ave ee outen thurr, ho urr."

The spies behind the rock slithered away to inform Marshgreen and his toads of what they had seen.

Tsarmina slept heavily after the night spent in Mossflower Woods. The nightmare visited her dreams again; once more she was engulfed by cold, dark, rushing water. It flooded her senses as she fought feebly against the muddy engulfing tide that filled nostrils, ears and eyes. At the very moment when she felt all was lost and drowning was inevitable, she came awake with a start. Stumbling heavily, she slumped on the floor, pawing the solid stones to reassure herself. Stone was real; it was good. These stones belonged to her, Queen of the Thousand Eyes. She looked gratefully at the floor.

That was when she saw the pawprints in the dust.

Two mice and two moles!

Fortunately, Ashleg was halfway up the chamber stairs when he heard the Queen screeching his name. As quickly as his wooden limb would allow, he hopskipped the remainder of the distance. Bursting into the chamber, Ashleg found himself confronting a Tsarmina he had not encountered before. The wildcat sat on the floor, hunched up in a cloak that had once belonged to her father. She was rocking back and forth, gazing intently at the stone floor.

Ashleg closed the door and bowed apprehensively.

"Your Majesty?"

Tsarmina did not look up. "Mice and moles. Search this room for mice and moles."

"Immediately, Milady."

Ashleg did not stop to question the order. Knowing how dangerous Tsarmina's mood could become, he set about the task. Peering into cupboards, looking beneath the table, behind the wall hangings and drapes, the pine marten searched the entire room thoroughly.

"No mice or moles here, Milady," he reported.

Tsarmina sprang up, pointing imperiously at the door. "Then go. Search the whole of Kotir!"

Ashleg saluted and hobbled swiftly to the door.

"No, wait!"

He halted, not sure of which way to turn next. Tsarmina was smiling at him. Ashleg gulped visibly as she put a paw about his shoulders.

"Ashleg, where is Gingivere?"

"He escaped, Majesty. You followed him yourself," he replied, puzzled.

"Oh, come now, you don't fool me," Tsarmina chuckled, almost good-naturedly. "First it was those two hedgehogs that escaped—but they didn't really, they were here all the time. Then there was the fox who was really an otter. Now my very

wn room is covered in the tracks of woodlanders. Come on,
ut with it, old friend, you can tell me.''

Ashleg began to be very frightened. ''Milady, I'm sorry, but
don't know what you're talking about. I'm only Ashleg. I
erved your father faithfully and now I obey and serve only
ou.''

Tsarmina smiled knowingly. ''Completely loyal to all my
amily, eh, Ashleg?''

''Oh yes, indeed, Milady.''

The murderous claws shot out, burying themselves into the
ine marten's shoulder through the feathered cape he wore.
sarmina's whiskers brushed against his face as she snarled,
''So, that's it. You're helping my brother now. Gingivere never
eally escaped, did he? It was all a trick. He's still here with
hose woodlanders. They're turning my army against me.
Maybe he was with me all the time I was in the forest looking
or him. Ha, he's a sly one, that brother of mine. I'll bet it was
im who pushed me into the water when the otters loosed the
ig pike . . . Ugh!''

Ashleg's face was a mask of frozen agony. The claws dug
leeply in him, blood was staining his cloak.

Suddenly Tsarmina released him and scrubbed furiously at
erself with the cloak she was wearing.

''Uuuuuhhhh, deep, cold, slimy, dark water,'' she muttered
ncoherently.

Ashleg backed quietly out of the chamber. The wildcat was
oblivious to his departure; she was battling the watery torrents
n her imagination.

As the pine marten hobbled swiftly down the stairs, his
Queen's ravings echoed about the spiral stairwell.

''Stay away! Stay away! You won't get me. I won't come
near the water.''

Ashleg's mind was made up: he could not stop a moment
onger. Tsarmina was a mad Queen. Kotir was a place of danger
o those who stayed there.

The late afternoon sun poured down over the ramparts of Kotir.
Silence made it frightening to the departing Ashleg; the large
areas of dark shadow and sunlit stillness unnerved him. He had
cast aside the plumed scarlet cape, exchanging it for a dull
brown homespun cloak. Hurrying across the deserted parade
ground, Ashleg slipped through the gates and began walking

south—away from Tsarmina, Mossflower and dreams of ambitious conquest. Maybe there was somewhere under a different sky where he could find a new way of life; maybe somewhere there were friends waiting who knew how to live simply, without delusions of grandeur.

Perched in his high spruce, Argulor opened one eye. Never too proud to scavenge, the eagle had satisfied his hunger with the results of the confrontation at the river. Argulor's eye closed again lazily. Feeling full and tired, he slept on in the mistaken hope that everything comes to him who waits.

Ashleg had flown the coop; that is, if a pine marten with a wooden leg does ever fly.

Dinny counted himself lucky. He had found the woven rush net that had carried them to Screamhole. Securing one end to a tree root, he pushed the remainder over the edge of the pit.

"Yurr below, grab'n 'old of 'ee net, Marthen."

Unfortunately the net fell short of the travelers' grasp.

From above, the mole's voice was calling urgently, "Burr, 'asten now. Oi 'ears they toadbags a-cummen."

Gonff jumped up and down with frustration. "Think of something quick, mateys!"

Snakefish poked his massive head up. "Sit on my head. I think I can reach it!"

"What? Not likely!" Log-a-Log backed into the cave.

"Urry, they'm nearly yurr!" Dinny called.

Sitting at the edge of the cave, Martin placed his paws on the huge reptilian head and braced himself against the skull ridge beneath the smooth skin.

"Push me up, Snakefish!"

The great eel thrust upward, slid back slightly, then with a colossal effort reared out of the water and shot up like a bolt. Martin grasped the net, keeping his purchase on the eel's head.

"Quick, bite!"

Snakefish's teeth clamped onto the bottom of the net. He hung there a moment, then began bunching his coils, the rough underskin finding contact with the fibers as he weaved his sinuous body into the meshes of the net.

Martin pulled upward. Snakefish secured himself, and called, "I can make it easily. Show yourselves, you two below. I'll loop my bottom coils around you and lift you up with me."

Log-a-Log and Gonff stood clutching each other, their eyes

shut tightly as they felt themselves enveloped in steely coils and lifted effortlessly.

Marshgreen and his toads loomed out of the cottony mists. Three of them waddled forward, trying to capture Dinny as the mole flayed about with heavy digging claws.

"Gurr, 'ee doant cum near oi, sloimy toadbags," he warned.

Deathcoil and Whipscale noticed too late the net fastened at the edge of the Screamhole. Martin came leaping over the edge, loosing stones from his sling, fast and accurate. He bounced a rock off Marshgreen's head, knocking him flat.

Gurgling screams of horror greeted the next arrival from the pit. The head of Snakefish appeared, dripping like some primeval monster from the abyss, slitted eyes and white rows of teeth confronting the terrified assembly.

"Toadflesh!" With a bunching serpentine motion, the slayer of the swamps pulled himself clear of the pit, shedding his passengers in the same movement.

Gonff and Log-a-Log sprang up, battling despite their bruised ribs. Pandemonium took over as Snakefish struck like a thunderbolt into the nearest group of toads. Regardless of tridents and firefly lanterns, the giant eel went about the business of satisfying his immense hunger.

Martin turned away, sickened by the grisly spectacle.

"Are you all right, Din?" he called anxiously. "Quick, Gonff, Log-a-Log. Let's get out of here right now."

Gonff stared wildly into the mists. "Aye, but which way, matey?"

"Hoo arr, this'n 'll show 'ee." Young Dinny had a fierce headlock on the groggy Marshgreen.

Martin grabbed a trident and poked the toad Chief.

"Good mole, Din. Come on, you. Lead the way due west, or I'll stick you on this oversized dinner fork and feed you to Snakefish."

Marshgreen waddled off pleading mournfully, "Krrgloik! Mousefur notkill Marshgreen, showyou waytogo."

In a short space of time they were blanketed on all sides by a mist so heavy it drowned out even the far-off squeals of Snakefish's victims.

Log-a-Log watched the green bulk of the toad waddling ahead. "Well, at least he seems to know which way to go. What's next in your rhyme, Gonff?"

Without hesitation Gonff reeled off Olav Skyfurrow's lines,

O feathered brethren of the air,
Fly straight and do not fall,
Onward cross the wet gold flat,
Where seabirds wheel and call.

Martin prodded Marshgreen lightly with the trident. "Do you
know that place?"

The defeated toad Chief turned, blinking his eyefilms.
"Krrploik! Notfar notfar, shorebad, seabird eatyou eatme."

Martin leaned on the trident. "Oh, stop moaning, Greenbot-
tom. We'll let you go when we're free of this mist. Though
it's more than you deserve."

Eventually they reached a clear running stream. They drank
some water while Dinny dug up edible roots.

"Gurr, rooten. They baint no deeper'n ever pie, no zurr."

Gonff perched on a rock. "Don't worry, matey. If we ever
come out of all this in one piece, I'll steal the biggest pie in
all Mossflower, just for you."

Dinny closed his eyes dreamily. "Urr, a roight big'n an' all
furr this yurr mole."

Gonff broke into song.

It will be great, I'll watch you, mate,
And you can dive right in.
But don't sing with your mouth full,
'This pie is all for Din.'
A crust as light as thistledown,
And filled with all you dream:
Fresh vegetables, the best of fruit,
All floating round in cream.

Dinny lay upon his back, waving stubby paws. "O joy, O
arpiness, an' all fur oi, 'ee say."

The trek was long and wearisome; time stood still in the land
of the mists. Martin longed to see natural daylight again, be it
bright and sunny, or clouded and rainy.

They were negotiating a particularly soggy stretch of ground
when Log-a-Log remarked to Gonff, "Here, d'you reckon
things have gone a bit darkish?"

Gonff jumped onto a tussock of dry reeds. "That's prob'ly because nighttime's coming on, matey."

Martin pointed. "Look, I can see the sky."

Sure enough, the mists were beginning to thin. Pale evening sky was plainly visible from where they stood.

Gonff made a further discovery. "See, on the other side of this grass, there's sand. Looks like miles of the stuff."

Hurriedly they jumped onto the tussock to confirm Gonff's sighting. Behind them, Marshgreen picked up the trident and waddled off, back into his domain of swamp and mist.

The questors gazed in wonder at the scene before them. On the horizon the sun was sinking in a sheen of pearl gray and dusty crimson. Martin's paw shot up, pointing northwest. "Look, the flames of Salamandastron!"

32

That same evening, the Corim assembled in the main room of Brockhall. There was much to be discussed. Goody Stickle bustled about laying the table, with Coggs firmly attached to her apron strings. The little hedgehog did not complain; besides, speaking through a mouthful of hot acorn scone dripping with fresh butter and damson jam was not quite the form for budding warriors and daring escapers. He waved in passing to Ferdy, who was seated in a deep armchair with Ben Stickle.

Between bites of his scone, Ferdy related a highly colored version of their adventures.

"So me and Coggs broke the door down and pounced on these three weasels—or was it stoats? No, they were weasels. Anyhow, there was six of them, great ugly vermin. Hoho, did we ever give them what for! The wildcat Queen was there, but she took one look at us and ran away. Good job, too! D'you know, Ben, me and old Coggs there, we had to carry four squirrels off through the trees—or was it otters? No, it was squirrels, I'm sure. Saved them from those Kotir soldiers, though."

Ben Stickle wiped jam and crumbs from Ferdy's mouth.

"Must have made the pair of you powerful hungry. You

haven't done anything but eat since you got back, except talk, that is. Are you sure you never chattered any of those stoats to death?"

When the table was laid, silence fell as Bella entered the room.

"My hall is your home," she said. "Please fill your platters and eat the excellent food. Thank you, Goody Stickle, for this splendid table."

There was an immediate clatter of serving and good humor.

"Pass that deeper 'n' ever pie. Mind you don't fall in."

"Hoho, is that leek and onion broth I smell?"

"Mmm, fruit pie. Ouch, it's hot!"

"Here, cool it down with some of this cream."

"Pass the butter, please."

"Nut pudding! My old mum used to make this."

"Aye, I remember Gonff pinching it from her oven."

"Hahaha. Here, have a go at this quince and apple crumble."

"Hey, who's used all the cream?"

"I say, Goody, you must give me the recipe for your plum pudding."

"Ask your gran—she gave it to me."

"Now, which will I have, October ale, cider or buttermilk?"

"None. You're fat enough, Ben Stickle."

A pleasant time was passed eating the celebratory supper.

When the dishes were cleared away, Abbess Germaine stood up.

"Pray silence for our host," she called.

Bella took the floor. "Where are Ferdy, Coggs, Spike and Posy?"

Ben pointed in the direction of the dormitory. "Well abed and snorin' like champions, marm."

Bella bowed her head. "Then let us give a moment of silence and thought to the memory of a very brave otter, the Mask, without whom none of tonight's joy would have been possible."

A respectful silence followed, broken only by an audible sniff from Skipper.

Bella took a sip of buttermilk, then she wiped her eyes on the back of a heavy paw.

"Now to business. First let me say it has been a good day in many ways, mainly because Ferdy and Coggs are back safe

with us. Also because we have a new friend in our midst—
Gingivere. I am sure you will all join me in saying that our
home is his for as long as he chooses to stay here.''

"Thank you, Bella, and you too, my friends. But this cannot
be,'' he said sadly. "Tsarmina is a very dangerous creature;
my presence here would only endanger you all. I would never
forgive myself if any of you suffered because of me. Tonight
I will stay with you, but tomorrow I will leave at first light to
go eastward through Mossflower, far away from Kotir and all
it stands for. I could not stay here, knowing that I would be
adding to your problems. If Tsarmina knew that I was here
with you, she would go mad for revenge on us all, and who
knows what evils her dark mind could think up. Somewhere
beyond Mossflower I will make a fresh start. Thank you for all
your help and kindness. All my life, wherever I am, I will carry
the memory of my woodland friends deep in my heart. If the
time should arrive when I can return the good treatment you
have shown me, then rest assured, you will not even have to
ask. I will help in any way possible, for I owe the woodlanders
of Mossflower a deep debt of gratitude.''

The wildcat sat down amid silence, which suddenly gave
way to loud applause for his noble words.

Ben Stickle shook him firmly by the paw.

"Mr. Gingivere, sir, it'll break Ferdy an' Coggs' liddle 'earts
to know you've gone away. But one day I'll tell 'em when
they're old enough to understand. Thankee for looking after
my liddle 'ogs, sir.''

Bella banged upon the table.

"As you are aware,'' she continued, "our friends from
Loamhedge and the Foremole's crew risked life and limb to
find out about Kotir. Old Dinny, I believe you have something
to tell us?''

The ancient mole tugged his snout to Bella, then spread a
barkcloth scroll across the table.

"Hurr, now this yurr's Koateer, see. We'm been a commen
an' goen all the wrong ways. See yurr, this'n's a map of b'low
cells. They's a gurt cave an' lake under Koateer, also a tunnel
wot'll lead 'ee out into an 'ollow stump in woods.''

There were murmurs of wonderment from the onlookers. Old
Dinny rapped a digging claw on the tabletop.

"Foremole an' oi bin a-plannen. 'Ee'll tell about it; oi baint
one furr speechen.''

Foremole threw up his paws and announced in a clear no-nonsense tone, "Fludd 'er out. Charmania woant stay in no floaten 'ouse."

Hubbub broke out. Columbine rushed to Foremole's side, waving the scroll aloft.

"Please, listen to what I have to say," she shouted over the noise.

Abbess Germaine looked proudly at her ward as she began to speak.

"I was with Foremole and Old Dinny when we made the plan. Let me explain. First, it relies on the fact that Kotir lies in a land depression. Mossflower Woods itself is actually on much higher ground. The moles have studied the landfall."

Columbine laid the scroll out, pointing at two areas of the table as if referring to a larger map.

"Over here and over here, the River Moss runs on a northeast course through the woods, then takes a sharp bend to the west. Sometime in the past there must have been a large lake where Kotir now stands, but this dried up when the river changed its course. We have since found the remains of that lake in the cave beneath Kotir."

Lady Amber did not see the point. "But how does that help us, Columbine?"

"Let the maid tell it," Skipper whispered in her ear. "I think I've guessed the plan, though."

"If the moles were to dig from where the river is closest to Kotir," Columbine continued, "they could make flood tunnels from the banks of the River Moss down to the lowland and straight into the cave beneath Kotir."

Realization dawned upon Lady Amber. "Then the old lake bed would fill up again!"

Excited shouts rang out.

"They'd be flooded!"

"Kotir would sink beneath the lake!"

"Good riddance too, I say!"

Skipper bounded up onto the table. "If we can make sluice-gates, me and my crew will sink them on the riverbank to hold the water back until the tunnels are complete."

Lady Amber leaped up beside him. "Leave it to the squirrels, Skip. We'll build your floodgates. You just see to it that they're sunk properly into the banks."

Foremole was not the greatest of leapers, but he clambered up on the table besides Amber and Skipper.

"Ho urr, an' us moles'll dig 'oles. We'll tunnel for 'ee, boi 'okey, us will!"

Columbine thought the cheering and paw-thumping would never stop. All around her, woodlanders were dancing, hugging each other and whooping at the top of their lungs.

Bella had to pound the table for a long time until order was restored.

"Congratulations, Corim. I think it is a good plan," she announced. "Best of all, it will save open warfare and loss of life. Now, does every creature present agree to the plan?"

There was a mass shout of approval. Every paw in the room shot up.

"Aye!"

"Then we shall carry out this plan. We must, for I fear that Martin and his friends are long overdue on their return. Having said that, I do not wish any of you to feel downhearted, for who can calculate the journey to and from Salamandastron? We must hope and keep the faith in our friends' promise to carry out their mission. Maybe one day not too far from now I will see my father, Boar the Fighter, come striding through Mossflower Woods—along with Martin, Young Dinny, and Gonff—to lead us to victory. Wherever the questers and my father are this day, let us wish them good fortune."

A rousing cheer rang through Brockhall as Bella sat down and crossed paws with the Corim leaders.

Abbess Germaine had the final word at this meeting.

"Yes, friends, good fortune to those who traverse afar and good fortune to us all. I think the plan is a good one," the frail old mouse told the assembly. "Even I and my brothers and Loamhedge, unused to fighting and war, can see that this will avoid unnecessary bloodshed on both sides, for friend and foe alike. A death is always a death. Bloodshed is an awful thing. What we are striving for is peace—keep this thought uppermost in your minds. If I had a wish, it would be that we lived in harmony with those at Kotir. But this cannot be. So let me say again, good fortune to the lovers of peace and right. Let liberty and freedom be the legacy that we leave to those who follow us in the seasons to come. May they find true peace in Mossflower."

There was a reverent silence for what was, indeed, a heartfelt prayer.

• • •

The four travelers were hungry.

They had risen before dawn and were on their way through the low sand dunes where little else grew but tough sand grass. Belts were tightened after the previous night's meager supper of a few roots which Dinny had managed to forage. The mole tried digging in the sand for edible material. He rubbed grit from his eyes with weary paws.

"Gurr, baint no gudd diggen in this sloidy sarnd. Moight as well try diggen 'oles in a river."

Gonff wiped a dry paw across his mouth. "I'm thirsty more than anything, mateys. What I wouldn't give for a good old beaker of cold cider right now."

Martin trekked on doggedly. "Look, it's no good going on about what we haven't got. We'll just have to keep our eyes peeled until food comes along. Here, let me show you an old warrior trick my father taught me." He rummaged some smooth pebbles from his sling pouch. "Try sucking one of these. I know it isn't as good as a drink, but a pebble will keep your mouth moist and stop you drying up."

Being woodlanders, they were not used to traveling through soft sand. Even Log-a-Log, who had made such a journey before, found the constant sinking of paws into dry shifting grit very tiring. All four soon sat exhausted on top of a dune. Martin picked up some sand. Letting it run through his paws, he scanned the distance to where the mass of rock stood, but there was no light issuing from it in daytime.

Gonff spoke his thoughts aloud. "There stands Salamandastron, mateys. And here we sit, as far away from it as ever. Not a crust nor a drink between us, and sand all round. It's certainly hard going."

Log-a-Log stood up, brushing his fur free of sand.

"Wait here. I've traveled in sand before. I may be able to help."

He scrambled off among the dunes.

Dinny scooped a small hole. He watched it fill up again. "Moi ol' granfer Dinny'd never b'lieve thiz, stan' on moi tunnel."

Martin stretched out upon the dune. "Well, at least we've come this far. Don't worry, mates. We'll make it somehow."

Log-a-Log returned carrying four thick pieces of wood—branches he had found at the edge of the dunes.

"Here, trim these up," he told them. "They'll make good walking staves to help us through the sand."

They set about trimming the branches with teeth, claws and knives.

Then they set off again. With the staves, the going was slightly better. Every once in a while they spotted a small toad or a frilled newt from a distance, but the creatures would either ignore them or scuttle off among the sandhills. There was also the odd small bird, which had to be shooed off with staves when it became too inquisitive.

Log-a-Log found some soft grass with a milky sap, and they chewed it as he conjectured what lay ahead.

"Pretty soon we'll be out of these dunes and onto the firm sand. Maybe then I'll find something to eat. No water, though. Trouble is that most things on the shore taste salty, and that makes you want water even more. Oh, test the sand with your staves as we go. Here and there you may find sinking sands. Watch out for those big seabirds too—gulls and such. They'll gobble up anything at all. Show them you're not afraid; whack out at them with your staves, then they'll leave you alone. Now, if you see any pools of water, don't drink from them—it's all seawater, full of salt, tastes very nasty. One last thing, stick together and don't wander off."

"That all, nothing else?" Gonff laughed and waved his staff. "Good, then what are we lagging for?"

To their amazement, the mousethief skipped off singing,

> I mustn't drink the water,
> And there may be nought to eat.
> Those gulls may see a mousethief
> As just a tasty treat.
> I step out bravely on the quest,
> Across this funny land,
> And when I disappear they'll say,
> 'He's found the sinking sand.'

"Nothing keeps our Gonff down for long," Martin laughed. "Come on, let's press on."

They came out of the dunes at midafternoon. Before them stretched the shore: flat solid sand, dotted with small rocky outcrops. The sun glinted like gold leaf on the shimmering sea.

Log-a-Log ignored it and walked on. His three companions, however, could not help stopping momentarily to stare in awe at the distant reaches of mighty water. It staggered the imagination of woodlanders who had never witnessed such a spectacle.

Dinny could scarce credit his first sight of the sea.

"Hurr, oi sees it, but oi doant berleeve it. Whurr do it all cum from, Gloglog?"

"They say it's always been there," the shrew shrugged. "Like the sky and the ground. See this sand here with ridges on it like little waves? Well, that's where the tidewater comes up to. You'll probably see it flooding in soon. Keep your paws on the smooth sand, here, this side of all these shells and suchlike. That's called a tideline."

Dinny was fascinated with the shells. He picked lots of them up; when he could carry no more he would throw them away and start his collection afresh.

Without warning, a black-headed gull swooped down at them. All four fell flat upon the sand. Log-a-Log lashed out with his staff, catching it on the beak, and as it soared away, Martin hit it hard on the wing with a sling stone.

The gull wheeled, screaming angrily, then more seagulls flew in to investigate. Soon the four friends were hard-pressed defending themselves against aerial invaders.

Waving his staff at an oystercatcher, Martin called to Log-a-Log, "I thought you said they'd go away if we showed 'em we weren't afraid of seabirds?"

Log-a-Log thwacked a common gull across its webbed claws.

"You can never tell with these birds. Quick, let's make a run for it. There's some rocks over yonder!"

Waving their staves furiously, they dashed along the beach to where a rocky outcrop thrust up from the sand. Finding a fissure between the rocks, they huddled in together.

The gulls wheeled and circled awhile, screeching threateningly, diving toward the rocks, but sheering off at the last moment. Finally they gave up and flew off in search of other, easier prey.

Martin poked his head out into the open. "All clear, they've gone now," he reported.

Log-a-Log climbed swiftly to the top of the rocks. "Look, mates—a rock pool. Get the fishing tackle out."

Locked tightly in by the rocks there was a beautiful miniature lake of deep seawater, crystal clear. They sat on the edge, gazing into the colorful depths.

"Look, there's shrimp, just like Skipper and the crew get from the River Moss," Gonff exclaimed. "What's that, Log-a-Log?"

"Where? Oh, that. I think it's called a starfish. Not very good to eat, though. See here, attached to the rock? These are limpets. They're a bit chewy to eat, but they'll keep us going."

Dinny shook his head. "Nay, Gloglog, them's shells loik 'ee picken up out of sarnd."

The mole was surprised when Log-a-Log managed to prise one loose with his knife. He scooped the flesh out and cut it up, giving them each a portion.

"Chew on this," he invited them. "Go on, it's not poison."

Gonff pulled a face at the unappetizing limpet flesh, but bravely he popped it into his mouth and began chewing.

"Tastes very salty," he commented. "I bet you could chew this until next harvest came around and it'd still be bouncing off your teeth. Best swallow it in one gulp."

Martin found some seaweed that tasted quite mild.

"Hey, try some of this! It's like Goody's cabbage with a bit too much salt on. Not bad though."

Between them, they explored the different tastes of rock pool vegetation. The shrimp were proving too difficult to catch, though Gonff sat determinedly, his line hanging in the water, baited with a piece of limpet. Gradually it was taken by something which pulled it beneath an underwater ledge.

"Haha, mateys, I've got a bite," he shouted excitedly. "Look out, here comes supper!"

Assisted by Martin, he pulled and tugged at the line. Finally they hauled up a small spidery object with a soft shell and two tiny claws.

"Throw it back. It's a crab!" Log-a-Log called urgently to them.

Martin took hold of the small crab as Gonff tried to unlatch its claws from the segment of bait. There was a scrabbling and clattering noise at the poolside, and a huge carapace emerged.

Log-a-Log slashed the line with his knife, leaving the baby crab to enjoy the bait.

The water splashed away, displaced by a considerable bulk.

Four blackish-gray armored legs clawed their way over the edge of the rock.

It was a fully grown crab!

The monster stood in front of them, its eyes roving hither and thither on long stalks. Two large plates opened, revealing a downward-slanting mouth that shed water and gaped open at them. But it was the creature's claws that caused the most concern. Large powerful pincers, held high, snapping open and shut with a noise like steel hitting stone, they were studded with horny nodules that resembled teeth.

"Back off. Don't try to fight it, you'll lose," Log-a-Log said, not taking his eyes from the angry crab. "Keep backing off until we're on the sand. Then we'll really have to run for it. Crabs can scuttle sideways very fast."

They retreated carefully. The big crab blew a bubble from its mouth, lowered its claws, snapped them viciously at the intruders and charged like lightning.

Now that Cludd was gone, Tsarmina needed a new Captain of the Guard, so she promoted Brogg the weasel.

At first Brogg enjoyed his position of power. But of late he was sorry he had ever donned the cloak of Captaincy, particularly when he was called up to be interviewed by the Queen in her chambers.

"Brogg, I made you Captain. You must find Gingivere. He has kidnapped Ashleg."

"Yes, Majesty."

"Find yourself another Captain. That stoat, Ratflank—he'll do," she suggested. "I want you to go through the entire army one by one."

"Go through the army, Milady?" he asked, puzzled.

"Yes, jellybrains. You and Ratflank take them one by one to the cells."

"Yes, Milady."

"Will you stop interrupting me and listen! All anyone ever says around here is 'yes, Milady' or 'no, Milady'."

"Yes, Milady."

"Shut up!" Tsarmina shouted irritably. "Get them one by one in a cell, pull their whiskers, then check their fur. Is their tail their own tail?"

"Er, is it, Milady?"

"That's what I want you to find out, nitwit."

"Oh yes. But why, Milady?"

Tsarmina paced the room, her voice rising to a cracked crescendo. "Because one of them is Gingivere in disguise, you clod. He's here, in my fortress, plotting against me. Get out and find him!"

Later Brogg sat at a barrack room table, joined by Ratflank and several other cronies. They were reduced to eating hard bread and woodland plants. Brogg sipped from a flagon.

"Huh, at least there's still a drop of cider left. I tell you, mates, the Queen has definitely taken a funny turn."

"Oh, I don't know," Ratflank smirked. "She's still got the sense to recognize a good stoat when she sees one. Look at me, I'm a Captain now."

One of the ferrets spat out a moldy crust.

"Is that some kind of ceremony you carried out, Brogg?" he asked.

"What ceremony, what are you talking about, Dogfur?"

"Well, the way you took Ratflank down to the cells and twitched his whiskers, then you pinched his fur and twitched his tail before you gave him the Captain's cloak."

"Oh no. Matter of fact, you've all got to have it done."

"What, you mean we're all going to be made Captains?"

"Caw, I wish old Lord Greeneyes was here now, mates," Brogg sighed gloomily as he cupped his head in his paws. "Or even the other one, Gingivere."

Warm sunrays cascading through the leaves mingled in harmony with the peace of Mossflower Woods. Somewhere a cuckoo was calling, and young ferns curled their tendril tops toward blossom on the bramble.

Gingivere had traveled east since early morning, never once turning his head to look back toward Brockhall. He sat with his back to a sycamore and opened the satchel of food given him by the woodlanders. The very sight of a homely oatcake brought a lump to his throat at the thought of the good friends he had left behind, especially of little Ferdy and Coggs.

With unshed tears bright in his eyes, Gingivere wrapped the food up. He continued walking east through the peaceful flowering forest.

33

Martin leaped to the fore as the crab came charging forward. "Hurry, get down to the sands," he shouted urgently. "I'll try to hold this thing off. Go on, get going!"

The three travelers would not run and desert their friend. They backed away slowly to the edge of the rocks, while Martin, facing the crab as a rearguard, followed them.

The crab would make a scurrying attack then back off, suddenly changing tack to shuffle in sideways. Not having time to use his sling, Martin hurled several well-placed stones at the maddened creature. They made a hollow clunking noise as they bounced off the tough crabshell. Each time it was hit, the crab would halt, pulling its eyes in on their long stalks. Holding one claw high and the other out level toward them, it advanced—for all the world like a fencer minus his sword. The huge claws opened and shut, clacking viciously.

From the top of the rocky outcrop where they stood to the sand below was a forbiddingly long drop. Log-a-Log teetered on the brink, shutting his eyes tight at the dizzy height. Without a second thought, Gonff grabbed the shrew's scrubby coat with one paw, held tight to Dinny's digging claw with the other, and jumped.

As Dinny felt himself being pulled from the smooth rock surface, he seized Martin's tail with his free digging claw.

The crab dashed forward, only to find its pincers nipping nothing. Clutching paw to fur to claw to tail, the travelers sailed out into midair and plummeted downward, narrowly missing the jutting rocks that projected from the main mass.

Bump!

They landed flat upon the beach sand with a dull thud that knocked the breath from their bodies.

Martin was first to recover. He sat up, rubbing his back, feeling as if his tail had been dragged out by the roots. Dinny lay face down. He lifted his head, snorted sand, and looked up at the rock face.

"Hoo arr. Lookout, 'ee commen doawn!" he warned.

Sure enough, the crab was scrambling and scuttling sideways down the rocks toward them with surprising agility.

Ignoring his injuries, Martin ran to face the armored menace as his friends recovered from the fall. Grabbing a stave, he hit out strongly at the creature.

With a loud *clack*, the crustacean caught the flailing stave between both its claws, immediately locking tight onto it, wrenching the weapon from the warrior's grasp.

Martin felt totally helpless as he readied himself for the crab's next move.

Whirling and prancing about on the sand with its slitlike mouth gaping and frothing, the crab clutched madly at the stave. Martin could only stare in amazement at the dancing monster as it jigged about, holding the stave high in its murderous claws.

Log-a-Log tugged at the warrior's paw. "Come on, Martin. Let's get going while we can. That crab doesn't seem to want to let go of the stave!"

"Ha!" Gonff snorted. "It's not a case of wanting. It hasn't got the sense to release the stave. Can't you see?"

As if to prove his point, the little mousethief joined the crab and actually began dancing along with it. Round and round they went, Gonff comically following his strange partner's every twist and turn. Furiously the crab waggled its stalked eyes, opening and closing its mouth as it pranced crazily around, still clasping the stave tightly.

Martin and his friends nursed their aching ribs, trying not to

augh too hard. Tears streamed down their cheeks at Gonff's
ntics.

"Oh hahahahooohooo. Stoppit, Gonff, please," Martin
egged. "Heeheeheehahaha. Come away and leave the silly
east alone. Hahahaha!"

Gonff halted and doffed a courtly bow at the enraged crab,
"My thanks to you, sir. You truly are a wonderful dancer."

The crab stood glaring at Gonff, with a mixture of ferocity
nd bafflement as the mousethief continued his polite compli-
ments.

"Oh, I do hope we meet again at the next annual Rockpool
Ball. Those shrimps are such clumsy fellows, you know. They
read all over one's paws. They're not half as good as you.
ncidentally, who taught you to dance so well? Keeping all
hose legs going together, you didn't trip once. My, my. We
eally must do this again sometime."

The crab stood stock-still with the stave held high. It watched
he four travelers depart along the shore, their laughter and
esting mingled on the breeze.

"Hahahaha! Wait'll I tell Columbine. Maybe he'll give her
dancing lessons if we ever chance this way again, hahaha!"

"Burr, 'ee'm a wunnerful futt tapper."

"What about you, Din? You could have joined them for a
hreesome reel."

It had been an eventful day. Now, as the noon shadows began
engthening, the tide flooded in. The friends wended their weary
way along the interminable shoreline. Salamandastron stood
firm in the distance, never seeming to get any closer.

Tired and dispirited, they trekked onward, feeling the pangs
of hunger and thirst. Apart from the odd seabird whose curiosity had to be fended off forcefully, they were completely
isolated.

Log-a-Log shielded his eyes, pointing ahead. "Look, what
are those birds up to over yonder?"

Some distance farther on, gulls were wheeling and diving.
There were two black shapeless objects upon the sand. The
birds were concentrating their attack on the smaller of these.

Eager to see what was happening, the travelers broke into a
trot. As they drew near to the scene, it became apparent that
the gulls were harassing a living creature. Not far from where
it lay there was a ramshackle lean-to.

Martin whirled his sling as he began running.

"Come on, mates. Let's drive those scavengers off. Charge!"

The creature was a thin ragged rat. Gulls pecked and tore ruthlessly at it as it lay unprotected on the sand.

Under the fierce onslaught of stones and staves, the seabirds took to the air, screeching and wheeling above the intruders who had robbed them of their prey, and finally flying off to seek easier victims.

Martin knelt and lifted the rat's head. The creature was very old and emaciated.

"There, there, now, old one," he said, stroking sand out of its watery eyes. "We're friends. You're safe now."

Log-a-Log touched the rat's limp paw. "Save your breath, Martin. This one has gone to the gates of Dark Forest."

"Dead?"

"Aye. Dead as a stone. He must have been on his last legs when the birds found him. Let's get him to his hut."

Between them they bore the rat into the tattered dwelling. Placing it gently in a corner, they covered the body with an old piece of sailcloth. Then Gonff explored the contents of the hut.

"Look, mateys, water and supplies," he said triumphantly.

There was a small quantity of dried shrimp and seaweed and a pouch of broken biscuit, but best of all there were two hollow gourds filled with clean fresh water. Dinny found a cache of driftwood. He began setting a small fire, using a flint from Martin's sling pouch and the steel of Gonff's dagger.

"Pore beasten. Oi wunder who'm'ee wurr." The mole shook his head sadly.

Log-a-Log poured water into cockle shells.

"Sea rat. No question of it. He's been chained to an oar, too. I saw the scars on his paws. Mine were like that once."

Martin found a thick deep shell, blackened by fire on its outside. He began shredding shrimp and seaweed into it.

"But you said they used other creatures as oar slaves, yet this one was a rat?"

Log-a-Log poured water onto the ingredients and set the shell on two stones over the flames.

"Aye, but there's no telling with sea rats. They're savage and cruel. Maybe that one did something to offend his Captain. I've seen them laughing and drinking together, then suddenly fighting to the death the next moment over some silly little incident.''

Night fell purple and gray in long rolling clouds; a stiff breeze sprang up from seaward as the four companions stood for a moment in silence around the pitiful canvas-wrapped figure in the small grave Dinny had dug in the sand. After the brief ceremony, they watched as the mole filled in the hole, decorating the mound with colored seashells he had found.

''Baint much, but far better'n sea ratten ud do furr 'ee.''

Salamandastron flared crimson against the dark sky as Gonff began to sing,

> Always the tide comes flowing in.
> Ever it goes out again.
> Sleep 'neath the shore evermore,
> Free from hunger and pain.
> Morning light will bring the sun;
> Seasons go rolling on.
> Questing ever far from home,
> For Salamandastron.

Log-a-Log shivered. He turned to the hut. ''Come on, you three. That soup should be ready now.''

Martin bowed his farewell to their benefactor and followed the shrew inside.

''Aye, life must go on,'' he agreed. ''A dry place to sleep, a warm fire, some food and a night's rest is what we all need. Tomorrow we go to the fire mountain.''

Far to the northwest of Camp Willow, the moles were making ready within sight of the river bank. The great tunneling was about to begin.

Chibb watched them from a plane tree. The feathered spy was now in semi-retirement. He had amassed a considerable store of candied chestnuts for his services. Still, he thought, there was no harm earning the odd extra nut by standing guard here.

Foremole and Old Dinny paced and measured; mole digging terms were bandied about freely.

''Needen furm ground. Roots t'make shorin's too, urr.''

"Ho urr, good down'ards gradin' t'make watter flow roight."

"An' rockmovers, Billum. 'Ee be a gurt rockmover."

"Aye, but moind 'ee doant crossen no owd tunnellen. Doant want fludd goen wrongways, hurr."

Above in the trees, Amber's crew were dropping down timber for the sluicegates.

"Mind out below!"

"Tip that end up, Barklad."

"Come out of the way, young un."

"Right. Let 'er go!"

On the ground, Loamhedge mice were stripping, cleaning and jointing the wood. Abbess Germaine rolled up her wide sleeves and joined in with a will.

"Columbine! Here, child, sit on the end of this log and keep it still," she called out. "I'll mark it here, where the joint should be."

" 'Scuse me, Abbess. Where do we put these pine branches?" a strong young mouse asked.

"Take them over there. Mr Stickle has his little ones pulling the bark and twigs off all the new wood."

"Hey, Ferdy, I think I might like to be a carpenter instead of a warrior. What about you?" Coggs decided.

"Oh, I'm going to be a warrior carpenter, Coggs. Posy, will you stop carving patterns and strip that bark."

"Ooh, look! Here's Miz Bella with some big stones. My, isn't she strong!" Posy exclaimed.

"Can I put these stones here, Spike? Whew! I'll have to go back for more now. I saw Goody coming through the woods—I think it's beechnut crumble and elderberry fritters for lunch."

"Hurray, my favorite!" Ferdy said delightedly.

"Don't forget to wash those paws in the river before you eat," Bella reminded them.

"But, Miz Bella, all us workbeasts get mucky paws," Coggs protested. "Shows we've been working hard."

"Oh, and what about littlebeasts? They get mucky paws just playing. You scrub 'em with some bank sand, young Coggs."

The woodlanders stood by after lunch until Old Dinny was brought to the spot where the tunnels would begin. Three young champion digging moles were there—Billum, Soilflyer and Urthclaw. They stood respectfully to one side as Foremole escorted Old Dinny forward. Billum presented the ancient one with a beakerful of October ale. He quaffed most of it in one gulp. Emptying the rest on the ground where the work was to take place, Old Dinny recited,

> Moles a-tunnellen, deep an' far.
> Moles a-diggen, urr that we are.

Foremole nodded approvingly. Old Dinny was quite a solemn mole versifier. He raised a gnarled claw to the three champions. They went to it with a will amid loud cheers. Other teams would follow up, widening and shoring in their wake.

The great tunnelling of Mossflower had begun!

Hidden by a screen of leaves in a high elm, a woodpigeon was witness to a very strange scene in the woods south of Kotir. Tsarmina, armed with a bow and arrows, was talking to the surrounding foliage.

"I know you're there, brother. Oh, it's no use hiding. The Queen of the Thousand Eyes will find you, you can be sure."

The woodpigeon remained perfectly still. No point in offering a handy target to a wildcat with bow and arrows, he decided, even if she were looking for someone else.

"Come on out, Gingivere. Show yourself. This is between me and you."

Silence greeted the challenge. Tsarmina smiled slyly.

"Think you're clever, don't you? Haha, not half as clever as your sister. I know your little game. I'll find you!"

The wildcat Queen continued padding through the still forest, sometimes hiding behind a tree, often doubling back on her own tracks, always on the alert.

Brogg and Ratflank were sitting in the larder. As Captains, they decided it was their prerogative to sample some of the remaining rations. The two officers stuffed bread and guzzled cider from a half-empty cask.

There was a knock at the door. Hastily, they swallowed and wiped their whiskers. Brogg stamped about kicking sacks and checking casks as he called out, "Yes? Who is it?"

"It's Squint the stoat, Cap'n," a thin reedy voice piped back at him.

The pair relaxed.

"Come in, Squint. What d'you want?" Brogg asked.

The stoat entered. He stood to attention before his superiors. "I followed Her Majesty, just like you told me to, Cap'n Brogg."

"Well, where did she go?"

"South into Mossflower. She took a bow and arrows with her. I kept well out of sight and watched. Funny though, she kept ducking here and bobbing there, hiding behind trees and so on."

"What for?"

"Her brother—you know, Gingivere. She kept calling out his name. Went on like that for ages. I thought I'd better come back here and report to you."

Ratflank wiped a crumb from his paw. "You did well Squint," he began.

Brogg silenced him. "You keep quiet. I'm giving the orders around here."

He turned on the unfortunate stoat. "You thought you'd better come back and report, eh? Who told you that you had permission to think? D'you realize that you've left your Queen out there alone in the forest, at the mercy of any roving band of woodlanders?"

"But Cap'n, you told me to—"

"Silence! Speak when you're spoken to, stoat. Now you get back out there on the double, me bucko, and don't come back until Milady does, and that's an order!"

Squint stood bewildered until Ratflank joined in the chastisement.

"You heard Captain Brogg. On the double now. One-two, one-two, one-two. Step lively, Squint!"

The stoat double-marched backward out of the larder. Brogg and Ratflank fell back upon the sacks, laughing.

"Hohohoho, proper thick'ead, that one. Hey, it's not too bad this officer lark, Brogg."

"I'll say it isn't," Brogg agreed. "Keep the troops on their mettle while I inspect the larder, eh?"

"Righto, Captain Brogg. I'll go up and turn them all out for an arms inspection and chuck a few in the guardhouse for having dirty spears. You keep checking round here."

"Heeheehee. That's it, Captain Ratflank. You make 'em jump."

When his companion had gone, Brogg rooted about under

some sacks. He came up with a stone jar half-full of strawberry jam. Upending it on his snout, he smacked the bottom with his paw to free the sticky sweet. Some of it actually went down his mouth; the rest stuck to his nose and whiskers, and he gave a jammy giggle.

"Heehee, hmmmm, mmmmm. Too good for the troops, this stuff!"

Squint dashed heedlessly through the woods, pushing aside bushes, cracking twigs and branches as he followed the trail.

Tsarmina was not aware that Brogg had ordered her to be followed. Stealthily she slipped behind an outcrop of furze, fitting the arrow to the bow as she followed her pursuer's noisy progress.

"Come to me, Gingivere," Tsarmina crooned softly under her breath. "Run quickly! Your sister awaits you."

Squint ploughed headlong past the furze bush. The string twanged mercilessly.

He lay facedown with the arrow protruding from the back of his neck. Tsarmina stood over the fallen stoat, her mad eyes seeing only what they wanted to.

"There's an end to it, brother. You'll never trick me again!"

34

The gourds of water had been lashed to both ends of a stave; any other food that could be packed was carried along. The four travelers had a new spring to their step, now they were free from hunger and the mountain was much nearer.

Since early morning they had been on the move, glad to be away from the hut and the memory of its dead occupant. The going was easier and lighter; the weather stayed fine. Late afternoon found them seated by a shallow rock pool.

Log-a-Log munched a biscuit, keeping a weather eye on a crab lodged beneath a rock.

"I don't like those things. You never know when one's going to do a quick scuttle at you."

Gonff wiggled his paws in the sun-warmed shallows. "Oh, I don't know. I quite fancy another dancing lesson, if our friend there is in the mood."

They laughed at the thought of their last encounter with a crab.

Martin glanced up at Salamandastron. "Look, you can just see the light faintly. Whatever it is must burn continuously. D'you suppose it is a fire lizard, Din?"

"Hurr oi doant be a-knowen of such creat'res. Burr, foir

dargons, indeed. Wot moi owd granfer'd say of 'em oi doant know.''

"Nor do I, but one thing I do know," Log-a-Log said, nodding toward the mountain. "That place is all that stands between sea rats and the land. They fear it and hate it."

Gonff dried his paws. "Then why don't they go around it?"

"Because it's there, I suppose." Log-a-Log shrugged. "It stands as a challenge. The ship I was on avoided it like the plague. But not Cap'n Ripfang, master of the vessel *Bloodwake*; he's the most black-hearted sea rat of 'em all. Ripfang's had many battles round Salamandastron. They say he swore a mighty oath never to rest until he rules that mountain."

Martin stood, stretching his limbs. "But what's up there? What do they fight against?"

Log-a-Log shook his head. "Some say one thing, some another. Fire dragons, armored monsters or phantoms that can strike a creature down without touching it, who knows?"

"There'll only be us to find the truth," Gonff remarked, shouldering the supplies. "What chance do monsters stand against a Prince of Mousethieves, a warrior and a champion digger, not forgetting a shrew like yourself, matey. Come on. Let's get going."

Toward evening, with the mountain burning bright above them, Martin first noticed they were being watched.

"Do you see anything, Gonff?" he asked, when he'd told his companions.

"No, matey, but I know what you mean. I can feel the hairs on my neck rising. What about you, Din?"

"Ho urr, moi diggen claws be a-tellen me summat, tho' wot it be oi doant know."

Log-a-Log was in agreement, too. "Aye, just a sort of feeling really. D'you see that lump of something or other out by the tideline? I could swear it moved a moment ago."

"Don't stare at it," Martin warned them. "Keep going. Shortly we'll make as if we're camping down for the night, but we'll lie down with paws to weapons, keeping our wits about us. Then let them make their move."

The travelers chose an open spot away from the rocks. They lit a small driftwood fire and lay around it, feeling very vulnerable.

Martin kept his eyes slitted against the guttering fire, clutch-

ing his sling in one paw and his sword hilt in the other. Ago-
nizing moments stretched away; still there was no sign of
movement. The friends began to think that their suspicions had
been groundless. Night had fallen and it was quite warm; there
was not even a breeze to disturb the loose sand.

The fire burned lower.

Despite himself, Martin began to feel sleepy. He fought to
keep his eyes open. Dinny's soft snores reached his ears. Gonff
was lying too still to be fully awake.

"I say, did you fellahs do a bunk from the jolly old sea
rats?" a voice said softly in Martin's ear.

"No, we've come all the way from Mossf—" Martin answered in a dozy murmur.

He sprang up, whirling his sling.

Lying amongst them by the fire were three hares.

The warrior mouse was shocked and angry with himself.
"Stand up and fight, you dirty sneaks!" he challenged them.

The nearest hare held up his paws to show they were unarmed. His companions smiled innocently at the travelers.

"Hello, chaps. I'm Trubbs."

"I'm Wother. Capital W and an O, dontcha know."

"I'm Ffring. Double F, no E. Howja do."

The sling dropped from Martin's paw. "Er, very well, thank
you. How did you get here?"

"Oh, this way and that, old chap."

"Dodge and weave, y'know."

"How the dickens do we ever get anywhere?"

Dinny scratched his nose and stared hard at the sand-colored
hares. It was hard to distinguish them from their background.

"Drubbs'n'oo, did 'ee say?" he asked sleepily.

"No, no. It's Trubbs, old sport."

"Wother, at y'service."

"Haha, then I've got to be Ffring, I suppose."

Gonff took the initiative. He saw immediately that the
strange trio were friendly. He made a deep bow.

"Pleased to meet you, I'm sure. My name is Gonff, Prince
of Mousethieves. This is our leader, Martin the Warrior. Here
we have Young Dinny, the world's best digger, with the latest
addition to our little band, Log-a-Log, a shrew and an excellent
boat builder."

Paws were shaken warmly, then the three hares were invited

to sit by the fire with the travelers. It amused Martin and his friends how the hares spoke in turn.

"Well, well. This is comfy. Tell us all about yourselves."

"Rather! What neck of the old county are you bods from?"

"Live far from here, do you?"

Martin explained the nature of their quest. At the mention of Bella's father, Boar the Fighter, a twinkle passed between the eyes of the hares. The warrior continued the tale up until the time they had found the rat on the shore.

"Well, that's our story," he concluded. "Now, what's yours? How do you three come to be out here in the middle of nowhere next to a fire mountain?"

"Actually, that'd be telling."

"Er, haha. I second that, old bean."

"Oh yes, quite."

Getting a straight answer from either Trubbs, Wother, or Ffring was difficult, to say the least. Gonff tried the casual approach.

"Well, you can either stay here with us, mateys, or be off about your business. We've got to get a proper night's sleep so that we can climb that mountain tomorrow."

The three hares shuffled about a bit, then their tone became more businesslike.

"Ah, the mountain . . . Actually, we've been sent down here to you."

"To lead you to the mountain, y'see."

"Would you mind awfully coming along with us?"

Log-a-Log clapped his paws in delight. "Haha, now you're talking."

The hares wiggled their long ears appreciatively.

"Yes, I suppose we are talking, really."

"Never alone, though. Always together, you'll notice."

"Silly, really, I suppose. Do hope you'll forgive us, what?"

"Mateys," Gonff chuckled, "we'll forgive you anything if you can take us up that mountain."

"Hmm, it's not actually up, don't you see."

"No, it's sort of under, dontcha know."

"But we are glad you're coming with us, chaps."

Dinny scratched his head. "Ho arr, us'ns be a-commen with 'ee awright. But who'm sent 'ee for uz?"

"You'll soon see."

"I'll say you will."

"Most definitely."

Martin kicked sand on the fire to extinguish it. "Righto. Lead on, Trubbs, Wother and Ffring."

"Oh, I say. Good show. Let's all go together."

"One never leads, triple initiative, what?"

"Jolly good idea, chums."

As they started toward the mountain, the three hares produced strangely shaped shells. They blew into them simultaneously, making a treble note not unlike that of three small trumpets. The sound echoed across the stillness of the shore. Immediately the scene lit up like daylight as a huge blast of flame rose from Salamandastron. A voice like thunder on a hot noon boomed out with an immense rumble.

"Come in peace to the mountain of fire lizards!"

Hearing the gigantic sound effect, Log-a-Log threw himself face down upon the sand with both paws over his ears, but the hares seemed hardly to notice it.

"Oh, golly. Old Log-a-Thing's fallen over."

"Must be in a blue funk about the boomer, eh."

"I expect so. Up you get, old fellah."

It was a narrow passage between the sand and the rocks; they went in single file. At the end was a small cave. Trubbs tugged at a concealed cord. They had to jump aside as a stout ladder clattered down from the darkened recesses overhead.

"Right. Up you go, laddie."

"No, no. After you, old chap."

"Oh really, I insist."

Martin jumped up to the rungs of the ladder. "I'll go first, if it'll save you three arguing."

"What a spiffing idea."

"Sensible chap, what?"

"Rather. Indeed he is."

At the top of the ladder they found themselves in a broad upward-running passage hewn into the living rock. The ladder was hoisted and they walked up the steep incline, lit by torches at regular intervals in wall sconces. From somewhere above there was a steady roaring sound.

"Wot be that gurt noise, maisters?" Dinny asked curiously.

"Could be the jolly old fire lizards."

"Then again, it might not be."

"You'll soon find out, old fellow."

Five flights of stairs hewn into the rock, one more cave and another steep corridor led them to their destination.

The very heart of Salamandastron!

Bane the fox came down the dusty road from the north with his band of mercenary plunderers.

They numbered about sixty in all, mainly foxes, with a scattering of rats and weasels—a motley group, part tramp, part scavenger, mostly thieves. All were well armed and capable, despite their ragged appearance. Food they had in plenty: fish, birds, and vegetables to cook with them. By craft, guile and murder they had crossed the boundless northern lands, seeking warmer climes and easier living.

Bane was weary of living on his paws, always on the move. He was on the lookout for some fat prosperous little community where he could hold sway without much argument.

Then he spotted Kotir. A grand ruin that had seen better days, but the possibilities were there. Backed by woodland, fronted by flatland, practically skirting a road used by travelers—it was a dream come true.

Leaving orders for his band to camp in the ditch at the roadside out of sight, Bane circled Kotir by himself to spy out the lie of the land. The more he saw of Kotir, the more he fancied it. There would be no more winters in the freezing northlands once he gained entry to this place.

Striding purposefully around the woodland edge at the south side, he practically bumped into Tsarmina returning from the forest. It would have been hard for a bystander to tell who was the more surprised, the fox or the wildcat. As Tsarmina quickly nocked an arrow to her bowstring, Bane's paw shot down to the curved sword he wore at his side. There was a moment's silence as they both stood still, gathering their wits. Finally Bane cocked a paw toward the fortress.

"Whose place is this?"

"It is mine. Who are you?" Tsarmina demanded haughtily.

"They call me Bane. I'm a fighter, but if there's an easier way of getting what I want I'll always try it."

"Hmm, a fighter. My name is Tsarmina, Queen of the Thousand Eyes. That is my headquarters; it is called Kotir."

"Thousand Eyes," Bane said thoughtfully. "There was only ever one with that name, old Verdauga Greeneyes. He was a wildcat, too."

"Yes, he was my father."

"Was?"

"Verdauga is dead now. I alone rule here. If you want, you may come into my service. Kotir is in need of fighters. Are there any with you?"

"Sixty in all. Trained warriors—foxes, rats and weasels."

"I don't trust foxes. Why should I trust you?"

"Ha, who trusts who these days?" Bane snorted. "I'm not particularly fond of wildcats. I've fought alongside your father, and against him, too."

"No doubt you have, but that is in the past now. You say you have threescore warriors at your command. What would be your terms if you came to serve Kotir?"

"Make me an offer."

"I'll do better than that. I'll make you a guarantee, Bane," Tsarmina told the fox. "There are certain creatures—otters, squirrels, mice, hedgehogs . . . woodlanders. One time they used to serve my family, now they choose to live in Mossflower Woods and resist me. Once we have flushed them out of hiding together and enslaved them, then you can have an equal place alongside me. We will rule Mossflower jointly."

Bane's paw left the sword hilt. "Done! I'll take you at your word."

"And I will take you at yours," Tsarmina replied, clasping the proffered paw.

Their untruthful eyes smiled falsely at each other.

Tsarmina saw that at least Bane had told the truth about his followers; ragged and unkempt, but fighters to a beast.

They entered Kotir together.

Bane felt as if the place had been built for him.

The uniformed soldiery of Kotir looked askance at the tattered but well-fed band of mercenaries.

Bane's fighters cast scornful eyes over the ill-fed soldiers in their cumbersome livery.

Tsarmina and Bane were closeted together in the Queen's chamber. She listened to his ideas with respect; treachery could come later, but for now she gave the fox full credit as an experienced campaigner.

Bane's plan was simple. "Don't give 'em an inch; show them you mean business; forget about subterfuge and spies— that only makes for prolonged war—strike hard and be ruthless.

We have the superior number of trained fighters. Start tomorrow morning, have the full strength out in skirmish line, comb the forest thoroughly, kill any who resist and take the rest prisoner. It's the only way to get results, believe me.''

"Bold words, Bane,'' Tsarmina told him approvingly. "But have you tried fighting squirrel archers? They can vanish through the treetops as quick as you can think.''

"Then burn the trees, or chop them down. I've seen it all before. If small creatures scurry off down holes, then block them up, fill every possible exit. That's all they understand. You take my word, it works every time. I know, I've done it.''

Tsarmina pointed out of the window at the vastness of Mossflower. "Could you do it again out there?''

"With our combined forces, easily.''

"Then we start tomorrow morning,'' she said decisively. "At first light!''

Columbine was learning to use one of the smaller squirrel bows. Lady Amber had set up a target while they patrolled the digging areas to protect the workers.

"Pull the string right back,'' Lady Amber instructed. "Look along the arrow shaft with one eye. See the target? Good. Now breathe out and release the arrow at the same time . . . Fine shot, Columbine!''

The shaft stood quivering near the target's center.

"Haha, I'm getting better at it all the time, Lady Amber.''

"You certainly are. Keep it up and you'll soon be as good as me.''

Foremole and Old Dinny came trundling up. The mole leader tugged his snout to Amber.

"Marm, Dinny an' oi filled up yon holler oak stump whurr 'ee got'n out Kotir from,'' he reported.

Old Dinny plucked the arrow from the target and returned it to Columbine.

"Hurr, that we'ave,'' he agreed. "Doant want fludden commen out thurr. We'm gotter fludd cat place, not 'm woodlands.''

Amber sighed. "It's a long dig. Let's hope we can do it before the cat and her army make any surprise moves.''

Skipper sprang dripping from the river.

"Never fear, Amber. My crew and I have done our bit. We've dug from under the water clear to the flood-gates your crew sunk into the ground, where the moles began digging. Mind, I wish we could tunnel as well as Billum, Soilflyer and Urthclaw. Strike me colors, you ought to see those lads shift earth.''

Foremole and Old Dinny smiled with pleasure, but Amber slammed her paw against the target.

''I just wish there was more my squirrels and I could do. Oh, I know we're patrolling and keeping watch, but we don't seem to be contributing any real work.'' She sighed again.

''Then why don't you let me and my crew do a bit of guard duty?'' Skipper suggested. ''We could certainly do with the rest after all that underwater diggin'. Listen, Billum reckons they'll strike some big rocks soon; why don't you see if you could rig up something that'll help the moles to move them?''

Amber was delighted with the suggestion.

''Righto. I'll get Barklad and Oakapple onto it. They could rig tree hoists. Thanks, Skip.''

Chibb had flown a wide patrol merely for the exercise, but soon he grew weary of such energetic practices. Perching on a branch not far from the sleeping Argulor, he listened to the eagle talking in its sleep.

''Hmm, pine marten, one little pine marten, that's all, maybe they taste like pine, hmmmmmm.''

35

Despite the feeling of awe, Gonff could not help smiling to himself. After watching Salamandastron from afar, seeing the column of fire that spouted from its top, and recalling the very name meant "mountain of the fire lizard", the little mousethief immediately saw it was a trick worthy of some mind as clever and resourceful as his own. There were no fire-breathing dragons here, but there was something equally as impressive in this great cave.

It was more than a cave, he decided. It was a huge mountain hall. At its center was a mighty furnacelike forge. A towering column of rockwork took it up to the ceiling, away out of sight. Surrounded by hares, there stood the father of all badgers. He was pure silver from tip to tail with a double broad creamy white stripe on either side of his forehead. Above the thickly muscled limbs and barrel chest, a pair of wild eyes surveyed the newcomers. Giving the mighty bellows handle a powerful downward swing, he tossed a red-hot spear-point with a quick flick of his bare paws. It landed in a water trough with a boiling hiss of bubbles.

As the badger stumped across to them, Martin could almost feel the reverberations through the rock floor. He towered above them, extending a calloused paw that resembled a chunk of rock.

"Welcome to Salamandastron, friends. I am Boar the Fighter," the big voice boomed and echoed about the hall.

His paw enveloped by Boar's, Martin felt very tiny. Now the full impact of Bella's words came to him. Here indeed was one to save Mossflower; the silver badger looked as if he could tear Kotir to pieces with his paws.

"I am Martin the Warrior. This is Young Dinny, and these two are Gonff and Log-a-Log. I have traveled from Mossflower with my friends to bring a message from your daughter, Bella of Brockhall."

Boar unfastened his apron and shed it.

"All this I know. Come, let us go to my cave. It is more comfortable there. My hares will bring you food and drink, and you can clean yourselves up."

As they followed Boar, Gonff whispered to Martin.

"How does he know, matey? Is he a magic badger?"

"Sshh," Martin silenced the mousethief. "Watch your manners. We'll get to know soon enough."

Boar's cave was indeed comfortable. There were ledges to sit or lie upon covered in velvety moss; plants grew around the walls and hung from the ceiling. There was a rough rock table and a pool in one corner with steam rising from its surface.

"The pool is heated from my forge," Boar said, noticing their surprise. "You may bathe there later. You will observe that it is never cold here, again thanks to the forge. But please be seated. Here comes the food."

The hares brought in new bread, fresh salad, baked fish, mint water and a selection of last autumn's fruits crystallized in honey. After the frugal seashore meals, the four travelers ate like a regiment many times their number.

Boar watched them with something approaching amusement on his gigantic face.

Gonff gave him a friendly wink. "So, the flames of the forge carry up that rock flue and shoot out the top of Salamandastron, eh?"

Boar winked back at Gonff. "You are a very perceptive little fellow, Gonff the thief."

"Prince of Mousethieves, matey," Gonff corrected him.

"But how did you know he was a thief?" Martin interrupted.

Boar leaned his chin on muscular paws, bringing his eyes level with Martin. "I know many things, little mouse. Later I will show you how. Now, is that young Dinny, grandson of my childhood friend Dinny the mole?"

"Hurr, Zur Bowar, that oi be. You'm know moi granfer Owd Dinny?"

"Of course I do. Is the old rascal still going strong?"

"Ho urr, 'ee be fitter'n a flea an' owder'n twenny 'ogs," Dinny laughed.

"Good, I'm glad to hear it. And what about you, Log-a-Log?"

"Sir Boar, I am a boat builder, one-time leader of the Northwest Shrew Tribe."

"Oh? Why one-time leader?"

"Because I'm all that's left of my tribe in freedom," Log-a-Log explained. "We were captured by sea rats. I was the only one to escape the galleys."

Boar's eyes hardened to a burning ferocity and the bones in his paws cracked audibly as he ground them together.

"Sea rats! Dirty, treacherous, murdering scum!"

Martin was shocked at the deep hatred in Boar's voice. He listened intently as the badger continued.

"Not only do they burn and plunder among honest creatures, but they are savage to their own kind. Sinking each other's ships, murdering their own companions for an extra pawful of loot."

"Log-a-Log has told me of a sea rat called Ripfang of the *Bloodwake*," Martin interrupted. "Do you know him?"

Boar pointed seaward. "That one, he's out there now—my spies have been watching him all spring—sailing from north to south of here, waiting his chance to attack Salamandastron. Ripfang is the most evil of all sea rats. He has fought and sunk all others who sail in these waters, pressing their crews as slaves in his service. He is also the cleverest and most cunning of them all."

"In what way is he clever and cunning?" Gonff asked, noting the concern on Boar's face.

"Well, he has never feared Salamandastron, or the legends that surround this place. Ripfang is very daring, too. He has personally been here and knows that it is only myself and a few hares who keep the myth of the mountain alive. Others we can scare off, but not Ripfang. It is written that soon he will mount a major war against Salamandastron.''

This was the second time that Boar had spoken of things that had not yet happened. Martin was curious.

''You say it is written, Boar?''

The badger stood tall, pointing at Martin. ''What is that broken weapon you wear about your neck like a medal?'' he asked.

The warrior mouse took it off and gave it to Boar, who inspected it closely as Martin explained.

''That was once the sword of my father. He was a warrior. How it came to be broken I will tell you, because your daughter Bella asked me to inform you about all that is going on in Mossflower.''

As they ate and rested, Martin told Boar how he came to Kotir, the plight of the woodlanders, and Bella's plea for Boar to return to his birthright and free the land. Throughout the narrative, Boar the Fighter said nothing. He paced the room, turning the broken sword hilt over in his paws, looking at it as if it carried some message for him.

Martin finished his recitation of the events. ''So you see, Mossflower has need of its son, Boar,'' he concluded. ''You must come back with us.''

There was silence. When the silver badger spoke, he did not answer the plea.

''This is a very ancient sword hilt, a good one. I can make it into a new weapon. I must give it a blade that will not be broken again by anything.''

Martin saw that Boar would not be pressed for answers; he decided to comply until the badger's mood changed.

''Thank you, Boar. I would dearly like to see my father's old sword forged into a new weapon. Since it was broken I have felt like half a warrior carrying half a sword.''

Boar shook his massive head. ''Your mistake, Martin. You are a real warrior, a full and true one. You have the heart—I can see it in you. But when I make this sword anew, you must always remember that it is not the weapon but the creature that wields it. A sword is a force for good only in the paws of an honest warrior. But enough now. You and your friends are tired. I will talk to you tomorrow and show you many things. Sleep here. If you wish to bathe the dust of travel away, I will send my hares with dry towels for you.''

Boar took his leave of the travelers.

• • •

he hot bath was deep and refreshing. Trubbs, Wother and
'fring turned up with huge soft towels.

"One each, you chaps. No splashing."

"Wash behind your ears, old sport."

"Night-night. See you in the morning."

Dry, full and warm, they lay on the moss-covered ledges.

"Hoo urr," Dinny yawned, "so we'm come to Samman-
astor at larst."

Log-a-Log stared at the high ceiling.

"A wonderful place indeed. Strange creature that Boar, eh,
Martin?"

"Oh, he'll tell us what he intends when he's good and
eady," Martin said airily. "Let's get some sleep. I've a feeling
omorrow's going to be a full day."

Gonff could not resist a rendition of his latest song.

At last the weary travelers
Have reached their hearts' desire.
We quested overland to reach
The mountain of the fire.
To meet with Boar the Fighter,
Who knows secrets dark and deep—

Gonff sat upright scratching his whiskers. "What rhymes
with deep, mateys?"

Three wet towels knocked him flat.

"You'm moight troi sleep!"

36

The woodlanders were caught completely unawares in the early morning.

Led by Bane and Tsarmina, the joint forces hit swiftly. Luckily the little ones were still abed at Brockhall and the Loamhedge mice were preparing breakfasts. The only creatures at the diggings were moles, otters and a few squirrels.

Bane's mercenaries dashed in, hacking madly, backed by Tsarmina's spears. Urthclaw, Billum and Soilflyer were deep underground. The rest were caught in the open.

It was chaos!

Skipper took an arrow in his side. Lady Amber lost an ear to a fox's sword. The woodlands were alive with yelling, slashing animals. There was only one thing to do: retreat with all speed. Disregarding his wound, Skipper stood fast with a small band of otters, hurling stones as he roared aloud, "Get away, quickly!"

Amber and her squirrels managed to escape through the treetops, leaving two slain on the ground. Skipper and his otters saw to it that the few moles were safely carried off across the river, before vanishing into the water themselves.

Tsarmina gave out howls of victory across the now silent woods.

Bane leaned on his curved sword breathing heavily. "See, I told you they're no match for us. Phew! But they can put up a tidy fight, even when they're outnumbered."

Brogg swaggered up and saluted.

"Two squirrels, three otters and a mole slain, Milady," he reported.

He was about to turn away when Bane tugged on his cloak. "How many of ours lost?" he asked tersely.

"Three ferrets, a stoat and a weasel, four rats and a fox."

Bane shook his head in amazement. "Good job, we outnumbered them. No prisoners?"

"No, sir, not a one."

"Hmm, pity."

Ratflank limped up, nursing a cracked paw.

"We've found three big holes over there by the river," he said.

The commanders strode across to the spot. Bane bent down and sniffed the earth around each hole, while Tsarmina stood watching.

"What d'you suppose they were up to?" she wondered.

Bane spat into one of the holes. "Your guess is as good as mine. We didn't get time to chop the trees or fire the woodland. Maybe there's some of 'em still down these holes."

"Then we can fill them in." Tsarmina grinned wickedly. "Brogg, get some big rocks, fetch that timber lying about there, use the spears, fill them in well and press the earth down hard. They'll be imprisoned down there until the air runs out."

Bane wiped his sword and sheathed it.

"Well, that's that. There's not much my band can do around here. We'll head back to Kotir and try another dawn raid tomorrow."

Tsarmina was right beside the fox leader. She was not about to stop out in the woods with her soldiers, leaving Bane to take over Kotir in her absence.

"Right, Bane. I'll leave Brogg with some of the others to get on with the job. The rest of us will go back to Kotir with you."

As they marched off through the morning brightness of Mossflower, one of Bane's foxes sniggered as he trod on the back of Ratflank's cloak.

"Yah, I think your pussycat Queen's frightened of us locking the fortress door on her."

Ratflank tugged his cloak free, sneering. "Oh yes? Well, you just try calling her pussycat to her face, hero!"

The first Bella knew of the attack was when the Corim leaders regathered their crews at Brockhall. Abbess Germaine and Columbine organized bandages and herbs. Loamhedge mice bustled about ministering to the wounded. Skipper refused to stand still, and Goody Stickle chased about after him, dabbing at his injury, trying to get a bandage around it.

There were tears of rage in the otter's eyes. "Six lost, by the fur. Where did they come from? Who was that fox with all those scruffy murderers? Tsarmina could never have done this on her own."

Lady Amber adjusted the bandage around her head so she could see properly.

"I heard someone call him Bane," she told him. "Get Chibb. Tell him to go to Kotir. He'll have to be very careful, but we've got to find out all we can about this other lot."

Foremole tapped a digging claw upon the table.

"Us'll avter do summat 'bout Urthclaw, Soilflyer 'n' Billum. They'm stucken down 'oles. Oo be a-tellen wot they villyuns do to 'ee."

"Yes," Bella agreed, "it's most important that we rescue the moles from the tunnels. Next on the list is to make sure that the area around Brockhall is completely hidden. If they don't know where we are, they can't attack us. Furthermore, we will need to find a second hideout, somewhere deeper into the east of Mossflower. If ever Brockhall is discovered, another refuge will be very necessary."

Messengers were sent out to find Chibb, and the woodlanders set about erasing the tracks around Brockhall, while Germaine and her mice tended the wounded with dedicated care.

The memory of the murderous ambush still lingered.

Lady Amber was not one to forget.

Neither was Skipper.

Before noon, Chibb had reported back to the Corim, but the news was not good.

"Er, ahem. Very serious, very serious. It seems that this fox Bane is an expert, a mercenary with a band of about sixty.

Harrumph. 'Scuse me. Evidently they are planning another ambush, as deep as they can get into Mossflower in one early morning march. Tomorrow, they plan to set out at dawn in a skirmish line, killing or capturing all before them.''

Columbine held up her paw. ''Then we must not give them any targets. Everyone should stay here, completely out of sight, in case Brockhall is discovered.''

Bella nodded approvingly. ''I second that. Good thinking, Columbine. Are we all agreed?''

There was a low murmur of assent. Nobody noticed the look that passed between Amber and Skipper.

In the early afternoon, Bella left command of Brockhall to the Abbess and Columbine. Alone, the badger set out eastward into the woodland depths to find a second place of refuge.

37

Martin woke feeling pleasantly fresh. He opened his eyes to see Boar supervising the laying of a beautiful breakfast table. Hares were wreathing flowers across the board; the food they brought had been grown in small gardens dotted about the landward side of the mountaintop. Boar had small rosebuds and sweet peas twined in his beard, and a garland of ivy leaves sat on his head. The huge badger looked like some benevolent spirit come down from the mountain, holding a green wand in his paw.

Pointing to a high arrow window that streamed down golden sunlight on him, he boomed out to the waking travelers, "Welcome to Salamandastron on the first day of a new summer!"

Young Dinny's heart leaped at the sight of Boar and the mention of his favorite season. "Burrhoourr, oi dearly loiks summertoid, Zurr Bowar!"

During a fabulous meal in which all took part, they were introduced to the other hares who lived in the mountain. Besides Trubbs, Wother and Ffring there was also Harebell, Honeydew and Willow, three doe-eyed beauties who could render Trubbs and company speechless with a single flutter of their eyelashes. There were four others, a huge fellow named Buffheart, his wife Lupin and their two young ones, Starbuck and Breeze.

"These hares are my eyes and ears," Boar explained. "I can stretch out my paws through them and feel what is going on for miles around. They are also fearsome fighters. Yes, every one of them. Don't let silly talk and pretty eyes fool you. They'll show you later. As for the present, they'll take your friends off and show them something of this mountain we live on. Martin, will you come with me? I would talk to you alone."

The warrior mouse followed the silver badger up through many caves, flights of rock stairs and long passages. High up the pair went, into the topmost cave. It was still warm from the heat of the forge. Martin looked out of a long open window to see the beach below and the waters beyond, sparkling and glinting in early summer sunlight.

"This is where you heard my voice when you were down on the shore last night," Boar whispered to him. "I must whisper now because if I were to raise my voice, the echoes would deafen you."

Martin nodded, fearing to speak lest his voice did the same.

Boar smiled, patting the mouse warrior lightly. "You are wise beyond your seasons. Now, do not be surprised by what I am going to show you. This is for our eyes alone, Martin— we two warriors."

The badger went to the left wall between the entrance and the window, where there was a long, deep crack that appeared to be a natural seam in the rock. Setting his great blunt claws deep into the fissure, he began to pull.

Martin stood in awe at the frightening brute strength of Boar the Fighter. Steely sinews and giant muscles bulged and strained as the badger pulled, grunting quietly deep in his chest. Froth appeared on his jaws with the exertion; still he pulled with might and main, platelike back paws set flat on the rock floor, ponderous claws gouging at the bare stone. With a low rumble, the entire wall started to swing outward.

Martin watched wide-eyed, paws and jaws clenched tight, willing the silver badger to perform this great feat of strength. Boar set his shoulders against one side and his paws against the other. He pushed hard, and the secret doorway stood wide open. Without a word they walked inside.

• • •

It was a narrow hall. One side of the wall was covered in minute carvings, the other was smooth, whilst the far end was a rounded alcove. What Martin saw there stopped him in his tracks so fast that Boar stumbled on him.

A badger in full armor was seated on a throne in the alcove! Martin felt Boar's paw upon his back. "No need to be afraid, little friend." The badger's voice was calm. "This is my father, Old Lord Brocktree."

Boar padded silently forward. He touched the armored badger reverently.

"I went questing for Salamandastron, just as my father did," he explained. "When I found this place, he was still alive and well. He ruled here, and we were happy together for many seasons. In the end he was called to the gates of Dark Forest because of his great age. Now he is part of the legend of the mountain, as he wished to be. I did this for him; this is his tomb." Boar gave the armor a gentle rub; it glowed dimly. Walking back to the entrance, he called Martin over.

"Let us start at the beginning. See here?" Boar indicated a carved line of badger figures. "Our kind have come here since creatures first felt the sun. Only warriors, the brave of heart and strong of will, are listed here. See: Urthrun the Gripper, Spearlady Gorse, Bluestripe the Wild, Ceteruler . . . the list goes on and on. Look, here is my father, Lord Brocktree; here I am, next to him. There are the spaces for those to come after us. I see you wish to ask me a question. Carry on, Martin. I release you from your silence."

Martin did not need to speak; he pointed at a block of picture carvings set apart from the others.

"They are good likenesses of you, I think," Boar whispered.

The scene was a small frieze depicting the activities of four creatures. Three were intentionally small, but the fourth was unmistakably Martin, even to the broken sword about his neck. Boar looked at Martin with a strange expression on his face. "Friend, believe me, I did not carve these pictures here, nor did my father. How long they have been here, I do not know. I accept it as part of the legend of Salamandastron; you must, too. You are the largest figure, and here are your friends. See, here you are leading them toward the mountain. Here is Salamandastron, and here are you again, emerging from it with your friends. You no longer carry the broken sword about your neck;

you are holding a bright new sword. As for the rest, well, your guess is as good as mine.''

Martin studied the picture closely. ''Here is the sea, there is a ship . . . Over here looks very faint. It could be a group of trees, a wood or a forest. This looks like a whip and an arrow. What does that mean, Boar?''

''Your eyes are far better than mine, Martin. The whip is the scourge of the sea rats, a sign of evil. As for the arrow, which way does it point?''

''Down the hall to where your father sits.''

Boar indicated the room of echoes. ''Martin, you must go out there and wait for me.''

Without question, Martin went, glancing backward once, to see Boar stooping in the alcove behind Lord Brocktree's throne. He was studying something carved low down on the wall.

Sometime later the badger emerged. He seemed older and tired-looking, and Martin felt concern for his friend.

''Are you all right, Boar? What was written there?''

The great silver badger whirled upon Martin, his face a mask of tragedy.

''Silence! Only Boar the Fighter must know that!''

The sudden shout caused a thousand echoes to boom and bounce off the walls with startling intensity. The sound was deafening. Martin threw himself to the floor, covering both ears with his paws as he fought against the flooding crescendo of noise. Boar's voice reverberated like a thousand cathedral bells. Sorrow and contrition creased the big badger's face; he swept Martin up with a single paw, bearing him swiftly from the room.

When the warrior mouse recovered, he was lying back in the badger's cave. Boar was bathing his brow with cool water.

''Martin, forgive me. I forgot to keep my voice down. Are you hurt?''

Martin stuck a paw in his ear, wiggling it about.

''No, I'm all right. Honestly I am. You mustn't blame yourself. It was my fault.''

Boar shook his head in admiration. ''Spoken like a true warrior. Rise up, Martin, and follow me. Now I will give you the means to fight like one.''

•　　•　　•

Trubbs, Wother and Ffring met them at the forge. There were lots of giggling and winking between the hares.

"Well, does he know about you-know-what, eh, Boar?"

"I say, let's show it to him now, Boar. Be a sport."

"Yes, otherwise the poor old bean might keel over with suspense."

There was a twinkle in Boar's eye as he turned to Lupin, the wife of Buffheart.

"What d'you think, Lupin? Is he ready for this?"

Lupin waggled her long ears humorously as hares do.

"Oh, I suppose so. Anyhow, we'll soon find out."

Boar had moved to the edge of the forge and was toying with something wrapped in soft barkcloth.

"While you slept last night, my hares and I worked until after dawn had broken," he said at last. "I have made something for you, Martin."

The warrior mouse felt the hairs rising on the back of his neck. He gulped with excitement as Boar continued.

"One night while out on patrol, our Lupin here saw a star fall from the sky. She found the spot where it landed. A lump of hot metal was buried deep in the sand. When it cooled she dug it out and brought it back to me. Last night I put sea coal and charcoal in my forge; more than ever before, I made Salamandastron glow so hot that it could be seen in lands far across the sea. I had to—half the night had gone before the metal became soft. I hammered it out, oiled it, folded it many times against itself on my anvil, all the time reciting the names of every great warrior I had known or could think of. I spoke your name on the final hammer blow. Here, Martin. This is yours."

Everyone gathered round, including the three travelers, who were back from their tour of the mountain. They held their breath as Martin carefully unwrapped the barkcloth, layer by layer.

It was the sword!

Double-edged, keener than a razor, it lay glittering and twinkling, a myriad of steely lights. Its tip was pointed like a mountain peak in midwinter, the deadly blade had a three-quarter blood channel. It was perfectly balanced against the hilt, which had been restrapped with hard black leather and finished with a ruby-red pommel stone and curving scrolled crosspiece where it joined the marvelous blade.

Never in his wildest dreams had Martin imagined such a thing. Since they left Mossflower on the quest, he had more or less forgotten the broken hilt that hung about his neck. Caught up in the adventures and perils they had been through, he had used whatever he had to—a sling, a piece of wood as a stave— never expecting to see his father's sword restored to a newness that far outshone its humble beginnings. Now, suddenly, he felt the warlike blood of his ancestors rising at the sight of a fighting weapon few were chosen to look upon, let alone own. The feeling of destiny lay strong upon him as he picked up the fascinating weapon in one paw. His hackles rose and the blood surged in his face, flashing across his eyes. Now he was the Warrior!

Everyone moved back to the walls as the warrior mouse took his sword in both paws. He held it straight out, letting the point rise slightly to feel the heft of the weapon. Suddenly Martin began sweeping it in circles, up, down, and around. The steel blade whooshed and sang eerily on its own wind; the bystanders followed its every move as if hypnotized. Martin leaped onto Boar's anvil, still swinging his sword. There was an audible *ping* as he sliced the tip from the anvil horn. It ricocheted off the rock walls. They ducked instinctively as it hummed past like an angry wasp, leaving the singing blade unmarked.

"Tsarmina, can you hear me?" Martin roared out above the voice of the howling blade. "I am Martin the Warrior. I am coming back to Mossflowerrrrrrrrrr!"

38

An hour before dawn, Brogg was rubbing sleep from his eyes. He flopped his Thousand Eye Captain's cloak about him and stumbled into the main billet with Ratflank. They kicked at prostrate forms, pulling tattered blankets from sleeping soldiers.

"Come on, you lot," they ordered. "Up on your paws. It's invasion time again."

Grumbling and protesting, the troops sat up, scratching at their fur, wiping paws across eyes.

"Gaw! I was havin' a lovely dream there."

"Huh, me too. I dreamed we were getting a proper hot breakfast."

"You'll be lucky, bucko. Bread and water, and be glad of it."

"Where's this fat of the land we're all supposed to be living off? That's what I'd like to know."

Ratflank kicked out at a huddled form wrapped in sacking. A rawboned fox wearing brass earrings leaped up.

"Keep your stupid paws off me, lumphead," he snarled. "I'm not one of your dimwit soldiers. We only take orders from Bane."

Ratflank hurried away, narrowly dodging the bared yellow fangs.

Bane and Tsarmina paced restlessly about in the entrance hall. The fox banged his paw against a doorpost.

"What's keeping them?" he asked impatiently. "It'll be noon by the time we get going at this rate."

Tsarmina gritted her teeth. Turning, she screeched toward the barracks, "Brogg, Ratflank, get them out here double quick, or I'll come in there and move you myself!"

The first bunch came tumbling out, adjusting tunics, clattering shields on spears.

"Here's mine. Where's your crew, Bane?" Tsarmina smirked.

Moments later, Bane's mercenaries strolled casually out in the rear of the uniformed soldiers. The fox commander struck his curved sword against a shield until he got order.

"Right, you lot. Same drill as yesterday—skirmish line, comb the woods, keep your eyes peeled and your wits about you. When we find them, remember: no mercy!"

The horde moved out toward the parade ground in the courtyard. As the first half-dozen soldiers passed through the doorway into the open, there was a harsh shout from the woodland fringe.

"Fire!"

A hiss of vicious weaponry cut the air. The six soldiers fell in their tracks, cut down by arrows and javelins.

"Retreat, retreat, get back inside, quick!" Bane ordered hastily.

There was panic as the back ranks coming forward stumbled into the front ranks retreating. More troops fell, transfixed by flying death.

"What's going on out there?" Tsarmina yelled at Bane.

Bane stood panting with his back to the wall.

"They've got us bottled up in here. Wait a moment. Badtail!"

The rawboned fox came trotting up. "Here, Bane."

"See what the position is out there. Pinpoint where they are and report back to me."

Badtail lay flat upon his belly. Sliding around the doorposts, he scrambled out onto the parade ground, tacking and weaving. Halfway across the courtyard, he bobbed up and down, checking the trees and scanning the low bushes through the open main gates.

"What d'you see?" Bane's voice rang across the open space.

Still lying flat, Badtail raised his head as he shouted back, "Squirrels and otters. They've got the main gates open and they're shooting from the tr—"

An otter javelin closed his mouth forever.

Bane poked his head around the doorpost. An arrow hummed its way viciously into the woodwork. He pulled back swiftly as two more buried their points in the doorpost where his head had been.

Skipper crouched behind a bush and signaled to Lady Amber, who was perched on the low branches of an oak.

"Eleven down and plenty more to go," he reported.

Amber drew back her bowstring and let an arrow fly.

"Make it the round dozen, Skip!"

Grim-faced and determined, the crews of both leaders tightened paws on bowstrings, slings and javelins, waiting for the next head to show around the doorposts of Kotir fortress.

Inside the building, confusion followed the panic of the initial attack. Tsarmina dashed upstairs to her chamber, dashing back down again when a fusillade of arrows greeted her through the open window. Bane sat at the foot of the stairs.

"Fortunes of war," he said philosophically.

"Oh, burn them out, come down hard on them. I've seen it all before," Tsarmina sneered. "Well, fox, what's your next move?"

"Is there another way out of here?"

"There's the scullery and larder entrance on the north side, but it's only a small door."

"It'll have to do. Let's give it a try."

At the scullery and larder entrance the door was shut tight with rusted bolts which took some considerable time to move. When it was finally opened, the troops hung about reluctantly. Nobody seemed very keen on dashing out to do battle. Bane prodded a Kotir soldier with his sword.

"Come on. You lot have got shields. Get out there!"

The stoat turned sullenly to Brogg. "He's not giving me orders. I've got six seasons' service here. Him and his lot only arrived yesterday."

Tsarmina rushed up the corridor, thrusting creatures aside. "Get out there, you and you," she ordered. "Form a barrier of shields the way you've been trained to do!"

Her word was final; there was no arguing with the Queen of the Thousand Eyes.

Three soldiers pushed their way out into the open, shields held up in front. A slingstone cracked the middle ferret on his paw. He yelped with pain, automatically dropping the shield. Arrows hissed in once more, reducing the ranks by a further three.

High in a sycamore, Barklad fired off an arrow as he remarked to his companion, "How long d'you think we can keep this up, Pear?"

Pear rubbed beeswax on her bowstring before answering.

"Lady Amber says until noon, then it'll be too late for them to go invading Mossflower. Personally, I think we should encourage them to come out at noon, then we could follow them back and pick them off in the evening."

Another squirrel swung in through the branches. "Are you two all right for arrows?" he asked breathlessly. "Here's another quiver full. Give a call if you're running low."

He swung off to the next tree with his supplies.

Bane tried every possible move, but at each new turn he was frustrated by the deadly accuracy of the woodlanders. Every exit tried, be it window or door, resulted in further loss of troops. The summer morning wore on, the high sun above impervious to the dead that littered the courtyard.

Tsarmina came up with the most sensible suggestion to date. "Why don't we just shut the doors and ignore them? With nothing to shoot at, they'll have to leave."

Bane was glad of the solution. He would have mentioned it earlier, had Tsarmina not been in such a towering rage.

Skipper was no mean climber. He stood on a low bough with Lady Amber. Together they considered the problem of the doors that were slammed shut and the bolted, wooden tables which had been placed across the open windows.

"Looks like a stalemate, Amber."

Lady Amber thwacked off an arrow at the closed door. "Cowards! They're very brave attacking defenseless wood-

landers and killing unarmed creatures, but they can't face real
warriors when it comes to a battle.''

Skipper looked up at the clear blue sky. ''Ah well, second
day of summer and all's well, me old branchjumper. Come on.
Let's withdraw and get back to Brockhall.''

A mischievous smile spread across the squirrel's face.
''Right you are, Skip. But not before I've left them with a small
token of our regard.''

Tsarmina sat eating woodpigeon with Bane in an inner room
with no windows. There was a tap on the door.

''Come in!'' she called.

It was Ratflank.

''Milady, Brogg says to tell you that the woodlanders are
setting fire to us.''

''What?''

''Er, yes, Milady. Fire arrows. They're shooting them into
the doors and window shutters. Brogg says it'll be all right,
though, 'cos it's a stone building and they'll only burn the
woodwork.''

Tsarmina sprang up knocking the table sideways. ''My
chamber! Bane, see if you can do something quickly. Organize
a bucket chain. Put those fires out. If they've touched my room
I'll, I'll . . . oooooohhh!''

She dashed from the room, taking the stairs two at a time.

The wall hangings were smoldering ruins and the door still
blazed merrily—Amber's archers had given it special attention.

''Get those buckets up here. Bring water!'' Tsarmina howled
down the stairwell.

''But we're trying to put out the fire at the front door, Milady,'' a dithering voice called up from below.

''I don't care what you're trying to put out! Get that water
up here on the double.''

''What about the door, Milady?''

''Spit on it, for all I care. This is my room—the Queen's
own chamber is on fire. Hurry up, idiot.''

''Idiot yourself!''

''Who said that?'' she demanded.

39

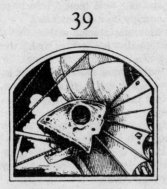

'Place your paw flat upon the blade, grip the handle tight, hold the sword flat above your head.''

Thwang!

Martin countered Lupin's blade as Boar roared out instructions.

''That's how to block the downward chop. Now let go of the blade. Sweep it down and under. Two paws on the haft, straight up and slice. Quickly, turn in and slice again at head height.''

It took Lupin all her skill to duck Martin's blade. She backed off, panting as she leaned on her sword.

''Whew. Golly, there's not a lot you can teach this warrior.''

''Can't I, though.'' Boar smiled. ''Watch this!''

The badger picked up a fire iron from the forge. Thrusting one paw into his blacksmith's apron, he adopted a ready stance.

''On guard, Martin,'' he called. ''Go for a direct thrust.''

Martin came on guard. Moving in swiftly to take the badger by surprise, he lunged and stabbed forward.

Boar hardly seemed to move. With a flick of his fire iron he disarmed Martin, sending the sword spinning and pinning Martin against the wall in the same movement, the fire iron hovering a fraction away from the warrior mouse's right eye.

"How did you do that?" Martin gasped with shock.

Trubbs and company were watching from the sidelines.

"Oh, he does it easily, old sport."

"No trouble to the jolly old boss."

"Quick as a wink, dontcha know."

Boar laughed aloud. "It's only a trick, Martin. Don't get discouraged. I'll show you a dozen more like it before this day's through. Pick up your sword, on guard again."

This time the silver badger ducked in under the blade, catching Martin's sword paw. Locking the point with the flat of the fire iron, he flattened the warrior mouse against the wall with the edge of the sword across his throat.

"See, just another bit of trickery."

That second day of summer, Martin learned more of swordplay than in his whole life. Nobody was more adept with a blade than Boar the Fighter.

Dinny, Log-a-Log and Gonff tried jointly to lift Boar's own sword, but they could hardly manage to get the big battle blade off the floor. It was immense, a real full-grown male badger's war sword, with double crosstrees and a ripping edge that had two sets of curved prongs halfway down the length of the extra-wide blade.

Boar performed tricks with it, slicing apples in the air and taking a whiskertip from Lupin as she stood stock-still. Martin noticed that the badger's mood became more light-hearted and jovial when he was around weapons, even allowing himself to be flattered by Harebell, Honeydew and Willow, who imitated Trubbs and company by speaking alternately.

"Ooh, you are clever, Boar old chap."

"And strong. My word!"

"We ladies would never be able to lift your big heavy sword."

Three special daggers had been forged for Gonff, Log-a-Log and Dinny, who wore them proudly about their waists. Gonff delighted the occupants of Salamandastron with his impromptu ballads.

Harebell, Honeydew and Willow,
Each a pretty thing;
Bold, brave and fearless,
Wother, Trubbs and Ffring;

Lupin, Buffheart, Starbuck, Breeze,
Swift as winds across the trees;
Rule o'er land and sea herefrom,
Sala-manda-stron.

Harebell and company fluttered their eyelids madly.

"Oh, Mr. Gonff, you are clever."

"And so handsome, too."

"You have a lovely voice."

Gonff waved a modest paw. "Save it for Trubbs and company, ladies. I'm promised to my Columbine."

"Is she pretty?"

"Very pretty?"

"Prettier than us?"

"Well, she's certainly prettier than Gonff," Martin, Dinny and Log-a-Log chimed in impudently.

"I'd say half as pretty again."

"Oi'd say twoice as pri'ee, hurr hurr."

Boar roared with laughter and raised his battle sword. "Cheek, shall I chop off their heads, Gonff?"

The mousethief flushed scarlet beneath his fur. "No, just their legs will do, Boar. They need their mouths to eat and make silly remarks with."

To ease Gonff's embarrassment, Buffheart beckoned the friends.

"Have you seen our fire lizard?"

"Fire lizard? No," Gonff chipped in quickly. "Let's go and have a look!"

They followed Boar and the hares, trooping up more flights of stairs until they were somewhere near the echo cave. Buffheart took them into a side cave that had a big open window slot. By the side of the window lay a great stone carving of a fearsome head, a grotesque parody of what its maker had imagined a dragon should look like.

"Nobody knows how it came here," Starbuck said, stroking it fondly. "Sometimes Boar lifts it up to the window at night and lights a fire in its mouth to frighten off the sea rats."

Boar exerted his great strength and picked up the stone head. "Yes, I put it about here, facing out to sea."

He rested the head on the window sill, then went strangely quiet. Boar the Fighter stared hard to seaward. The rest joined him at the window to see what it was.

Halfway between the skyline and the shore, a ship was sailing in toward land. It was a large black galley with double oarbanks and twin square-rigged sails. At the tip of the prow was the bleached skull and fin of some large seafish, standing out like a figurehead.

Boar whispered a single chilling word.

"Bloodwake!"

He was oblivious of all about him, remaining with his gaze riveted on the craft in the water.

Martin turned to Lupin. "Is that Ripfang's ship?" he asked.

She nodded distractedly, pulling at Boar's heavy paw. "Come away, Boar, please. Can't you see he's taunting you again?"

The silver badger shook her off and dashed through to the echo cave.

Even though they shielded their ears, they could hear Boar in the other room, roaring out like thunder at the vessel, "Ahoy, *Bloodwake*. Ripfang, are you there? This is Boar the Fighter. Why don't you show your rotten hide near my mountain again? How about tonight? I'll be waiting, seascum!"

As they watched, a red flag embellished with a scourge was hauled to the foremast peak. It dipped up and down twice.

Buffheart's teeth ground angrily together. "He'll be here, make no mistake about that."

Boar strode heavily in from the echo cave, stretching himself up until his head brushed the ceiling. He gave a huge sigh of satisfaction then recited aloud,

> The second night of summer,
> The second visit since spring,
> The rat from the seas
> Meets the Lord of the rock,
> To settle everything.

Martin saw the wild light of battle in Boar's eye. "Then you're going to fight Ripfang tonight?" he surmised.

Boar departed from the cave, calling as he went, "No, I'm going to kill him!"

They pursued him down the stairs to the forge hall. Taking a rough file, the badger began putting a slashing edge to his war sword.

The happy time was at an end.

Martin picked up his own sword. "We're coming with you, Boar."

The badger shook his head. "No. This is not your fight. This one was written long ago on the wall behind my father. It must be."

Martin was obdurate. "Say what you like, Boar. When night falls, I'll be there at your side."

"Aye, and I."

"Me too."

"I'm coming with you."

"And me, matey."

"Boi 'okey, an' oi too."

"Count me in, old chap."

"Rather, what ho!"

"Wouldn't miss it for the world, what?"

Boar put the file aside. "So be it. Come if you feel you must, and thank you, my friends. But you, Buffheart, and you, Lupin—you must remain here with your young ones. The fires must be kept burning, you understand?"

Buffheart nodded, biting his lip so fiercely that a trickle of blood coursed from the side of his mouth.

"As you say, Boar." Lupin spoke for both of them.

The silver badger stood with his paws resting on the top crosstree of his sword, every inch the commander.

"The rest of you, listen to me. No matter what happens, you must obey the warrior's code. I give the orders, no one else. I know it may be difficult for you to understand, but you must trust me completely. If you obey me, then you are my true friends; disobey, and you are my enemy. Do you understand what I say?"

The heads nodded in silence.

Boar hung the great sword back on its wall spikes.

"Good. Now go and rest," Boar told them. "But first see to your weapons and eat."

When they had gone, Martin lingered awhile with Boar.

"That verse you spoke," he said curiously. "It was written on the wall. Did you recite it all?"

Boar shook his head. "Not all. The last lines are only for me to know. Once again, Martin, thank you. It will be good to have a real warrior at my side tonight."

They clasped paws, the mouse's dwarfed by the badger's.

"Good luck, Boar, my friend."

"Luck has little to do with fate, Martin. You follow the warrior's star. Be true to yourself and your friends."

So the creatures of Salamandastron lay down to rest, each one with his own thoughts.

The second glorious day of summer rolled on toward night.
The black ship *Bloodwake* sailed closer with every wave.

40

Bane had an idea.

"Now that the woodlanders have gone," he suggested cunningly, "why don't we sneak out of Kotir and hide ourselves in the bushes at the edge of the forest? We could hide right behind the position they held this morning. That way, we'll be able to turn the ambush on them if they come back tomorrow for another dawn attack."

"Huh huhuhu, good idea, fox," Brogg chuckled encouragingly.

Tsarmina turned a frosty stare upon the Captain; the chuckle died to a gurgle in his throat. Near open enmity was the order of the day now between her and Bane. She was sorry she had ever let him and his band inside her gates.

"Fool, Brogg," she snarled. "Can't you see this fox only wants us out of Kotir so that he and his raggedy band can slip in behind our backs?"

Bane spread his paws wide disarmingly. "Hoho, if that's what you think, lady."

"Yes, that's exactly what I think, fox!" Tsarmina snapped back.

"That's a problem easily solved." Bane shrugged. "You

stay in here with your deadhead Captain; I take the forces out into the woods. In fact, I'll take them tonight, so that we can be well hidden by the time the woodlanders arrive.''

Tsarmina sniffed. ''That's a better idea. I'll agree to that, Bane.''

The fox laughed. He drew his sword and held it out. ''Think you can trust me, or would you like to confiscate my sword?''

Tsarmina's eyes slitted dangerously. ''If I take that sword, I'll take your head with it, fox.''

Bane sheathed the sword and spat. ''If you ever try to take my sword, it'll be your head that comes off, cat.''

''We shall see.''

''Aye, we shall see.''

Chibb saw, too. He heard all as well.

A swift flutter of his wings took him out across Mossflower, back to Brockhall.

Foremole was pacing around in deep leaf mold with Old Dinny. They were trying to remember the exact location of a disused tunnel.

''Thurr it may be. Moind, oi only sez maybe.''

''No, tis yurr. Oi'd swurr on moi tunnel it's yurr.''

''Nay, may'ap it's midway 'twixt they two.''

''Wo urrhoops, urthenquaker. Look out!''

The ground beneath them trembled and heaved. Both moles were tipped flat on their bottoms in the loam.

Soilflyer's head popped out of the ground. He blew dead leaves from his snout, grinning broadly.

''Hurr, good morrow to 'ee, zurrs,'' he called cheerfully. ''Us'ns found that crossways tunnel as used to be yurr.''

Foremole tried hard to preserve his dignity. ''Thurr 'ee be, Owd Din. Oi did tell 'ee it wurr thurr.''

''Oo, fer a 'spectable Foremole, 'ee be a gurt fib bag!''

Soilflyer pulled himself free of the loam, followed by Urthclaw and Billum. They tugged their snouts in mock respect to their elders, Billum stifling a bass giggle.

'' 'Ow summ of these owd lads do enjoy loif, a-setten about playen in 'ee leaves loik liddle 'ogs, it do surprise oi.''

Foremole shook a stern claw at Billum. ''Lessen thoi cheek. Get 'ee over to Brocken'all an git 'ee vittles.''

•   •   •

Over at Brockhall, things were running smoothly. The little ones played games with Columbine and Goody, while the Abbess helped Ben Stickle and her mice to fletch arrows, which they tied into bundles. As deputy in Bella's absence, Abbess Germaine was not too pleased that Skipper and Amber had disobeyed a Corim decision, but she made allowances for the fact that they had lost friends in the ambush at the diggings. Nevertheless, she felt it was her duty to upbraid them.

"You had no right to go off like that after electing to stay here. Both of you might have been killed."

Skipper was fishing pieces of hazelnut and leek out of a pan of stew that had gone cold beside the hearth. Germaine rapped the table sharply with an arrow.

"Skipper of otters, are you listening to me?"

"Oh aye, marm, I'm all ears," he said abstractedly. "Are these last season's nuts or the one before? Right nice sweet taste they've got."

The Abbess snorted in exasperation. "Now, I want you, both of you, to promise me that you'll never do anything so foolish again. I'm surprised at you, Lady Amber—you a squirrel Queen, too. That's not setting a very good example to others, is it?"

Amber cocked her severed and bandaged ear stump toward Germaine.

"Eh, what's that you say?"

All three dissolved in helpless laughter.

Chibb arrived with the moles, saving the miscreants further scolding; reports were made to the Corim leaders present. Ferdy and Coggs had arrived at a decision to become warrior carpenter cooks, so they served refreshments for everybody.

As they ate, the Abbess mulled over the situation. "Well, if the forces of Kotir are hiding in the woods, it would be unwise for you two to try a repeat performance of today's attack."

Skipper grinned broadly. "Why, perish the thought, marm. They'll be keeping themselves busy, by the sound of it. We'll just let 'em lie uncomfortable like out there all night, then they can shiver through the dawn waiting for us not to turn up. What a damp squib."

Foremole banged the tabletop with one of Ferdy's biscuits. "Hurr, an' iffen they varments think us'ns stopped a-diggen, burr, they'm doant know moles. Us'll 'ave 'ee tunnels worken agin afore eventoid, mark."

• • •

Bella of Brockhall had wandered far in search of a second hideout. If ever Brockhall were discovered by the army of Tsarmina, it was imperative that the woodlanders have a place of safety to flee to. The good badger was always conscious of her responsibility to the woodlanders. She felt she must undertake this search. Bella enjoyed the solitude of the far Mossflower stillness after the close confines of Brockhall in the company of woodlanders. By midday she was traveling east through vast tracts of field country. The badger knew instinctively that the River Moss would be winding its way somewhere near, and her good senses were confirmed in due course.

Bella seated herself on the bank of the broad swirling water. She did not resist taking a short nap in the early summer warmth.

"Bella. Hey there, Bella of Brockhall!"

The badger sat bolt upright, blinking away her tiredness. Gingivere was running towards her, and there was another cat with him, a sleek reddish female.

The badger jumped up waving her paws joyfully.

"Haha, Gingivere, you old rascal, who's your friend?"

The female cat smiled and waved back.

"Oh, you are just as I imagined you, Bella," she said warmly. "Gingivere has told me all about you and his woodland friends. I'm Sandingomm."

They sat on the bank together as Bella brought them up to date with the news and explained her mission. As she talked, Bella noticed how strong and happy Gingivere looked. The reason why soon became apparent.

"Look at me, Bella. Would you believe it, I'm a farmer now. Yes, me, Gingivere, son of Verdauga. We've got a nice little piece of land farther up the bank and the fishing is good in this river."

The badger was delighted. "Well, you certainly fell on your paws this time, friend. Though you deserve it after all you've been through. Congratulations to you both."

Sandingomm thanked Bella. "Anytime you please, you may bring the woodlanders to stay with us. This place is too far away for Gingivere's wicked sister to find."

Bella stood up. Dusting her coat off, she refused an offer to stay for lunch.

"I wouldn't dream of intruding on two such happy creatures

any longer,'' she said firmly. "Besides, I've got to get back to Brockhall and give them the good news. Not only have I found a second hideout, but I have rediscovered our friend Gingivere and made yet another new friend in Lady Sandingomm.''

Gingivere smiled understandingly. "As you will, Bella of Brockhall. Give my best wishes to all the woodlanders, and don't forget to tell Ferdy and Coggs to visit Uncle Gingivere and Aunt Sandingomm sometime.''

"Oh I will, never fear,'' Bella assured him. "Thank you, it's good to know that we of the Corim have two great friends always ready to help.''

The badger set off westward, back toward the leafy glades of Mossflower in the noonday sun.

"Goodbye, Bella of Brockhall. Good luck to you,'' the cats called after her.

"Thank you. Take good care of each other now. Goodbye, Farmer Gingivere. Goodbye, Lady Sandingomm.''

41

Night had fallen over Salamandastron.

The war party climbed down the roof ladder onto the sand. Gonff, Dinny and Log-a-Log had been outfitted by the hares. They were helmeted and armed with long pointed pikes, smaller versions of the arms carried by fighting hares.

Martin looked around, checking out the company. There were Trubbs, Wother and Ffring, Harebell, Honeydew and Willow, his three traveling companions and Boar the Fighter. The silver badger towered above them all, looking fearsome enough to chill the blood of any sea rat's veins. He wore heavy spiked armor across his back and front, topped off with a shining metal headpiece that came forward into a badger war mask.

Boar pointed his great war sword up at Buffheart as he gave final orders.

"Make sure you pull that ladder back up safe, slide a rock over the entrance hole and don't open it to any creature."

"But supposing you want to get back in again, Boar?" Starbuck asked, gazing down from behind his father.

The badger chuckled drily. "Don't worry, Star. A short climb and a rock slab won't stop me."

Lupin appeared at the opening. "Breeze is at the forge sob-

288

bing herself silly. Will you be all right, Boar?''

The badger did not look up. ''I'm fine, Lupin. You're the strong one. You know what to do.''

''I do, Boar.''

''Good. Then come on, you lucky lot, follow me. We're going to a party with some sea rats.''

As they moved off, Gonff nudged Dinny. ''What a happy badger. He seems to get merrier when he's closer to a battle.''

''Urr, wishen oi did,'' Young Dinny gulped. ''Moi young paws be all of a-trimble.''

''I'm glad I haven't got that trouble, Din,'' Gonff giggled nervously. ''Mine froze solid with fright some time ago.''

In silent file they made their way out to the shore, keeping close to the rock face. The party halted when they stood with their backs to the mountain. It was deserted, though *Bloodwake* bobbed at anchor close to the land.

Trubbs twitched his whiskers. ''Don't like this at all, chums. Not one little bit.''

''I'll second that, laddie.''

''Thirds for me, old scout, wot?''

Gonff peered toward *Bloodwake*. ''Maybe they're still on board.''

Log-a-Log gripped his pike tighter. ''No, mate. She's riding too high in the water for that.''

''Log-a-Log's right,'' Martin whispered to Boar. ''What do you think?''

''Oh, they're here, somewhere,'' Boar chuckled softly. ''I can smell the stink of sea rat fouling up my territory. Trubbs, you take the left. Harebell, around the mountain to the right. See if you can spot anything.''

The hares slipped off like sand on the breeze. ''Look, there's a small band of 'em,'' Boar exclaimed, pointing straight ahead. ''Been lying low where the waves lap the sand. Ha, they don't fool me. There's some kind of ambush being rigged up around here, but don't worry, we'll be ready.''

Trubbs and Harebell arrived back at the same time. ''Boar, they're around the back of the mountain, hordes of them!''

''Harebell's right. I saw 'em too, all skulking in the shadows.''

Boar remained calm. ''Huh, Ripfang seems to be using his brains more and his mouth less these days. They must have

dropped off farther up the coast and come overland, circling to
get behind us. I told you that band up ahead was only a blind.''

Dinny gave a hoarse shout. ''Look out! Yurr they'm a-
cummen!''

From both sides of the mountain they filtered out in a swift
pincer movement. Trubb's estimate was right: there were
hordes of them. Martin watched in silence as they formed a
semicircle. He had never seen so many sea rats.

Villainous faces, wreathed by black headbands and adorned
with brass earrings, snarled at them. Strange sickle-shaped
swords with small round target shields were brandished high.
Daggers and whips bristled where there were no swords. Martin
thanked the fates that there were no archers.

Boar stood forward smiling hugely, leaning idly on his battle
blade. ''Well, well. The gang's all here. Where's old snotwhis-
kers?''

The ranks parted, allowing two standard bearers carrying sea
rat banners to come through. Standing between them was a rat,
half as big again as any of the others, carrying a sickle sword
and a long whiplash. A single fang grew overlong from the left
side of his mouth, giving his face a grotesque sneer.

''Here I am, mountain Lord. We have you surrounded and
ready to die.''

Boar did not give the courtesy of a reply. He whirled his
giant war sword aloft and charged with a thunderous battlecry.

''Yoooohaaarrraallaayleeeeee!!!''

Both sides surged forward, meeting with a crash of steel
upon the churning sands.

Martin felt the madness of combat searing through his veins.
He leaped and struck, hacked and thrust, stabbed and slashed
like a flash of hot summer lightning. Shields were shorn
through by his flying blade, sea rats went down before him like
corn to a reaper. They crushed inward, swinging their sickle
swords. Dinny took a gash upon his shoulder. He was about to
go down when Trubbs heaved a squealing rat high upon his
pike, tossing him onto the blades that menaced Dinny. Gonff
had lost his pike, but he went at them with a dagger in each
paw, flailing like a windmill, up, down, across, over, his fear
forgotten in the boiling melee of battle. Ffring was hemmed in
on all sides, his bobtail shorn off; but Wother and Log-a-Log
came vaulting over the sea rats' heads on their pikes to save
the beleaguered hare. Jabbing left and right, they were joined

by Harebell. Foursquare back to back they fought, turning in a ferocious circle, spearing and ripping like a carousel of doom.

The rats on the tideline had begun to move. Boar swung low at the feet of his enemies. As they jumped, he carried the sweep high, the immense war sword slicing through at head level. Blood-spattered, pierced by steel in a dozen different places, he fought on, oblivious to his wounds, trying to reach Ripfang, who stood at the back urging on his sea rats.

"Come to me, Ripfang," the silver badger chanted as he battled. "Meet Boar the Fighter. I am the son of Old Lord Brocktree, ruler of Mossflower, Chief of the mountain. My blade is singing your deathsong. Let Boar take you and your vermin crew to the gates of Dark Forest this night. The summer sun cannot stand the sight of you darkening the earth!"

Now the rats packed in harder at Ripfang's command. The roiling mass of enemies seemed endless. Martin and his comrades wiped sweat and blood from their eyes as they battered heroically away at the tide of sea rats which threatened to engulf them.

The warrior mouse found himself back to back with Boar. "Boar, we're hard-pressed and outnumbered," he yelled over the noise of war. "It'd take us all season to slay this pack, even if they stood in line and waited."

The silver badger made a rat into two half-rats with his sword. "I know, little warrior. I told you this was my fight. I'm sorry I got you into it."

Martin extinguished a spitting face with his blade. "Not your fault, Boar. It was written."

The badger used his sword hilt to pulp a rat who came too near. "Listen, Martin. Get the crew around you. I'm going to force a way through, then we'll run for it. There's only that single group standing between us and *Bloodwake*. Are you ready?"

It took a few moments in the battle until Martin had mustered his comrades in a group. There was a momentary lull as they stood ringed on all sides by sea rats.

Like chain lightning, Boar made his move with a furious charge. The mad onslaught carried them forward to the edge of the horde. Hewing ceaselessly, Martin and the rest broke through. They began running toward the small advancing band of sea rats.

Pikes clashed with sickle swords as they met. The astounded

vermin were so taken aback by the ferocity of the attack that they broke and scattered.

Rushing onward, the friends made the water's edge.

Honeydew looked back. "We've left Boar behind!"

"No, he never came with us."

"Let's go back."

"Stay!" Martin's shout was a cold command.

They turned to stare at the warrior mouse.

"Remember your orders from Boar. Do as he said; it is the way of the warrior. Boar has seen his own fate written; there is nothing we can do to stop it. We must capture that ship."

They slid into the surf with the sounds of battle still ringing in their ears.

There was only a token watch left aboard to guard the galley slaves. They leaped overboard at the sight of the roaring fighters who sprang dripping to the deck of *Bloodwake*.

Panting with exertion, Martin turned to Log-a-Log. "Get this vessel under way with all speed!"

The shrew rapped out commands to the new crew. "Slash that anchor cable. Hoist those sails. Martin, take the tiller— steer her out to deep water. You below, row for your lives if you want to taste freedom again."

Pushing the tiller over, Martin felt *Bloodwake* respond. She turned on the ebbing tide with a stiff breeze at her stern, riding the waves out toward the open sea. The rest of them joined him as he stared over the after end, across the smooth wake to the shore.

The silver badger's voice carried to them on the wind.

"Sail away, my warriors. Tell Bella and Mossflower of Boar the Fighter. Come closer, sea rats. Let my blade kiss you to sleep. Ah, Ripfang, my old enemy, got you! Now I embrace you as a friend. See."

They watched as Boar went down under a mob of sea rats who were howling and screaming. The badger wielded his sword with a single paw. The other mighty paw held Ripfang close to his studded metal armor, crushing him to death.

Martin turned away, blinded by tears. He could look no more.

Nor could his companions.

Before them lay the deep open sea. Behind them, the flames

of Salamandastron burned bright over a shore piled and littered with dead and wounded sea rats.

The spirit of Boar the Fighter lingered on the sands, reluctant to leave a good battle and travel to the gates of Dark Forest.

The silver badger had seen the writing on the wall. He had fulfilled the legend of the mountain!

Tsarmina and Bane watched each other like pike eyeing a water beetle, the wildcat Queen from her high window, Bane from where he crouched shivering with the troops, drenched in morning dew, completely dispirited after a fruitless night spent in the forest. The rift was widening between cat and fox.

Bane squatted in the wet grass beside Brogg.

"See how your Queen treats us? We shiver out here all night while she lies in luxury, warm and snug."

Brogg squinted dully. "She always has. Milady is a Queen, you know."

Bane spat at a small insect. "If I ruled Kotir, the troops would get the same treatment as me. Ask my crew. We always had plenty to eat. I never hid in safety and let them take all the risks."

"Is that why you pushed them out of doors, in front of all those arrows and javelins?" Ratflank sniggered.

Bane cuffed him soundly across the snout. "Who asked your opinion, snivelwhiskers? I didn't notice you volunteering to dash out and fight those woodlanders."

Brogg stood up, brushing dewdrops from his cloak. "Ah well, they won't be showing up this morning. Wonder how they knew we'd be lying in wait?"

Bane winked and tapped his muzzle. "Maybe she got word to them. That way she could have Kotir and the rations to herself. There's enough supplies in there to keep one cat happy forever."

Brogg scratched his chin. "Really? Do you think she'd do that?"

"Well, look at the evidence." Bane laughed mirthlessly. "From what I hear, the garrison was in a right old mess before I arrived with reinforcements and rations. They say she was acting strange. You should know—she had you pulling tails and checking whiskers. What normal creature does things like that?"

As the force moved back to Kotir, Bane and Brogg were deep in quiet, earnest conversation.

Tsarmina watched them from her high window. She also scanned the surrounding treetops for signs that the eagle might be abroad. An idea was forming in the wildcat's mind.

Later that morning, while Bane was supervising a team to replace the burned door and window timbers, Tsarmina had Brogg come to her room. She fed him on cider and roasted woodpigeon as she wormed information from him.

The weasel Captain told his Queen all.

Tsarmina resumed her position at the window, watching the telltale quiver of a spruce top. When she turned to Brogg her voice dripped sincerity.

"You have been a good and loyal Captain, Brogg. Make no mistake, your Queen will reward you. This fox forced his way in here while we were distracted by the woodlanders. He countermands my orders and whispers lies about me to my soldiers. Do you realize that if he had not barged his way in with his ragged mob, I was going to promote you to act as Supreme General?"

"Me, Milady?" Brogg could hardly believe his ears.

"Yes, you. Say nothing of this to any creature, especially Bane. Let him carry on repairing our woodwork. He thinks he will rule Kotir one day. You stick to doing your job, Brogg. Keep my Thousand Eye soldiers loyal to me. As for Bane, leave him to me. If he speaks to you, tell him that I wish to see him, up here in my chamber."

"I will, Milady. You can trust me."

"I do, Brogg my good friend. Now go."

The weasel did not stop backing up and bowing until after he was outside the room.

By midafternoon most of the repair work was well under way. Bane strolled up to the high chamber and slouched against the table where Tsarmina sat.

"Well, what d'you want me for now, cat?" he asked insolently.

Tsarmina pushed a beaker of elderberry wine across the table to Bane, and poured one for herself.

"To you, Bane. A good job well done on the doors and windows. I could not have done better myself."

The fox watched carefully, not taking a sip of the wine until the wildcat had drunk from her beaker.

"Why this sudden honor, Tsarmina? What are you up to?"

The wildcat Queen shook her head sadly. "How did we ever come to this mistrust and enmity, Bane?" She pointed a dramatic claw to the open window. "Out there is where the enemy is. The woodlanders are the ones we should be fighting, not each other."

The fox took a mouthful of the rich dark wine. "I'll agree with that, but what's brought about this sudden change? Tell me, if we are to trust each other."

Tsarmina passed a weary paw across her brow. "Until you came, I had not won a single victory over the woodlanders. Even when they attacked us yesterday you did all you could, but still I did not trust you," she confessed. "I made you wait out in the open all night and you never complained once. Today I looked from my window and saw you helping your band to repair the damage to Kotir. That was when I changed my opinion of you."

Tsarmina refilled Bane's beaker with wine. When she spoke again there was something approaching a sob in her voice.

"Forgive me. I have misjudged you, Bane. You are a true friend."

The fox quaffed the wine, then took the liberty of pouring himself some more.

"You like the work that we are carrying out on the fire damage?"

Tsarmina pushed the wine jug so that Bane would not have to stretch when reaching for it.

"Indeed I do. It's ten times better than my bumbling lot could have done," she assured him.

Bane nodded agreement. "Aye, my band can turn their paw to most things. They're still working round at the larder and scullery entrance."

"Good," Tsarmina said over her shoulder as she rummaged in a wooden chest. "But what I'm worried about is the main gates between the courtyard and the woodland edge."

The fox finished his wine, banging the beaker down decisively. "Right, let's go and take a look at 'em, though I don't think they'll need much repair. They're a solid old pair of gates."

Tsarmina produced a cloak from the chest. It was a long

trailing garment made from bright red velvet trimmed with woodpigeon feathers. Recently it had been cleaned and brushed.

"I want you to take this cloak, friend," she insisted smilingly. "Wear it as a token of our new alliance. As you can see, it is not the plain cloak of a Captain; this was made for a Lord."

Bane took the cloak. Twirling it round, he admired the color and weight of the velvet. He swept it up, draping it around his shoulders. Tsarmina fastened the clasp at his neck.

"There! How handsome you look. More like the Ruler of Kotir than I do."

Bane's paw stroked the feather edged velvet. "Thank you, Queen Tsarmina. This is a splendid cloak. Hoho, wait'll my gang see their leader decked out in his finery. Come on, let's take a look at that gate."

There were many admiring and envious glances from Bane's mercenaries as he strode across the courtyard.

"By the fang. Look at old Bane. What a fine cloak!"

"He certainly cuts a dash in it. I'll bet he's been promoted."

"Haha, he looks more like the Chief here than the cat does."

Brogg and Ratflank leaned out of the barrack room window. The weasel Captain could not help remarking under his breath, "What d'you suppose the fox is doing, wearing Ashleg's cloak?"

42

Dawn brushed pale streaks of pink and gold through the gray mist on the calm sea waters.

Rasping sounds from a file could be heard on deck from the oarbanks below. Gonff was freeing the slaves.

Martin and Dinny assisted the pathetic creatures onto the deck. Some of them had not seen daylight in seasons. They were a mixed bunch, ragged shrews and emaciated mice, together with some bedraggled hedgehogs and the odd gaunt squirrel.

How could any creature treat another in this cruel manner? Martin wondered. It made his blood boil as he tended them.

Dinny was doling out food from *Bloodwake*'s well-stocked pantry. "Yurr, get sum vittles down 'ee, us'ns fatten 'ee up."

Martin was supporting a tough mouse who seemed on the verge of collapse.

"Thank you, Martin son of Luke," he said, nodding gratefully at the young warrior.

Martin's paws gave way. He sank to the deck of *Bloodwake*, taking his burden with him. They sat staring at each other. Martin could find only one word to say.

"Timballisto?"

Tears ran freely down the mouse's whiskers. "Martin, my friend."

A shrew who was gnawing at a ship's biscuit came and sat by them. "Martin, the young warrior mouse, eh? Timballisto here was always talking about you."

Timballisto threw a paw about his friend's shoulder. "How did you know I was aboard this floating rat trap?"

Martin hugged him. "I didn't, you old wardog. I thought you'd gone to the gates of Dark Forest long ago, fighting enemies off outside our caves in the northlands."

As they sat talking, Log-a-Log came from Ripfang's cabin aft. He was studying some sailcloth charts. Immediately a great shout went up from the shrews who had been freed.

"Log-a-Log! Chief, it's us, the old gang from the village!"

Preoccupied with something he had discovered among the maps, the Shrew Chief waved distractedly to them. "Ha, hello, you lot. Well, eat up and get fit again. The boss is back now. Told you I'd rescue you, didn't I."

Gonff heaved himself up from the galleybanks below. "Whew, matey! It could do with a good scrub down there. Hey, Log-a-Log, found some booty?"

The shrew spread charts upon the deck. "Look, it's all here—the way home."

Martin could make little of the charts. "Show me."

"Righto. It's simple really. See here, that's Salamandastron," Log-a-Log explained. "Keep the setting sun to your left and follow the coastline until we sight a river flowing into the sea from the right. It's the River Moss, see, flowing from east to west."

Dinny's digging paw tapped the canvas. "Hurr, well oi never did, stan' on moi tunnel! It be our river as flows thru Mossfl'er. Lookit, thurr be 'ee woodlands marked up over yon. Burr, 'ee ratbag knowed it all."

Log-a-Log pinned the canvas down against a breeze that was springing up.

"I'll say he did. That's how he came to capture my tribe. There's our village marked up on the northeast fringes of Mossflower. Banksnout, shin up the mast and keep your eyes busy for the river flowing in from landward. Gonff, take the tiller and hold it seaward a point to bring us closer into shore. Shrews, break out all sail so we catch this good breeze."

Under the eye of the summer sun, *Bloodwake* scudded across

the foaming whitecaps like a great seabird. Timballisto leaned over the deckrail with Martin.

"I wish I'd had the chance to meet Boar the Fighter," Timballisto sighed. "He sounds like a great warrior, from what you say. What a pity he won't be coming back to save Mossflower."

Martin drew his sword. He pointed it east toward the land. "It is my duty to save Mossflower. I swore it to Boar and I intend keeping that oath."

Timballisto watched him as he held forth the beautiful blade. "You will, Martin. You will!"

A hedgehog poked his head around the door of the forward cabins. "Ahoy, there's a full armory here, lads—swords, spears, knives, everything an army could wish for."

"Gurt loads o' vittles, too." Dinny chuckled. "Oi tell 'ee, Gonffen, liddle boats make oi sick, hurr, but this'n's a noice big shipper. Oi'll call 'er *Wuddshipp*. Harr, that be a foin name."

Gonff watched the forepeak respond to the tiller.

"*Wuddshipp* it is then, Din. Though personally I'd have named her *Columbine*."

Trubbs and company chimed in.

"I say, that's a bit strong, Gonff, old sailor."

"Has Columbine really got a wooden bottom?"

"And two ears that stick out like sails?"

They narrowly ducked the pail of seawater that Gonff hurled.

Banksnout roared out in a gruff shrew bass from atop the rigging, "Ahoy! River in sight up north to landward!"

Martin climbed the bowsprit. He stood on the bleached fish skull figurehead, looking eagerly.

Sure enough, there was the river, boiling across the shores in the distance. He turned to the crowd of eager faces watching him.

"Take her head up and round the shore, Gonff. We're going home!"

Shrews, mice, hedgehogs, squirrels, hares and a single mole roared out in one voice that rang across the waves,

"Mossflowerrrrrrr!!!"

43

Argulor was awake.

Shifting on his high spruce perch, he glared down greedily through his old watery eyes at the red-cloaked figure crossing the parade ground of Kotir.

"At last, pine marten!"

Tsarmina pushed hard against the gates. "See, they're rocking on their hinges," she pointed out to Bane. "Those woodlanders have been meddling with them, I'm sure of it."

Bane gave the gates a kick. "Do you think so? They seem solid enough to me. Huh, even fire arrows didn't make much impression on these gates."

Tsarmina unbolted the locks. Opening the gates cautiously, she peered around them at the woodlands. It was safe.

"All clear out here, but I don't like it. I'm sure they've done something to these gates from outside. Just think, if these gates blew down during the autumn, we'd be at their mercy."

"Huh, I don't know what you're fussing about," Bane said, swirling his new cloak impatiently. "The gates look all right to me."

Tsarmina gnawed her lip. "Are you really sure, though?"

The fox sighed in exasperation. "Oh, I suppose I'll have to go and take a look to keep you happy."

He strode briskly outside.

Tsarmina dodged inside, slamming the gates and bolting them.

Bane was puzzled momentarily. "Hoi, what's the matter with you, Tsarmina?"

There was no reply. Tsarmina was racing across the parade ground to watch from her high window.

Suddenly Bane sensed he had been tricked, but it was too late.

Argulor had already launched himself from his perch. He homed in on the red-cloaked figure like a bolt from the blue.

On the other side of Kotir, Bane's mercenaries worked away on the scullery door, blissfully unaware of what was taking place outside.

Bane did not see the eagle swoop; he was trying to find pawholds as he clambered up the oaken gates.

Argulor struck him hard from behind, burying powerful talons and vicious hooked beak in the prey that had eluded him for so long. The fox was transfixed, frozen with cruel agony; but as the eagle started to carry him off, Bane's fighting instincts took over. Freeing his curved sword, he struck upward at the feathered enemy.

The sword hit Argulor, once, twice!

Doggedly the great eagle sank talons and beak deeper into his prey. Beating the air with his massive wing-spread as he did, both hunter and quarry rose skyward.

Tsarmina at her window danced up and down in fiendish glee. Attracted by the screams, the occupants of Kotir looked up. Bane slashed wildly with his sword; Argulor stabbed madly with his beak. All the while the combatants rose higher, and soon they were above the treetops.

Chibb fluttered in circles some distance away. He watched the amazing sight as eagle and fox rose into the sky.

Far above Mossflower, Argulor won the battle. Bane gave a final shudder and went limp, the curved sword falling from his lifeless paws. The ancient eagle felt cheated; this was no pine marten, it was a fox. Argulor's heart sank in his breast. It did not rise again. The rheumy eyes shut in the same instant as the

great wings folded in death, and only the talons remained fixed
deep into the dead fox.

Tsarmina watched as both creatures plunged earthward.

Two enemies defeated in a single brilliant stroke.

Ratflank dashed for the gate. Brogg shouted after him, "Where
d'you think you're off to?"

"Ha, to get that cloak, of course. That's a good bit of velvet.
It can be repaired, y'know."

"Get back here, frogbrain. See what happened to the fox—
he wore the cloak. D'you want the same thing happening to
you?"

"Frogbrain yourself, dimwit. Can't you see the eagle's dead?
Any creature can wear that cloak now."

"Hoi! Don't you call me dimwit, droopywhiskers."

"I'll call you what I like, dimwit. Nitears! Fatnose!"

Tsarmina smiled inwardly, a third victory today. Now that she
heard Ratflank shouting she could identify the insolent voice
that had often insulted her from the protection of the ranks or
the bottom of a curved stairwell.

Later that day, she instructed Brogg.

"Take Ratflank, and find the bodies of the eagle and the
fox."

"Yes, Milady. Shall I bring them back here?"

"No, Brogg. Bury them."

"As you say, Milady."

"Oh, and Brogg . . ."

"Yes, Milady?"

"How do you feel about that insolent Ratflank these days?"

"Oh, him. He's a cheekybeast, Milady. Called me lots of
nasty names."

"Yes. Me too. How would you like to bury him with the
fox and the eagle?"

"Huh huhuhuh," Brogg chortled. "Can I, Milady?"

"Yes, but not a word to any creature about it."

"Can I have the red cloak too, Milady?"

"Yes, if you want it."

"And Bane's curved sword, Milady?" Brogg pressed her.

"If you can find it."

"Where d'you think it fell, Milady?"

Tsarmina turned her eyes upward as if seeking patience.

"Brogg, I wouldn't know where the sword fell, or the eagle, or the fox. Just get out of my sight and don't bother me with details."

"But what about—Yes, Milady."

Urthclaw was first to reach the underground foundations of Kotir. Tunneling steadily, he made his way along the underground wall until he met up with Billum. Together they continued until they linked up with Soilflyer, who was waiting for them.

"Burr, 'day to 'ee moles," he greeted them. "Foremole an' Owd Dinny be along wi' tools soon, us'ns can brekk throo 'ee rock then."

Lady Amber had sunk the floodgates at the other end of the tunnels; they were to be lifted by rope hoists attached to rock counterweights over high branches. Skipper and his crew had dug fresh tunnels from the river, sloping down to meet the floodgates which separated them from the main tunnels. All the workings had been shorn up with stone and timber. Foremole supervised the removal of rocks from the foundations of Kotir. The moles pried away the soft, damp stones with bars and chisels until they felt the cold fetid air on their snouts. "Burr, oo, durty owd place needen a gurt barth, hur hurr."

Shortly before nightfall, the moles climbed out of the tunnel workings, back in Mossflower, where the woodlanders and Corim leaders had assembled. Bella rolled three large rocks over the holes from which the moles had emerged. Others moved in to pack the bung-rocks firmly in with wood and soil.

Now everything was ready.

Between the lower depths of Kotir and the distant river in Mossflower Woods, all that stood was three timber sluicegates.

Lady Amber laid her tail flat on the lower branches of a sycamore.

The woodlanders held their breath.

Skipper nodded to Foremole.

Foremole nodded to Bella.

Bella nodded to Amber.

The squirrel's tail rose like a starter's flag. There was a creaking of rope pulleys as squirrels launched the rocks from the high trees, riding down to earth on them, holding to the ropes. The counterweights traveled fast, humming across the heavily beeswaxed branches.

The wooden floodgates made a squelching sound as they were pulled free of the earth, then water began rippling through into the tunnels.

The flooding of Kotir had begun!

44

Driving *Wuddshipp* inland against the flow of the River Moss was a difficult task.

All paws manned the oarbanks, and Martin sat alongside Timballisto.

"Phew! I never realized rowing was such heavy work," Martin groaned.

"Pull, my friend, pull. It's twice as bad when you have to do it on half-rations with a sea rat's whip cracking about your ears and you chained to the oar."

The vessel had been built for coast raiding. Though it was a large craft, it had a flat bottom for taking shallow draught; thus it was able to travel upriver without a deep keel sticking in the shallows.

Inland they traveled, sometimes aided by a breeze when the sails were hoisted. Other times saw two teams dragging her forward on headropes from the riverbanks.

It took a day and a half of hard work to get across the flat beach and into the dunes, where the river was tighter-channelled and flowed faster against them. Log-a-Log solved the problem by using the long galley oars from the deck. Two crew to each oar, they punted and pushed *Wuddshipp* through the dunes, keeping her head upriver with great difficulty. Gradually the dunes gave way to hilly scrubland and the sand began to disappear.

It was a weary crew that sat upon the bank that night, watching the ship riding at anchor.

Gonff hurled a clod of earth at the fast-flowing water. "We'll never make it this way, mateys. Why not abandon ship and march the rest of the way?"

Harebell and company smiled sweetly.

"Oh, you are a silly, Mr. Gonff. We must take the ship."

"The river flows back to the sea, you see."

"And we may need that to make a quick getaway if we are pushed."

Martin winked at Gonff. "The ladies certainly know their strategy. By the way, has anyone seen Log-a-Log Big Club?"

As if in answer, the shrew strode up out of the gathering gloom. "Aye aye. I've been scouting ahead. Found the old village, too. Come on, you lucky lot. There'll be a hot meal and a warm bed with a roof overhead tonight. Banksnout, you wouldn't recognize your little ones now—they're taller than me. Oh, Martin, I forgot to tell you, we've gained another hundred able-furred recruits."

Delight awaited them at the shrew village as families were reunited amidst cheering and shouting.

"Daddy, Daddy, it's me, Emily, your baby shrewlet."

"Hoho, look at you! You're bigger than your mum."

"Sharptail, you said you were going for acorns. That was four seasons ago! Where have you been?"

"Sorry, m'dear. Sea rats y'know. What's this, grand-shrew babies?"

"Aye, you're a grandpa shrew now."

"By the fur! Here, give me a hold of that little fat feller."

"Gluggabuggaluggoo!"

"Haha. See, he knows me already."

The hares joined Martin and the others around a fire. Two plump shrews served them with hot fruit pie, dandelion salad and bowls of fresh milk. Gonff sang around a mouthful of hot pie,

O the *Wuddshipp* is a goodship,
And we'll sail her anywhere,

Rowed by mice, crewed by shrews,
And often steered by hare.
So hoist the anchor, loose the sails,
Give me a wind that never fails,
And we'll sail the goodship *Wuddshipp*
From here to old Brockhall.

He had to sing it twice again whilst the shrews danced a
hornpipe with the hares.

As the fires burned low, they settled back with full stomachs
and renewed hope for the morn.

Martin and Timballisto slept side by side beneath the stars,
each wrapped in a colorfully woven shrew blanket.

Dinny dug a flattish hole for the hares.

"Oh, thank you kindly, Mr. Mole."

"Such charming manners and swift digging."

"Ooh, and that beautiful velvety fur and strong claws."

Dinny wrinkled his face and tugged his snout, slightly em-
barrassed. "Burr, bless 'ee, baint nought but an owd 'ole, miss-
ies."

The moon rose like a white china plate over the peaceful
scene on the banks of the River Moss.

Tsarmina faced the troops gathered in the large mess hall. She
had specially arranged the gathering by sending Bane's former
mercenaries in first; her own soldiers, led by Brogg in his red
velvet cloak, ringed the mercenaries by jostling them to the
center of the floor. Brogg held up Bane's curved sword for
silence as the wildcat Queen addressed the assembly.

"Bane is dead. Those who served under him have nowhere
left to go now. Move from here, and you do it without supplies
or weapons. Besides, those woodlanders out there would take
care of you in short order. Any creature want to say something?"

There was silence.

"Right," she continued commandingly. "From now on you
take your orders from me. Brogg will see that you get rations
and a billet each. Later I'll see about appointing more officers
and getting you some proper uniforms. Take over, Brogg."

The weasel Captain stepped up, twirling his new sword. "Altogether now. Hail Tsarmina, Queen of Mossflower!"

The response was less than enthusiastic.

Tsarmina made them repeat it until she was satisfied. "That's better. You can learn my list of titles later."

They stood in awkward silence, not knowing what to do next. In the hush that followed, Tsarmina's ears rose visibly. Something was beginning to disturb her.

"Dismiss, all of you. Brogg, you stay with me."

When the hall was emptied she turned to Brogg with haunted eyes.

"Listen, can you hear it?" she asked fearfully.

"I can't hear a thing, Milady."

"Listen! It's water, flowing, dripping, spilling somewhere. Ugh!"

Brogg gave careful ear. Suddenly he brightened up. "Haha. Yes, I can hear it now, Milady. You're right. There is water about somewhere. Damp d'you think?"

The sound of water produced so distressing an effect upon Tsarmina that she forgot to chide Brogg. She cowered in a corner, paws covering her ears to shut out the dreaded noise. Flowing water, seeping water, creeping water, dark, icy, swirling water!

"Brogg, quick, get as many troops together as you can," she ordered desperately. "Find out where that water is coming from and stop it. Stop it!"

Brogg saw the terror on his Queen's face and fled the room.

The whole of the garrison searched high and low. But not too low; nobody, including Brogg, was overkeen to venture beneath the cells. Down there it was dark and cold; down there was the lake where Gloomer used to be kept.

And goodness knows what else!

That night, as Tsarmina sat huddled in her chamber, dripping water echoed in her imagination, never letting up. When the fear of water was upon her, the daughter of Verdauga was no longer Queen of Mossflower, Lady of the Thousand Eyes or Ruler of Kotir.

She was reduced to a crazed, terrified kitten, trembling at the sound of dripping water in the darkness, longing for morning light to come stealing over the horizon.

Something had gone radically wrong with the flooding.

Bella slumped in the grass by the river with Skipper.

"No joy, marm?" he asked solicitously.

"I'm afraid not, Skipper. There seems to be only a trickle oing down the tunnels."

Lady Amber joined the pair. "Aye, it seemed to be going so vell at first. D'you think it's because it's summer and we aven't had much rain?" she suggested.

Skipper chewed a blade of grass. "Maybe so. There's not a ot we can do about it, anyway."

"Maybe we could dam the river?" Bella offered tentatively.

"Impossible, marm," the Skipper of otters snorted. "Dam he River Moss? Stow me barnacles, you couldn't hope to stop a river that size from flowin' to the sea."

Columbine stopped by to join the discussion.

"Perhaps it will fill gradually."

"Aye, missie," Skipper chuckled drily. "We could all sit ere growing old and watch it doin' just that. No, we'll give it a bit more time, then if things are still the same we'll have to hink of another scheme."

Lady Amber whacked her tail down irritably.

"After all that underwater digging and tunneling, then here's the lives that were lost, too. Huh, it makes me mad!"

The river carried on flowing its normal course, only a thin rickle diverting down the flood tunnels.

t was the evening of the following day. Abbess Germaine and Columbine were helping Ben Stickle to take the little ones out or an evening stroll along the river bank. Ferdy and Coggs played with Spike and Posy, together with some young mice. They were sailing miniature boats that Ben had made for them.

Germaine watched fondly as the young ones dashed boister-ously up and down the bank, bursting with energy after being confined to Brockhall the past few days.

"Be careful, Spike. Watch you don't fall in," she called.

"See my boat, Abbess. It's faster than Coggs's."

"Ooh look, Ferdy is cheating. He's pushing his boat with a stick."

"No, I'm not. It's the wind. Mine has a bigger sail."

"Columbine, mine has gone down the hole. Can you get it back for me, please?"

"Sorry, Spike. It's gone for good now. Never mind, I'm sure Ben will make you another."

Ben Stickle crouched to look down the hole where the boat

had vanished. He stood up, wiping his paws and shaking his head.

"Flood tunnels, they're about as much use as an otter in a bird's nest. Now far d'you suppose they'll have filled up the lake under Kotir? A paw's height? A whisker's level?"

The Abbess watched the rays of the setting sun through the trees. "Who knows, Ben. One thing is certain, though: Kotir still stands, dark and evil as ever it was. What a shame that Foremole and Old Dinny's plan never worked."

They turned back to Brockhall.

"Bella says there's no likelihood of rain; the weather is staying fine," Ben added.

Ferdy tucked the boat under his small spines.

"Maybe they should have done it in the winter, Ben," the Abbess observed unhelpfully.

Ben ruffled Ferdy's head. "Maybe frogs should have had feathers. Come on, young 'uns. Get your boats. Back to Brockhall and wash up for supper."

It was a warm night. As the Corim sat about in the main room, an air of defeat hung over the company.

Bella yawned, stretching in her deep armchair.

"Well, any more suggestions?"

There were none. The badger searched one face then another. "Then we must explore the possibilities open to us. But let me say this, I do not want to hear any more plans of mass attack or open war."

Skipper and Lady Amber shifted uncomfortably.

"Foremole and Old Dinny still think that the flooding will work, if they can figure out certain alterations to the original plan," Bella continued. "I know a lot of us do not agree with this, but personally I think that the flooding is our only hope. With this in mind, I propose we visit the site tomorrow morning. Maybe with all the Corim there we might come up with a good idea. If not, then there is only one other sensible thing to do."

Goody Stickle wiped her paws on her flowery apron. "What might that be, Miz Bella?"

"To move all the woodlanders and everything we can carry away from here. We would travel east to Gingivere's new home. I have told you that he and Sandingomm will accommodate us. We would find a welcome there, far away from Kotir.''

Skipper jumped up, unhappiness written on his tough features. ''But that'd mean the cat has won.''

Cries of support rang out for the otter leader.

''Yes, why should we be driven out?''

''We already left our homes to come to Brockhall.''

''It wouldn't be the same in a strange place.''

''I was born around here. I'm not moving!''

Abbess Germaine banged a wooden bowl upon the table to restore order, but it broke in two.

''Silence, friends, please. Let Bella speak,'' she shouted above the din.

Bella picked up the two halves of the bowl, and smiled ruefully at Germaine.

''Thank you, Abbess. Friends, there is more to my plan than first meets the eye. If we were to make this move I am speaking of, then think of its effect upon Kotir. Tsarmina would not have won; she would not have chased us through the woods—we would have left of our own free will. Now, what would it accomplish? Imagine for a moment if we stayed in the east until next summer, or even spring. All the time we were gone the water would continue to run down the flood tunnels. In autumn there is more rain and the wind drives the river faster. Winter would see the current run under the ice, and on warm days the snow would feed the river and swell it. Finally when the thaw arrived in spring, the river waters would flood, mighty and unchecked, then we would truly see the lake rise beneath Kotir. One other thing. Between now and next spring my father, Boar the Fighter, may arrive. He alone can face Tsarmina and defeat her. That is all; I have spoken my piece.''

Foremole rose and came to the table. Taking the two broken halves of the wooden bowl, he held them up.

''We be loik this hobjeck—splitted up we'm baint much use. But if'n us sticken t'gether, then we'm useful, hurr.'' He pressed the two halves together for all to see.

Old Dinny seconded him. ''Foremole be roight, Miz Bell. 'Tis wunnerful molesense.''

Columbine was allowed her say.

''Let us do as Bella suggests. Tomorrow we will go to the flood tunnels, then if nothing can be done we will follow her plan.''

Immediate agreement followed.

"See, Columbine," the Abbess said, picking up the broken bowl in her frail paws, "old and weak as I am, yet somehow I managed the strength to perform a small bit of magic. Let us sleep now. It is late, and tomorrow we can tidy up here and wash the dishes—all except this one."

The Abbess placed the broken halves carefully on the table.

"Maybe a lesson in mole logic would not be a bad thing for a wildcat Queen to learn."

Log-a-Log was in his element as leader of his tribe once more. He roused the entire village an hour before dawn to get the ship under way. With a hundred extra shrews to help, *Wuddshipp* fairly flew along the river. When they were not rowing, they were punting, pushing or hauling on ropes.

"Come on shrews, hoist sail," Log-a-Log commanded. "Two of you on this tiller. Make yourselves busy. Double up on the oars there. You two in the crosstrees, stir your stumps, the Chief is back. Let's show these bunny rabbits how to move a craft up our own River Moss."

"I beg your pardon, old Log-a-Thing."

"Steady on with the name-calling there, O Mighty Leader."

"Indeed, we're hares, not bunny rabbits, d'you mind."

T. B. sat on the deck sharpening pikes. "Odd lot those hares," he remarked.

"Seasoned warriors though," Martin said, as he counted swords and daggers. "Boar the Fighter taught them personally. Don't let their silly talk fool you. I wouldn't have them as an enemy at any price, and I was proud to fight alongside them against the sea rats."

Gonff sniffed the air. His whiskers twitched in the predawn darkness that shrouded the riverbanks.

"Trees, Din. We must be in Mossflower. Dawn will soon tell."

The young mole was painting a crude sign to cover the name *Bloodwake*. It bore the legend *Wuddshipp*. He shook his head admiringly, wiping paint from his paws.

"Hurr, Gonffen, we'm 'ome again, oi'm a-feelen it."

The gruff voice of a shrew in the crosstrees confirmed Dinny's words. "Sun arising eastward, trees growing close, we're in the forest."

"Keep her head straight," shouted Log-a-Log, standing out

for'ard. "Furl those sails in before they snag on the branches. Lively there!"

Martin joined him at the prow.

"At this rate we should make Camp Willow around midday. I never noticed us navigating the ford that crosses the path."

Log-a-Log patted the rail. "I chanced it in the dark. Good sailoring, see. Old *Wuddshipp* skimmed the shallows with her flat bottom. Nice and deep here though, easy going on the oars."

The sun rose above the woodland mists, revealing another hot summer day. Patterns of water light played along the bulkheads, leaf and branch shadow mottled the decks. The oars pulled strong against the deep slow current as the big ship nosed its course, farther into the depths of Mossflower.

45

Brogg watched Tsarmina as she lay flat upon the parade ground with her ear to the floor.

One of Bane's former mercenaries, a rat named Chinwart, tugged at Brogg's cloak and asked, "What's she up to, Cap'n?"

"Can't you see, she's listening for water."

"Water?"

"Aye, water, wormbrain. What d'you suppose she'd be listening for, strawberry cordial?"

Tsarmina sprang up, hurried across the parade ground and lay near the wall of the building. Listening intently, she waved a paw.

"Brogg, over here!"

"Yes, Milady."

"Get down, press your ear to the wall—not up there, down here by the ground."

"Oh, right. Here, Milady?"

"That's it. Tell me what you can hear."

"Er, nothing, Milady."

"Are you sure, Brogg?"

"I'm certain, Milady."

"Well, I can hear water running."

"But I can't, Milady."

"Hmm, perhaps it's my imagination."

"Strange thing the imagination, Milady."

"Are you sure you searched below the cells last night?"

"Positive, Milady."

"Brogg, if I thought you were lying to me . . . You did search there, didn't you?"

The weasel Captain noted the look of fear that flitted across Tsarmina's features. He took full advantage of it.

"Your Majesty, I personally went alone to the place beneath the cells where it's all damp and green with slime and fungus. I searched around that underground lake where the Gloomer lived. The place was full of strange echoes and dripping sounds. Maybe that's what you've heard. The place is always full of odd echoes and dripping noises down there in the blackness. Shall we go down there together and recheck it, Milady?"

Tsarmina could not stop her whole body shaking; she sat on the ground, unconsciously wiping her paws across her coat. "No, no, Brogg," she said nervously. "I won't be going down there. I'll be up in my chamber if you need me for anything."

She hurried indoors, brushing roughly past Chinwart, who had been lingering nearby, eavesdropping on the conversation.

He winked knowingly at Brogg. "I was with you last night. We never went anywhere near that place under the cells. What a pack of old fibs you fed her there, mate."

Brogg grabbed the rat savagely by his ear and pulled him close, twisting hard.

"Listen to me, bonebrain. You keep your skinny mouth shut. I'm giving the orders now, not Bane."

"Owowowow, leggo, you're pulling me lug off!" Chinwart whined pitifully.

Brogg twisted the ear more cruelly.

"I'll rip your tongue out too if I hear another word from you," he said menacingly. "Let her go and search the deep dark places if she wants to. I'm not going down there, not for all the cider in Kotir. Unless, of course, you're volunteering to go down there alone?"

Brogg released the rat, who stood nursing his ear tenderly. "All right, all right! I haven't seen nothing, heard nothing, and I won't say nothing. It's none of my business."

Brogg contemptuously wiped the claws that had been nipping Chinwart's ear on the rat's tunic.

"Good. Now get about your business, pigsears."

When the rat had scurried off, Brogg stood sunning himself. He held the larder keys, had a new red velvet cloak and a dangerous-looking curved sword. To all apparent purposes, he was the only Captain at present serving in Kotir.

Life was beginning to feel fairly good.

A packed lunch was served at the river's edge.

Bella tossed an apple core into the water; they watched it bob to one side then stick in the shallows.

Skipper plucked it out and flung it far. "All I can say is that somehow the River Moss is at a low ebb. Those holes were underwater when we dug them, and now they are high and dry."

Ben Stickle lay flat out on the bank, gazing up at the cloudless sky. "Must be the mild spring we had. Look at it now, hardly a week into the season and it's like midsummer. Huh, it'll be late autumn before we see a drop of rain at this rate."

"So, what is to be done?" Abbess Germaine asked, putting her milk beaker aside.

Lady Amber stroked the space where her ear had been. "What d'you think, Skip? Would it be possible to dam the river now that the level's fallen a bit?"

The otter picked up a pawful of banksand. It ran freely through his claws.

"Marm, even as things are now, it'd be like trying to stop the sunrise at dawn. We don't stand a chance of even trying to block off a river the size of old Moss."

"Er ahem!" Chibb perched on a young chestnut shoot.

They continued talking, ignoring the robin.

"Maybe if we dig the channels a bit deeper."

"Tunnels, you mean."

"Channels, tunnels—it's all the same, isn't it?"

"Ahemhem harrumph!" Chibb called again.

"It is if you're a squirrel, but to a mole or an otter a channel and a tunnel are two completely different things."

"Humph, ahem, harrumph!" Chibb was becoming impatient.

"Hurr, that be correck. 'Oles is 'oles an' furrers is furrers."

"Harrumph, ahemhemhemhem!"

"What d'you mean, furrows, a channel isn't a furr—"

"*Ahem!*"

"Chibb, what's the matter with you? Some nut stuck in your throat, is it?"

"Er ahem, no. But I thought you'd like to know there's a ship coming up the river."

"A ship!"

"What, you mean a boat?"

"Harrumph, I beg your pardon, but I'd have said a boat if I meant a boat. It is a ship, full size, all black, white skull thing on the front, rolled up canvas sails, lots of oars. Ship!"

Bella leaped up, spreading her paws wide. "Every creature take cover. Abbess, you stay with them. Be ready to make a dash for Brockhall if you hear my signal. Skipper, Lady Amber, come with me. We'd better go and investigate. Chibb, did you see who was on the ship?"

"Ahem, 'fraid not. Soon as I sighted it I came here to report."

"Good work," Bella congratulated him. "Come with us. We may need you to carry word back fast to those in hiding."

The woodlanders concealed themselves behind trees, in bushes and under deep loam. The badger, the otter, the squirrel and the robin struck out west along the bank, leaving the scene apparently deserted.

Traveling light, they made swift progress. It was not far to the stretch of water where the ship was.

Chibb was the first to sight it. He fluttered up and down excitedly. "Ahem, see, I told you so. Look at those two big poles sticking up above the trees. They're, er, harrumph, big poles that stick up on ships."

Skipper saw them, too.

"Masts, they are, matey," he explained. "Let's get in closer and take a better look."

On all fours, they crept to the river's edge, concealing themselves in the bushes as the ship hove into view.

"You there, come no farther," Bella called from her hideout, in the forbidding boom of a warlike badger. "If you mean harm to any creature in Mossflower, put back to sea—or deal with me!"

There was silence from the black ship.

•　•　•

On board *Wuddshipp*, Martin and his friends lay on deck, hidden by the ship's sides.

Dinny clapped a paw to his mouth, stifling a chuckle. "Hurr-hurrhurr, oi know oo that be a-shouten."

"Bella, good old Bella of Brockhall." There was a distant look in Martin's eyes. "For a moment there she sounded like Boar."

Log-a-Log nodded toward the shore. "Well, we can't lie here all day. Who's going to answer her?"

Young Dinny solved the problem by standing up and bellowing, "Yurr, thurr be a beast aboard oo's a-perishen frum luv fer one called Combuliney."

The creatures in the bushes dashed out in time to see the mole hit the water with a splash as Gonff heaved him over the side.

"Oo arr, glub, 'elp! Oi baint much gudd at swimmen!"

"Hold fast there, Young Din!" Skipper called, and he was in the water like a flash. He held Young Dinny up as eager paws hauled them on board.

"Skipper, you old waterwalloper!"

"Gonff, you young piebandit!"

"Hallo, Bella. Ahoy, it's me, Martin!"

"Martin the Warrior, welcome home. Look who's here!"

"Lady Amber, where's your ear?"

Log-a-Log's voice rang out, and suddenly *Wuddshipp* was swarming with shrews, mice, hedgehogs, squirrels and hares.

"Bring her hard over. Steady to the bank. Mind those masts on the trees. Steady that tiller. Watch her head in the shallows!"

Chibb flew to the ship and perched importantly upon the rail. "Ahem, I must fly and conduct good tidings to those languishing in concealment."

As he flew off, Skipper chuckled. "Does that mean he's going to tell the others? Strike me colors, but this is a fine 'andsome vessel. I never seen the like of it afore on old River Moss. You didn't steal it, did you, Gonff? Is that two sails I spy? Wonderful. Blow me, look at the size of that tiller! This is a real seagoing craft, all right. What's that big skull on the for'ard tip? A fish! I don't believe there's a fish that big in all the world."

As *Wuddshipp* berthed alongside the bank, Timballisto held up his paws laughing heartily. "Hold steady, otter. You must

e Skipper. I'm Martin's pal Timballisto. We'll answer all your
uestions soon enough."

Bella and Lady Amber came aboard, gazing about in awe as
ªey hugged Martin, Gonff and Dinny.

Bella smiled fondly at the warrior mouse as she patted his
ack. "Martin, you've grown. You really look like a full-
looded warrior now. What a beautiful sword that is! Is my
ather here? Where's old Boar the Fighter?"

A silence fell over the ship's crew. Martin gently took
¡ella's paw.

"Come into the cabin with me, old friend. I have a long
tory to tell you."

here were many stories told that summer afternoon while Mar-
¡n and Bella remained in the cabin. Ferdy and Coggs, Spike
nd Posy sat among a group of woodlanders on the deck. The
¡ttle hedgehogs wore brass sea rat earrings and carried a round
hield each. Their eyes were wide and mouths agape as Gonff
elated the events which had befallen the travelers since they
eft Mossflower to go questing for Salamandastron. Ben Stickle,
¡oody and the Abbess were equally impressed, smiling broadly
vhen Gonff could not get his paw loose to illustrate a point
ecause Columbine was clasping it tight.

"Toads, mateys. You've never seen toads as wicked as this
ot. But when that eel came slithering out of the Scream-
ole . . ."

"Was the eel as big as a tree, Mr. Gonff?"

"Twice as big, Spike. He'd have eaten you without even
pening his mouth."

Lady Amber chuckled drily. "Are you sure you saw mice
vith wings, Gonff?"

"Oh, I never saw them. But Martin and Dinny did. Isn't that
ight, Din."

"Burr aye. Gurt leathery burdmouses, a-flyen about inside
ee mounten."

"Was that Salamandastron mountain, Mr. Dinny?"

"Indeed it was not. Batchaps inside our mountain? Never!"

"Fat chance, young feller me hog, what!"

"Only fire, hares and badgers inside our mountain, old lad."

Gonff looked severely at Trubbs and Company. "Who's tell-
ng this story, me or you?"

"Yes, please be quiet and let Mr. Gonff tell the story Trubbs."

"Rather, he's a much better storyteller than you."

"Indeed, and isn't little Columbine pretty."

"Then there was this beach," Gonff continued enthusiastically. "Huge, big as Mossflower, nothing but sand as far as you could see, besides the water and the crabs."

"Ooh, what's a crab, Mr. Gonff?"

"Well, it's like a spider, only a hundred times bigger, with great nipping claws and lots of hard armor."

"Did you and Martin slay the big crab, Mr. Gonff?"

"Er, well, no, Ferdy. Actually I ended up dancing with it."

"Hahahahahaha!"

"Was it a pretty lady crab, Gonff?"

"No, I think it was a jolly sort of male crab, Columbine."

"Oh, then that's all right."

"Here, I nearly forgot, this is a necklace of shells I made for you. Put it on."

"Oh, thank you, Gonff, it's beautiful. Are they crab shells?"

"No, missie, them's shell shells, c'llected 'em moiself, oi did."

"While Gonff was busy dancing with the crabs, I suppose. Thank you very much, Dinny."

The mousethief chose to ignore the reference to his dancing talent and continued the narrative.

He told of the sands, the movement of mighty sea tides, of the scavenging seabirds and the dead rat whose provisions saved their own lives. He described the meeting with Trubbs and company and how they led the travelers to the mountain. Gonff went on to tell of the fabulous place called Salamandastron, its halls, caves, stairs and passages. He related to his amazed audience the saga of Boar the Fighter, of his roaring forge, gigantic battle sword and his colossal bravery in the war against the sea rats. Gonff told of the struggle that ended with Boar and Ripfang going together to the gates of Dark Forest, and finished with the capture of the ship *Bloodwake*, now called *Wuddshipp*.

There was a moment's complete silence, then the woodlanders flocked about him, babbling questions.

T. B. and some former oarslaves saved Gonff from further harassment by lugging large copper tubs out from the galley.

"Right. Form a line here. It's skilly and duff time!"

The young ones sniffed the savory odors as he explained, "Seafood and potato stew, that's skilly. It'll put hairs on your chest like a giant sea dog. There's plenty of pepper and sea salt in it, too. Finish it all up and show me a clean plate, then I'll dish you up some of my own warrior's recipe: plum and chestnut duff in cream and beechnut sauce. Come on, there's plenty for everyone."

Night fell as *Wuddshipp* rode at anchor, kedged safe in midstream. Martin emerged from the cabin looking pale and sad after the news he had related to Bella. He called the six hares to him.

"Go to the cabin, Bella wishes to talk with you," he told them. "Tell her all you know of her father and the time you spent in his company on the mountain."

"Rely on us, old chap."

"Only the good times. Mum's the word, y'know."

"That's the ticket. How strong Boar was."

"Like a father to us. A handsome badger, what!"

"He taught us all so much. He was so understanding."

"How could we forget such a dear friend."

Before they slept, the travelers were closeted with the Corim leaders to hear how Mossflower had fared in their absence. When they had learned all, they went out onto the deck. The little ones had been bedded down in the cabins, but the novelty of hammock sleeping lost out to weariness. Outside on the deck, every creature was assembled, packing the rails and rigging.

Bella stood with her paw upon the tiller, red-eyed with grief but calm and composed.

Martin took command instinctively. The warrior mouse seemed to have grown in stature and confidence since his return. Every woodlander now looked upon him with a respect that bordered upon awe. He stood on the peak of the after end gallery, the sword glinting under a full moon.

"Friends, I have heard all, and my companions have told you everything that happened to us on our quest. Now I am back."

Abbess Germaine nodded approvingly at the commanding figure. "Tell us what you want us to do, Martin."

The warrior mouse drew his sword and leaned on the pommel stone as his blade pierced the deck timbers.

"Trust me, Mossflower will be saved. I have been thinking of a plan that I will not explain at present. First I must see certain things before I know it can be executed properly. Now we must sleep until the morning. Tomorrow, after the little ones are somewhere safe, you will see what I intend. Do not worry anymore. Our force has been doubled by the numbers who have sailed back with us, and we have seasoned warriors with us now. Boar the Fighter cannot be here tonight, but I know that his strong spirit watches over us. From beyond the gates of Dark Forest he has sent me with this sword to make an end of Tsarmina and all who follow her. I promise you that I will."

Every creature who saw Martin the Warrior that night knew, without a shadow of doubt: he was the one chosen to keep that promise.

BOOK THREE

Of Water and Warriors

46

Deep beneath Kotir the water level had risen gradually. Now it was above the rock sections removed by the moles.

Hour by hour it had risen fractionally. To the casual ear the trickling had stopped, but it was still adding silently to the volume, as it seeped in from below the surface of the gradually rising lake.

Standing at her high window, Tsarmina breathed deeply, filling her lungs with the soothing summer breeze that blew in from Mossflower Woods.

At last the accursed dripping had stopped!

She felt light-headedly happy. Dark, fearful night had given way to this beautiful calm sunlit morning, taking with it the haunting sounds of the water.

Brogg was right, she thought, even though he was only an oafish weasel. There was a certain sense to his logic. Imagination was a strange thing, which played odd tricks upon an overwrought mind.

Now a new resolution was forming in Tsarmina's devious brain, one she considered worthy of her talents.

Mossflower must be conquered!

The eagle was gone; Bane too. And her forces were stronger now with the addition of his one-time mercenaries.

Tsarmina allowed herself an audible snigger. That Bane! He had even taken the trouble to restore and repair all the Kotir woodwork, in anticipation of taking over from her, the Queen of Mossflower. Stupid fox!

Furnishing herself with a bowl of milk and a roasted woodpigeon, she mentally thanked Bane for his supplies, adding another point to her favor. She sat down to breakfast and some earnest thought as to the final solution of the woodlanders.

Tsarmina rang the bell to summon Brogg.

"Your Majesty?"

"Ah, Brogg. Put aside that sword and sit over here at my table."

"Thank you, Milady."

"This morning I was thinking of appointing some new Captains. However, I have since changed my mind, Brogg. You will remain as the one and only officer, giving out my orders, of course."

Brogg sat to attention, his chest puffed out proudly. "Oh, thank you, Milady, thank you. I'll make you proud of me. You won't regret this. Wait and see, I'll—"

Tsarmina silenced the babbling Captain with a wave of the woodpigeon carcass.

"Enough chattering, Brogg. Let me tell you what you must do to earn this great honor."

"I am yours to command, my Queen."

"Good. I want traps, lots of traps. Snares, nets, pits—anything we can think up."

"Traps, Milady?"

"Yes, traps, you great buffoon. I want traps laid all over that forest out there."

Brogg grinned as recognition dawned. "We'll capture some woodland prisoners."

"Capture, kill, maim—I don't care, as long as it makes those creatures afraid to set paw outside their hiding place, wherever they may be. I'll turn the tables on them, and they'll never pen us in again. Give them a good long summer of my scheme, and they'll be only too willing to accept my terms—those who are left after the traps begin their work."

"Right, Milady. I'll start today. How about some covered pits with sharpened stakes at the bottom?"

"Excellent, Brogg. At last you're talking my language. Also, we could arrange some thin strangling nooses concealed in the deep loam."

"Great idea, Milady. How about some big nets and trip ropes?"

"Splendid. Make sure you have lots of poisoned hooks tied in the net meshes. Oh, and don't forget the old bent sapling trick with the hidden noose. You can always bank on some lumbering badger or hopping squirrel to step into it, eh, Brogg."

"Yes, Milady. Imagine all those woodlanders dangling upside down by their back paws. Huhuhu!"

"Hmm, just like apples waiting to be picked."

"Oh, huhuhu. We might just leave them to ripen until autumn before we pick 'em, Milady."

"Heehee. Very good, Brogg. I never imagined you had such a sense of humor."

"Oh, I have my moments, Milady."

"Well, make sure your moments are all victorious ones from now on, my one and only Captain."

Brogg saluted awkwardly, knocking the chair over as he rose. "Yes, Majesty. I'll get right down to it this very morning."

Tsarmina caught the end of his cloak, pulling him back. "There you go, rushing and dashing about like a sparrow after a fly. Priorities, Brogg. If you must do a job, do it properly. Take your time. Gather the right equipment together, organize the troops into squads, give each one a team leader and offer rewards for the most ingenious traps and the best results. Do you see the idea?"

Brogg's face brightened at the power he was about to wield. "You're right, Milady. I'll spend all today organizing, then we can make a start first thing tomorrow."

He departed, leaving Tsarmina back at her high window, still clutching the woodpigeon. She destroyed the carcass by crushing it with a single blow and hurled it out of the window toward the forest.

"Here, have something to eat, woodlanders," she shrieked. "You'll need it by the time autumn comes. I'll keep you penned up in your holes. We'll see who runs out of supplies first."

• • •

Abbess Germaine and Columbine were taking the little ones to stay with Gingivere and Sandingomm. Bella drew a map to direct them. Ferdy and Coggs were torn between visiting their uncle Gingivere and staying behind to become warrior seadogs. Gonff had a word with them.

"Listen, mateys, Martin and I can't be spared to guard the little uns, that's why we thought of sending you two. Imagine how much safer the Abbess and Columbine will feel, knowing that Ferdy and Coggs are along to protect the convoy. I've made you a sling each and a pouch of throwing pebbles apiece."

"Honest to goodness real ones, Mr. Gonff?"

"Aye, the same as Martin and I carry."

Ferdy had only one thing to say: "Right, Coggs. Let's line these creatures up. I'll tell the Abbess and Columbine to lead, we'll protect the rear."

They departed amidst much cheering and paw-waving, both warriors getting their snouts wiped soundly on the corner of Goody's apron.

The Corim leaders set about the distribution of arms. Log-a-Log and his shrews were proficient archers; they used the squirrel shoulder bows as standing longbows, and Lady Amber saw to it they were well supplied. The six hares fell gladly into Skipper's company. They were well liked by the otters, and proved to be as efficient with javelins as they were with their own big pikes, which were greatly admired by the otter crew.

The Loamhedge mice were unused to any sort of weapon, so they joined Goody Stickle to help in any way possible—healing, repairing, and running the field kitchen. T. B. and Young Dinny took the moles. They banded together with the former oar slaves; between them there was an amazing variety of weapons.

Bella strolled over to review them.

"Well, well, who's in charge of this bloodthirsty crew?" she asked, receiving two salutes.

"Captains Timballisto and Young Dinny of the Mossflower irregulars reporting for duty, marm."

Young Dinny brandished a dagger. He was decked out in a many-colored fringed silk sash and brass sea rat earrings.

"Haharr, we'm a roight drefful rabble an' ready furr foighten owt."

Bella returned the salute as she tried to hide a smile.

In the for'ard cabin of *Wuddshipp*, Martin spoke secretly with five strong, experienced otters. When he emerged, the banks were thronged with a horde waiting upon his word. Every eye was upon him as he sprang from the side of the vessel and waded ashore through the shallows. Timballisto had found his old battle armor in the sea rat lockers. He came forward and buckled it on his friend in silence. Setting the round war helmet firmly on Martin's head, he strapped the breastplate on and buckled the greaves about the warrior's paws. Bella and the hares presented Martin with a scabbard and swordbelt which matched his sword to perfection.

Martin turned to his army.

"Let us go and settle the score with Kotir!"

Brogg cursed in the half-light before dawn as he tripped upon a coil of rope lying in the main hallway. The place was a jumble of snaring equipment. The weasel Captain rubbed a bruised paw and wished he had not been so enthusiastic on the previous day. Picking up the rope, he hurled it at Chinwart, as the rat was settling down for a quick nap in the corner.

"Come on, dozychops. On your paws. I thought you were supposed to be helping me sort this mess out?"

"What about the others?" the rat yawned. "Why aren't they all awake and helping?"

Brogg paused, letting go of the net he was dragging to the doorway. "Good idea. Why should I have to do it all myself? Chinwart, go and kick them out of their billets, say that anyone who isn't ready to parade smartly will be reported to the Queen."

The threat worked. A few moments later the hall was filled with sleepy soldiers; but seeing Tsarmina was not about they offered no help. They lounged about, sitting on the stairs.

Brogg remembered Tsarmina's advice.

"Attention," he called. "First one out on the parade ground carrying a trap gets double supper this evening. Anybody who lies about will be sentenced to half bread and water."

Chinwart grabbed three stakes and scuttled outside. The rest began half-heartedly picking up nets.

Chinwart came hurtling back inside.

"Cap'n, they're out there!" he said wildly.

"What are you yammering on about now, rat? Who's out there?"

"Woodlanders! Go and see for yourself!"

Recalling the last woodlander raid, Brogg acted with caution. He poked his head around the doorway nervously, ready to pull back swiftly in case of arrows.

The main gates had been flung agape. Standing in the open with the dawn mist evaporating in the sun around them were a number of creatures: a badger, a mouse in armor, and that brawny otter. Brogg did not linger to see if there were others.

"Chinwart, go and rouse the Queen, quickly!" he ordered.

Tsarmina came bounding down wide awake. She peered round the doorway with Brogg.

"So, at last they're showing themselves. Maybe we might not need the snares, Brogg. Perhaps they've walked straight into a trap."

"But, Milady, they're carrying a white flag. Doesn't that make them peaceable?" Brogg protested.

"Don't believe all you see, Brogg. You're carrying a sword, but that doesn't make you a soldier. Let's hear what they have to say."

As she stepped boldly out into the open, Tsarmina whispered out the side of her mouth at Brogg, "Get the archers. Wait for my signal."

None of the deputation was armed, except the mouse who carried a sword at his side. Tsarmina recognized him immediately, also the cheeky mousethief standing behind him. She curled her lip in scorn.

"Escaped prisoners and woodland rebels, what do you want?"

"We are the leaders of the Corim come to deliver an ultimatum." The warrior mouse's voice was hard and clear.

Tsarmina's mind was racing. All the leaders here in one place; they must not be allowed to escape alive. Had Brogg organized those archers?

"Well, here I am, speak your piece." The wildcat Queen kept her voice deceptively calm.

The warrior pointed a mailed paw at her. "Listen carefully to what I say, cat. You and your creatures have no right to tyrannize or try to enslave woodlanders. We are honest and free. Mossflower is our home."

"You insolent upstart!" Tsarmina laughed harshly. "I

should have killed you when I had the chance. Do you realize who you are threatening? I am Tsarmina, Queen of the Thousand Eyes, Ruler of Mossflower.''

Her adversary did not seem impressed. ''I am Martin the Warrior, and I have not come here to make idle threats. This is what I have to say: leave this place by sunset today, take your army with you, go where you will, but stay clear of Mossflower and do not try to harm any woodlander.''

Tsarmina glanced over her shoulder; she could see the archers standing ready inside the doorway.

''If I do as you say, what then?''

''You will be allowed to leave in peace and none of your creatures will be harmed. You have my word as a warrior.''

Tsarmina shrugged. She held her paws open wide. ''What happens if I choose not to leave?'' she asked.

Martin's tone was like Boar's hammer striking the anvil. ''You will die here, you and all your vermin. I will bring this evil place down on your heads. Again you have my word as a warrior.''

Tsarmina remained silent for a moment, as if considering both offers. When she spoke again her voice was flat and dangerous. ''Big words for a little mouse. I will make no promises save one: you will all be slain where you stand.''

At her signal a score of archers leaped forth, ready to fire.

She folded her paws, smiling sarcastically. ''What do you say to that, little warrior?''

Martin stood like a rock, showing no trace of fear. ''Then we will stand here and be killed by your arrows. But look behind me at the trees and on your outer wall. Every woodlander who can draw bowstring or throw javelin is aiming straight for your treacherous heart. You would not get a paw's length before you were sent to the gates of Dark Forest. So carry on, cat. Tell your archers to fire. We will die so that Mossflower can be rid of you.''

Tsarmina's eyes shifted, dodging back and forth. Otters, mice, squirrels, hedgehogs, even hares—there seemed to be as many of them as leaves in an autumn gale. Each with a weapon trained on her, every face grim with determination.

''Down bows!'' she called to her archers in an urgent hiss.

The soldiers pointed their bows to the ground, allowing the strings to slacken off.

The Corim leaders began walking backward out of the gate-way.

Tsarmina extended a quivering claw. "This isn't where i finishes," she threatened, her voice shrill with rage. "Oh no this is only the start."

Martin's response rang back at her. "Until sunset tonight We will wait outside for your answer."

Brogg popped his head out. "Don't forget to close the gates after you, huhuhuh!"

As the gates closed, Bella's voice was loud and clear. "These gates are being shut, not to stop us getting in, but to keep you from getting out."

Tsarmina dashed inside. "Get those nets and ropes out of my way. I want everybody up to the top of Kotir, the very top Hurry!" she urged.

Gonff stood in the shadow of a sycamore with Martin.

"Well, matey, it's done now. We're all in it, win or lose No second chances. You heard the cat—this is only the start."

"She's planning something, Martin," Lady Amber said from up in the branches. "It's gone too quiet in there for my liking."

Martin looked up. "Mine, too. Tell the leaders to draw their companies back under cover. Let us wait and see what move she'll make."

Whispered orders went out, and the woodlanders moved back, blending into the green shade and mottled shadow. The outside wall was deserted; not a whisker, paw or weapon showed anywhere. Eerie silence fell upon the soft morning warmth, broken only by a faint rustle of breeze through the treetops.

Filing silently up a wooden loft staircase, Tsarmina led her forces out onto the flat, square, battlemented roof of Kotir. Signaling them to lie low, she peered over the top of the wall.

"Quietly now. Archers come forward. Keep your heads down and station yourselves around these battlements. Be ready to fire at my command."

The archers deployed stealthily. They lay waiting.

Tsarmina nodded to them.

"Fire!"

A deadly hail of arrows flew earthward. She watched as they vanished into the treetop foliage. There were no screams or cries from below; silence reigned.

"Fire again!"

A second volley of shafts plunged down into the green fastness.

Still nothing.

Farther back in the woodland, Skipper munched an oatcake. "I wonder if the cat's allowing her troops an early snack?"

Timballisto polished an apple on his fur. "Shouldn't think so. Look at those arrows peppering the trees where we stood a moment ago."

The woodlanders sat eating, watching scores of arrows striking the branches and soft earth, just out of range of where they sat. A Loamhedge mouse was sharing a bowl of milk with Gonff.

"Shouldn't we be firing a few arrows back, sir?" he asked boldly.

"No, matey. Waste of time. Too high. Besides, we'd give our position away to them. Let 'em waste more shafts awhile yet."

"Unless we could get high up in those trees on the north side," Barklad said as he nibbled a stick of celery.

"Could you hit them from there?"

"What! Good squirrel archers! Of course we could, Martin."

The warrior mouse pondered. "Hmm, possible I suppose. But we'd need something to decoy them into concentrating their fire over this way. Any ideas, Amber?"

Tsarmina waved her paw for the archers to cease fire. Some of them did not see her and kept shooting.

"Stop, that's enough, fools," she shrieked. "Can't you see they're not there!"

The arrows stopped. A fox called Bentbrush turned to his companion, a rat named Whegg.

"Bane would have thought of something to weed 'em out," he said nostalgically.

"Like what, for instance?"

"Well, like, er. I don't know. But he'd have thought of something."

"If he was so smart, why is he so dead now? Look, the bushes are moving down there!"

Tsarmina was alongside the rat in a flash. "Where? Show me!" she demanded eagerly.

"Down there, right by where we were shooting."

The fringe bushes at the wood's edge were indeed shaking and rustling.

Tsarmina smiled with satisfaction. "So, we weren't just wasting arrows; some of them are hit. Over here, you lot. Give those bushes a good raking with arrows. I don't want anything left alive down there. Ready, fire!"

The shafts went through the bushes like a shower of rain.

Lady Amber climbed high in an elm until she glimpsed the back of the soldiers over the battlements. Notching an arrow to her bowstring, she murmured to the twelve stout squirrels who were following her example, "Three shots, quick as you like, then away from here."

The shafts flew straight and true, striking the huddled group who were firing upon the bushes. Tsarmina was saved by the body of Bentbrush, who fell across her, two arrows protruding from his back. There was nowhere to run on the open roof, and a score of soldiers were struck by arrows.

Before they could recover and retaliate, the squirrels had gone.

Log-a-Log and Foremole sat some distance from the bushes. Well hidden, they tugged vigorously at lengths of rope that were attached to bush and branch.

"Yurr, 'ow long do us'ns keep a-tuggen 'ee ropes?"

"Take a rest now, Foremole. They've stopped firing."

Lady Amber and her squirrels swung in from the high branches.

"Good decoy, Martin," she congratulated him. "We gave them something they won't forget in a hurry. Nearly got the cat, but a fox fell across her."

"Yes, a clever strategy, but you must keep on trying to think one jump ahead of Tsarmina. She'll come back at you with something else, if I know anything of warfare. That cat is as cunning as any sea rat, you'll see," Log-a-Log warned.

Martin pointed to Chibb descending from the blue. "Here comes my spy now."

"Er, ahem, I overheard the cat giving orders."

"What was she saying?"

"Well, harrumph, ahem. Most of it wasn't fit for the ears of

ny decent creature, but she's left a token force on the roof and
s taking the rest downstairs.''

Martin unsheathed his sword. "That may mean she intends
oming out to make an attack on us."

Bella nodded. "Well, she can't get through the gateway. I've
ocked and wedged that gate myself."

"Then they'll probably be coming over the walls," Skipper
nterrupted. "This is what I've been waiting for, hearties—a
;ood chance to use my pike hares."

"Oh, we'll be there, old bean, pikin' away."

"Rather. Done this sort of thing before, dontcha know."

"Jab, thrust and whatnot; all part of the game."

Young Dinny waved a dagger at his crew. "Ho arr, we be
oight aside 'ee. Wudden miss et furr nuthen."

Martin called order. "I want no pitched battle or wholesale
;illing," he told them firmly. "You must do just enough to
lefend our position and send them back in retreat over that
vall. Lady Amber, keep squirrels high in the trees; have them
ake brushwood shields for protection. They must keep those
archers on the roof pinned down."

\ weasel called Foulwhisker peered around the doorway to the
arade ground.

"All clear, Milady. They think we're still on the roof," he
eported.

"Good. Get across the open ground quickly and don't drop
hose ladders."

The attack force was a large one. Brogg led them across the
arade ground to the wall.

"Right, you lot. Set the ladders up and get climbing," he
rdered.

They scaled the walls until the top of the stonework was
hick with soldiers. Nervously they watched the trees, until
Brogg came up last, panting hard.

"See anything?"

"No, Cap'n. All clear."

"Then haul these ladders up and let them down the other
side."

As the last troops set paw on the woodland side, Martin appeared from the trees. He was backed by six hares carrying
pikes. Brogg grinned; not a very large reception.

"Troops charge!"

Otters poured out of the undergrowth from behind Martin and the hares. From the left and right flanks, a horde of Mossflower irregulars sprang from hiding, closing like pincer jaws.

Pike clashed upon spear as the two sides met, and battle cries arose.

"Death to the woodlanders!"

"Martin for Mossflower!"

A fox struck down an oar slave. He was about to finish him off when Skipper thwacked him hard with a rock-laden sling, knocking the spear from his paws. The six hares were causing devastation, with their pikes easily outreaching Kotir spears. Soldiers facing fierce otters ran to the left or right, only to see the way barred by mobs of shrews, mice, moles and oar slaves.

Brogg was no coward when his blood was roused. He fought madly to reach the warrior mouse who carried the whirling sword.

Martin took a stoat low down, whipping the blade up and round at head height as Boar had shown him. Turning, he felled a weasel. Then Brogg was upon him, bulling forward. Unable to use his spear, the Captain threw himself at the warrior mouse. Martin saw him coming. Falling backward and throwing his paws up, he caught Brogg off balance, tossing him neatly. Skillfully, Brogg landed on all fours. Grabbing his curved sword, he came thundering back with the point held low. Martin rolled to one side, leaped straight up, and chopped down with a double-pawed swing. The weasel Captain found himself holding a sword handle from which the blade had been completely shorn. He backed up to a tree, with Martin's sword at his throat.

"Back over that wall. Now!" The warrior mouse's voice snapped like a whip.

To Brogg's surprise, the blade lowered. He found himself dashing for the wall, shouting aloud, "Retreat, retreat. Back to Kotir!"

Skipper hefted a javelin, taking aim at Brogg, but Martin's sword pushed the weapon aside.

"Enough, Skip. Let them go."

The vanquished troops fought tooth and claw among themselves to be first over the wall lest the warrior mouse change his mind.

Loamhedge mice moved in to help the wounded. Martin, Skipper and Gonff stood breathing heavily.

"You should have let us finish it, Martin."

"No, Skipper," Martin said firmly. "The only time I would have allowed that was if the cat had been here."

Gonff sheathed his two fighting daggers. "Blow me, matey. We had them whipped there. Why did you let 'em go?"

Martin wiped his sword on the grass, staring at the slain of both sides strewing the woodland floor.

"To show them we are not evil," he said at last. "We only want what is ours, and now I think they know we're strong enough to get it. Could you not see, the fight is going out of those soldiers? They are beginning to look as if they need food. Their larders must be just about empty, and only the fear of their cruel Queen keeps them going. Besides, when I put my plan in motion with the help of some otters and my friend Timballisto, Kotir will be truly broken and defeated until it is only a bad name to frighten little ones off to bed with in the seasons to come."

Bella shook her head sadly as she picked up the limp form of a squirrel who had been a former oar slave.

"You did right, Martin," she told him. "There is no greater evil than killing. I don't care whether they call it war or justice. Life is precious."

A Loamhedge mouse wiped away a tear as she turned to Timballisto. "I think Bella's right," she added.

"Aye, and so do I, young missie. But what can Martin do? He has to lead us to a lasting peace against a cruel and cold-blooded cat," Timballisto said gently.

There was no more fighting that day. Both sides halted to lick their wounds. Martin waited for sunset, whilst Tsarmina berated her soldiers as she tried to think up fresh schemes for victory.

47

It had been a hot afternoon. The sun started to redden again a dusky purple sky as Tsarmina ventured to stand at her hig window. There was the warrior, standing armor-clad on top the wall. He had probably used one of the ladders left behin by the cowards who had retreated. Tsarmina raked her claw across the window ledge in helpless fury.

"What do you want, mouse?"

As she asked the question, she was groping furiously for th bow and arrows which she kept close to paw.

"The sun is nearly set, Tsarmina. Remember the ultimatu I gave you this morning?"

The wildcat Queen played for time as she fumbled with bow and arrows beneath the window ledge.

"Tell me again, mouse. Refresh my memory."

"The message has not changed. There is still time for yo to take your army out of here and leave us in peace," he sai reasonably. "You will not be harmed if you leave before th sun is down."

The arrow came speeding through the air and struck Marti in the side. The warrior mouse flinched and swayed with pai but he stood firm. Tsarmina bit her lip until blood flowed.

338

Martin turned and painfully mounted the ladder, with the shaft still sticking in him. As he went, his words were like a final knell:

"Then it is finished. I will bring this place down around you stone by stone. You will travel to the gates of Dark Forest."

The troops sitting in the mess hall heard every chilling word in the failing light.

"We should have got out of here long ago," a ferret called Ditchpaw snarled at Brogg. "With an army our size we could live off the fat of the land anywhere."

Others joined him.

"Aye, why should we fight for this old ruin? It's hers, not ours."

"I was with Bane. He let us fight and keep our plunder sacks filled. There isn't even enough to eat in this stinking place."

"I don't know what the mouse has planned, but you can bet he really means business."

"Aye. We must have been mad ever to think woodlanders were soft."

"Right. Look at the mates we lost today, and where was she?"

"Hiding on the other side of the wall like a worm from a fish."

"More like a cat from a mouse, hahaha—"

Tsarmina stood in the doorway. "You were saying?"

Silence fell across the mess hall.

"Well?" Tsarmina's eyes narrowed.

The rat called Whegg stood up. "We want to get away from this place," he whined.

Tsarmina prowled across to him, her face almost touching his nose. "Too late, rat. The sun has set. However, there is one way you could get out: by the gates of Dark Forest. Do you want me to send you that way?"

Whegg stood trembling with fear as Tsarmina slid back to the doorway. Turning, she smiled disarmingly.

"Look at you. All of you panicking because of a mouse in armor and some woodland creatures. You've heard what they want. They don't want a war, they wish to leave us in peace. Why?"

The troops gazed dumbly at her.

"I'll tell you why, because they cannot get us out of here! Kotir is too strong. Take no notice of mouse threats," she urged. Ditchpaw swallowed hard and dared to speak. "But the mouse said he was going to destroy Kotir stone by stone. We all heard him."

Tsarmina beckoned to Ditchpaw and a hefty-looking fox.

"You and you, push against that wall," she ordered.

Puzzled but obedient, they shoved against the wall with their paws.

"Oh, you can do better than that. Harder! Push with all your might!"

The two creatures pushed and strained until they fell down gasping.

Tsarmina laughed. It sounded almost jolly. "Well, did anyone see Kotir budge, even a tiny bit?"

Troops shook their heads, and there was a chorus of no's.

"Of course not, you great load of ninnies." The wildcat spoke like a mother hedgehog to her infants. "It would take more than all of you and the woodlanders together to make a single dent in these stones. Kotir will outlast even the forest outside. Now, listen. I'm going to break my golden rule and tell you about my plan. First let me say there is no shortage of food. In fact, starting tomorrow, you are all on extra rations."

Brogg jumped up. "A cheer for the Queen, mates!"

"Hurray!"

Tsarmina nodded gratefully to her Captain. "We will last out the summer. It has been a drier season than ever before," she continued encouragingly. "Just before the first rains of autumn come, I will have my archers prepare many fire arrows, exactly like those the sly woodlanders shot at us. Can you guess what I'm going to do?"

"Burn the woodlands, Milady."

"Who said that?"

"I did, Milady."

"What's your name?"

"Foulwhisker, Your Majesty."

"Well done, Foulwhisker. Good weasel. Yes, we'll stay safe in Kotir all summer, with plenty of supplies for everyone. Then in autumn we'll burn the woodlanders and their forest together."

Brogg was on his paws again. "Well, mates, I'm all for it. A lazy summer with lots of grub. I vote we stay here with our Queen. She's not afraid of woodlanders. Huh, she even shot their boss tonight."

•

A cheer rang out from the troops. It was not wildly enthusiastic, but at least it carried a note of optimism.

Bella and Lady Amber bent over Martin.

"Looks as if he's coming round," the badger reported thankfully.

T. B. held the sling pouch with the arrow still sticking from it. "It would have been a different story without this stone carrier."

Bella bathed Martin's brow with cool water. "Even allowing for that, it's not exactly a scratch, is it?"

Martin opened his eyes and immediately tried to stand, but Amber pushed him back. "Be still," she said firmly. "It's only by luck you weren't really injured. Bella, stick some herbs on his wound and bind it up."

"What hour is it, Gonff?" Martin asked, looking at the sky.

"Not long before midnight, matey."

"Bella, thank you. But please stop fussing over me like a mother hedgehog. I must get up. There is important work to be done."

Bella extended a paw. "Then up you come, warrior. Gonff and I will help you. What is this important work that cannot wait?"

Martin tested his leg experimentally, and winced. "I must get to *Wuddshipp* tonight."

"Well, jump up on my back. It's quite broad enough to bear a mouse—even a wounded warrior."

With Gonff walking in front to clear the path for Bella, they made their way through the warm woodland night.

Bula the otter lay crouched on the foredeck. She watched the dark shapes materialize silently from the trees by the bank.

"Who goes there?" she challenged them.

"Corim of Mossflower."

"Advance and be recognized."

"Bula, you old shrimp-chaser!"

"Gonff, you little pie bandit. Hello, Miz Bella. What news? Martin, are you hurt? What happened?"

Martin slid from Bella's back and leaned on his sword. "It's nothing, Bula. Is everything ready?"

"As ready as it'll ever be, Martin."

Bula gave a short bark, and her four companions appeared on deck.

Martin gave a last fond look at *Wuddshipp* as she rode at anchor on the River Moss, then he nodded to Bula.

"Sink her!"

"Scuttle *Wuddshipp*, matey? Are you out of your mind?" Gonff blinked in disbelief.

Bella laid a heavy paw gently on the mousethief. "Martin knows what he's doing, Gonff."

With a splash the five otters dived into the river and were momentarily lost to sight in the dark water. When they surfaced they were at opposite ends of the craft, three for'ard, two astern. Clamped in their jaws were rope hawsers which ran to the ship. They began swimming strongly, tugging *Wuddshipp* around so that she drifted until stem and stern faced opposite banks. Now *Wuddshipp* stood side on across the River Moss.

The otters emerged, dripping. Passing the headropes to Bella, they dived back in and joined their friends on the other bank. "Make those stern ropes fast to that big oak," Martin called out to them. "Give some slack to allow for sinkage. We'll make her fast to this beech over here."

Diving back into the water, the otters boarded the vessel amidships. Bula handed out wooden mallets, and they went below. She pointed out the inlets under the oardecks.

"Knock those spigots and seacocks wide open, crew. Let the water in."

They went at it with a will. Soon the river was gushing in from eight different points and the bilgewater level rose swiftly. Bula took one last look around, satisfied that the job was done.

"She's filling fast, crew. All ashore!" she ordered.

Martin stood on the bank with them. They watched *Wuddshipp* list slightly with the flow, then the black ship began sinking lower in the water. Above the gurgling flow and creaking timbers, Gonff could be heard singing a mournful farewell,

> You carried us safe o'er the water,
> So proudly you sailed the blue sea,
> Now lie on the bed of a river,
> To help make old Mossflower free.
> But here in our hearts we will keep you, *Wuddshipp*.
> Like a great bird of freedom upon that last trip,
> With the wind in my whiskers,

Surrounded by friends.
Sleep deeply, old *Wuddshipp*,
Your voyaging ends.

The little mousethief sniffed as he wiped a paw across his eyes. "It's a good thing Log-a-Log isn't here, matey."

Stem and stern sank levelly as the vessel went down. With a cascading ripple the waters broke over her midship rail.

Martin turned away. "Come on, Gonff. I can't bear to watch her anymore."

A pale silver moon dappled the forest floor as they made their way back to the camp outside Kotir. Bella, with Martin on her back, lumbered through the calm summer night, flanked by Gonff and Bula.

"Don't fret. It was a great act of sacrifice, a brave thing. Boar would have been proud of you both," she consoled them in her gruff, gentle voice.

Bula was a little more cheerful. "I'll bet you when this is all over that Skipper will find a way to refloat your *Wuddshipp*."

Gonff looked across at the otter. "D'you really think so? You're not just saying it to make us feel better?"

Bula winked. "Of course not. We never stoved her in, just opened the inlets. She's not damaged. Don't you worry, matey. Skipper'll sort it out. He's got other things in his head beside water in his ears, that's for sure."

Back at the river, only the tops of stem, stern and masts were showing. The bilges had settled deep into the river bed under the steady pressure and weight of inflowing water.

Now the River Moss was blocked. It began overflowing its banks, backing up and pressing against the sunken ship that barred its course. In less than an hour there were only three points where the dammed-up river could find escape.

Straight down the flood tunnels!

The swirling waters gushed in with a thunderous rumble. A creamy brown deluge poured underground, sweeping earth, loam, twigs and rocks along in its mad rush. It ripped through the tunnels, tearing and battering at the walls until the shorings were swept away and the whole thing was welded into one great torrential underground bore, hurtling toward the lowlands where Kotir stood.

• • •

Foremole and Old Dinny were dozing over the crusts of a deeper 'n' ever pie when they felt the ground reverberate under them. Foremole pressed his snout into the loam.

"Thurr she goes, Owd Din. Doant need no diggen claws to tell 'ee wot be 'appenen unnerground."

"Ho urr, they varments soon be getten a gurt barth o' thurr loives, oi do b'leeve."

"Harr, stan' on moi tunnel, oi'd 'ate t'be they!"

Mossflower slept on through the night, which was still and calm.

But only on the surface.

Whegg the rat yawned and shivered. He tugged the old grain sack which served as a cloak tighter about his skinny body against the afterdawn freshness. The morning had started cloudy, with little sunlight to provide warmth up on the flat roof where he was stationed on watch. Brogg came stamping up. Rubbing his paws together, he glanced over the battlements at the still woodland.

"Quiet night, eh, Whegg?"

"Aye, bit chilly though, and they're still out there," Whegg reported.

"Those squirrels been shooting again?"

"Nah. They don't if we don't. But I think there's something going on down there."

Brogg squatted down beside Whegg.

"Ahh, what can they do? You heard the Queen. We'll just sit tight here until the moment's right."

"Huh, sez she! Those woodlanders aren't as green as they're grass-colored," Whegg answered back cheekily.

Brogg shoved him playfully. "You let me and Milady worry about that. Had your breakfast yet?"

"No, not yet. I'm starving. Any chance of slipping off for a bite to eat, matey?"

"Matey! You mean Captain, don't you?"

"All right. Captain, then."

"Aye, go on. But send a relief up here. I've got other things to do besides standing guard for the likes of you."

Whegg rubbed the stiffness from his limbs as he hobbled downstairs, making for the pantry rather than the mess as there was more chance of food down near the larder. A fox passed him, wiping and scrubbing its paws against the stones.

"Damp down there, mate. Water's coming up between the pantry floorstones," he warned.

"Water? Where?"

They both looked up to see Tsarmina coming down the stairs. The fox beckoned over his shoulder.

"Down there, Milady. Anyhow, it's always been damp below stairs."

Whegg shook his head. "Only in the cells and beneath them, not on ground level. Besides, it's summer, and there hasn't been a drop of rain since spring."

Tsarmina pushed past them urgently. "Follow me you two!"

They hurried down to the pantry passage. Water was leaking through the floor, and all three jumped back onto the bottom stairs.

"It was only damp when I was here a moment ago," the fox said in surprise. "Look, you can see the water covering the floor now!"

Whegg touched the water with his paw. "But how? I mean, where has it all come from?"

Tsarmina's eyes were riveted on the water. "Get through to the dungeons, rat," she said shakily. "Tell the guards there to come up and report to me. They'll know."

Whegg saluted. Stepping gingerly down, he slopped off along the wet passage.

Tsarmina backed up several stairs and waited.

Moments later, Whegg came swishing hurriedly back, his face a mask of disbelief.

"Milady, the staircase to the cells is completely underwater. It's like looking into a well. Ugh! There are two drowned weasels floating in there."

Wild-eyed, Tsarmina began rubbing her paws as if trying to dry herself. Suddenly she turned and bounded upstairs. Soldiers' voices were shouting everywhere.

"The parade ground's like a lake!"

"Bottom barracks is flooded!"

"The supplies will be ruined!"

"Front hall's awash, mates!"

"All the cell guards have been drowned!"

Screams and cries rang in her ears as the Queen hurried to her chamber. Grabbing the bow from the wall, she began firing arrow after arrow at the empty face of the woodlands.

"Show yourselves! Martin, come out and fight!" she shrieked.

In the high branches of a poplar, Martin stood, supported by Lady Amber and four squirrels.

Barklad patted him resoundingly. "Look, Martin, it worked. Kotir is flooding!"

"How high is it, matey?" Gonff called up from ground level.

"Oh, it's looking pretty wet, Gonff."

"And still rising?"

"Aye, still rising, all right."

The squirrel Queen signaled her crew to take the warrior mouse back down to earth.

"What now, Martin?" she asked.

"Now the real plan goes into action. I've never told you about my friend Timballisto, or even how he comes to have a strange name like that. Well, you just wait and see what he has in store for Kotir, he'll help it to sink, all right.

"I'm going to get my sword and armor. Tell the Corim leaders to have every available fighting creature gathered at the edges of the land rise. There's bound to be a final charge."

Whegg the rat and a weasel named Slinkback threw their armored mail tunics and shields over the rooftop battlements. There was a faint splash as they hit the water below.

Brogg faced them, his curved sword at the ready. "Here, what d'you think you're up to? You can't do that."

Slinkback laughed openly in the Captain's face. "Haha. Listen, Brogg, you'd do better to chuck your stuff over too, or do you want to be drowned in full armor?"

The Captain looked at his Thousand Eye tunic and red velvet cloak. "But what will Milady say?"

Emboldened by his companions' actions, the weasel called Foulwhisker skimmed his round shield over the battlements. "Don't listen to Brogg, mates. We've heard enough lies. That mad cat will get the lot of us killed to save this old ruin." The weasel whirled at a sound behind him, but too late.

Tsarmina was standing there. She dealt him a furious blow, killing him where he stood. Lifting the body effortlessly, she threw it contemptuously over the battlements, then turned upon the rest.

"Who's next?" she challenged them. "Does anyone want

to join him? Come on, step up. Let's see who wants to disobey the Queen of Kotir.''

They backed off fearfully; the slightest scowl or mutter now would mean instant death.

Tsarmina snatched up a fallen spear and jabbed it toward one group, then at another. The troops cringed, cowering close to the walls. She laughed insanely as she snapped the stout weapon with a single fierce movement.

''Look at you! Call yourselves warriors! I could break you as easily as I snapped that spear. But I won't. I'm going to use you to break those woodlanders out there. The time has come for you to act like proper soldiers. You'll fight or die, either victory or death. I'll show you how to make wa—''

Whump!

The whole roof shook.

Terrified, the troops fell flat.

Tsarmina dashed to the edge, in time to see a second boulder come whizzing through the air like some giant shapeless bird.

Whoom!

It struck halfway up the wall. Masonry fell, splashing into the water from the gap left by the striking missile.

As the roof shook under the impact of another boulder, the wildcat Queen grasped the battlement, staring wildly across the deep flooded area.

Skipper patted the rough timber frame. ''What do you call this thing again, mate?''

Timballisto was helping squirrels and otters to lay the next boulder in the cradle.

''A ballista, Skip. I built them in the wars up north many a time when I was young. Great idea, isn't it?''

Skipper shook his head admiringly as the system of pulleys and counterweights creaked under the winding handles. A long throwing arm fashioned from three silver birches strained and bent against the brake lever.

''You're a cunning old wardog, Timballisto. Ha, a baby hedgehog could operate this big catapult.''

Young Dinny jumped up and down, clapping his paws. ''Let oi do et. Oh, please give thiz young mole a shot, zurr.''

Timballisto shut one eye, sighting along the line the rock would take when it was fired.

''Aye, why not? Be my guest, Young Din,'' he agreed.

The mole could hardly release the lever pin for chuckling. He threw himself face down in the grass as the lever snapped back; the long arm pitched forward as the rock shot away overhead.

"O joy, O arpiness! Whurr'd et go? Wot'd oi 'it?"

The watchers on the shore saw the tower shudder. A hole appeared as the rock hit Kotir with tremendous force. Rubble and masonry showered into the water as another gap was made.

A loud cheer went up from the woodlanders.

48

Tsarmina turned from the battlements to give an order to her soldiers, but they were gone. The roof was deserted.

Below in the water were foxes and weasels, ferrets, stoats and rats. Some were swimming, others were hanging onto doors they had hacked off with their weapons. Wooden window shutters, tables, benches, anything that could float was being utilized by the fleeing army.

The rooftop shook from yet another assault by the siege catapult.

Brogg stood faithfully at the head of the stairs.

"You had better come down, Milady. The whole building is starting to crumble inside. Hurry, before the stairways collapse," he advised.

Tsarmina turned left then right. She ran to the battlements, looked over and ran back in agitation.

"You'll see, we'll win yet. It's that traitor brother of mine, Gingivere. He must still be alive. A single mouse couldn't have thought all this up. I should have killed them both and made sure they were dead when I had the chance," she ranted.

Leaping the spaces where the stairs had been demolished, the Queen and her Captain made their way to the high chamber.

It was still intact. Beneath their paws, Kotir rumbled and crumbled in its death throes. The whole place was beginning to disintegrate into the massive, rapidly rising lake which surrounded it.

Brogg lifted a table and slid it out of the window. It did not have far to go before it splashed into the water.

"Hurry, Milady. We can both make it out of here on the table!"

Helped by Brogg, Tsarmina made an undignified scramble over the window ledge. She lowered herself onto the upturned table. It rocked crazily in the water, but stayed floating.

Brogg climbed up on the window ledge. "Hold it steady, Milady, closer to the wall so that I can get on."

Tsarmina ignored the Captain. She pushed farther along the wall until the table was beyond Brogg's reach.

"Milady, wait for me!"

"Don't be silly, Brogg." Tsarmina sounded almost condescending. "You can see there's only room enough for your Queen on this thing. Two of us would sink it."

The Captain scratched his head dully as if trying to understand.

"But, Your Majesty, what about me?"

Tsarmina pushed farther along the wall. "Oh, you'll find something, Brogg. Get ashore and regroup the army. I'm going to find that mouse warrior and my brother Gingivere. Don't you worry, I'll make them pay for the loss of Kotir."

Tsarmina floated off round the sinking stronghold, propelling herself along the walls by paw, to the other side, where there were no woodlanders.

Brogg crouched miserably on the window sill, trying to make up his mind which surprised him more—the desertion of Tsarmina his Queen, or the arrival of a huge ballista boulder which put an end to his bafflement forever.

It was a tranquil summer morning far to the east in Mossflower. On the farm the small creatures were out tending crops with Gingivere and Sandingomm. It had become a second home for the young woodlanders who had made the trip to this peaceful haven of refuge.

Abbess Germaine and Columbine sat upon the riverbank together. Columbine was busying herself with roots she was drying; it was a good area for medicinal herbs and plants. The

Abbess had charcoal and parchments; she was drawing something. Columbine watched from the corner of her eye. She remembered Loamhedge. The Abbess used to draw a lot in those far-off days, often translating her thoughts onto parchments which she kept in a journeying satchel—a thing she had not done since their arrival at Brockhall.

Now the old mouse took up a dried reed. Using it as a straight edge, she worked busily with her charcoal sticks, rubbing here, altering there, shading and curving the lines until a clear outline of a great building began to emerge. Germaine peered over the top of her spectacles as she worked. Columbine smiled fondly at her.

"That's a fine big house, Abbess."

"I suppose you could call it a house, child. I've had this idea in my mind since we left Loamhedge."

"Ah yes, poor old Loamhedge. I was just thinking about it myself. Perhaps we could have built your big house there, had we been able to stay," Columbine suggested.

"No, that would not have been possible, Columbine. There was very little local stone around the Loamhedge area."

Columbine put the roots aside and looked at the drawing with renewed interest.

"Then this great house is not just a dream. It could be built if we had the right material and location, plus, of course, the creatures to build it."

Germaine nodded decisively, spreading the plans out between them. "Oh yes, indeed. Let me explain. This would not be a mere house. The building I am planning will be a real Abbey for all our woodland friends who wish to live there, a peaceful place where all would exist in happiness."

"How lovely. Tell me more about your Abbey," Columbine said excitedly.

The old Abbess explained eagerly, pleased to have Columbine showing interest in her brainchild.

"See here, this is the outer wall, with its gatehouse, small wicket gates and big main threshold. Here is the main building—bell tower, Great Hall, kitchens, dormitories, infirmary, store rooms, cellar spaces . . . I have thought of everything that a proper Abbey needs. These areas around the large building are enclosed within the main walls—they are orchards and fields to grow crops in, a pond, and everything it would need to be self-supporting. This is a dream that could become reality if Mossflower were freed.''

Columbine gazed in wonder at the well-outlined plan. ''You say it could become reality?''

''Oh yes.'' The old Abbess nodded emphatically. ''When we first saw Kotir I noticed that though the stones were darkened and slime-covered, it had been built of red sandstone. There are outcrops of it all over the Mossflower area. Yesterday I crossed the River Moss on a log, and there is an old quarry over there. We could hew an endless supply of good stone from it.''

''A beautiful dream, Abbess, maybe someday—''

''Abbess, Columbine, hurry up, we've made you a lovely cheese and apple salad, but Coggs says he'll eat it all unless you come right away,'' Spike said breathlessly as he and Posy dashed up. Sandingomm followed, looking mock-seriously at the two mice.

''I think you'd better do as they say, Abbess. I'll go and get Uncle Gingivere. We don't want him to miss his salad because of that fat little Coggs.''

Germaine allowed Spike and Posy to help her up.

''Cheese and apple salad—my favorite,'' she told them. ''Lead me to it. I'll show that wretch Coggs a thing or two about putting salad away. Did I ever tell you, when I was a young mouse long ago, I once ate three great bowls of cheese and apple salad at a sitting?''

''Oh, hahaha. Then why aren't you fat like Coggs? He says he's not going to stop eating until he's twice the size of Skipper.''

''What d'you mean, twice the size? My goodness, look at you, young Posy. You'll be bursting out of your fur soon.''

''Hahaha. Oh, stoppit, Abbess. That tickles. Haha-heeheehee!''

The first Kotir soldiers were hauled dripping to shore by the woodlanders. Dispirited, disarmed and soaking wet, they were made to sit at the water's edge by Skipper and the six hares, who fished them out with fearsome-looking pikes.

''Sit down there, you great wet weasel.''

''Steady on, Trubbs old chap, that's a stoat.''

''Oh, I say, sorry. Sit there, you soaking stoat.''

''Saturated stoat, don't you mean, old bean?''

"Hmm, what about the weasels?"

"Oh, actually they get wringing wet, both begin with W, you see."

"Righto. Sit over there, you wringing wet weasel."

"Oh golly, I've got a rat now. How d'you address these blighters?"

"Easy, old thing—rats are rancid."

"Rancid? That doesn't mean wet."

"No, but the wretched cove does look pretty rancid."

"So he does. Splendid. Sit here, you rancid rat!"

Skipper patrolled the ranks of defeated troops and eyed them sternly.

"Sight tight, vermin," he said sternly. "Keep your paws on your heads, where I can see them. First one to make a funny move goes straight back into that water on the end of a pike. Understood?"

Young Dinny and Ben Stickle fed them bread and milk.

"Here you blaggards, eat this and drink up. Though the way you've behaved toward us, we shouldn't be giving you anything."

"Hurr, too roight. Oi'd give' 'ee ditchwatter an' frogtails if'n oi 'ad moi way."

A weasel tried to snatch the bread from a stoat. Dinny cuffed him soundly round the ears with blunt digging claws. "None o' that yurr, please, or oi'll sett 'ee atop o' yon cattingpult an' shoot 'ee into middle of 'ee lake," he threatened.

There was no fight left in the vanquished Kotir troops. Most of them looked grateful to be fed and treated civilly by their captors. Lady Amber and her archers sat in low boughs, bows and arrows ready in the event of an uprising.

Martin was otherwise engaged. He made his way farther along the bank, away from the bustle and noise. Standing at the north edge of the lake, he watched Tsarmina's progress in silence. The wildcat Queen was obviously making her escape bid, leaving her army to its fate. She paddled between Kotir and the shore, whilst behind her the fortress crumbled and splashed into the water under the ballista's constant battering. The wildcat Queen floated steadily toward land on the upturned table.

Martin drew his sword. "Boar the Fighter, help me this day," he whispered, remembering its maker. Then the warrior mouse limped along the shoreline as fast as his injured limb would permit, on his way to intercept the enemy.

Tsarmina paddled in to land and sprang ashore. Ignoring the activity on the east side, she stared miserably at Kotir. There was no further need of rock missiles; the flood had done its work. With a rumbling crash, the last of the roof caved in. The whole structure disintegrated, splashing into the great lake. There was a boiling of muddy brown bubbles, then the lake surface went still under the gray midday sky, rippled only by the soughing wind.

Kotir was gone from sight forever!

Tsarmina threw back her head in an anguished yowl and ran to the water's edge, drawing back swiftly as the wetness touched her paws.

"I have kept my promise to you, cat. Kotir has fallen!" A stern voice called out from behind her.

The wildcat Queen froze, fearing to turn around.

"Gingivere, is that you?"

Martin strode to the water's edge and stood a short distance from his mortal enemy.

"I am Martin the Warrior, son of Luke, friend of Boar the Fighter."

Tsarmina turned to face her foe. "So, it is you. Well, my little warrior, where are your woodland allies? Not here to help you?"

Martin leaned upon his sword. Now that the moment had arrived he felt only contempt. "Tsarmina, you are the Queen of an underwater fortress, Ruler of the fishes." His voice had a mocking ring to it. "Cat, you are scum, floated ashore on an upturned kitchen table, nothing more!"

Stung by the scathing insult, Tsarmina gave a scream of rage, and dived straight upon Martin. Digging her claws into his back, she gave a mad yell of triumph, which was swiftly followed by a howl of pain as the keen blade slashed her ribs to the bone.

Martin winced as he swung his sword. Feeling Tsarmina's claws pull free of his back, he stabbed furiously at the great furred bulk of the wildcat. She leaped back a pace.

Maddened by the same berserk rage that had driven Boar onward, Martin hurled himself upon the surprised wildcat. This time Tsarmina took two thrusts in the flank before she raked the warrior's face savagely with vicious claws. The helmet was torn from Martin's head, armor flapped loose as Tsarmina disentangled herself, but he managed to pierce her paw right through.

They crouched panting for a moment, both sorely wounded. Then Martin dashed the blood from his vision, and with a bellow of rage he charged the wildcat.

This time she was ready. Tsarmina nimbly side-stepped, cruelly striking Martin's back as he plunged by, opening further the wounds she had already inflicted.

The warrior mouse fell heavily upon his face and lay still. Tsarmina licked her wounds, chuckling evilly. She had finally finished her enemy off.

Then Martin stirred.

Shaking himself, he stood upright. Gripping his battle blade with both paws, the warrior went headlong at Tsarmina.

Despite the shock at her opponent's recovery, Tsarmina swiftly gathered her wits, sidestepping once more.

This time Martin sidestepped with her, striking a mighty blow to her back.

The wildcat Queen screamed in agony, rounding suddenly on him. Paw grasped claw, teeth bit fur; kicking, scratching, gouging and stabbing, they rolled over and over on the bank in a shower of flying earth.

Tsarmina freed herself, leaving Martin prone on the ground. Once more she backed off licking her wounds.

"Got you that time, woodlander!" she crowed.

Digging his blade into the earth, Martin heaved himself up, breathing raggedly. Exerting all his strength, he whirled the war sword aloft.

"Mossflowerrrrr!"

Fear was etched in Tsarmina's eyes as she tried to fight off the wild onslaught. Here was a warrior who would not lie down and die.

Locked in combat, they strained and flailed at one another, the warrior mouse hacking at the wildcat Queen, who gave back slash for thrust, bite for cut.

Her hide open in a dozen places, Tsarmina kicked out with her four paws, sending Martin flying into the water. She grabbed a piece of driftwood to push him farther in, only to find him standing in the shallows, waiting to attack. Covered from head to tailtip in mud, blood and water, Martin struck the branch that Tsarmina thrust at him, breaking it in two with a single swipe. His next backslash splintered the remains deep into Tsarmina's paw.

Crouching low with the sword point held out in front, Martin waded out of the water toward his foe, the red glitter of total war shining hot in his eyes, his teeth bared in a wild laugh.

Tsarmina's craven heart failed her.

The wildcat began circling nervously as Martin closed in. Like a dream from the past, she recalled that winter evening in her father's bedchamber when she had smashed the rusty sword of a captive mouse. She remembered the words he had spoken as he was dragged off to the cells at Kotir: *You should have killed me when you had the chance, because I vow that I will slay you one day!*

Unaware of the water behind her, Tsarmina retreated, backing off as the little warrior came toward her, bloodied but unbowed, the mouse who would not lie down and die. Martin, the one that fought like a great male badger.

Back, back, she paced, her eyes shifting from the gleaming blade to Martin's piercing eyes. Deeper and deeper into the waters of the lake went the Queen of the Thousand Eyes.

Even though Martin had halted upon the lake shore, he seemed to be getting larger, towering in her vision. She had to get as far away from this threat as she could.

Suddenly Tsarmina realized she had gone too deep. The energy drained from her body; dry land seemed miles away. Water filled her world, dark, swirling, eddying, tugging, longing to fold her in its wet embrace, pulling her down, filling her mouth, nostrils and finally her eyes.

The dream had come true. The nightmare was alive!

Back in the shallows, Martin dragged his wounded body onto the land. Trying to lift his sword one last time, he managed to gasp out, "Sleep in peace, Boar. Mossflower is free!"

The shining sword slid from the warrior's grasp and he fell to the earth, a limp sodden bundle.

The captives on the lakeshore were seated in ranks. Paws on heads, they disputed in low voices with each other.

"I think we're safe. These woodlanders are not killers."

"Huh, if we'd been captured by Bane or Tsarmina it would have been a different story, mate."

"I'll say. We'd all have been floating face down in that lake by now, those who hadn't sunk."

"Aye. Instead the woodlanders fed us and cared for us."

"Better grub than I ever had at Kotir."

Bella forestalled any further comment by standing upon a mound and calling for order.

"Attention, all of you. Listen to me!"

Murmuring died away as the former army of Kotir listened to hear what was in store.

The badger pointed over their heads at the lake. "Look! Turn your heads and see—Kotir is gone forever. Now you have no leader or walls to hide behind. The war in Mossflower is at an end. You are defeated."

Late afternoon sun emerged through the clouds as Bella continued. "We do not make total war upon you because we are not killers. However, that would not be the case a second time. Remember that."

A timid paw showed in the ranks. It was Whegg the rat.

"Then we're not to be sentenced to death?" he asked anxiously.

Bella held her breath a moment before speaking.

"No."

There was an audible sigh of relief from the prisoners.

Whegg could not resist a second question.

"What will happen to us?"

Skipper stood on the mound beside Bella.

"Right," he said. "Clean up your lugs and listen hard, mateys. I'll only say this once. You will each swear an oath that you will never again carry a weapon or come near Mossflower country, though if I'd had my way none of you would have got out of that lake alive today. Be that as it may, Bella of Brockhall here has said that you be spared, so you have her to thank for your lucky escape. But I'll tell you this: any creature that doesn't agree to our terms, let him show a paw now. The lake is still here, and so am I."

The captives immediately sat upon their paws.

"Good!" Skipper nodded his approval. "Now you will remain here until tomorrow, when you will be escorted under guard to the flatlands west of here. You can travel west or south, but not back up north and certainly not back here to our land. That is all for now. Be still and behave."

Bella and Skipper stepped down to join Amber and the others.

Amber looked concerned. "Where has the big cat got to?"

Timballisto was worried too. "Where is my friend? Has anyone seen Martin?" he asked anxiously.

Ben Stickle nodded. "Just before Kotir fell into the lake, I saw him on the bank. He headed up that way, yonder."

"Then he must be found straightaway," Bella interrupted. "Gonff, you and I will search the water's edge. The rest of you stay here and keep an eye on this lot."

Before they moved off Bella issued a warning:

"Watch out for Tsarmina."

Young Dinny, Bella and Gonff halted farther up the bank. Timballisto joined them, refusing to watch captives while his friend was missing.

Bella looked about. "I don't think he would have come this far with his wound. In all that armor he couldn't possibly have traveled fast enough."

"Aye, besides, what would he have wanted all this way along the shore, when we were capturing prisoners farther down?" Gonff agreed.

"If I know my friend, I think he must have spotted the cat."

"Hurr, moi diggen claws be a-tellen me Marthen be about sumwhurrs. Oi do feel et."

"Well, we'd better trust you, Din. The old digging claws haven't been wrong yet, matey."

"Lookit, thurr!" Squinting hard, the mole pointed farther along the shoreline to where the sunlight was clearly glinting off a shining object.

Gonff broke into a run. "By the teeth and fur, matey, that must be the sword!"

The little mousethief was first to reach the fallen figure of his friend. Dinny, Timballisto and Bella came as fast as they could to the spot where the sword lay. They found Gonff blinded by tears, his whole body shaking with grief as he knelt by the pitiful bundle that was his friend. "He's dead, they've killed our Martin!"

Dinny knelt beside him, burying his face in the earth. "Hoa nay, letten et doant be true!"

The two friends wept bitterly.

Timballisto would not, could not, believe that after the short period they had been reunited, his friend had been taken to the gates of Dark Forest.

Timballisto turned Martin gently over, laying his limbs straight. Swiftly he hurried to the water and filled Martin's helmet. Soaking a cloth, he dabbed feverishly at the fearsome wounds that covered his friend's body.

"Who could have done these awful things to a living creature?"

Gonff wiped his eyes. Picking up a long broken claw from the earth, he held it out to them. "Tsarmina, that's who," he said grimly.

Dinny squinted at the claw. He cast about, sniffing and sifting with his paws, finding many traces of blood on the ground. "They'm fought a gurt battlefoight yurr. Lookit, catbludd on Marthen's sword, ground all a-ploughed up."

Gonff followed the tracks to the water's edge. "You're right, matey. The cat went backward, into the lake. I think our warrior won the battle."

Once more the tears sprang to the little mousethief's eyes. "Martin, we went through everything together. Why couldn't I have been here to help you, matey?"

Bella was cradling Martin's head, when suddenly she leaned closer to the warrior mouse's lips.

"He's alive! His mouth is moving!" she exclaimed joyfully.

T. B. began dabbing furiously at his friend's paws with the wet cloth. "He's alive! My friend is alive! Bella, is it true? Oh, please say yes!"

The badger's eyes were misted. "He's talking to Boar my father at the gates of Dark Forest," she said in a strained voice.

"Don't let him go there, please. Do something to help him!" Timballisto begged, seizing Bella's paws.

Bella thought hard for a moment. "Wait, I have not got the knowledge as a healer for something as serious as this. But I know one who has—Abbess Germaine."

Gonff paced up and down, shaking his head. "But she's taken the little ones over to the east of Mossflower. It would be too late by the time we found her."

"Then send Chibb. He can fly there," T. B. said in a desperate voice.

Even in the urgency of the situation, Bella of Brockhall took command. Restoring order and good sense, she provided a solution.

"Friends, here is the only way we may save Martin. Listen carefully. Gonff, hurry back to our camp and send Chibb east. He must tell the Abbess to gather her medicines and herbs together. Meanwhile, you will get blankets and bring them back here. Do not move Martin, just keep him warm and dry. Abbess Germaine is old and cannot travel fast, but I will follow Chibb and bring her back from Gingivere's farm as speedily as I can."

Without another word, Bella dashed along the shore with a speed surprising for a badger. Cutting to the east, she crashed into Mossflower Woods like a juggernaut, disappearing in a welter of churned-up ground and flying foliage.

Night fell upon the lakeside. A fire burned bright as Goody Stickle tended Martin, tucking the blankets gently but firmly around his injured body. Ben Stickle hurried hither and thither gathering firewood.

T. B. stood by, feeling totally useless as he listened to the fevered voice of his friend.

"Carry on the sweep of the blade," Martin whispered. "Up and across, eh, Boar, you old battlebeast. Who will wield our swords for us now, warrior?"

T. B. was about to speak, when Goody held a paw to her lips. "Hush now, Mr. T. B. He's a-sleepin'. I'm doin' all I can to keep the life in the poor mouse until Abbess gets here."

Trubbs and the hares built a bower of reeds and willow about Martin and Goody, speaking in whispers as they did so.

"Keep the old night breezes off, what!"

"Rather. Can do without the bally wind, y'know."

"Nothing worse than a chill on the paws when a chap's not on top form."

Pale moonlight glimmered off the surface of the lake as Martin lay still, scarcely breathing. The woodlanders sat waiting.

49

An hour before dawn, the occupants of the small farmhouse were up and about. Columbine checked the Abbess's satchel.

"Comfrey, elmbark, motherwort, verbena, rosehips. . . . I can't think of anything we've missed out, can you, Abbess?"

The old mouse stood facing the western woodlands. "No, child. I've got everything I need. Now stop upsetting yourself and prepare breakfast for the little ones."

Chibb perched on the farmhouse window sill, listening to Gingivere and Sandingomm.

"We must not let the little ones know," Gingivere was saying. "Let them play. Soon enough they'll grow up and have to face life's problems."

"You're right, Gingivere. Spike, Posy, would you set the bowls and spoons out, please."

"But Lady Sandingomm, you said it was Ferdy and Cogg's turn today. We did it at supper last night."

"You're right. It's not fair. Hey, you two, come on. Your turn for setting the breakfast things out."

Ferdy and Coggs came running from the woodland edge. "Hurray, it's Miz Bella. Look out or she'll knock us all over."

361

Bella came pounding out of the woods, lathered in foam and breathing heavily. Ferdy ran alongside of her.

"Miz Bella, have you been running all night? Have we won the war?"

"Come away, little one. No time for games now."

Gingivere led Bella to the farmhouse, but she collapsed near the front doorstep, panting.

Sandingomm dashed indoors. "I'll get something to dry you down and you can have breakfast."

Bella shook her head as she caught her breath. "No time, friend. Some water to drink, then I'll be on my way. Abbess, are you ready?"

Germaine patted Bella's heaving flank. "Oh, I'm ready. But you're not, Bella. You need rest. You'd never make it back like that, so lie still awhile."

Still panting with exertion, the badger took a sparing drink of water and lay upon her side.

"Right. It won't take me long, Gingivere. Get some stout cords and be ready to bind the Abbess on my back. We don't want her being swept off in the woods."

Chibb decided to forego breakfast. "Er ahem. I'll fly back and tell them you're on the way."

Sandingomm turned to Columbine. "We'd best leave breakfast. Pack some food to eat on the way. I'll close up the farmhouse and we'll go back together."

Posy tugged Gingivere's tail. "Did you hear that, Uncle? We're going for a trip and taking a picnic with us."

"Of course we are, Posy." Gingivere smiled distractedly.

A short while later, the Abbess sat upon Bella's back, securely roped together with her satchel of herbs.

Bella took a deep breath. "Good, I've stopped blowing like an old frog now. My legs are feeling steady. Hold tight, Germaine. Here we go!"

Goody Stickle tried hard not to let her concern show. She had done all she could, even following her instincts and allowing the delirious warrior to clutch his sword as he lay raving. Timballisto stood by her, gnawing worriedly at his claws. "He's still trying to get past those gates into Dark Forest. Goody, what can we do?"

Wiping her paws on her old flowery apron, the hedgehog tried to look busy.

"Well, for a start you can stop hangin' about an' botherin' me, Mr. T. B. You go and gather some firewood with my Ben." She softened at the helpless look on Timballisto's face. "My dear, you can't do anythin' for your friend, nor can I, really, until proper help arrives. You go and help our Gonff on lookout. Go on, I'll call you if he wakes."

When he had gone, Goody wrung out more cloths to place on Martin's brow. He was feverish, shivering, sweating by turns, and constantly murmuring.

"Bring her head around," he muttered. "Sail for the shore. I'll rescue Boar from those sea rats. Give me my sword. Watch out for those seabirds and the crabs, Gonff. Leave the rest to me, matey."

Midmorning brought a shout from Gonff. "It's Bella! She's got the Abbess with her. Hey, Bella, over here!"

The badger came thundering across the lakeshore. Stopping in a shower of earth, she parted the ropes with a slash of her big claws and a few snapping bites. The Abbess tumbled from the badger's back. Pausing only to grab her satchel, she ran to Martin's side.

"You did well, Goody Stickle, go and rest now," she said comfortingly. But Bella was shocked by Martin's appearance. "Abbess, he looks dreadful. Do you think he'll live?" she asked, looking over Germaine's shoulder.

Germaine was already ministering to Martin.

"Gonff, put some water to boil on the fire. Bella, open my satchel and give me some feverfew—yes, that one there. Now a touch of nightshade; not too much. Ben, can you gather some fresh dock leaves for me?"

As she tended the warrior mouse, the Abbess answered Bella. "Do not worry, old friend. This mouse will live, if I have anything to do with it, though it will take all my skills and a long, long time before he is completely out of danger. Columbine will be here soon. You go and rest; the race that you ran to save Martin's life would have killed a lesser creature. You must get some sleep."

The three female hares were not fond of the idea that prisoners should be fed and cared for. Prodding the defeated troops of

Kotir with their pikes, they drove them ten at a time to the lake. Harebell, Honeydew and Willow thoroughly approved of cleanliness.

"Come on, slimeface. Get in there—you won't drown."

"Use plenty of sand and scrub hard, you mucky lot."

"You there, fox, wash behind those grubby ears."

The fox turned away muttering insolently, "Huh, why should I?"

Trubbs and company were practicing with slings. Ffring bounced a sharp pebble off the fox's bottom, causing him to jump.

"Because you won't get any tuck if you don't, you filthy rogue."

"Hear hear! Now get those ears washed—both of 'em, laddie."

"Then you can wiggle 'em in the sun until they dry, what!"

Skipper inspected a rat. "Show me those paws. Turn 'em over. Right. Go and get fed. Hoi! Where d'you think you're sailing off to, scruffbag? Get back in and scrub those whiskers, or I'll come and do it for you with a cob of spruce bark."

He leaned on his pike, discussing the prisoners with Dinny and the hares.

"This miserable lot will eat us out of crop and woodland, the way they're scoffing," he objected.

"Burr, they'm gotten a dozen stummicks apiece, narsty vurrmen."

Log-a-Log pushed a half-washed weasel back in with his stave. "Not to worry. I heard Bella mention to Lady Amber that we're marching them out of Mossflower tomorrow."

"Urr, zooner th' better, sez oi."

"Any news of Martin yet?"

"Bella said he's still the same, no change, though the Abbess has decided to have him moved down here after this lot have been banished."

"I still find it hard to believe that he slew the big cat. That must have been a battle and a half, matey."

"Urr, ee'm a wurrier, our Marthen, tho' the battle be furr 'ee loif of 'im now."

It was noon of the following day. The sun beat down on the dusty path that separated Mossflower Woods from the flatlands rolling away to the west.

On the far side of the ditch stood the defeated army of Kotir, each one carrying two days' supply of food and water. On the woodland side of that same ditch stood the hordes of Mossflower: shrews, mice, squirrels, hares, otters, hedgehogs and moles, together with Gingivere, Sandingomm and Bella.

The badger stood tall. Pointing to the horizon, she addressed the freed prisoners.

"You must go now. Travel together or split into groups, as you will. If any of you are thinking of finding more weapons and coming back here, I would strongly advise you to listen to what these creatures have to say."

The six hares stood forward, brandishing their long pikes.

"Hello, you rascals. We're the border patrol now, y'know."

"Yes, first regiment Fur and Foot Fighters at y'service."

"Woodlands are splendid, but the old flat country, this is the place to be, what!"

"So, you've got until sunset to vanish into the distance, savvy?"

"Actually, if we can still sight you then, there's going to be another jolly old battle."

"Rather. We hares and these woodland chappies will be only too happy to pursue you."

There was silence from the other side of the ditch. Some of the Kotir troops began shuffling nervously, unsure of what to do.

"Count of ten to be on your way." Skipper's gruff call rang out. "Them that stays here gets buried here. Right, mateys. Altogether!"

Every woodland voice was raised in deadly unison.

"One!"

"Two!"

"Three . . ."

The leaderless foxes, weasels, stoats, ferrets and rats ran. They ran as they had never run before, stumbling and pushing to get out in front. Not a word was spoken amongst them. All that could be heard was the harsh panting of breath as they sped away into the far sunlit distance, each one feverishly hoping that, regardless of the others, he would be out of sight by sunset, away from Mossflower and its grim horde of dangerous woodlanders.

• • •

Halfway through the long afternoon, Lady Amber and Skipper approached Bella.

"Couldn't we just go after them one last time, Bella?" Skipper pleaded.

The badger shook her head at the Corim leaders. "No, friends. We've won, Mossflower is ours again."

"Hurr, let's go 'ome!"

Foremole's words in his rough molespeech sounded like the sweetest music ever heard.

50

A score of days had gone since the banishment.

The lakeshore rang to the sounds of late evening merriment. Colored lanterns were hanging from the trees, reflecting a mass of orange, pink, blue and gold lights upon the calm waters. Stars twinkled above, woodlanders danced below, garlands of flowers were strewn everywhere and delicious smells came from the great fires at the lake margin.

Martin awakened to the sounds of Gonff singing.

Let no foul beast give one command,
I'll say, 'O no not me,
My back bends to no tyrant's rule.
Hey, friends, this mouse is free.'
Free has a sound, it rings around,
A lovely way to be.
So dance or sing, do anything,
You're free free free free freeeeeeeeeee!

"Hurr, that's wot 'ee think, Gonffen. You tell 'im missus."

"Gonff, come and help me to get the stopper off this strawberry wine, right away."

"Immediately, my Columbine, O nurse of warriors and charming mouselet. I'm coming, my little candied chestnut."

There were roars of laughter.

Timballisto flopped down on the edge of Martin's blanket.

"So, you're awake, mate. The Abbess said it'd be sometime today."

Martin smiled and grasped his friend's paw.

"Don't worry, I'm back now. How long have I lain here?"

Before Timballisto could answer, Ferdy and Coggs dashed up.

"Ha, so you're awake, sleepyhead," Ferdy teased.

"Yes, fancy dozing off when there's a party," Coggs added.

The Abbess and Bella came over, decked in flowers and carrying a bowl of woodland vegetable soup, which the old mouse started feeding to Martin from a ladle.

"Good evening, Martin. Don't answer, just keep eating; we want you up and about as soon as possible."

The warrior mouse did as he was bidden. Soon all the woodlanders had gathered around him.

"Look, Martin's awake now!"

"My, my, doesn't he look well!"

"Urr, loivly as pepper 'n' strong as ale."

"Haha, ahoy there, shipmate."

"Well, how do you feel, Champion of Mossflower?" Bella chuckled happily.

Martin gazed about him at the friendly faces and smiled through the tears falling from his eyes.

"Good to be alive, Bella!"

There was a loud cheer, then the voices poured in thick and fast.

"Guess what, matey—while you were asleep I wedded Columbine."

"Yes, Gonff's given up being a thief—I've seen to that."

"Ha, we found them a place, y'know, while we were out on border patrol down south along the path. It's just inside the woods."

"Yes, it's a tiny old church called Saint Ninian's or somesuch. How it came there, goodness knows. It's all overgrown and rickety."

"Oh, my Gonff will soon fix that up."

"Hey, matey, have you noticed that the lake's gone down a

bit? Skipper and Log-a-Log have practically refloated *Wudd-shipp*."

"Indeed they have. Before summer's out we'll be shipping stone down from the quarry near Gingivere's Farm."

"Have you heard? We're going to build a great stone Abbey."

"A huge place where we can all live together."

"Right at the side of the path, not far from where Gonff will be living with Columbine."

Bella waved her paws for order. "Hush now. Go and enjoy yourselves. Our warrior has fallen asleep listening to your chatter."

The fires burned low, though the festivities continued on the lakeshore as the sounds of happiness drifted up into the soft summer night, traveling onto the places beyond the stars, where legends live.

51

Some creature was knocking on the gatehouse door.

Bella of Brockhall rose slowly from her armchair by the embers of the fire and shuffled across to the threshold.

A fine plump mouse stood framed against the star-strewn night. He entered, nodding toward the small mouse who lay asleep, propped up on the arm of the chair by a cushion.

"I knew he'd be here listening to your stories, marm."

Bella squinted closely at the plump mouse. "You must be Gonff, son of Gonff and Columbine from Saint Ninian's. I thought I recognized your son. He's the image of his grandfather."

The plump mouse chuckled. "Aye, you'd better check your candied chestnuts and cheese, marm. There's nothing safe while he's around. Lucky he's asleep, eh."

Bella picked up the sleeping mouse with great gentleness. "Little rogue. Look, his tunic's full of acorns. Wonder where he got them from. Come on, I'll carry him back home for you."

Together they made their way south along the dusty path, Bella talking quietly as they went.

"Pity he went to sleep like that. I never told him of the great vow that Martin made when he hung up his sword to become

Redwall mouse. Or of the wonderful feast when the main gate was raised. That was when you were born, y'know. Hoho, we certainly made a double celebration of it that summer. Skipper of otters ate so much that he sank in the Abbey pool, and Lady Amber dived in to fish him out. Did your mum and dad ever tell you about it?''

Gonff, son of Gonff and Columbine, nodded, smiling in the late autumn night.

"Aye, at least a hundred times, matey!"

52

The last day of autumn was hot and bright as midsummer. Still as a millpond, the sea reflected a cloudless blue sky. Seabirds wheeled and called, soaring lazily on the warm thermals above the sun-baked sands of the shore.

Two hares stood shaded by the cave entrance, watching a fully grown male badger plough his way wearily across the beach toward them. He was big and dangerous-looking; the fierce light in his eyes glinted off the metal tips of an immense warclub which he carried easily in one paw.

The hares stepped from the shadows of the rock into the sunlight. The stranger stood before them, pointing at the mountain.

"What do they call this place?" he asked.

The oldest of the hares, a male, answered him.

"Salamandastron, the place of the fire lizard."

The badger gave a huge sigh. Leaning against the rock, he rested his club on the sand.

"I feel as if I've been here before," he said strangely.

The female hare produced victuals from within the cave entrance. "Rest awhile. Eat and drink. I am called Breeze, and this is my brother Starbuck. What do they call you?"

e badger smiled. He touched one of his headstripes, which
yellow rather than white.

ome call me Sunflash the Mace. I am the son of Bella and
stripe. I'm a traveler."

arbuck nodded in satisfaction. "Your traveling is at an end,
ash, you are the grandson of Boar the Fighter and great
lson of Old Lord Brocktree. It is written on the walls of
nountain that you would come here someday."

nflash straightened up. He stared hard at the hares.

Vritten, you say. By whom?"

eeze shrugged. "By whoever wrote that other hares will
w after us. That is the way it has always been and always
oe."

th hares stood in the cave entrance. They bowed to the
er. "Welcome to your mountain, Sunflash the Mace, Lord
lamandastron."

e high sun above watched as the badger and the hares
together into the mountain on the shores below.

e badger smiled. He touched one of his headstripes, which
ellow rather than white.

ome call me Sunflash the Mace. I am the son of Bella and
tripe. I'm a traveler.''

rbuck nodded in satisfaction. ''Your traveling is at an end,
ash, you are the grandson of Boar the Fighter and great
son of Old Lord Brocktree. It is written on the walls of
ountain that you would come here someday.''

flash straightened up. He stared hard at the hares.
Written, you say. By whom?''

eze shrugged. ''By whoever wrote that other hares will
after us. That is the way it has always been and always
e.''

th hares stood in the cave entrance. They bowed to the
r. ''Welcome to your mountain, Sunflash the Mace, Lord
amandastron.''

e high sun above watched as the badger and the hares
together into the mountain on the shores below.